WELCOME TO THE OLD SCHOOL

In your hands is a one-way ticket to the Old School.

It is a literary world that is shadowy and unknown. A fiction few today remember or have read.

This original "pulp fiction" represents an edgy and extreme chapter of black literary history. It is at once dangerous and deeply transgressive, gritty yet bold and experimental.

Your tour guide—a lost generation of black authors with street credentials born of hard times and tough luck.

Your destination—the charred remains of urban America. Places like Flatbush, Hell's Kitchen, South Philly, and, most ominously, a federal warehouse for repeat drug addicts. But in the Old School even suburban tree-lined streets can play host to violence, and a perfectly nice young man can become a twisted psychopath thanks to one small problem: his mom.

It is an era whose time has come and gone. It begins as early as 1958 and leaves off about 1975. But this is not a sentimental journey. Get on board and you will visit a world inhabited by original players and hustlers . . . mack daddies and racketeers . . . police and thieves . . . cops on the take and girls on the make. Flawed little men with big dreams, bad guns, and no hope for redemption.

It is a world of the desperate and the deranged, the doomed and the damned, a world where the sun never shines.

You get the idea.

America wasn't ready for these hard-boiled dispatches when they first appeared, and they were lost to history. Reclaimed in the Old School they join Stax Records, 70s gangsta chic, and the blaxploitation flick as cultural artifacts to be embraced by a new generation.

These books deserve a second chance, and in the Old School, they get one. So get on board.

Marc Gerald and Samuel Blumenfeld, Editors
Old School Books

The Scene

OLD SCHOOL BOOKS

edited by Marc Gerald and Samuel Blumenfeld

The Scene   CLARENCE COOPER, JR.

Portrait of a Young Man Drowning   CHARLES PERRY

Corner Boy   HERBERT SIMMONS

The Angry Ones   JOHN A. WILLIAMS

CLARENCE COOPER, JR.

The Scene

SB

Old School Books

W · W · Norton & Company
New York · London

Whispering Grass, by Doris Fisher and Fred Fisher. © 1940 (Renewed) EMI Mills Music, Inc. and Doris Fisher Music. All rights reserved. Used by permission. Warner Bros. Publications U.S. Inc., Miami, FL 33014

The text of this book is composed in Sabon, with the display set in Stacatto 555 and Futura.
Composition by Crane Typesetting Service, Inc.
Manufacturing by Courier Companies, Inc.
Book design by Jack Meserole.

Library of Congress Cataloging-in-Publication Data
Cooper, Clarence L.
     The scene / by Clarence L. Cooper, Jr.
        p.   cm.—(Old school books)
     ISBN 0-393-31463-4 (pbk.)
     I. Title.   II. Series.
PS3553.05799S34   1996
813'.54—dc20   96-8036
                                                                      CIP

W. W. Norton & Company, Inc., 500 Fifth Avenue, New York, N.Y. 10110
http://web.wwnorton.com
W. W. Norton & Company Ltd., 10 Coptic Street, London WC1A 1PU

1   2   3   4   5   6   7   8   9   0

CLARENCE COOPER, JR.

ON THE BASIS of his two great masterpieces, *The Farm* and *The Scene*, the reputation of Clarence Levi Cooper, Jr., should be secure. And they are masterpieces, too. Not quite crime fiction, not exactly serious literature, these unrelenting novels about the mindset of the drug addict reside uneasily in that somewhere in-between place. You know, the one which is usually synonymous with commercial death. And so it is with Cooper. For in a perfect world he would be mentioned alongside the names of the greatest writers of the postwar era. Meanwhile in the real world he's a complete unknown.

Cooper's life was a bad dream from the start. Born in Detroit in 1934, Cooper, a boyhood pal of Malcolm X, got married, developed a monstrous drug addiction, did a two-year stretch in the Iona Penitentiary, wrote and edited for the black daily newspaper *The Chicago Messenger*, and published two novels, all before his twenty-seventh birthday.

His first, *The Scene* (published in hardback by Crown), was set in a nameless, faceless city populated by dope fiends, lesbians, whores, and pretty boys, and written in a style that evoked an unholy mix of Jim Thompson and a jailhouse reading list. More than just a document of petty lowlifes, it was, as you'll soon see, a formally inventive work, one that gave more than just a passing hint at the direction his future writings would take. It was blunt as a sledgehammer and welcoming as a barbed-wire fence. The critics noticed. The *New York Tribune* remarked: "Not even Nelson Algren's *The Man with the Golden Arm* burned with the ferocious intensity you'll find here. [Cooper) writes with a personal authority that can only be called shattering and the searing exactness of one who has lived through the horror."

Unfortunately, Cooper was still living through the horror, and by the time *The Scene* hit the streets in 1960, he was serving another lengthy stretch.

Over the course of the next two years, Cooper was a busy man. Not only did he play bass in a jailhouse band, he turned out three more impressive manuscripts and a slew of whacked autobiographical notes that prove far less truthful than his fiction in reporting the details of his life.

"How these books ended up in the slush pile at a low-end house like Regency is something of a mystery," says famed novelist Harlan Ellison, who during the early 1960s was doing it all for the Chicago-based publisher. While the two men never met, through their correspondences Ellison formed the opinion that Cooper was a "very literate, very troubled individual."

Cooper's troubles only multiplied. Released from jail, and unable to write in a world of temptation, Cooper again fell into drug addiction and petty theft, and would spend much of the mid-sixties in lower Manhattan, haranguing former friends and associates for money and looking for a place to hang his hat. John A. Williams, who knew Cooper at this time, describes him as a "disappointed man who was unable to override his frustrations at the reception of his books." Less romantic is Cooper's longtime agent, Charles Neighbors, who suggests "Cooper was brilliant but utterly committed to mind-altering drugs. Cheap and intoxicating was his favorite combination."

Not that Cooper didn't have a few bright moments. For a time, he had a radio show, and served as the first president of the Fortune Society—a foundation devoted to facilitating ex-offenders' entry back to society. "Sadly," says former executive director of Fortune Society David Rothenberg, "the demons were still inside him. Success as a writer, admiration as a catalyst for change, and love from friends were not sufficient to protect him."

"So much of what we know of ourselves is such a lousy God Damn Lie," explains John, the hero of *The Farm*. Released in 1967, it was Cooper's last book and his most personal. This enigmatic statement would foreshadow the final years of Cooper's life, the few details of which include a failed stint as a Hollywood screenwriter, eventual return to New York, rumored decline into homelessness, and slow suicide through alcohol and drugs.

In one of the few reviews of *The Farm*, the *Negro Digest* savaged the book for its "flawed characters," "over-writing," and "gratuitous and affected prose construction" while admitting "there is a small coterie of readers who swear by Clarence Cooper, Jr., . . . [who] is, they maintain, one of the most underrated writers in America."

Unwilling to compromise his scorched-earth point of view for fame, Cooper died at the 23rd Street YMCA in 1978, penniless and alone. Now that *The Scene* is back in print, with other novels soon to follow, one can only hope that he will finally receive his due.

TO MY WIFE, IRENE
AND TO JACQUES CHAMBRUN,
WHO UNDERSTOOD

If thou shouldst, along the way,
Meet the Hungry Hunters,
Avoid them,
Else they wouldst devour thee.

The Scene

January

1

*T*HAT NIGHT, for the first time, Rudy Black was painfully aware of the street. Its strange, disassociated rhythms sang through the cold night air; it settled about him from the click of his expensive shoes on the pavement to the halo of shining marcelled hair on his head.

All the elements of the Scene—the lights, the whores, the tricks in their cars, the razzle of jazz music from the record shop on the corner of Seventy-seventh and Maple—repelled Rudy, the pimp and pusher, made him feel alien, a person without stable ground or purpose, although he knew no other atmosphere but this.

The Scene's touch was like dead flesh. He remembered touching a dead person, an old woman. She had died alone in a flat above the one in which he and his mother and father lived. One day his mother went upstairs to find out why the woman never called, why she never cackled her greeting any more on the evenings when she should have come back from the open-air market. His mother found the old woman dead in the bathroom, swollen fat.

The doctor had come—and that's when he touched her. The doctor was old and gray, weak. "Get her legs, boy," he said over the body. "Help me get her into the other room."

"I ain't," Rudy had said. "You can't make me!"

"I'll beat your ass," his mother said. "You do like he tells you." But she never touched the body herself. "I'll beat your black ass," Rudy's mother said.

In fear of his mother, he touched a dead thing.

Now the Scene was like that woman; the life was leaving it and it was beginning to swell. And again there was something like his

1 9

mother forcing him, trying to make him defile himself, pushing him toward death.

He left his car on Seventy-eighth, far back off the corner so that no one would recognize its broad fishtails, and walked up Maple, shrinking inwardly at the thin-faced people, the cars and buses.

The lights seemed dimmer, glowing cheaply from bars with their double shots and glasses of shell beer.

His steps faltered; his legs trembled uncontrollably. He began to curse himself, lighting a cigarette, drawing in the harsh tobacco taste and the coldness of the tainted wind simultaneously. Then he noticed his woman, Nina, working the other side of the street with two other women.

He crossed over, disregarding the careless, searching drivers whose eyes were averted to the passing women, waiting anxiously for a hail, a whistle or call.

Rudy stood in the shadows of a barred pawnshop window and called after the women. "Mama, come over here."

The shortest of the trio broke away, recognizing him. She came over quickly, hips twisting pretentiously under the straight lines of her red coat. She was fleshy to the point of chubbiness and her face, though noticeably young under the brazen whore make-up, appeared yellow and aged, like newsprint that has lain too long under the sun.

The other women waited while she came over.

"Yeah, Daddy?" she said, a hesitant, frightened smile on her wide red mouth.

"What are you doin?" he said.

She jerked her head as though it were obvious. "I'm workin, Daddy."

"Haven't I got eyes?" he said. "What do I see? Do I see you workin, Mama?"

"I—I was just talkin."

"You was just screwin around!" he cried, unmindful of the stares of the women and passers-by.

"For real, Rudy Daddy—I was just talkin for a minute—"

"You ain't out here to talk! You're out here to pull them tricks and cop that bread, dig? Now get your ass on the other side of the street and keep it there!"

She nodded dutifully. "O.K., Daddy."

She started away, but he pulled her back. "How much money you got?"

She hesitated. "I . . . not much, I—"

"Give it here."

"Awww, Daddy."

"Give it here!" he said.

She gave him some bills from her change purse, pouting. "I can keep my bread just as good as you can!"

"You ain't got the brains." He counted for a moment. Give me the rest of it."

"Rudy baby—"

"Give me all of it, Mama! No arguments! No Rudy-baby nothin! Give me the bread and shut up!"

She opened her coat and fingered down the neck of her sweater, pulling out several bills from between her wide breasts.

"Now get across the street in a goddamn hurry," he said, pacified. "And if I catch you screwin around when I show again, I'm gonna break both your legs!"

She left, and he looked up to find both the women looking at him. "What are you bitches lookin at?" he said. They turned away without answering, their hips tight under the flaring coats, their eyes shifting to the passing traffic and lonesome men who watched them from car windows hungrily, shyly. Passing.

Still he felt the death; his fingers ached with it as he gripped the money Nina had given him. He shoved it into his deep overcoat pocket, feeling the round nobs of capsules through tissue paper at the bottom of the warm pouch. He shivered at the touch of them, unable to squeeze back the fear, the queasy twisting of his entrails, impelled to call Nina back and further debase her, as though that in some way could push the night and its terrors away.

I told The Man—I said I'd kill the snitch and The Man's paid me . . .

21

He passed the Garden Bar and Poolroom without entering, knowing how the faces would look if he had. The fear . . . *Sonny—Rudy—Sonny* . . . the voices, the dirty hands with fingers blue from the chalk, palms white from the cue-stick powder, missing an easy shot because he had entered.

The stupes.

He didn't need guys who could believe that he had busted Sonny Tubbs, the crippled pusher. What reason could he have for busting Sonny? They were both in the same business, but they weren't hurting each other. Even the dagotown pusher was wary of him now, just because of Sonny.

Rudy wondered how the bad mouth about him had started, although he'd arrived at the point where he didn't much care. He had his regular customers and he didn't have to worry about keeping his own habit straight.

Well, they'll be talkin outa the other side of their mouths after tonight!

He could feel trouble in the air: Sonny busted by the Feds, Black Bertha slowing up on her trade, Dell, the Scene's senior pusher, freezing up on all but a few of his regulars. It was all in the air, like the smell of death which had been troubling him. But now *he* had the boy; he could lie around up in his crib, twisted, drugged to the verge of insensibility—*To hell with them junkies!*—and listen to jams with his mind blank and the music written on the long, hump-shouldered ridge of his consciousness, with no hunger and no need to cop, gone into his shell of security like a turtle, like a bear in its hibernation, like a bullet, resting, waiting for the moment to joyously explode itself out from the chamber of a forty-five automatic . . .

He turned off the street, thinking of his purpose tonight, the lights and noises of the Scene enticing him.

You can't make me!

And his mother was gone. Bitch, he thought.

He could see his father in a cheap casket, laid out in a $37.50 suit: "Condolences of McPherson Cement Co." Thirty-seven fifty for twenty years of forgotten toil. He hated the memory of his parents. He refused to think of them further.

Ninety-seventh, he noticed, looking up at the street sign. He crossed over to the next corner and waited, his back against a tree.

He lighted another cigarette; it tasted raw in his mouth. He would have to have a fix soon. He could have that almost anywhere: there were works stashed at the Garden Bar, the poolroom, near a small bush off the sidewalk on Ninety-second, in the awning of the Century Barber Shop on Seventieth, in the mailbox of a deserted house on the corner of Seventy-first and Maple . . .

Works were getting hard to buy, too, he thought idly. Some new city rule forbade the sale of hypodermic needles without a prescription. But there was a druggist downtown who would sell Rudy a hypodermic needle any time, knowing he was doing something contrary to the law but anxious to increase his earnings by thirty-five cents.

Thirty-five cents. It was a good price. Fellows he knew who'd been to Chicago said that works cost a dollar there, just for the needle and eye-dropper. Only to junkies; when you had a prescription you could get them for the regular price.

Rudy had a new needle tonight, and an eye-dropper.

He began to feel scared again, like the times he'd shot too much air into a vein and the bubbles refused to come out when he pressed down on his arm.

A car passed, music coming from a half-opened window, softly in the cold night.

The winter-stiff bark of the tree bit into his back deeply, like the teeth of some wild animal. He felt the fear quicken.

I said I'd do it . . .

With a chill, he thought back to the afternoon at the junkyard on Sixtieth, where bed mattresses sold for a dollar.

"Batt'ry?" the small Jew had said. "You got car?"

"I gotta Cadillac. I don't want it for my own car."

"You want good one? Good secondhand?"

"No. Just an old one, real old, the oldest one you got. One with

23

the acid running out—get me one like that, with the white crust on it."

And he had taken it up the back stairs to his room in Lou's Hotel, for one dollar. One capsule of heroin.

Sonofabitch, he cursed himself. What are you gettin scared about? Look. See? The snitch is comin out. He trusts you. Just like he trusted you over the phone. Here he comes. It's all set up, real crazy.

"Whadda you say?" said the police informer.

"Whadda you say, Andy?" Rudy said.

Andy Hodden came over so he could see Rudy's face in the darkness. He was nineteen, two years younger than Rudy, and short, almost stunted, with a harried, little-boy terror in his eyes and gaunt features.

"What's happenin?" he said.

"Heaven," Rudy said.

"I've had heaven, man."

"I got a bomb to knock your nuts out." Rudy smiled. "It's really grand, my man, the choicest to come along my way for a long time. You hip?"

Andy shook his head. "I'm bogue, but I ain't gonna indulge. I'm tryin to kick."

"I've heard that wire a thousand times. Remember who you're talkin to, man."

"I'm talkin to another junkie," Andy said. "I'm tellin you I haven't had no stuff for four days; I'm clean. I'll never get hooked again. I don't know why I said I'd come out when you called. I had company—"

"A broad?" Rudy raised an eyebrow. "Thinkin about turnin her out, huh?"

Andy shook his head again, almost plaintively. "She's not that kind of girl. I'm thinkin about marryin—"

"You wanna get high," Rudy cut him off. "That's why you come out; because you *want* some drugs. Nothin can stop you when you want some drugs, not even a broad."

"No . . ."

"Don't pull my leg; you're bogue and you know it. You want some stuff so bad the veins are poppin out on your head; and they're poppin out in your monkey tracks the same way."

Andy's shoulder jerked nervously. "Why? Why do you wanna turn me on, man? You froze on me every time I ran into you before."

"I went for you real tough, though," Rudy said testily, becoming impatient. "I like your style. I just never had a chance to pull you in and have a long talk."

The youngster's face seemed to turn a sickly gray in the darkness. "You don't have to larceny me—I won't flip on you. I'll never flip on nobody again."

"What about Popeye?"

"I—It was a forced bust. Detectives Davis and Patterson, the Rollers, they made me. I had to set somebody up. Popeye'd just got in town; I didn't know him."

"You're too weak to take your own weight!"

"It was him or me! The Rollers have a secret indictment against me from that time with Big Earl."

"I remember Big Earl," Rudy said softly, staring hard at him.

"The hammer can fall any time!" Andy said. "Why should *I* go to the joint?"

Rudy's lips smiled tightly. "I guess you got somethin there." Then quickly, convincingly: "I'd have done the same thing in your place. Nobody wants to go to the joint when someone else can go, takin the weight. Right?"

Andy turned away. "I'm goin, I'll see you later."

Rudy was almost relieved. "I wanted to turn you on, baby," he said carelessly. "I got some new stuff in today. Why don't you bust a cap with me? It's choice. I used this mornin and I'm still nice. I haven't been sick all day."

Andy paused, and Rudy became frightened again.

Go on, you punk, you little punk!

"I've kicked," Andy said, but this time without conviction, his voice lowered a trifle, his breath beginning to show whitely in the coldness.

25

"One or two things couldn't hurt you," Rudy tried lamely. He waited, hoping: He's gonna walk away in a minute; I know he will.

But Andy came back. "I *couldn't* get hooked with a deuce, could I?"

"No, you couldn't." Rudy watched the expression of greed come over the boy's face.

"You got some works?"

"A new set."

Andy stood undecided. His eyes had grown smaller in the darkness; they glowed as his head made several senseless, effort-filled jerks on his neck.

"Two things couldn't hurt me," he said, repeating Rudy's words. "Where can we use?"

Rudy said, "Wait a minute," then stood there with his mouth open and heart pounding, wondering why he had said anything like that, listening to the loud thumping within the walls of his chest. "If you really wanna kick—"

"This is nothin," Andy said. "Two things?" He laughed scornfully. "Two things won't hurt me. Look, I can use ten things a week and not get another bee."

"But I thought you wanted to kick."

"I *have* kicked," Andy said, grinning stupidly, forgetting his words of a few moments before, his vows of a few days before, returning once more to the drug, innocently, like a mindless infant, aware of nothing save his hands and mouth and genitals. He rose up as though trying to make himself taller, his feet tilting him forward. A gland in his neck was making the ducts in his mouth water at the thought of drugs: cooker, matches, needle, eye-dropper, and pacifier. "Where can we use? Nobody's home at my crib—let's go by there."

"I—I got a room at the Quality Hotel."

"Don't you live at Lou's, you and Nina?" Andy said, his eyes becoming suspicious for a moment. "Why did you get a room at the Quality?" He canceled out this question with the next: "Why go way over to the Quality when here's my pad right across the street?"

"I—" Rudy stumbled. "Listen, if you wanna kick—"

"C'mon, I got another pair of works in the stash at home. C'mon!" He begged now, becoming afraid that Rudy would take back his offer of free drugs.

"I wouldn't blame you a damn bit," Rudy said, his fingers touching the tissue and its nest of capsules in his pocket.

"You wouldn't blame me about what?"

"About kickin. I wouldn't blame you if you did."

Andy watched him. "You look like you're leery."

"I'm not leery. If we're gonna use, I'd just rather use my pad."

"I don't see any sense in it."

Rudy bit his lip. "Is—is anybody around at your place?"

"My sister's gone to a square-settin with her chump; they won't be back till late. Nobody'll bother us."

"What about the broad you was keepin company?"

"I told her not come back tonight. She won't come back."

Rudy tried to seem doubtful. "I don't know . . . I—well, I just don't feel—I mean, in your crib."

Andy waited a long time before he answered. "I wouldn't bust you, if that's what you're leery about."

They waited, then Rudy sucked in a deep breath. "Let's go."

He was no longer afraid now. Until this moment everything had been unreal and unsubstantial. But with this final movement, their voices, their mouths pushing out the words, letting them become hard objects in the air to fall useless to the ground, there was substance.

In the apartment Andy put on a record:

> *Somebody done stole my gal,*
> *The dirty mother———*

And their own voices sang the weird, illogical worldly words, their bodies moved with a wonderfully primitive, inherited rhythm, as they dropped two capsules in the cooker on each double-slap of the bass and drums, and the alto horn pleading like a human voice:

Somebody done stole my gal,
And I wonder did he———her?

. . . Until it was all deliciously ready, the raw smell of cooked heroin permeating the room.

Andy used first. "Crazy."

"I told you so."

Andy's head dropped. "I'm . . . *twisted!*"

"It's dyno, baby."

"Go on and use."

"I will."

"It's crazy!"

"I told you it was nice."

Andy raised up, raised the iron shutters that were his eyelids. "Baby, it's TERRIBLE!"

They sat there, not hearing the music, with a half-filled glass of bloody water in which an eye-dropper and needle sat clouded by the redness.

Andy's mouth became an alligator's maw: "TERRIBLE!"

And that explained it all, established their reason for existing here in a room with a record player playing a filthy record, a cooker with a small mound of waste sugar half-mooned on one side, the bloody water and the eye-dropper filled like a fat, red leech.

Now this was the time for action, but Rudy sat in his chair immobilized by heroin, his eyes fighting their own heaviness and losing the battle, sitting for a full hour with a deep sickness in his belly which refused to come any higher, doing everything in slow motion. Once he lighted a cigarette, then nodded; when he opened his eyes again he found the cigarette smoldering in his jacket pocket, and when the fire was extinguished there was a great hole in the fabric. . . . The movement, the cool movement of nodding . . .

I told The Man I'd do it . . . I said . . .

He forced his lids open, and the room seemed to swell. Then he saw clearer: Andy sat facing him on the bed, head down, almost touching his knees, arms limply held by his sides.

"Flip," Rudy said, using the name given to Andy by those of

the Scene who hated and feared him, his lips tired from the one word suddenly, tired from the sensation that was no longer terror but only a real, heavy knowledge in his mind.

"Flip," he said again. "You sonofabitch!" feeling the anger course up in him, the anger he needed to impart strength to his vaguely reluctant hands and mind.

"*Flip!*"

Andy started up, his mouth gaped open, straightening his back slowly from its usual slump. "Yah, babeee?" His speech impaired by heroin, his tongue thick. "What's matter, babeee? The record player, my man?" He reached for it blindly. "Oooo, I'm twisted!"

This, Rudy seeing him like this, became all important. He felt his hand move over the lethal capsules, filled not with heroin but the white crust of pure battery acid. He felt his mind knowing the unoriginality of another junkie. He saw two tiny white things in his palm.

"You wanna do again?" he asked.

Andy nodded, jerking to himself as the nod developed. He rubbed his nose vigorously, arousing himself. "Yeah, daddy, I could stand another deuce."

Andy took the capsules.

He took them in his greed, not really wanting them or needing them, just as Rudy knew he would.

He cleaned the bloody dropper and dropped the contents from each capsule-half into the cooker, even tapping them for any residue that might have clung to the gelatin.

Sure, trusting, he put on a new record and was humming its tune when he shot the clear liquid into the worn, black depressions of his left arm's antecubital vein. Then, as the blood of the vein carried hot death quickly to his heart, he looked at Rudy in shocked surprise, frozen by the almost instantaneous blow.

"Snitchin bastard," Rudy said, more out of horror than out of the power he suddenly felt.

Andy's mouth opened and moved and gulped, but no words came out.

"Punk sonofabitch," Rudy said, standing, bursting with his new

29

ou can't carry your own weight, huh? You bust people
u're good enough to live when you take their lives,

Andy grunted like a pig and threw up a greenish muck on the
floor.

Rudy wavered unsteadily. "You ain't good enough to live, you
punk! In this world you carry your own weight. You die if you
ain't strong. You won't testify against Popeye—me and The Man'll
make sure of that. You'll be dead!" A twisted core in Rudy's throat
gagged him, squeezed involuntary tears to his eyes. "I'm killin you
'cause you're a junkie what ain't got no right to be a junkie."

Andy tried to stand up, fell over in the mess that had erupted
from his belly. He stared up at Rudy, not understanding.

"I was . . . supposed to . . . to get married . . ." he gobbled. His
forehead twisted and bounced loudly against the floor. He rolled
over in an agony of pain, both legs shooting up like bows to his
chest, his eyes wide in their sockets, staring away and away until
they saw nothing.

"Don't you understand?" Rudy cried, trembling over the life-
less body. "YOU GOT A HOT SHOT! YOU'RE DEAD, YOU
SNITCHIN BASTARD!"

The music played on. Automatically, Rudy went over and shut
the machine off, standing for a long time with his back turned.

He felt weak; his legs wobbled under him. Finally he mustered
the courage to turn back and look at the body. He thought: That's
it; it's all over, just like The Man said. . . .

But The Man did not exist here, in this room. There were only
two people here.

Rudy trembled, unable to gain complete control of himself. He
found his coat and stumbled out of the room blindly, fearful of
every shadow as he tripped down the tenement steps. His heart was
bursting, and it seemed for a while almost impossible that he would
get away.

Then he was on the street, and the Scene was not far off, warmly
beckoning to him with its lights as though it could save him.

He did not feel safe until he had lost himself in its myriad-neoned insanity.

Sitting in an unmarked car at the corner of Ninety-eighth and Maple, Detective Virgil Patterson nudged his partner, Detective Sergeant Mance Davis.

"Isn't that that junkie, Rudy Black?" Patterson said, pointing over the steering wheel.

A big man, Davis twisted in the front seat to get a better look. "Yeah, that's him. So what?"

"He might be heavy with drugs. Maybe we ought to pull him in."

Davis, with a wide red mustache peeking out under a thickly bandaged nose, presented a threatening and formidable picture to the younger man.

"Are you trying to give me some more of your lip?" he said.

Patterson sighed. "I don't know what you mean, sir."

"You know damn well what I mean. Who makes the decisions around here?"

Patterson felt helpless anger burn in him again. "You do, sergeant."

"Then why don't you let *me* make 'em?" His authority established, Davis settled back in his seat. "You know what happened the last time we pulled Black in. The Man's got a dozen connections. We couldn't hold the punk more than forty-eight hours if we caught him with a kilo."

They lapsed into a silence, waiting. One of the neighborhood pushers, Black Bertha, had been enlisted as an informer several weeks before and was due to report her latest activities with The Man, the bulk supplier in the area.

In his short time with the Narco Squad, Patterson had learned to respect his immediate superior, even if he didn't like him personally. He sat back under the wheel and lit a cigarette resignedly. If Davis said leave Rudy Black alone, they'd leave Rudy Black alone; he could have poppies growing out of his lapels and they'd still

31

leave him alone. It was funny the way Davis did things, but the results were invariably effective.

With a side glance, he saw the sergeant's bandaged nose again and decided to salt the wound a little. At least that was one way he could get back at him until his transfer came through. "That Georgie Barris . . ." he began.

Davis threw him a wilting look. "What about that Georgie Barris, college boy?"

"I was just thinking about him," Patterson said deliberately.

Davis twisted around in his seat. "Do you think you're being funny?"

Patterson tried not to betray his grin. "No, Mance, you know I'm not."

"You've been raking at me ever since that sonofabitch busted my nose," Davis accused. "Maybe you haven't seen him since the boys picked him up the other day."

"No."

"Well, maybe you ought to go over to County and take a look, college boy. I told you that night when it happened on the playground—I told you it'd be that junkie's birthday when I caught up with him. If you don't believe it, just go see him!" He settled back with a grunt, but not satisfied he resumed again. "All you bastards think I'm too old, that's what you think, isn't it? All you *young* guys! You think you know so much 'cause you been to college—but, brother, I had to rough my way!"

"I don't think you're old," Patterson said unconvincingly. All at once, he felt ashamed of himself. He had taken advantage of Davis, neglecting to remember that Georgie Barris, alias Popeye, also had soundly thumped him along with Davis and Andy Hodden, who had arranged the buy. He didn't feel very proud of his needling then.

He puffed on his cigarette, turning its coal into a bright, angry glow. It was a damned shame, he thought, he and Davis being the only two Negro detectives in the Sixth Precinct and disliking each other so. Where it began, he couldn't say. Maybe on Patterson's first night with the Narco Squad, the first time he met Davis and

32

got a glimpse of the complexity of the big man's ego. Or maybe it started when he goofed on the Bertha Travis set-up, his first real active duty with Davis.

He shrugged. Wherever it began, he and Davis were caught in this thing called the Scene, clinging to each other with double strength, one supporting the other. Davis needs me, he thought, even if only to shoot off a little steam. And, God knew he needed Davis! Although Patterson refused to admit that he was afraid of the Scene, at least he acknowledged that this assignment would call for a great deal of getting used to.

"Got a call-in from Captain Beeker today," Davis said through his thoughts, sounding almost genial. "Remember that Halsted case? The kid who got run down by a police cruiser at headquarters?"

"Vaguely," Patterson said, trying to recall the particulars in the case. "Picked up speeding, or something, wasn't he? Had some heroin on him?"

"That's it," Davis said. "The kid died last week and Beeker's catching hell about it. The heroin the boy was picked up with was high, almost a hundred per cent. They think it came from the Scene."

"Where would he get stuff like that?"

"Not on the Scene, I can tell you." Davis hesitated for a moment, as though newly appraising Patterson. "It was probably from Mexico, or one of the ports. I didn't tell Beeker, but I think I've got a small line."

Patterson became interested.

"That junkie we got, Barris—he had high stuff, too."

"Does that say anything?" Patterson asked.

"Dope doesn't come like that, college boy. After you've been around a while, you'll see what I mean. Those high percentages usually come from the same bag."

"Then Barris and the Halsted boy—"

"Maybe," Davis said. "They were social worlds apart—Halsted was white, Barris colored."

"There must be a tie-in somewhere," Patterson said, but his momentary enthusiasm was quickly deflated by Davis.

"Just suppose you let me do the figuring." The red mustache closed tightly over the straight mouth.

Patterson knew the congeniality had come to an end. He was surprised at how easily he had intimidated Davis.

Bertha Travis' progress along the Scene was surreptitious. She came quickly from The Man's apartment on Pennsylvania, periodically glancing behind her as she walked up Ninetieth to Maple. Maybe it was her imagination, but it seemed that Dell Swiggins, her boy friend and close confidant of The Man, had been watching her closer than usual lately.

She pulled the collar of her coat tight about her throat, her belly turning with the quick fear. They mustn't ever find out! And, anyway, it wasn't Dell Sergeant Davis was interested in—it was The Man. Who could blame her for trying to save her own neck?

The thought of her two daughters, Edna and Ginny, reassured her for a moment. They were just *babies*. If she went to jail, what would happen to them?

She danced away apprehensively from the crooked fingers of a tenement's shadow, looking behind her quickly again.

It was driving her almost crazy! Why couldn't the Rollers have picked on somebody else? She wasn't doing anything, only selling drugs, just like Rudy Black or Ace or Sonny Tubbs—or Dell himself. Why couldn't Davis have set one of them up for a prop?

The darkness of Ninetieth closed in against her back as she neared the muted, rhythmic roaring of the Scene, the twinkling dazzle of its cheap lights. The night was dying and she was surprised; she had been occupied with Dell in dope talk for over two hours.

She thought of Dell's bragging manner, now that The Man had given him a seat at the foot of the throne. She remembered his penetrating look as he suggested that something other than indifference was the cause for the latest drop in her drug trade.

Could he know? she thought frantically.

She had tried to remind him that she wasn't a junkie herself, that she dealt only because of the children, only because there was nothing else for her to do. There was no need for her to scramble after those dirty junkies . . .

But could he suspect it was because of the Rollers, because the Rollers had shot her a prop, one that was impossible for her to resist: her own freedom?

Without warning, the Scene spread open its arms. She ignored the greetings of whores, the requests for service from various junkies, the pimps who were addicts eying her anew in consideration, wondering what approach would be likely to loosen the strings on the black woman's dope bag.

Davis had said Ninety-eighth, she remembered. Even the cold was unable to quench the Scene's fire. Closing time was at hand for the various bars, and the people wormed themselves along the broken pavement.

Ninety-sixth, Bertha said to herself.

From here on, the Scene stretched endlessly red: the death-mask faces of whores in the black wounds of each building.

"Hi, Bertha."

"How ya doin, Bert?"

"How's business, honey?"

"Stop by on your way back, Bertie."

"Nothin's happenin," Bertha said irritably. "Ain't nothin happenin!"

She saw the car on Ninety-eighth, but they spotted her first. The Ford started up. She cast one last look over her shoulder and turned on the corner.

The car was sitting beyond the dim beacon of a street lamp, on the right-hand side. She crossed over and hurried down to it.

Davis opened the door and let her crawl in the back. "What the hell took you so long?"

"I had to wait," she said breathlessly. "The connect ain't come through the last week, and The Man's downtown. Sylvia didn't have nothin on hand."

Davis kept his gaze on the front window, while Patterson idly surveyed the street behind.

"What's happened to The Man's pipeline?"

35

"I don't know," Bertha said, twisting her hands nervously. "Somethin happened, I don't know what. The Man's pulled Dell in. I have to go by what Dell tells me, and he ain't gonna tell me everything."

"He's not getting set to put the freeze on, is he?"

Bertha shrugged in the darkness. "Maybe, I don't know. Since Sonny Tubbs was picked up by the Feds, The Man's been real leery. Sonny used to cop from him."

"The grapevine around here says Rudy Black fingered Tubbs," Davis said.

"The Man don't believe that," Bertha told him. "Dell told me tonight. He said The Man has a way to find out about Rudy. He'll find out for sure—one way or the other. Dell says he don't believe Rudy did it, either. Maybe the word got around because Sonny was shootin his mouth off about Rudy the night he got busted."

"What else did you find out, Bertha?"

"That's all—except that there ain't gonna be no drugs in quantity until The Man gets himself set up again."

"The Man could be getting ready to suspend operations completely," Patterson suggested. "Then we'd be left out in the cold."

"Oh, no he won't," Davis said thickly. "I've been after that sonofabitch for over five years. I won't let him cheat me *that* easy!" He turned to Bertha. "Okay, honey. Let me know the first time something comes up. You're doing fine—just keep it up." He leaned forward and pulled up the front seat, opened the door.

Bertha clambered out.

"Oh, Bertie," Davis said.

"Yeah, Mr. Davis?"

"How're the kids?"

She was lost for words for a moment. "Oh . . . they're just fine."

"Good," Davis said.

Bertha was relieved. She felt almost as if she'd taken a lifesaving purge. She could feel the network closing in now; she could tell it in Davis' voice. She was amazed at how well the man knew the business of dope, being a cop, and she knew that her involuntary enlistment into his service hadn't come a day too soon.

At last the whole mess was coming to an end. Maybe one day she would have a clean apartment, one with gas heat and even a garbage-disposal, a big living room and TV, in another section of town where the girls could go to good schools with large playgrounds. The most important thing was to get the girls away from the Scene! At least dope had provided money enough for that.

Dell was waiting for her on the corner of Ninety-eighth and Maple. His big yellow face towered over her without its usual smile, and the slickness of his konked head looked hard and clublike.

She was frightened into speechlessness.

"On your way to the pad, Bert?" he said slowly. His hands, in the pockets of his overcoat, threatened her with their bigness.

"Dell . . ." She tried to grin and seem delightfully surprised, but the attempt was blunted by her fear. "I—I was just—"

"You was just in a car," he said. "I saw you."

She didn't know her next answer, didn't know what lie to summon up in order to save herself.

He began to laugh suddenly. "Don't mean to tell me you turnin tricks at *your* age, Bert!"

She grasped it quickly. "And why not? I *have* tricked, my man, and I got just as much to offer as any whore on the Scene."

He continued to laugh, but it was subdued now. "You're a long way from home, Bert. C'mon, I'll walk you."

He took her arm firmly and started down Maple.

The dying lights of the Scene laughed unsympathetically at Black Bertha.

As Davis and Patterson entered the squad room, Lieutenant Stuart, the officer in charge of plain-clothes men, came over to them.

"Beeker's got a bug in his ass," he said. "A couple of very important citizens have just made a nighttime survey of the Scene. We'd better get over there right away."

They went over to a frost-paneled door on which *Captain* appeared in small letters.

Captain Claude Beeker popped up quickly from his seat. He

was a bald, nervous man, with a body that was lost inside his expensive business suit.

"This is Mr. James Flaubert and Donald Halsted," he said in a high voice, gesturing to a redheaded little pumpkin of a man and a younger, hawk-faced fellow, both of whom sat in front of his desk. "Mr. Flaubert, as you know, is district manager of this section of the city. Mr. Halsted is the brother of Richard Halsted, whose son died a short time ago. . . . Have seats, won't you?"

They all sat down. Beeker looked around at them with jerky little motions of his head. "We're all here?" he said.

"Garver is on detail, sir," Stuart offered.

"Well, dammit, get him on the radio and tell him to get the hell in here!" Beeker said. "It's way past these gentlemen's bedtime."

"Yes, sir." Stuart got up quickly and left.

Flaubert watched Patterson and Davis placidly, his hands hanging limply between his thighs. Donald Halsted squinted at them with what might have been disapproval.

Flaubert beat a rapid finger tattoo on his legs and then began. "We want a cleanup. There'll be no hees and haws about it; we're going to work on it right *now*."

Beeker shifted a bit in his chair. "You remember, Davis, I was talking to you the other day about the very same thing."

"Yes, sir."

"I recommend an immediate drive right here in my district, first off," Flaubert said. "I've talked to the commissioner about it and we're both in agreement."

Stuart came back in, closing the door very quietly. "He's on his way in, sir," he told Beeker.

"Good. Go on, Mr. Flaubert."

Flaubert shrugged. "I've covered the whole thing in one word, captain: drive. Drive dope out of my district. I never realized how far this thing had gone until word of the Halsted incident reached me. This gentleman is a very old friend of mine"—he nodded toward Donald Halsted—"as is his brother. Tonight we took a turn together around my district, and I'll have to admit that conditions are deplorable. My investigators tell me that my area is the city's central dope outlet. If Ricky Halsted got dope anywhere, they assure me, it had to be in my part of town." He paused. "I won't waste words. I want every drug addict or drug handler in the vicinity picked up and behind bars as soon as possible. Don't regard this as a reflection on your capabilities, but I want this district cleaned up once and for all."

Beeker said, "There'll be obstacles, of course. I've got the best men on the force, but dope isn't a thing you can clear away in days. A few months, perhaps—"

"May I say something, captain?" Lieutenant Stuart said.

"Go right ahead, lieutenant."

"Well, sir, I don't mean to sound pessimistic," Stuart began, "but narcotics isn't as easily erased as all that. You see, our biggest problem when we make an arrest is that another peddler or addict is next in line for the empty place. We've got four squads under my swing-shift command, and four under Lieutenant Speer: thirty-two men, working from twelve to fourteen hours. These men can't even begin to cope with the scores of dope violators. Eventually, with Federal help, we will. But not right away—unless we have an extremely good break." He looked toward Davis. "Detective Sergeant Davis has made more arrests than any other officer in the precinct. Maybe he can give you the over-all picture."

Davis got up and went over to a wall-map of the city. He picked up a wooden map-pointer and, as if lecturing to rookies, began:

"This is 'the Scene,' addicts' jargon meaning the place where everything's going on, where dope, women, or any other commodity can be bought or stolen. This area east and west, embraces Pennsylvania, Lippert, Maple, and Cambridge streets. North and south includes every cross street within these four thoroughfares, from Hundred-and-sixth and Maple to Sixty-ninth, which I believe, Mr. Flaubert, is the border of your district."

Flaubert nodded. "There're fifty thousand voters in that area."

"Then it might interest you to know that one out of every twenty or thirty voters is an addict or an occasional user of narcotics," Davis said. "I can't say when the influx of dope began in this part of town, but it must have been a bit before the war; the fast-money,

39

fast-life time. Now it's in there deep, and we're having a hell of a time trying to dig it out." He tapped the map with the pointer. "The property here has depreciated until it's almost worthless, and when one bad bunch moves out or we bust 'em out, another slips right in. This is a part of town where almost anyone can live, except the best citizens. We have three groups of people in these thirty-five or more streets: Negroes predominate; then there are Italians here in this section called dago-town; Polish here." He indicated all the sections with the pointer. "They've segregated voluntarily, but they intermix; the influence of heroin is interracial. We've got something like a syndicate in this part of town, with the central connection being handled by a character called The Man. He's got an out-of-state pipeline that hasn't failed to get in less than eight ounces a month. This is pure stuff. When you break it down, it comes out to something like eighty ounces after cutting, or enough to give thirty-two thousand addicts a single fix at a buck a head."

"Can't you get that pipeline?" Donald Halsted asked. "Seems to me, if you know so much about it, it wouldn't be any trouble at all to knock the slats right out from under this thing."

"The method varies," Davis told him. "That's why we have so much trouble with it. Sometimes the stuff is brought in direct, while at other times a 'drop' is made at an outlying area. Someone picks it up and brings it across the state line. Then the stuff is taken to an unknown center, cut up, and distributed to The Man, the kingpin. He in turn distributes it to various pushers and middlemen, and the drugs find their way into the addict's possession in less than twenty-four hours."

"We're working in conjunction with the Treasury men in this drop thing," Stuart added. "But the drops are so complex and well organized that we've run into a blank wall so far."

"Look, I don't see where it's so difficult," Flaubert said with a sigh of impatience. "Knock out this kingpin, the fella you call The Man—get *him* out of circulation."

Davis walked over in front of the desk. "All right. All right, let's say we knock off The Man. We go over to his apartment, the one he has on Pennsylvania—he has several, but this is where he generally sleeps. We search it, and more than likely we find nothing; even if there is dope on the premises it won't *belong* to him—somebody else'll have it and he won't know a thing about it. Why should he? He's a respected businessman with a fleet of trucks." He walked back over to the map. "So what can we do? Book him for investigation, which is not a legal charge and one which his army of lawyers can have him released on within the next hour? Charge him with possession of drugs, when we couldn't produce enough evidence to get a true bill? With a sale, when he won't touch money directly or keep it on his person immediately after a sale? He's got a woman by the name of Sylvia Dutton who handles all this for him." Davis grinned knowingly under the red mustache. "You see, we're right back where we started. The Man is where we can see him and watch him, but he's untouchable. I've been after him quite a while now, and I should know. But he can't last forever; the odds are finally going against him."

"Well, if you can't touch him, get those pushers!" Flaubert said. "Those are the ones we want—the same bastards who sold junk to young Rickie Halsted. If you get them, this Man creature won't come out and sell narcotics himself. The whole organization will fold!"

Donald Halsted broke in smoothly. "I'd like to say I'm inclined to side with Mr. Davis. You know how I feel about the death of my nephew; I want to help all I can. However, as I told Richard, we can't be precipitate. I'm sure the police know what they're doing."

Flaubert would not be appeased. Getting up, he leaned across the desk toward Beeker. "At the moment, I'm guided by Mr. Halsted, captain, but I just want you to know I'm expecting results. *Results.* Am I understood?"

Beeker reddened, pressed for an adequate reply. "I'll do all in my power—"

"You just make sure you do," Flaubert warned.

The door opened just then and a tall, blond man in baggy pants came in.

41

"Garver!" Beeker exploded, relieved to be able to give vent to his pent-up rage and frustration. "Where the hell have you been?"

"Sorry, Captain, but something came up. A woman called in a little while ago about some kid named Andy Hodden. We thought at first it was an overdose, but all you had to do was look in the kid's face to see it was a hot shot."

"A hot shot?" Donald Halsted said.

"An injection of poison," Garver told him matter-of-factly. "Usually it's strychnine, or any soluble rat-killer."

"You said Andy Hodden?" Davis said in surprise.

"That's right," said Garver. "Flip."

"Does this have something to do with dope?" Flaubert demanded.

"Yes sir," said Garver. "The boy thought he was getting a fix."

Flaubert looked at all of them. Then, without a word, he and Donald Halsted walked out of the room.

The message had been delivered.

The eyes from windows watched.

The last snow lay melting under the blank white stare of the sun.

The traffic moved lethargically down Maple, slushing the asphalt to a dirty gray foam. Drivers averted their eyes.

The fat owner of the Garden Poolroom sat upon a popbottle case in front of his establishment. The great scarred door stood padlocked, the lock not his own.

The daylight people ambled along the thoroughfare, shopping, their eyes bright, the wives talking, the husbands—afternoon workers and laborers—confident, assured; they owned the Scene. The meek had inherited the earth.

The eyes from windows watched.

Children, like strange, other-world beings, appeared from their school places, skipping and yelling, their hearts screaming in this new freeness, their mouths and eyes opened wide, their hands strong and destructive, pushing, hitting, scratching, their legs pumping in their galoshes, weirdly distorted, short, fat, chunky bits of flesh in the baggy trousers of snowsuits.

The Scene purred.

The streets seemed happy to receive the new life, the elated feet and faces, the free voices, the sound of car horns honking, the brisk buying at corner stores and the greetings between people, the surprise in every eye that sensed the *difference*, the sensation of health.

A woman with her child stopped on the corner of Ninety-third and Maple and stared, lost for a moment in the unfamiliarity of the street although she had lived there for years.

The Panic had come.

The period of No Dope.

The time when junkies lined the counters of drugstores to buy paregoric, to take it and boil its sweetness into a brownness for its opium content, to shoot eye-dropperfuls into their veins until their arms swelled, red and stinging, and the sickness was abated momentarily.

The time when people who had drugs kept their doors shut to all but a select few.

The time when heroin, when available, cost a dollar and a quarter more than usual. Because of the risk.

The time when dozens of addicts were arrested for holding up doctors, for walking into their offices boldly, with only the need to satisfy the bee, demanding drugs at the point of a knife or gun.

The time when junkies became the people of the night, and C was their eyes, O their arms, P their bellies drawn up tight and empty with the grainy feel of diarrhea.

This was the Panic: people dying unseen, scraping the sugary bottoms of cookers, licking the bitter taste away with their tongues, frightened and cursing the unknown torment within their intestines, their eyes watery and twisted, their mouths yawning into big raw gapes.

Outside, the day held no relief. The Good People ruled, enjoying the legacy of a deposed clan—until nightfall.

The eyes from windows watched.

And hungered.

December

2

WINTER, WITH heavy feet, stepped into the city.

These were good days for Rudy Black. They were days measured in satisfying the need for drugs. They were crazy days.

Nina, the prostitute he owned, was working and making money, and he had a car, a Buick. He made nice side-money chauffeuring the boosting girls around. Chauffeur to the stars. He would have a booster someday. He had made up his mind to that. A boosting girl made twice as much money in an hour as a whore made in a week. It was something to strike out for, a goal. . . . *You need a change, baby. Even a car needs a tune-up.*

Rudy Black, a new, shiny, twenty-one-year-old machine, with all the working parts in order.

This is Rudy Black in winter. . . .

One of the girls georged him, just for kicks, just to see if he was as good a producer as a braggart. Her name was Alice, and her face was like that of a baby's but deeply lined and warped with the pressures of life. Still, her body was youthful and she stood planted firmly on big, sexy, yellow legs.

She took him to the apartment she shared with the other girls one afternoon, on the pretext of picking up some hot goods. Then she got on the bed and threw up her skirt over the fleshiness of her hips, and he fell for it just like any trick from the mines. He crawled right in beside her and made a hump in his back, without even being asked.

Alice told all the girls about it, and eventually the episode got back to Nina.

"You can't even bring it here to me, you bastard!" Nina shrieked, and to prove his pimp role, to re-enforce his dominance over her, he tried to prove he could—but he was too high at the time.

So what?

But the thing stuck with him, and all the boosting girls became chilly and demanding in their attitudes. In his weird little mind, he began to conjure a sort of revenge on Alice.

Saturday afternoon was a fast day downtown. At noon, all the clerks knocked off for lunch, leaving substitutes to cover one or more counters. It was ideal for boosting, and the girls had picked one particular store simply because everyone considered it a hard touch, being one of the oldest establishments in the business section. But it wasn't hard at all: it was the sweetest sting in town. The exclusive women's section especially was good at lunchtime because only two women were left on the floor, and they were too busy with other customers to keep their eyes on the trio of experienced boosters.

Alice, Marsha Lee,and Leslie had all come from the Apple, home base for a seasonal boosting tour around the country. Alice was from Washington originally, poised and careful; Marsha Lee was from New York, talkative and quick-fingered, eternally grieving about the new arrivals to her man's stable, outdoing both the other girls in an effort to prove herself capable; Leslie too was from New York, black, homely, unimposing, with a very foul mouth when she was aroused. All were addicts, and that meant that they had to work twice as hard, filling the funnel.

"Yes, ladies?" the saleslady, a petite woman in her early fifties, said with a smile.

Marsha Lee pointed. "That dress there."

"Susy Mae, you don't want that," Alice said, standing next to Marsha Lee. She smiled at the saleslady. "We're just looking. Susy Mae, you don't want that, dear. I've tried to tell you—"

"The wool?" the saleslady said. "Isn't it just *beautiful*? Would you like to try it on, madam?" she said to Marsha Lee.

"Susy Mae doesn't—"

"I'll try it on," Marsha Lee said stubbornly.

"Now, Susy Mae—"

48

"Isn't there something for you too, madam?" The saleslady cut her off purposely. Yakking her out of the damned sale. . . . "Over here is our new fall selection . . ." She waved at Marsha Lee, "The door on your right, madam, that's the dressing room." Then back to Alice: "And it's really quite lovely, you know."

Alice looked at some of the tags. "One-seventeen . . . Oh, they are rather attractive, but the price—"

The saleslady took a closer look at Alice's clothes and went on with added vigor. It was easy to see that the ape who was sleeping with her or married to her wouldn't be one to let a mere hundred and seventeen dollars stand in the way of something this yellow bitch had her heart set on.

"But, really, it's scandalously *cheap*, my dear," she hawked, "and it's this store's very own exclusive. And with your figure"— she appraised Alice enviously—"it'd be a perfect crime if you didn't own it. I mean that, right deep down from my heart. This is a creation that was intended for a woman just like you."

Leslie came in then and walked over to them. "I'd like to see your new stock of cashmere toppers," she told the saleslady, who began looking around for the other assistant. But she was standing near the dressing room talking to Marsha Lee.

"Eunice," the first saleslady called. "Eunice, *Eunice* . . . Oh, my goodness—Eunice, please come over here! Excuse me, please, ladies." She went off toward Marsha Lee and the other salesgirl.

Alice and Leslie copped. Three seventy-five dollar velour toppers and four of the hundred-dollar suits. They worked very fast. Alice short-folded and hooked two of the suits to her wide, flaring overcoat and short-folded one of the shorties between her thighs. Leslie did the same. They short-folded the extra topper and placed it at the bottom of a shopping bag Leslie carried.

The saleslady came back and smiled at Leslie. "She'll be over here to take care of you in just a moment." Then to Alice, "Now, as I was saying, this gorgeous little piece of heaven is just the thing for you. Really, if I had *my* way, I'd make it a crime to sell them under two hundred, an absolute crime!"

Alice shook her head helplessly. "I really didn't intend to spend anything when I came down here," she said. "William swore if I brought in anything else this week, clothes, I mean, that he'd shut me out of the house. But Cousin Susy Mae just arrived from Augusta, and she wanted to buy something *really* good, so naturally I brought her here first. . . ."

"Naturally," the saleslady said, doing what Marsha Lee called "jeffing." Looking at her, Alice got sick before it was time for her fix.

"I must admit I am fascinated by this suit," she said, "but— just thinking of William, and he can be so mean when he wants to be . . . Let's look at something a little cheaper, huh?"

They did spend money, approximately a hundred dollars in all.

But they left the store with over eight hundred dollars in suits and coats and shoes, in a bag, under their coats on hooks, and between their thighs, close to the worm that was beginning to gnaw at their bellies.

They had an exceptionally good fence, the owner of a real estate office, a highly respected citizen. He was a comfortably fat man, thinning on top, with a round face that smiled all the time—an occupational disease. Actually he never felt like smiling, except when Alice came. He had big eyes for her, and each time he saw her and the other girls he started playing with an expensive brooch, looking at Alice.

He had tried to go to bed with her several times, but she didn't like him. She told him she didn't like to yard on her man, who was living in New York.

Marsha Lee said she was a goddamned fool. She said Alice's man was yarding full time, why shouldn't she? Especially when here was a man who could do her a lot of good, who had the bread to support her bee and give her almost face value for the goods she pulled, all for a little grooving. Marsha Lee didn't like Alice anyway, and she was drugged because the fence didn't go for *her*. She needed the money more than Alice, so she could keep her man Mickey in Stetsons and Brooks Brothers suits, keep his nose full of cocain so that when she got back to the Apple he would ignore the other whores in his stable.

They fenced separately, although they worked together. This way they got more money out of the fence than if they'd sold him everything at once. They made a hundred each for eight hundred and twenty-five dollars worth of goods. If they had sold it in bulk, they would have received only twenty per cent.

This way was better. One hundred dollars to the good. Each took from this what she thought her man was worth, putting it away in a bulging fund—"My Man Fund"—putting it away faithfully, keeping what she knew was necessary for her sustenance, her drugs: *Remember, tomorrow is Sunday.*

The fence said, "You girls are wonderful." He was looking at Alice. "You girls are worth a million dollars. I keep saying it, but I don't believe it until you show up on good days like this." He held back Alice's money in his fist, paying her last.

"Gimme my bread," she said.

"Come here," the fence said. "In the back room. I wanna talk to you."

"I'm bogue," Leslie said. "Let's get Rudy to cop and get the hell on back to the pad."

"Just a minute," the fence said. "I wanna talk to her. Don't rush away. Just a minute."

"G'wan, talk to him," Marsha Lee said.

Alice's eyes were hard and sick; she was sicker than either of the other girls. "I want my money," she said.

"Come on back here, I ain't gonna hurt you. What's the matter, you afraid of me or something? I got nothing but love in my head and money under my bed mattress for you."

"G'wan," Marsha Lee urged.

Alice went into the back with the fence. Marsha Lee and Leslie went out front and got into the car with Rudy, who was beginning to get sick and touchy. "What the hell's she doin in there?"

"She's talking to the fence," Marsha Lee said.

"Well, you go tell that bitch I ain't got all day to wait."

"She'll be right out," Marsha Lee said.

51

"I don't give a goddamn. I ain't got all day to wait."

Leslie got out of the back and got into the front seat with Rudy. "Let's pull," she said. "They're probably grooving."

"We'll wait," Marsha Lee said.

Rudy started the car. "I'm pullin."

Marsha Lee opened the door and got out. "Let's ease this punk," she told Leslie.

"What the hell did you say?" Rudy said.

"I said you're a punk, and we're putting you down. You're nothing but a young, trick-ass punk."

Leslie got out of the car. Rudy shut off the motor and got out on her side. "I want my money, bitch," he told Marsha Lee thickly. He was getting set to sucker-punch her. She was big and he didn't feel like rumbling on the street with her. He'd just slap her and take his money.

"You get nothing," Marsha Lee told him, and backed away. She had been sucker-punched before. She went in her purse and wrapped her fingers about her hoss.

"Let's get back in the car," Leslie whined. "I'm freezing."

"I want my money, I'm telling you, *I want my money!*"

"We're gonna wait on Alice," Marsha Lee said adamantly. "And I don't think I wanna ride in your short anyway. You're nothing but a jive, trick, junkie-ass punk, and you know it. That's why you're so drugged!"

"I'm a cold sonofabitch," Leslie said. "Let's get the hell back in the car."

"I want my money!" Rudy almost screamed. "I want my money, or I'm gonna get in my short and run over both you whores!"

"Let's get back in the car," Leslie pleaded.

They got back in the car, forgetting after a while that they were angry. It was just the tension, the all-day copping, the haggling with the fence. It was their brains running and noses running, their bowels running and their eyes watering all day long for one thing: the fix. The anticipation of it was sweet, but it was an anticipation that could not be held back a moment longer than necessary to make the moment sweeter.

Alice's being away was like that, increasing the nervousness, joining all three of them in a silent human bond of hope: that she would come soon, and they could get the hell out of there and cop.

Cop, Rudy thought. One was good and one was bad.

Cooker, Leslie thought. She could see it plainly, partly filled with water and heroin, feel it burn the tips of her fingers deliciously.

Money, Marsha Lee thought. She had to have more. She was going to send Mickey half of what she made today, just to let him know she was still on the case. Smack was a dollar twenty-five a thing, and her shot was six, twice a day. She HAD to have more money. . . .

Then Rudy thought of money, the money owed him.

Leslie thought of copping—four girls and four boys. A speedball.

Marsha Lee thought of cooking up four things instead of six.

Alice came out soon, and they all became happy.

"Let's pull," Leslie said anxiously.

Alice got in the back seat with Marsha Lee. She had put on new lipstick and she was smiling. Rudy started the car and pulled out from the curb, tires screaming. Everyone felt like screaming along with them, screaming like children.

"Oh my man, I love 'im so," Leslie began to sing.

Rudy turned on the heater. The car became warm and expectant. This was now, going now to do what they had wanted to do all day, going to heaven. . . . *Oh, I'm on my way to Heaven and I'm so glad . . . The world can't doomee no harm . . .*

Alice finished counting her money. She gave five to Rudy. "For me," she said. Leslie gave Rudy five. Marsha Lee wavered. Five would hurt her, but five was worth the ride, and she felt exceptionally good now. She went in her purse and took out five, noticing, as she handed Rudy the bill over the front seat, the brooch on Alice's arm, the one the fence played with every time they came.

She touched it experimentally. "He give it to you?"

Alice looked guilty, then said, false-smiling, jeffing, "He sold it to me. Kind of crazy, ain't it? The two big blue stones are for real."

Marsha Lee didn't say anything. She was thinking about waiting and being sick while Alice turned a trick with the fence. The tension

53

had been unbearable, but what made her maddest was that Alice hadn't said anything about the brooch, hiding it.

Damn right she was hiding it! If she hadn't looked at Alice's wrist right at that moment, no one would have ever known about it. That goddamn brooch! It made Marsha Lee so mad she could hardly see. A yellow whore. And her with all that talk about no yarding, even though she yarded with Rudy for nothing, and being such a thoroughbred for her man, while Marsha Lee sat there in the car and damned near blew to pieces all the time she and the fence were rubbing bellies.

She hated Alice then.

Leslie said, "We waited a goddamn hour on you." But she didn't care, now that they were going to cop. Rudy didn't care either. He was driving fifty miles an hour down Seventy-first, keeping an eye out for cops, missing several oncoming cars by inches. He was going to heaven. . . .

"We were talking, me and the fence," Alice said, beginning to count her money again indifferently.

"If you're gonna be a whore," Marsha Lee said, "BE A WHORE! I didn't want to team up with you in the first place! Don't hold us up! Get on your goddamn own and turn tricks on your own time!" She had forgotten that she had urged Alice to stay on with the fence; she was glad of this excuse to release her animosity.

"My man told me to work with you and Leslie," Alice said. "I'm doing what my man told me. If Leslie don't wanna work with me, all right. But I'll go back to the Apple and let your man know how you treated me, you watch and see."

Leslie became frightened suddenly. "I hope to hell you don't do that. I don't mind working with you." She was afraid of what her man would do if he found out how much money she was actually making. The fear of such a thing struck deep in her, far deeper than her addiction to the white poison. It never occurred to her that her man was hundreds of miles away and that she could make the distance even wider if she cared to. It seemed that death was far better than her man knowing the truth. "Shut up," she told Marsha Lee. "If anybody pulls, it'll be you."

Rudy turned off on a side street. "Get your money ready."

They scrambled for their purses, surprised that the moment had come so quickly. They became happy again, tittering like a bunch of schoolgirls.

Only they weren't girls, having acquired through the years and months of practice the names: Four Caps, Six Caps, and Eight Caps.

The money did something to Rudy. His steps away from the vehicle were mincing, then hastened to a trot, then he was fairly running when he reached the corner.

In that moment, on this late Saturday afternoon, they almost loved him, his haste was their haste. Rudy was their black god.

Alice held up the brooch. "I brought this, if anybody wants to know. Fifty now, two hundred later."

But Marsha Lee and Leslie had forgotten her, and soon Alice herself forgot, joining them in the rapt observance of a neat brownstone on the corner of Eighty-third and Maple, next to a theater where children were lining up for the matinee. It was here that Rudy had gone to make the connection.

They were being carried steadily to a climax, somewhat like that felt in a man's arms with his body pressed close and the muscles of his back bunching under their fingers. The sensation was exquisite, and the excitement would come when Rudy returned with eighteen capsules of diacetyl-morphine. That would be the *real* climax. The shooting of the drugs would be anticlimactic.

Rudy came back. "Nobody home," he said.

Leslie began to curse and moan about the pains in her back. Marsha Lee lit a cigarette, bit it off angrily at the tip, and mashed it out in the ashtray.

Alice felt her stomach fold over and under in a cramp, and she did the thing she knew she was going to do all day; she vomited.

Later, on Ninety-third, Rudy went into the Garden Bar and Poolroom and sat down at one of the rear tables, waiting. He knew if he waited long enough, someone who had some drugs would come in. It was inevitable; sit and wait and pray long enough, and somebody with some drugs would *have* to come through.

5 5

His anger increased by the minute, thinking of the many pushers who had narcotics and would not make themselves available. The sonsabitches. Always blowing their hot breath in your face when you were still trying to get your bread together, and then disappearing when you finally got made. It seemed as though they did it on purpose!

He vowed to get himself a bag. He was going to see The Man tomorrow and tell him just how it was. He wanted to have as much power as the rest of those bastards; then *he* could make people wait and run their asses off up and down the Scene looking for him.

He was really sick now, and his stomach was cramping. He would have got up to go to the bathroom, but he might miss someone—Ace or Dell or Bertha—might miss the thing he needed more than a square meal or a thousand dollars or a boosting girl with three arms . . . or a place just to sit down and nod.

His life was crammed into a moment. There were no days in his junkie's world. There were only moments to cop and moments to use and moments to nod and cop again.

Nina came in. She didn't see him. Her eyes were big, sick, and watering. Rudy knew she was terribly sick to come out so early, but he didn't call her. To call her would mean to give up some drugs.

What the hell? He couldn't explain to her why he'd buy ten things for himself and eighteen for the stash. She wouldn't believe they were for the girls. She'd think he was just holding out, buying twenty-eight things for some bitch. It wasn't another woman that would bother her so much; it would be Rudy's hiding stuff. That's what she'd think.

It was easy to rationalize—about why not to share drugs.

He put his head down on his arms, pretending he was a drunk. When he looked up after a while, she was gone. The waiting had become too much for him now. He got up and went out on the street. The bar was filling with the lames and fools of Saturday-workday, loud and boisterous, living it up and acting like people.

He was jealous.

For the first time all day he noticed the cold biting through his overcoat, penetrating the thin leather of his shoes. It was foreign to him, the weather. He could not remember when he had made snowballs (before the reformatory, when his mother and father had found him too much trouble, shoving him off to live on the generosity of relatives), nor throwing them, or drinking hot sweet chocolate at a friend's house, made from a package stolen at the corner grocery. Nor could he remember sledding, or going to school with the wind whistling up his pants legs, or a potbellied stove in a long, straight, squeaky house, or his aunt, Mama Mee, with a face like an old horseshoe and a knot on her forehead, calling him from around the corner, away from the vacant lot. . . .

You little no good chinch!

Yeah, Mama Mee . . .

You get in the house, you!

Yeah, Mama Mee . . .

You little debbil . . . With a smile like soft brown linen on her withered lips.

He did not remember; he couldn't have. It all came to him unassisted with the smart smack of wind, uninvited. Mama Mee came back, and Elisa too, and Lucas, two cousins who lived like himself, unwanted by their parents, needed by Mama Mee.

He could see Lucas choking to death on a chicken bone one Christmas long ago. A boy of six, and Rudy nine, and the dying clinging to Rudy's mind. He could see Lucas even now, his face blue-black and his eyes big, leaning across the matchwoodlike kitchen table, coughing a cough that sounded like "huffff," like a cow spitting up its cud or a horse blowing its fat lips.

A Chicken Ain't Nothin But A Bird . . .

Somewhere the cacophony of the evening traffic reached his senses, bop music intermingled and dominant; an old cut by "Fats" Navarro. The trumpet entered a bridge like magic, the notes executed with pure genius. Rudy wondered how a junkie could think like that, where he'd get the time.

He stood listening entranced until the record was over, then he grew conscious of the ever present hunger. It seemed as though *it* had been listening too, charmed for a moment, saying proudly of the trumpeter, "I made him do that, I made him blow like that. Me. I did it."

He walked on, searching each face that passed him. Somewhere there were some drugs! He could see it now: smooth capsules, white or red, all laid out in a row, like miniature dead men; in a Sal Hepatica bottle, curled up together like little cocoons; in a pants pocket or a shirt pocket or a deep overcoat pocket, wrapped in a piece of Softskin; in The Man's stash, as yet uncut, a wonderful white bulk in a cellophane package; between Black Bertha's breasts, in a matchbox, sticking together with the heat of her body; in the police safe downtown . . .

He walked.

Yesterday it had seemed so easy, copping! Then today, nothing. No one with the bag in sight. The dirty bastards, hiding on purpose! They *had* drugs, so they didn't have to come out and cop. They could lay up in their cribs and shoot with somebody in the bed with them and say to hell with them junkies.

A trolley bus whirred by the corner and he hailed it suddenly, knowing with the suddenness of his actions where he was going. He was going over a high hill with a street two blocks long that had no trees anywhere, a little house on a faraway street, right near the corner, with a white-lighted crucifix in the one tall front window, burning day and night. *My God, my God, sweet Jesus, my God . . .*

It was early evening now, but darkness was settling fast. The city was settling, having lived a long life, another day. People on the bus were going, like people on buses went, to unspecified destinations, carrying with them happiness, hatred, and hunger.

Of all the hungers, none could have possibly been more acute than Rudy's.

Somebody behind him said, "What's happenin, Rudy?"

He turned and saw a young man he knew only as Penny, one of the many shifting faces of the Scene, a nobody except in that he used drugs in league with the other nobodies on the Scene.

"Where you goin?" Penny said. He was sitting alone in the seat behind Rudy, his eyes partly closed, a vaguely blank expression on his thin, dark face.

Rudy turned halfway around with interest. "You look like you're made," he said jealously. His sickness became worse and he began to feel sorry for himself. "I'm bogue. I went hustlin this mornin and I been tryin to cop since two o'clock. This is twistin me."

"I'm goin home," Penny said. "I got off work early today."

"You're straight. I can tell."

"I went right to The Man's pad. I told his woman, 'Listen, baby, I'm bogue and I need some drugs,' I said. I said, 'You gonna sell me some drugs or I'm goin downstairs and cut my goddamn throat and die right on your doorstep,' I said. And she knew the Feds was right down on Ninety-first. Me dyin on her doorstep with the Feds on Ninety-first?" He smiled. "She gave me some drugs like I told her."

"The Feds was on the Scene?"

"From nine till one-thirty."

"That's why nobody showed today, then," Rudy said. He was growing sicker, looking at Penny. "You got some drugs, Penny?"

" 'Bout six things."

"Sell 'em to me."

Penny shook his head. "Tomorrow is Sunday, man. You know how hard it is to cop on Sunday. Nobody comes out on Sunday. I'd be wasted if I sold 'em to you."

"Baby, I'm bogue. Why don't you do me the favor?"

"I can't do it, Rudy."

"I been sick all day, baby, I need some help," Rudy said pleadingly.

"Tomorrow is Sunday. Death day. I wish I could, but I ain't."

"Nina is sick, too," Rudy said, forming a lie. "She's so sick, I'm goin to get my Aunt Mee to stay with her while I can find a doc to do her some good. Nina's my bread, man."

He knew Penny respected him for being a pimp, just as he regarded The Man in almost the same light with God. Rudy was a nobleman to Penny, with Nina for a slave.

Penny said reluctantly, "I could cut loose two."

"Nina's shot is four things. I don't care about myself, my man, all I care about is Nina. What would you do in my spot if your woman was all twisted up and couldn't work or nothin? You'd do the same thing I'm trying to do, wouldn't you, knowin your woman is the star of the Scene? We both got oil burners, especially Nina."

Penny was impressed, but he shook his head determinedly. "Tomorrow is Sunday. I can cut loose two things; that's all I can cut loose, and you know I would do more if this was any other day but Saturday. Why don't you go to The Man like I did?"

Rudy felt like hitting him—sitting there flying while Rudy was sick as hell. If Penny wouldn't sell him the drugs, he was going to get off the bus with the little punk and knock him down and take them. There wasn't much Penny could do, high as he was.

"Sell me that stuff, Penny."

"I can't, Rudy. I'll sell you two things."

"I'll give you a dollar four-bits each, that's a half over what I pay."

"I'll sell you three things; that's *all* I'll sell you. You and Nina could get the sickness off till you get time to cop."

"Why act like a goddamn fool?" Rudy said, losing his temper. "That's just what you're acting like, like you'll be shot in the face with a shotgun if you sell me the goddamn six things. I'll be givin you three cents extra—what's wrong with that? What do you want, just what the HELL do you want?"

"People are lookin," Penny said nervously.

"To hell with people! I want that stuff, Penny!"

"Rudy—"

"I'll give you ten dollars!"

"Rudy, listen—"

Rudy got up and came around to sit next to him, pushing his thigh hard against Penny's. He was breathing hard, at the thought of the six caps.

"Listen," he said between his teeth, "if you don't sell me those six things, I'm gonna cut your throat. For real, I mean it. I'll kill you, I *mean* it!"

Without hesitating, Penny gave him the caps. Rudy gave him

ten dollars. He got up and got off the bus, feeling wonderful. He could see Penny looking out of the window after him as the bus moved on.

Rudy felt wonderful! He had his works with him and he wanted to stop at a filling station and use, but he was in a white neighborhood and it would probably look suspicious.

He walked until he saw children playing in the street together, white and Negro. Poor white, poor Negro. They were playing a form of hide-and-seek, the advancing darkness providing cover in an area where there were no trees, where the tottering houses of the last century rose up straight, with innocent Puritan confidence, allowing no hiding places for the frivolity of children's games.

The long block seemed to walk crookedly over a hill underneath which train tracks laid rusty arms through a tunnel, a wide cavernous jaw in the hill, a trysting place of adolescents.

From the corner, from beside a window of a musty little confectionery—where paper dots and ice cream, Baby Ruth boxes turned yellow with age, cream soda and ginger snaps in bowls, and the smell of the cigarillo smoked by the wizened little proprietor, all conglomerated in a weblike, tangy odor—Rudy could see the lights from Maple, felt somehow far removed from them and their urgency, and an aloneness twisted up in him as he listened to the cries of the children playing. He had a sense of not being, of floating in limbo. Nearby, a train bellowed majestically over the silence, chopping into him like the need to use, to put at rest the wildness of his brain and body.

"Can I use your bathroom?" he asked the old man.

The proprietor, who sat on an orange crate, half-hidden behind the hugeness of the ancient, cryptlike showcase, said, "You gonna buy anythin?"

"No," Rudy said.

"I cain't let ever'body use my bathroom. Might catch somethin." He went on puffing unconcernedly, staring unseeingly out of the thick cataracts in his eyes.

Rudy left, feeling vaguely irritated that the old man didn't remember him, didn't remember the hundreds of penny suckers and thousands of punkin seeds and tater chips bought just a few years ago. . . . *You spen* MO *pennies, boy! Where'd you get 'em all?* . . . And the evenings, the days like this, cold ones, with all the fellas crowded around the central-heating plant, a potbellied stove, and eating peanuts by the pound, talking, laughing, saying things, happy boy things, that would never be remembered . . .

On the street he sought, the wind was brisker, finding no obstruction on the long bare sidewalk, gathering force as it swept over the hill, rushing down like the cold angry fist of God. In the house near the corner, the crucifix still burned, Christ perpetually dying.

Rudy went up the straight, porchless steps and knocked, waited, and knocked again.

"Who is it?" a voice came from inside, like a voice from the grave, to Rudy.

"Me," he said.

"Me who?"

"Me, Rudy," he said.

"Rudy?" The voice sounded puzzled, then hopeful, "Rudy who?"

"Open the door," he shouted.

The door opened. "Come in," Mama Mee said, opening the door wider, seeming unbearably frail and old and black and weak.

They stood looking at each other. They could see the death in each other and it shocked them. Rudy felt ashamed coming here now after so many years, finding Mama Mee in the same old housedress and he with twenty-five dollar shoes on his feet that were useless against the cold; with slacks that cost the same, inadequately housing the decreasing substance of his hips and thighs and calves; with a hundred and twenty-five dollar overcoat that provided draft instead of warmth.

He came in. "Hello, Mama Mee."

The house smelled the same: the odor of cabbage and ham hocks cooking, incense and witch hazel, the deep warm smell of old furniture and charm water in the bare corners with their paper peeling.

"What you been doin, boy?" Mama Mee said.

"Same old thing."

"No, I mean to yourself. What you been doin to yourself, Rudy?" Her eyes, sharpened instead of injured by the years, filled with pain. The tumor on the smooth double-deep brownness of her forehead moved like a rock under the skin as her brow wrinkled with the hurt. "You ain't the same Rudy," she said. "Somethin's happened to my boy."

"Lemme use the bathroom."

"You know where 'tis."

He went back to the bathroom, which was little more than a closet, with a toilet that flushed sometimes and a chipped porcelain washbasin that had a crack in the bottom and leaked all over his shoes, soaking them. But he didn't care. Using the drugs now was more important than anything in the world—it *was* the world. This meant more to him, this filling of the cooker, this burning of his fingers, this drawing up of the liquid, than anything—even life. Without drugs he could not live. Without them he would not want to live.

He tied his belt around the upper part of his left arm quickly, making the veins puff up blackly under the well-worn crusts. His nervousness caused him to miss the vein in the bend of his arm, and blood erupted from the hole in a quick spurt, running down his arm and staining the left leg of his trousers. He hit successfully the second time. When he shot the drug in, it felt as though something smashed him sharply in the stomach. He nearly fell over from his seat on the toilet, but he righted himself and did not back the blood into the dropper. The drugs were good. If he played with them he might pass out. He might die.

No better way to leave this world.

He cleaned the works in slow motion. His actions were clumsy. He felt like lying down on the floor. In the middle of some movement he would fall into a nod, his head bending slowly toward his chest, his arms falling slowly in front of him. Nodding was unpremeditated; it came all of a sudden, without warning, dulling the senses, arresting and killing off any message from the brain to the motor nerves, destroying all thought.

63

In a while, he could stand straight and hold his thoughts together long enough to finish cleaning his works. He did it diligently, like a soldier cleaning his rifle, knowing that just as in battle all depended on the trustworthiness of the weapon, his life depended on his works.

He came out of the bathroom

from far off, a thumping sound

and went through the straightness of the sameness of the poor, neat house.

his heart's accelerated beating

Mama Mee stood near the door to the kitchen, near the small room which used to be his own, with tears in her eyes, her little body bent in the old housedress.

it was the finest he had ever felt

"Come here," she said softly, looking at him.

a warmth, a satisfaction so choice, so nice, so oo blah dee

"My baby," she moaned, her hands exploring the boniness of him, and

a junkie's work is never done, he hustles for drugs from sun to sun

the knot on her forehead pressing against his chest. "What you done done to yourself, Rudy, what you done, tell me, God?"

"I'm all right."

wellallright, wellallright

"You left that jailhouse and you never come back to Mama Mee. I cry my old heart out, just athinkin and wishin." Her face pressed deeper into him. "What I do wrong? 'Fore God, I try to do my best. . . . What I do wrong? I loves you, Rudy, and I loved Lucas and 'Lisa the same way. Tell me what's wrong."

"I'm okay, Mama Mee."

'cause the hotness burns your brains out!

"Don't lie to me. I can see it in your eyes, boy! You sick! Please come home to Mama Mee! Let Mama Mee take care of her baby."

"I'll be back," he said.

"Please," Mama Mee begged, "please don't go 'way from me, Rudy."

"I'll come see you."

"Don't, Rudy—"

He roused himself, pulling away from her. "I'll be back."

"No. I know you won't. It'll be just like the last time, I just know it. This time you'll go away, but you won't come back." She turned and went into the kitchen slowly.

Rudy was feeling good now. He went to the front door with long wide steps, his belly warmed over, like it was filled with whiskey but without the taste. With the taste of heroin.

"I'll be back, Mama Mee," he called to the kitchen, and went out, almost stumbling down the steep steps.

He'd be back.

If he was ever in this part of town again and had to have some place to use, he'd be back.

He walked all the way back to Ninety-third, and it seemed like nothing.

Marsha Lee said, "You trick sonofabitch, if I knew this town well enough, I'd go cop myself."

"You call me somethin like that again and I'm gonna kick the hell out of you," Rudy told her.

"Did you cop?" Alice asked him. She was lying on the bed, so sick that she could barely move. Rudy knew her bee hurt her worse than the other girls'.

"Yeah, I copped." He had too; after all the trouble he had gone to, he had bumped into Ace, who was loaded. Ace sold him all the things he wanted.

"Let's have them drugs," Leslie said. She had been in the bathroom. She came out now in her brassière and panties, her black little body shivering. "I got six things coming."

Rudy put the drugs on the table, ten capsules. He held back eight. Marsha Lee pounced on the capsules. Leslie snatched up six caps and ran into the bathroom, Marsha Lee close behind.

Alice tried to get out of bed, but she was very weak; her back was aching and her stomach was knotted with cramps. The lines in her face seemed deeper; the strain of every muscle showed clearly on her features. Her eyes were blue around the edges and puffed, the blood gone from them. Her lips were dry and cracked and bloodless. Her efforts to move were feeble.

"Help me, Rudy."

He stood watching her dispassionately. "C'mon, you'll make it."

"Don't be like that, baby, please. Come help me."

"You'll make it. You don't need help from me."

She got to her feet shakily, her body bent over in the thin slip she wore.

"C'mon," Rudy said. "C'mon." It was nice, this. It was part of the revenge he wanted—only part. "C'mon, you can make it. There's drugs over here. Pick up your goddamned feet." Trick, was he? A trick to be georged and then told on?

Alice reached the table, and Rudy pulled up a chair for her and gave her the last of Ace's caps. He went into the bathroom, where Marsha Lee and Leslie were using, and came back with a glass of water. Alice had put the powder in the cooker. She drew up the water from the glass in the dropper, her fingers trembling, and sprayed it across the powder. Then she took several matches from a book and struck them, placing the cooker over the flames.

"What's the matter?" Rudy said, when he saw her pause.

"Look." Alice's voice sounded disbelieving. *"Just look."*

"What is it?" Rudy looked into the cooker, where a thick pulpy mass sizzled and boiled like wet dough.

"That's what I *want to know*!" Alice screamed. "What is it? What the hell is it?"

Rudy looked puzzled. "I can't understand why your stuff is bogue; Marsha Lee's and Leslie's is okay."

Alice began to moan and cry and beat on the table.

Rudy turned and smiled to himself. "I musta got burnt," he said.

He knew he hadn't been.

3

IN THEIR BEDROOM, Maxine Patterson watched her husband get dressed. It was as if her eyes were seeing him anew after so many years: the fine brown leanness of his shoulders, the crooked, inquiring tilt of his closely cropped head. It's funny, she thought, he's almost thirty, but he doesn't look like he's aged a day. It's like that when you love somebody so much, I guess.

She cocked her head to the argumentative voices of Lonnie and Virg, Jr., downstairs in the living room, ascertaining that their play hadn't taken a dangerous turn; then her eyes went back to her husband again. A glow of instant pride made her get up and halt him in his movements.

"A kiss," she demanded, rising up under him on tiptoe.

He bussed her impatiently. "You'll make me late, Max."

"With just one kiss?" she said.

He seesawed a navy-blue tie under his white collar. "I want to get started right. Three years I've been waiting for this promotion. I don't want anything to go wrong."

"Nothing will."

He turned to the dresser and straightened his tie in the mirror. "When you wait three years for something, you get to feeling it's all a dream when it finally comes true. And being chastised by a desk sergeant for being late can be a rude awakening, my dear, let me tell you."

She turned him around and rapped his forehead soundly with her knuckles. "You're not responsible to desk sergeants any more, sweets, can't you get that through your crankcase? You're a full-fledged detective now!"

"More the reason for being on time," he said. "The guy I'm going to work with is an old vet, been with the force for years. I want to prove to him that I'm on my toes."

"You were on your toes when you passed the exam three years ago," she said soberly. "If he's the vet I think he is, he'll be able to see by your appointment that the police department is no stickler for punctuality!"

"If you'd seen my old man rushing to beat hell every morning to get to that three-wheeler downtown, you'd change your tune."

"That was twenty years ago. Times have changed," she said, lighting a cigarette for him as he got into his coat. "When your old man was a cop, the closest a Negro got to the detective bureau was with a mop and a pail. Just think of it, Virgil," she glowed, straightening the lapels of his coat, "you're a *detective*!"

"Big deal." He grinned.

She grabbed him by the arm. "C'mon, I let Virg and Lonnie stay up extra late tonight, so they could see you off."

"Just a minute."

"What is it?"

He opened the dresser drawer and took out a new, black leather hip-holster, the pungent smell of it thick in the room. In the pocket was a dull gray, snub-nosed thirty-eight.

"Like it?" he said. "There's a shop right across the street at headquarters. Costs a fortune, but you've got to have your own when you go into plainclothes."

She watched in silence as he strapped it on.

"The gun is issue," he went on, "just like the Special, only this one is lighter by almost a pound, and it's got better action; I tried it out on the range this afternoon." He looked up to find her watching him strangely. "What's the matter, Max?"

She looked away from him. "Virg, what kind of work will you be doing with the Narco Division?"

"I don't know yet. I don't guess it'll be any different than the squad car."

"Will—will it be dangerous?"

He came over quickly to gather her in close to him. "Honey, there's a certain amount of risk in any job, you know that."

"I didn't mean that," she said, drawing security from his nearness. "I was just thinking about the gun—those things you hear about drug addicts . . ."

"Look," he said firmly, chucking her under the chin, "I've been one of this city's finest for six years and I've never shot anybody once, not even accidentally. The Narco Squad is no different, Max, believe me. It's a job like any other—like washing windows. And you can't say we don't need the money. There's the car, the new breakfast set—"

"I know, I know," she said wearily. "The mortgage, the TV. If we could only make money as fast as we make bills!"

"That's my girl!" he said, catching her smile. "Let's get down to the boys. I've got to hurry."

The boys were watching TV quietly when they came down. Lonnie and Virg were eight and nine respectively, but looked almost like twins, with the same long, lean resilience of their father, the same dewdrop faces on square shoulders.

Lonnie was first to notice his mother and father. "Hey!" He poked his brother, who sat next to him on the couch. "Here's Pop."

Virg snapped up in his seat. "Yea, Pop!" Then his eyes faded with disappointment. "Where's the uniform?"

"Detectives don't wear uniforms, stupid," Lonnie said. "That's what makes them detectives."

Virg was disgruntled. "I liked the uniform better!"

"You got uniforms on the brain!" Lonnie told his brother. "Hey, Pop, you gonna investigate murders and things like that, like they do on TV?"

"If I ever get a role on TV," his father said.

"Aw, Pop, I'm serious!"

"That shows how much you know," Virg, Jr., said. "All that stuff on TV never really happens for real."

"Listen, fellas," their father said, leaning down to kiss them both on the cheek, "I've got to go. I'll tell you all about the detective bureau tomorrow morning. Take care of your mother now."

Maxine held his overcoat ready for him. She helped him on with it and lingered under his kiss for a long time, as though she were afraid to let him finally depart.

"Be careful," she told him, a tremor of anxiety in her voice. She and the boys stood in the doorway as he got into the Chevy and drove down the neat, interracial street.

"Boy!" Lonnie murmured to no one in particular, "Pop's a detective—a real live detective."

Mance Davis was just finishing up an arrest report when Patterson came over to him in the squad room. He gave the younger man an uninterested glance and continued pecking the twisted keys of the obsolete typewriter in the lap of his desk.

The report concerned a belligerent junkie who had given Davis a bit of trouble during his apprehension, swallowing some thirty capsules of heroin. Davis was trying to explain, as best he could, the manner in which he had throttled the man until he spat the evidence out, and how several of the addict's teeth had been punched out in the process.

He had an idea who Patterson was. He hadn't had a partner for nearly six months, and now they decided he needed help. He thought of the man as something dredged up from the Urban League, who'd been singled out because his teeth were whiter and the butt of his pants didn't shine. Oh, yes, he knew they'd been trying to ease him out of his job for a long time. But what they didn't know was that he wasn't budging, not until he was good and damned ready.

He looked up from under his thick brows and surveyed the man. He was young, with a face like a simp, with nothing on top probably but the nap of a wire brush.

He punched the keys angrily. It was getting so everybody was against you, even the goddamned Police Department. After seventeen years, you'd think they'd leave a man alone!

The report was finished too quickly, despite his bad typing; he wanted to make the man wait a bit longer. He took his time rereading the copy, pleased at how tersely accurate he'd been. He finally snapped the sheet over to the outgoing basket and took time out to light a cigar from the humidor in his desk, although smoking was something he did very rarely.

70

Gradually, he condescended to look up at Patterson, puffing intently on the cigar.

Patterson shifted in front of his desk. Davis let him wiggle around a while before he spoke.

"Sit down," he said at last.

Patterson opened his mouth. "You're Mr. Davis?"

Davis pointed with the foul-tasting cigar. "That's what the sign says."

"Well—" Patterson put his hat on the desk, then quickly took it off at Davis' disapproving stare. "They sent me here from downtown. I just talked to Lieutenant Stuart—"

"What's your name?"

"Virgil Patterson, sir."

"How long you been on the force?"

"Six years."

"How old are you?"

"Twenty-nine. Thirty next birthday, sir."

"That's good," Davis said dryly. "It wouldn't turn out so well if you were thirty-five. How long have you been on the force, did you say?"

"Six years, sir." Patterson fidgeted nervously.

"Married?"

"Yes, sir. Wife and two boys, sir."

Davis leaned toward him. "What's the matter with you?"

"What, sir?"

"That's it," Davis said, waving the cigar distastefully at him. "That *sir* stuff. You think you're in the army or something? You must have been in the army."

"Yes, sir, but only a short while, during Korea—"

"Well, you're not in the army now! Remember that. I don't like formality, do you understand? And I like the men I work with to be on time," he said, looking at his watch. "You're twenty minutes late."

"Well, sir, you see—"

"And I don't like excuses," Davis said. "You're either wrong

71

or you're right, one or the other—there's no in-between, do you understand?"

"Yes—er, sergeant," Patterson said, his nervousness turning to irritation.

Davis swung his big bulk back in the chair, watching the young man closely. "Been to school, I bet."

"Yes—sergeant. Central College."

"Majored in criminology, I s'pose."

"It was my minor."

"Know anything about stuff?"

Patterson looked at him questioningly.

"Know anything about boy? About girl?" Davis went on, taking pleasure in Patterson's ignorance. "What about pot? Know what a set of works is? A stash? Know what an addict means when he says he's bogue? What about a bee? A bag? A junkie says he's gonna cop—what's he gonna do?" Seeing Patterson's blank look, he puffed on the cigar with new vigor. "I'll give you a quick rundown, college boy. Boy is the junkie's term for heroin; they call cocain girl because it gives 'em a sexual jab when they take a shot. Pot is marijuana; works are the equipment an addict uses to give himself an injection. A stash is where he hides his drugs. When a junkie's bogue, he needs a shot; he feels like hell. A bee is what he calls his habit; it's always stinging him to get a fix. A bag is his supply of drugs. When he goes to cop, he goes to buy drugs, to connect."

Patterson felt his face burning, and his feeling of irritation was heightened. "Anything else I need to know?"

Davis smiled around the cigar. "Sure, if you think you can take it all in one lump. The junkie's terminology is almost like code. He calls money bread. He cons somebody out of some money for stuff, and he calls that a burn. A mackman is a pimp, among other things. A champ is a junkie who won't snitch or inform, although no such animal exists. The bomb is high-potency heroin. When a junkie's drugged, he's mad at somebody or something. When he's twisted, it's almost the same thing; but he can be twisted in another way on narcotics: that's when he's so high he doesn't know where the hell he is." He paused, chewing at the cigar. "A haim is a job, but junkies don't bother with 'em. Smack, smock, stuff, horse—they're all heroin. A short is a car, probably a hot one. A silk is a white person. A junkie makes a sting, he's made a heavy theft. When he's got some things, he's got heroin in capsule form." He shrugged. "I could go on all day. I can see all this is new to you. Maybe you should have *majored* in criminology, college boy—they didn't teach you a damned thing."

"I'll have to disagree with you there, sergeant," Patterson said angrily. "I learned a good many things in college."

Davis leaned toward him again. "Seems to me a man should know something about his job. Just what do you know about heroin?"

"I know," Patterson said, neglecting to take the sting from his voice, "that it was discovered by a German chemist, Gerhardt Dressen, in 1898, that it's a derivative of opium and it's been raising hell with the world ever since Dressen stumbled on it."

Davis choked slightly on the unfamiliar tobacco smoke. The discovery of heroin was something he'd never known about. He stubbed the cigar out in an ashtray and stood up.

"Let's get out in the street, college boy, and I'll show you something they never thought about in them goddamned schools."

First sight of the Scene repelled Patterson intolerably. He was conscious, but not entirely aware, of the fact that in the city where he lived prostitutes openly displayed themselves on street corners, and that dealers and junkies could operate conspicuously in full view of the public. He had always lived in a good neighborhood, gone to good schools, found his recreation in the community center. To see children of the Scene playing into such a late hour of the night, exposed to the net of addiction, shocked him.

"Pretty, huh?" said Davis, who was driving slowly down Maple. "It's called the Scene." He grunted to himself. "You'll find out why soon enough."

Their progress took them from Fifty-fifth to Seventieth. In that distance, Patterson counted at least twenty-five prostitutes and a score of suspicious-looking characters.

"You look surprised, son," Davis said, looking over at him. "Never seen anything like this before?"

Patterson shook his head numbly. "I've been downtown—you know, drunks and vagrants. This is the first time I've been to this part of town."

"Boy, you been protected! We've got more types here than a wild hare can shake his ass at. You should have been in the Sixth Precinct a long time ago." He laughed. "Grow some hair on your chest!"

At the next stop light, he pulled over to the curb and parked. They sat there in silence until Davis spotted a man coming out of a bar.

He jabbed Patterson. "See that little slick-headed punk? That's a guy called Ace. He's one of the biggest dealers on the Scene, but he's a weak spot; I know him. One day he's gonna break and do me a lot of good, you watch and see. He cops from The Man, and he's got a connection over in dago-town." Davis watched the man amble disjointedly down the street. "I won't even have to touch him. He's gonna break for me—he's gonna get ripe, just like a melon, and split wide open. I've seen it happen before."

Patterson noticed the whores, like a shift of some human tide, move farther down the street, changing their places of business.

A car with white faces passed next to them, the eyes of the occupants investigating them curiously.

"Those are more punks," Davis said, pointing after the vehicle. "Just a couple of kids with big habits. I've noticed them in the past couple of weeks. See how they looked us over? They want to cop, and anybody looks good to them. They're having trouble on the Scene: nobody wants to sell to them because they're white. Must be a couple of protégés of Coke Prado, another dealer who used to be here on the Scene. The dump squad picked him up sick as hell a few weeks back, right on the street—heroin poisoning. He used to be big; I thought he even handled the Mexican pipeline," Davis muttered to himself. "Wonder how come he fell out with The Man? But those kids," he said for Patterson's benefit, "they'll turn up, too. You just watch. Somebody's gonna make a mistake and sell 'em some drugs; then he'll be saddled with them—and he'll be saddled with a lot of time for selling drugs to minors when we find out who he is!"

Silence again, and Patterson's eyes were assailed by the Scene, the Babel of strange voices, the many wild words, the pulse of life in the strangely twisting street, a life as twisted and distorted as the Scene itself, sensually infectious.

"Now there's a queer one," Davis said, indicating a slump-shouldered little man who'd just passed. "Name's Lou Tyler. Got a hotel down the street a ways, regular dope hangout. The place is called Lou's, but his wife Ella runs it. Don't look like much, does he? I betcha he's loaded down though, him and his old lady both. No legitimate businessman houses ten or fifteen rooms of junkies for nothing. I'm gonna talk to Stuart about him. Maybe we can shake that place up a little bit, find out what's going on."

"It's amazing that you know all these people by name," Patterson said.

"I've been around here for five years and more," Davis said, almost proudly. "You wouldn't understand it, but this is my element. I can tell you more about these people than they know about themselves." As if to prove this, he nodded toward the other side of the street. "See that fella? The one with his head down, walking fast? You've got to keep your eye on him—that's Rudy Black, a small-time junkie with a big habit, but he bears watching. He's got a whore named Nina Moten, just a kid—a big, dumb kid." Davis nodded his head after Rudy. "Yeah, we've got to watch him. His woman is making *some* ends for him! Every time I come past her corner, she's not around, so business must be good." He twisted his lips thoughtfully. "Just look at him go! I bet he's loaded down with drugs; probably just copped from somebody."

The taste of bile came to Patterson's mouth. "If you know these people have drugs, why don't you arrest them?"

"Because it's not *them* I want, college boy. I want somebody a lot bigger than these little maggots, the junkies and pushers. I want The Man, that's who I want." He pointed after the vanished image of Rudy Black. "These people are going to help me get him. I leave

them alone. I let them act naturally. I *pick* my times to bust them."
He seemed suddenly angered, starting up the car. "You just watch
me, college boy, and follow suit. This is no simple job, this is nothing
that happens in a minute. You want to find yourself some neat
little assignment," he finished derisively, "maybe you should wash
windows or something instead of being on the Narco Squad."

"Maybe I should," Patterson mumbled to himself, the horror
of the Scene threatening to swallow him alive.

4

AUGUSTIN PRADO recognized the boy through a haze.

He was conscious that the nurses and many of the doctors had
been doing something to him earlier that day, but he still could not
figure out what. He felt as though he couldn't move, as though
something heavy sat in the middle of his chest. There was no feeling
in his arms and legs, but the pain in his intestines had lessened
somewhat.

In this lucid moment, his first thought was the unquenchable
desire for a fix. He had been perpetually high in his dreams. He
and The Man were together again, they were friends again. There
was no longer any disagreement between them; Coke Prado was
the same trustworthy pipeline he'd always been, and there was no
problem about money, no demands for percentages, no refusals, no
expulsion from the syndicate. . . .

Now he was awake and none of it was true, only the thin angular
face of Frankie Wysocki hovered over him, the boy's wild eyes
begging for something he could not give.

"En el nombre de Dios!"

76

Frankie grabbed at him. "Don't try to move, Coke—they got your arms tied down. You been pulling out your hair."

His body collapsed under the boy's hands.

"I woulda brought you a fix," the boy was saying, "but Coke, I can't score anywhere around town! Tony Caseri's got some stuff, but it's mostly sugar, and he charges two dollars a cap. I just ain't got it, Coke! I just ain't got the money! You know I'd do it for you if I could."

"Tal Adele . . ." Coke said, his lips sticking together with their own moisture. "Tal her I say come . . ."

"I stopped where she worked last night, me and Tippy. She wasn't around anywhere."

Coke barely heard the words. His stomach was burning again, and the feeling was returning to his arms, itching under the bonds.

"The Man . . ." he gasped. "Go to The Man, tal him Coke need him bad. Tal him—"

"But, Coke, I don't know The Man! I couldn't go up there."

"He help me," Coke said with strength. "He owe me much. . . . I make big connection for heem. Go to The Man. . . ."

Frankie straightened up helplessly. "I'll try, Coke. But I'm telling ya, it won't do no good."

But Augustin Prado did not hear him; he returned again to the realm of dreams, where everything between him and The Man was just as it used to be.

It was snowing when Frankie came out the wide swinging doors of Municipal Hospital. The flakes fell thick and sharp around his face and the wind blew his brown, uncut hair into his eyes.

Ahead of him, parked at the curb in the circular drive, was an Olds, its top piled high with snow, the exhaust puffing blue smoke lazily.

As Frankie got in, the youth under the wheel looked up. His body was branchlike, and his face, sharply defined in the car's dark interior, was smooth and handsome.

"Let's go," Frankie said. "Let's move, fast."

The car pulled out from the curb, slipping momentarily as its

77

wheels failed to get traction, then pulling ahead powerfully as the automatic shift made the rear wheels dig away at the snow.

"Turn right," Frankie directed.

The big car pulled out on Pennsylvania Avenue, the largest street in town.

The eyes of the boy under the wheel stared ahead of the traffic. "We going uptown, huh?"

"Just drive, will ya, Tippy?"

"Well, I need some gas. We gotta stop sometime and get some gas." Driving occupied him for a moment. "What did the spic say?"

"He said we should go to The Man and score for him."

"How can we do that?" Tippy asked. "We don't even know The Man."

"We gotta go *somewhere*, dumbhead! We haven't scored a decent fix since Coke's been in the hospital. Like last night, even—that guy you know from school hit the heads of those caps. When he got back to us, it was three caps instead of five."

"What I'm saying is, why should we worry about the spic?" Tippy said. "Another shot of stuff'll kill him, won't it? Why should we worry about him?"

"Because we *need* him," Frankie explained patiently. "We're *nowhere* without his in, don't you understand? We don't *know* any other dealers except Coke."

"Look at the needle," Tippy said. "It's on empty now. My old man don't even know I got the car. I'll catch hell if he finds out."

"To hell with your old man," Frankie snapped. "At the next filling station you see, pull in. I'll buy the damn gas."

At Pennsylvania and Mt. Vernon, Tippy turned into a gas station. It was deserted except for two cars raised on the racks in the garage, and the snow had piled up heavily in the driveway.

"Nobody here," Tippy said.

"Let's wait."

No one came out of the station.

"C'mon," said Frankie.

"Wait. Look, there ain't nobody there."

"So what?"

"So what? So what? There's a cash register in there, just begging to be taken. We could really score if we had a nice wad with us."

"Don't be dizzy!"

"But we can, and you know it! All I have to do is pull around the corner where nobody can hawk the license plate. One of us can go in and do it. How about it? There's nothing to it, Frankie!"

Frankie was beginning to see the advantages. The light was dim at the front, and the oil cans in the window obscured the view from the street. It was about fifty feet from the station to where Tippy would park the car.

The thought excited him queerly. Their thefts had never yet approached this in daring.

"O.K., Tippy, you go. I'll wait under the wheel."

"Me?"

"Yeah, *you*! *You* go."

"Why me? Why do I have to front myself off when it's my idea?"

" 'Cause it's *your* idea, that's why!"

Reluctantly, Tippy backed out of the driveway and parked the car near the corner, leaving the motor running.

"All right, go ahead," Frankie told him.

Tippy held back, eyes flashing rebelliously. "Listen, what makes you think I should always be the fall guy? When we lifted the whiskey at Farnham's today, it was the same thing."

"This is the way you show your appreciation," Frankie said, sounding injured. "All over a few lousy bucks! What about me? Look at the chance I been taking for the past couple of months, scoring from the spic just so's you could make up! That's enough to go to the can for," he said, gathering a handful of Tippy's collar. "I don't have to put up with you," he warned. "I was using smack a whole year before I turned you on in high school. I don't need you."

Tippy's eyes became frightened. "What do you mean?"

"I mean you can score on your own if you want to, without me helping you to."

It was an ultimatum, and Frankie knew it. There was no immediate way for Tippy to establish a connection. Coke was in the hospital, and Tippy, like Frankie Wysocki, was the kind of person whom pushers were wary of, the desire plain on their faces: *Beware*! it said. *I use drugs but I am too young to be responsible.*

"Aw, what the hell!" Tippy tried to say it lightly. "I'll go—just to show you I ain't chicken."

He stood for a long time outside the car, adjusting his coat collar, afraid. Then he bent his head under the light flurry of snow and disappeared around the bend.

Frankie slid under the wheel, tested it, liking the feel of it—big in front, on all sides of him. A real sugar-baby, the Olds.

He relaxed, and the effect of the drugs he'd used earlier that day pounced on him like a big, furry jungle animal. He slipped away in its softness, nodding. . . .

"You're seventeen, Frankie, I'm sixteen."

"So what?"

"So we're too young for it."

"I still say so what?"

"So a lot of things. You think you're smart."

"I am smart."

"Not smart enough to get me."

"I've got you."

"Not *here*, not in your mother's living room."

"She's not my mother!"

"Your stepmother, then. What difference does it make?"

"A lot of difference."

"*Don't*, Frankie!"

"I'm not hurting you."

"They're just tender—on all women they're tender."

"Let me kiss 'em."

"Oh, Frankie, *don't*! Your mother might—"

"She's *not* my mother! She's a lousy old country Polack!"

"So'm I Polish. So are you."

"I mean deep down Polack, with the straw still in her ears. I'm American, that's what I am!"

"Well, your father *loves* her!"

"Sure, that fathead would. Anything old country he goes for, from the goddamned *kielbasa* to the People's Community Club!"

"Let me go, Frankie. . . . Please, Frankie, don't—you're tearing it!"

"Never let me hear you call her my mother again."

"Please, Frankie, I swear I've never done this before . . . *Frankie*! . . ."

His head snapped up. He was fully aware of himself.

For the briefest moment he had nodded, and he had been with Helen again. Over a year ago. That had been the night he'd met Coke at Lenny's Poolroom, after they'd come back from the dance at the Arcadia and stopped off at his house.

Later he had left Helen standing on her doorstep, smiling. She had acted as though it were nothing that first time. She had liked him a lot.

And afterward, he had gone to the poolroom because he didn't want to get home early and listen to that gush between the old man and Kathrina, his bride of two months. She had come from Kuty, near the Romanian border in Poland, and the old man was from Kolomyja, which wasn't too far away.

He had shot three games of snooker with Coke, and later they went to the rooming house where Coke and Adele lived, and Frankie was introduced to drugs for the first time in his life.

It was the mostest the most could be! It was like Stan Getz lying in a million dollars, blowing "Too Marvelous For Words." Nothing had ever affected him like that, not reefer, whiskey, or anything. It didn't make you giggly like reefer did, or loud and crazy like juice. It was crazy, man, crazy cool!

Later on, maybe four or five days after using, you got a little sick. Like a cold. But it wasn't anything, not anything like they'd made it up to be in books, with crazy lights going around in your head and committing suicide and all that crap.

Man, *it was a way to get cool*!

Coke had scored and kept turning him on. Coke liked him, didn't he? He kept turning him on and scoring and turning him on and scoring.

8 1

Then turned him off. The Man had suddenly found Coke no longer indispensable.

Afterward, his body was racked with a torment far worse than he had ever imagined possible. His school attendance declined; he was too lethargic to compete with his classmates.

And as he continued to be alone, to be apart from the reefer-smokers and juicers and Happy Others who did nothing but be square, his drive to be needed made him seek out a companion, a victim, another like himself.

Ain't Tippy my best friend? he thought.

Tippy *was* his best friend. He had done him an honor, then, hadn't he—introducing him to the craziness of the Wild Horse? Hadn't he told him, "You don't have to use, you know, unless you're chickenshit."

Well, so what if it was something a guy shouldn't do to his worst enemy? Tippy wasn't a kid. He didn't have to if he didn't want. And furthermore, he had showed the big chump the greatest kick in the world: STUFF.

STUFF

STUFF

STUFF

Stuff me up a little tighter and call me a kielbasa!

His head dropped to his chest with the thought.

Sometimes he felt like crying. He got so sick, he felt like crying. The stealing taxed his nerves, for he was not a thief. He could not work long enough on a job to sustain himself; the eight hours passed so slowly. The bee didn't know about hours. It slept like a great, ugly baby, breaking forth irregularly with monstrous insistence.

He remembered that morning, after his father had gone to work and his younger brother and sister were off to school. He had cornered Kathrina in the kitchen.

"I'm sick," he told her. "I need some money."

"No money I have, Franik."

"Don't lie, I've seen it. The old man gives you everything."

"Franik—"

82

"No, not Franik—Frank! F-R-A-N-K. That's my name. Like tank, like stank, like what I smell every time I look at you!"

She recoiled from him, her eyes filling with anger at the intensity of his voice. "Thees I no onderstand—"

"You understand money? *Money!* What you're bleeding my old man for. Give it to me! *Pieniadze!*"

"I no have—"

He grabbed her by the arm, his thin fingers biting the firmness of her flesh. "You think—" he started.

At that moment her fist came around and struck him soundly across the cheek, a wiry, quick force behind it. She moved over behind the kitchen table, staring at him with pleading and anger. *"Co ci jest, Franik? Co ci jest!"*

"Nothing's wrong with me!" he screamed at her. "It's you. Bitch!" he cursed. "You think you can take my mother's place? You young whore, you make a fool of my father!"

She came around the table and swung at him with a heavy porcelain plate, but she missed.

"Pies krew pieklo!" she cried furiously, standing flushed, her eyes flashing. "My children, all I love! You tell me! *Ty pies!* I love you, I kill you!"

He had been frightened. He backed away, the whole side of his face stinging where she had struck him.

When he was safely outside the doorway, he yelled, "Get back! G'wan back to the old country, you strawhead!"

Then he had run away, frantically, knowing that he could not return for a long time, probably never, knowing that his father would kill him.

The door opened suddenly on the passenger's side, and Tippy got in quickly. Frankie threw the gears into Drive and mashed down hard on the gas pedal. The car slid away swiftly.

"What happened?" Frankie asked, his heart beating fast.

Tippy just sat with his eyes on the half-frost of the rear window, watching the street behind.

"Well, what happened, damn it? Did you get the money?"

"I—I didn't get anything."

"You *what?*"

"The guy *saw* me, Frankie. He was greasing a job in the back and he could look right out to the front."

"You didn't get *anything?*"

"How could I? He was standing there watching everything I did."

Frankie felt the beating of his heart subside. In a way, he was glad. This was too close, this was almost like the books and pictures said: two guys sticking up a filling station to buy drugs.

The next stage really frightened him: killing for drugs.

And it really wasn't like that. A guy didn't just kill people. For nothing. If a person killed, it was usually for something, wasn't it?

Stuff wasn't like that.

Adele noticed them when they came into the bar. They hesitated at the doorway, obviously unsure of themselves because of their age, and this gave her a chance to move away from the bar to one of the tables at the rear. She tried to keep her face hidden after she'd sat down, but they spotted her anyway and came over to her table. She felt her heart sink under the mixture of heroin and cocain she'd used an hour before, knowing that it was because of Coke that they'd come, hoping that they brought news of his death.

Since Coke had been away in the hospital, Adele had not known such freedom. She hadn't been to the Scene to work one night. As a pimp, Coke had been a hard taskmaster. For nearly ten years he had blasted away every vestige of her former life: the Arizona desert, the School of Our Blessed Mother, the compassionless social wasteland of Tucson.

It had all meant nothing since she met Coke. They fled together, like wild rabbits, from the scorn people felt toward a Mexican and a white woman.

Absently, she listened to Frankie's high young voice.

"You tell him I'll come tomorrow," she said.

"We already been there once today," Frankie said. "He's in the psycho ward. He needs some horse. You should see him—he's dying."

"Don't he know it's poison, stuff is?" she said, content. "Don't he know he'll die if he has anything now? You tell him I'll come over sometime."

"He told me I should go and see The Man for him," Frankie said.

Adele's lips smiled faintly. "What does he think that bastard will do for him? As far as The Man cares, Coke's dead already." Her laugh was barely audible. "That's gratitude for ya. Coke, he made the Mexican borderside connect for The Man when he first got started here in the city, years ago. For years that bastard got fat offa what Coke did for him, then he don't want 'im anymore. Just 'cause Coke wants more money, The Man don't want 'im." She laughed again. "That's gratitude for ya, kid."

Frankie watched her, and she could feel the junkie's envy of another addict who had successfully scored. It was good to be a woman, she thought, remembering her recent alliance with Tony Caseri, one of the richest dealers in dago-town. If you were nice to Tony, he was nice to you; he came up with dynamite when you were nice to him.

"You're supposed to be Coke's broad," Frankie said. "Why can't you look out for him right? He'll die if he doesn't have some stuff."

Adele looked at him, irritated. "He'll die if he *does* have some stuff. I'm catching hell, you know what I mean? Aside from the monkey, I got room rent and meals and all that stuff to take care of. Coke knows what I gotta do."

"Why don't you cop for us?" Frankie asked her. "Since Coke's been gone, we don't have a regular connect. You know where to cop—you're high already."

"Why should I? Don't you guys know Tony Caseri, over on Seventieth?"

"His stuff is no good," Tippy put in.

"What's the difference? It's *like* stuff, ain't it?" Tears of self-pity came to her eyes. "My God, what do you guys expect me to do? The world is walking on me, I ain't getting help from nobody."

85

The barkeep, a big fat man, over six feet, came over to the table. "You know these guys, Adele?" he said.

"Get 'em outta here," she mumbled against her sleeve. "They're punks, they're just babies."

"Let's go," said the barkeep. "You tryin to get my license took? What's it, the cops send you punks around to set me up? *Geddow- dahere!*"

He forced the boys out into the coldness of the night, then came back over to where Adele still sat, her arms nestling the cheap- peroxide blossom of her head. "Hey," he said, shaking her roughly. "There's a guy over at the bar. Might mean a couple bucks for ya."

Adele raised her head. She cleared the dryness of her mouth with her tongue.

With an effort, she got up to meet the three-dollar challenge sitting at the bar.

I've been watching you—that's what The Man had said. *I've been watching you on the Scene, Black, and I think you'd make a good pusher.* . . .

Rudy's feet sank deep in the plush carpeting of the hallway as he left The Man's apartment. In his overcoat pocket, wrapped in a slick packet of cellophane, were one hundred capsules and a quarter-ounce of heroin. For each dollar of heroin sold, he was to get forty cents. Though his capacity for arithmetic was bad, it wasn't too difficult for him to figure out that his portion of the drug sale would come to better than one hundred and thirty dollars.

All he had to do now was get to the Scene and let the rest of the junkies know he had the bag. He knew trade would be slow for the first couple of hours, but after everyone had tested the drug and found it effective, he'd be swamped with business.

He felt good, and he could hardly wait to get back to his room at Lou's and give the stuff his own test.

The stuff couldn't have come through at a better time. Nina had gone off somewhere for a couple of days, so he hadn't been getting those ends. To add insult to injury, the boosting girls had found another junkie to chauffeur for them, so he was minus whatever he might have got from them. He still had some hot goods Marsha Lee had stashed in his closet, though; he wasn't going to let them go under any circumstances.

Everything was turning out crazy for him, just *crazy*! After he got himself going, really got straightened out, he was going to trade the Buick in on a Cadillac. Did those oldhead mackmen who hung out at the Garden Bar think they were the only ones who could drive Hogs? He'd show them! Rudy Black, the Thoroughbred, the Regular. He could almost see their faces when he showed up with the bag, their wide grins when they came to him, looking for a deal for ten or twenty dollars.

He heard voices at the bottom of the stairwell and stopped, listening carefully for a moment. His hands gripped the bag of drugs tightly. It couldn't be the Rollers! The Rollers wouldn't dare come up here to The Man's place.

Footsteps came up the staircase. He retreated back up to the landing, a tight snare of fear grabbing his heart. Of all the nights the Rollers might pick to come up to The Man's place, they had to pick the night Rudy got his first bag!

He squeezed back the fear, looking for a place to hide. It *couldn't* be the Rollers. Didn't The Man say that he had the Sixth Precinct sewed up? Didn't he tell Rudy if he ever got picked up, not to worry and not to cop out to anything, that he would be released in a couple of hours?

He looked down to The Man's apartment, the last one on the right-hand side of the hallway. Several feet away was the door to the rear stairway. Rudy rushed down to the door. The back stairs dropped sharply from the stoop, and he almost tumbled over headlong. He got his balance and leaned with his back against the door. He could hear the footsteps in the outer hall.

Cautiously, he opened the door a crack and peered out. Two white boys, just youngsters, were knocking at The Man's door. Rudy could hear Sylvia answer.

"Is Floyd there?" the tallest of the boys shouted.

"No," Sylvia called back, without opening the door.

"When will he be back?"

"I don't know."

"Who is this?" the boy asked.

"Why?"

"I want to see Floyd. Tell him to come to the door."

"Get away from here!"

"I wanna see Floyd first."

"I *told* you he isn't here! Now get away from this door!"

"Not until I see Floyd first," the boy said stubbornly.

The door was snatched open a slit, and Rudy could see the small, brown-skinned, ratlike face of Sylvia Dutton. "What the hell do you want?"

"Look, lady," the tall boy said, "Coke sent us over. He said we should talk to Floyd for him. He's sick at Municipal, and he told us to come by—"

"You look," Sylvia said, "if you boys know what's good for you, you'll get away from here."

"But, lady—"

"I'm telling you," Sylvia said, "I've got a gun right here. I'll shoot the hell out of you if you don't get away from here."

The boys began to back away.

"Get away and stay away!" Sylvia said, slamming the door.

The youngsters started downstairs.

Rudy came out in the hall. He followed them quickly, fingering the packet in his pocket. Obviously they weren't policemen, but he was puzzled how they had found out where The Man stayed. Even most of the junkies on the Scene didn't know that.

Maybe Coke Prado really had sent them. Everybody knew he was in the hospital, sick.

He made up his mind quickly, hurrying down the stairs before they were out of the building. He caught them just at the front steps.

"Hey," he called, "hey, white boys! C'mere a minute."

This would be his first sale, and maybe he could make steady customers of the boys. Every dealer had five or six silks who spent a lot of money.

Then Rudy saw their faces, and he knew instinctively that the boys were novices. With his calculating junkie's mind, he pounced on them.

"You want some stuff?" he said. "I gotta bag, but it's so good it'll cost you two-fifty a thing. . . ."

"You saw most of the Scene last week," Davis said, pulling the Ford out on Pennsylvania, swiftly moving through the light scatter of snowflakes. "Now I'm about to show you the base of operations."

They went down several blocks past Eighty-eighth. Davis slowed down as they neared Ninety-second.

"Over there," he said. "See that trucking firm—Angelo's Transit? That belongs to Floyd Angelo, The Man. Perfectly legit. It does light hauling and has a couple of semis leased to a steel firm downtown."

"Looks big," Patterson said.

Davis grunted. "It is. You'd think a man making fifty thousand legitimate dollars a year would be satisfied, wouldn't you? Not The Man—he's not built that way."

"Makes you wonder," Patterson said thoughtfully.

"Where's the wonder?" Davis said. "The Man is a hog, pure and simple. He's one of those dirty little people who never get full, no matter how much you feed 'im. Only thing, he's smart as he is hungry." He drove on a little farther, down past Ninety-fifth. "See the apartment house there on the corner? It belongs to The Man, too. Hundred-thousand-dollar building, thirty units. He bought it from a management company three years ago: nominal down payment, five hundred a month. It grosses him about two thousand a month. And that's not all; he's got three other places, single homes, where he shifts the dope business around."

"I can't understand it," Patterson said. "He could quit right now and be straight for the rest of his life. Why does he continue, taking a risk that could get him years behind bars?"

"Some people are worse addicts to money than the most confirmed junkies," Davis said. "Then, too, The Man is a syndicate boy. I still say he's a hog, because you can quit anything if you really want to—but maybe the Big Boy won't let The Man ease out. It figures: the dope trade is so big here in this part of town, if The Man closed up shop it'd mean a loss way up in the millions." Davis broke off and stared hard at the apartment building. "Still, Floyd Angelo *could* quit, but he won't. He's hooked, really hooked."

As they came past the neat entrance of the building, Davis jerked his head. "Well, bless my buttocks! There's Rudy Black!"

Patterson snatched around in his seat. Davis pulled over to the curb and shut off the motor.

"There," he said, pointing through the rear window. "With those two kids. Looks like the same two punks who've been tramping the Scene the past couple of weeks."

"He's giving them something," Patterson said, squinting.

"Damned if he ain't!" Davis said. "I believe that punk's got a bag, do you figure? Yeah, he's got a bag!"

Patterson readied himself for action. "How do we take him?"

Davis waved the suggestion away impatiently. "We don't. We're gonna play him, like a big fish. The worst thing we could do would be to bust him right on The Man's front doorstep."

Davis closely watched the transaction between Rudy and the boys. "Something's wrong; they're bickering. Rudy's trying to burn 'em, I'll bet. Stuff is only a dollar and a quarter a cap on the open market. Rudy's trying to make 'em pay more."

"They're minors," Patterson said. "You said yourself the first dealer who sold them drugs would be due for a long stretch."

"Listen to me," Davis said tightly. "I know what I'm doing, do you understand? Now keep your mouth shut and maybe you'll learn something, college boy."

Patterson lapsed into silence. He was beginning to learn that the less he said and did in Davis' presence the better off he would be.

"Ahhh," Davis said, almost passionately. "They copped. Now they're leaving." He struck the back of the seat with the heel of his hand. "That's good! They'll be back to see Rudy, you can count on that. The Man's slipping! He's got a door up there in his apartment you couldn't get through with a riot gun. Every time we think we've got a case against him, one of his lawyers greases the right palm. We don't even know where his stash is, he's that smart." He started the motor and pulled off slowly. "But Rudy Black is something else again, I got a feeling. You just watch and see—I got a feeling!"

Patterson didn't say anything, burning inside.

The older man sensed his frustration. "Tell you what—there's a little black woman who deals on the Scene, Bertha Travis. I think she's about right for plucking; she's only been at it a few months, since her man got sent up on a robbery beef. In a week or so, I'll let you try to pull her in, just to see how much you learned in college."

From now on, Patterson resolved, I'll just keep my trap shut. I won't give this bastard any more chances to step on me.

It sounded all right, but for some reason it was illogical to place all the blame on Davis. He couldn't admit to himself it was the assignment, the offal-like contamination of these people obsessed by narcotics. There was something dirty about it all which you were never entirely rid of.

"Let's check up on our traps before we turn in," Davis said.

Patterson stared back at the neon fury of the Scene, as if to prove that he was bigger than it was.

OUTSIDE THE RAIN sliced into the dirty snow of the side street, chopping away at the blackened, shoveled-back mounds, flooding the sway-chested sidewalks with water. The slow cry of the box factory's whistle could be heard faintly, signaling four o'clock.

The winter rain fell steadily, splattering the indelible face of the neighborhood.

From her seat by the front window, Constance Purtell could see Ace and Rudy Black walking quickly toward the house. She felt her flesh crawl, thinking, it's worth it, I *know* it's worth it.

She rose impulsively, pulling tight the buttonless housedress she wore, wrinkled and split about the dark ampleness of her.

She went over to the phone in the hallway and dialed a number. She heard the receiver come up on the other end.

"Hello, Ma?" she said. "It's me, Connie."

"Yes, I know, dear. Where are you? Is anything wrong?"

"No, Ma, I just—well, I thought I'd call and see how you're doing, that's all."

"Are you working?"

"Just got off work." She bit her lip, for the lies came so easily now. "I'm at the apartment. Velma—you know, my roommate— she'll be in pretty soon. We're going to a show."

The front door opened and she could hear the low voices of the men.

"*Ma . . .*"

"Yes, dear? Connie, what's wrong?"

"Nothing—nothing, Ma. I just thought I lost the connection is all." Her voice rose in an exaggerated cheerfulness. "How've you been doing? How's Clara and the kids? I saw her at the supermarket the other day—"

"Clara's fine, dear. Little Haywood's got the whooping cough, though. She called just a while ago to say Seymour's going to drive him over to the doctor when he gets in from work."

"Seymour?"

"Clara's *husband*, Connie. My God, what's wrong with you? You don't sound right."

She could hear the footsteps behind her, advancing. Her flesh crawled again, clear up to her scalp.

She laughed with a nervous affectation. "Hell, what makes you think that, Ma? I'm O.K.; I never lived better. I wouldn't trade the way I'm living now for anything, not anything."

"But I never see you anymore, Connie," her mother said, the worry apparent in her voice. "You're only nineteen, dearest. I respect what you're trying to do, trying to live on your own, but, Connie, I've got a feeling everything isn't the way you want me to believe it is." A heavy tiredness suddenly entered her voice. "I'm all alone in this big house, Connie. Why—why don't you come back home?"

"Who you talkin to?" Ace whispered hoarsely in her ear, his breath hot and disturbing. She put her hand over the mouthpiece, then uncovered it quickly and spoke.

"I'm coming over soon, Ma, I swear I will!"

"You don't have to get angry—"

"I wasn't, Ma, I swear I wasn't! I just meant it, that's all. It was just the way I said it."

"Give me your address, dear, and I'll come over there."

"How many times have I told you that I can't? It's so irregular—well, you know what I mean."

"Your job?"

"Yes, that's it."

"I could come over on Sundays—"

"But *no*, Mother, I'm telling you what *I'll* do! Dearest, do we have to go through all this when I call? It's the easiest thing in the world for me to do like I said, and you know it."

"Connie, I haven't seen you in nearly a year. Something's wrong, I know that, too."

"I think we've talked long enough, Ma."

A pause.

"If you think so, Constance."

She waited, her heart expanding with a dull ache. "I'll call you again soon."

"I'd appreciate hearing from you, dear. When you get a chance, please stop by."

"Moth—"

"And bring your friend, dear."

"My friend?"

"Whoever he is."

The phone clicked in her ear. She stood there a long time. Then, overcome by a wild, vicious anger, she turned to Ace and Rudy

Black, who stood wet and dripping with the rain. Ace, his konked head soggy and shiny, came close to her, his piglike eyes flashing with a stupid anticipation.

Rudy Black watched disinterestedly as Ace's wet hands tore her housedress apart, drying their coldness on the warmth of her flesh.

She snatched away from him.

"Hey, hey, don't get chilly on me, little baby." He was almost on tiptoe, trying to reach her mouth with his own. She pushed him back toward the smirking face of Rudy Black.

"Now what'd I do?" he begged helplessly.

"I was *talking* on the phone!" she shouted.

"I didn't do nothin!"

"You inter-*rupted* my conversation, stiffy!"

"What the hell you get so mad about? I didn't do a damn thing, and you know I didn't." He stood, rain-soaked, pitifully short and black beside her tall slimness.

"I was talking on the *goddamned* phone!" she screamed. "I can't stand you *sneaking* up behind me!"

Over his shoulder, she could feel Rudy's appraising glance, and instinctively pulled the housedress around her tighter. Until recently, she had never known Rudy Black, and now each time he accompanied Ace home it was as though something unutterably despicable had slithered in from the Scene. She hated him instantly. Not because of the drugs, or the knowledge that his insatiable addiction was abnormal even among addicts: but because she knew intuitively he embodied something from her environment that was unspeakably evil and vile.

Ace came over and tried to put his hand in her dress again, but she twisted away, her flesh jerking, and went over to stand near the window.

Outside, the rain pounded with new fury against the quietness of the house. She heard Rudy go off into the living room; she heard the chair scraping back from the big round table: the sound of a Vaseline cap tinkled on its surface, and she knew he was getting ready for a fix.

Behind her, she could still feel the repentant shell of Ace. She relaxed; her lips smiled very beautifully, independent of the repulsion she felt.

"Give me some stuff," she said, turning to him.

He had taken off his coat, his face dark and sullen like a small child's.

"You act right, you get stuff," he said.

"What did you say?"

"I said—" he started, but found he did not have enough nerve to repeat himself. "We don't have to do all this, baby." He moved toward her again, his brows tilting high in sorry, comic furrows of pleading. "Why is it? Why can't we get along, me and you?"

She forced herself to go halfway, as though meeting an opponent on a battlefield, every muscle steeled. She had to accustom herself to this, this evening, like yesterday evening and all the other evenings past for more than eight months. Daily, she had to prepare herself for the wild needs of him, hypnotize her mind until she lost herself.

She reached him and smiled. "I just been bogue all day, Tommy, and when you came in I was talking on the phone with my mother, and I"—she drew taut at the touch of his fingers on her breasts— "I—I couldn't hear so good."

He nuzzled his head between her breasts, his hair cold and dead. "Baby, I had a hard day. You just believe it, I had a hard day. I'm gonna quit it, I'm gonna give this bag up, you just watch and see, baby."

. . . A long time ago she had been a very fast girl, quick to catch on, popular in the girls' club at school, sought after, kissed and petted and loved. Right now it seemed almost silly that she should be hooked, with scars on her arms, with nothing but a housedress on because she felt too lazy and sluggish to dress in the mornings, with an ugly little black man who held the bag containing all the riches and loves and romances she had ever dreamed of, held them in condensed version, powdered form. . . .

They reached the living room, where Rudy sat at the table with his left sleeve rolled up, eyes closed, the needle still anchored in the crook of his arm, filled with blood, the elastic belt still tied around his upper arm, the veins knotted under the skin like twisted, elongated worms.

Ace went over and shook him. "Hey, man! Come out of it, man!"

Rudy roused himself slowly, taking note of the needle in his arm, squeezing the fat bladder of the pacifier until every bit of blood had spurted back into the puffing vein.

"You wanna die?" Ace asked him. "I can't have you dyin around here."

"All right, all right," Rudy mumbled, his tongue thick, eyes half-closed. "All right, all right . . ." He snatched the needle out, sucking his arm where the blood was spurting. Like a drunk, he dragged his arm across the table, knocking to the floor the gaping white cups of the six capsules he'd just used.

"I'm glad I don't use," Ace told Constance proudly. "I'm glad I don't do nothin but joy pop." He fixed up a place at the table for her and began to take capsules out of an empty cigarette pack. "How many you want, baby?"

"Make it four," Constance said, staring vaguely at the thing that was Rudy Black.

. . . A long time ago she had gone with a fellow named Roy, a toy to twist and turn. She had a lot of fun, but it never became serious with her because she always fell back on her widowed mother when the situation became dangerous. She couldn't marry and leave Ma all alone, could she?

Anyway, it was extremely comfortable that way, just her and Ma, with her sister Clara married. She had a good job with the Negro insurance company downtown; she was having a lot of fun and meeting the best people.

Anyway, who wanted to get married anyway? . . .

"It'll be Christmas soon," Ace said. "What do you want for Christmas, baby?"

"I want a whole ounce of stuff to myself," Rudy Black mumbled, staring at Constance while she used. "Ain't that what you want, Connie? Tell your man you wanna ounce of stuff for Christmas."

"I want an ounce of stuff for Christmas," Connie said, getting the first hit of the narcotics, feeling her belly warm over and her fear of Rudy Black disperse with the good feeling. "My daddy's gonna get me an ounce of stuff, won't you, daddy?"

Ace ignored her, looking at Rudy jealously. "You may not be around at Christmas, man. You keep sellin stuff to them white boys, you won't be around for no Christmas."

"Be cool," Rudy sneered.

"I been tryin to pull your coat," Ace said. "You ain't had your bag but around a week. You don't know how the Rollers gobble you, man. Everybody gobbles you on the Scene."

"I'm not scared of no Scene," Rudy said defiantly. "I'm not scared of the Rollers or nobody. I'm thoroughbred! I step on 'em, step on 'em!"

"You crazy, man," Ace said. "Them silks is gonna get you in a world of trouble if you don't freeze."

"I already froze," Rudy said. "They didn't like it 'cause I wouldn't give 'em no deal on stuff. They told me to go to hell. They'll be back—nobody'll sell 'em no stuff. They come back, I'll tell *them* to go to hell!" He began to laugh insanely.

Constance's head wobbled on her neck, the blouse of her dress coming open, exposing the brown, neatly-tipped fineness of her breasts. "You ain't told me about that ounce for Christmas," she said to Ace, clutching at him roughly.

Rudy watched the jerking of her breasts.

. . . A long time ago she had gone to a bar on Twelfth with Roy and listened to the combo: vibes, bass, piano and drums. The combo was genuinely unique, with solidly organized arrangements, quietly penetrating. Like the Chinese water-torture, she had said: you wait for the next drop to knock your brains out. That's the way they were, with the latest in progressive.

Newton had played vibes. His name and picture were on the poster out front: FEATURING NEWTON LEWIS ON VIBRAPHONE. He was good; his was a crude, fluctuating rhythm and a mind flush with grotesque ideas. He was very dark and handsome, a skin olive-textured, and neat clothes smelling of apple-blossom scent.

The way he stared at her was potent, casually meaningful, with an urgency that caused her to make Roy take her home.

But she returned later, alone. . . .

"What's gonna happen to you when the hammer falls?" Ace was asking Rudy. They were opposite each other, Ace sitting on her right, his hand caressing the inside of her thigh from time to time. "A stud don't seem to realize that there's only so long you can sell stuff without gettin a bust. Then—shupp! it's all over, it's really solid mellowreeny the finish. I been tryin to pull your coat, man," Ace finished earnestly.

"I ain't worried," Rudy said. "The Man is tops, you know that. I don't have to worry about nothin. He springs me if I get busted."

"I cop over in dago-town from Puck just as well as I do from The Man," Ace said. "Puck couldn't do a thing for me if I got busted, and he's strong, man, really strong."

"Not as strong as The Man."

"He's syndicate," Ace swore. "They don't come any stronger."

"He's not as strong as The Man," Rudy said stubbornly. "Nobody in the city is that strong. You should cop regular from The Man; you'd get protection, too."

"I've been coppin from The Man as long as anybody; I was born right here in Dope City. I say nobody can stop the Rollers when they want you, *nobody*, man!"

"I'm gonna get big off The Man," Rudy said dreamily. "I'm gonna get me a big Hog and I'm gonna have the biggest bag on the Scene. I'm gonna be bigger than anything on the Scene. Everybody'll be talkin about how big Rudy Black is—you watch, you punk-out—you'll be talkin about how big Rudy Black is, you and every-body else."

"I'm thinkin about hangin it up," Ace said, "and just coppin enough from Puck to keep Connie straight until she can kick." He squeezed her thigh tightly. "Do you wanna kick, baby? Do ya?"

She raised her head and looked at him. "Yes."

Unmindful of Rudy, he went on. "We'll stick, won't we? Me and you?"

She didn't answer.

98

"We'll think about it," he said.

. . . A long time ago she had gone up to the apartment over the bar with Newton, and they had ordered shrimp in sauce, hot potato chips just cooked, with crackers and chow mein and cold beer that froze her teeth.

The apartment was small, provided by the management for all the show people on the current bill, nicely decorated, with a picture-window in the tiny kitchen which framed the glow of the river front several miles away: the deep, moving expanse of water, the hundred lights of tugs and barges like so many brilliant, misplaced eyes.

Their talk touched on everything except them, limiting how much they should know of each other. Their smiles were intimate repositories of what they knew to be inevitable. Her body became hot, and the beer left a sharp, fragrantly sensual odor in her nostrils.

Newton lay on the floor, watching her, his head propped on a pillow from the sofa, his clothes sprouting around his slim body like leaves, revealing now the too-thin core of him.

She remembered how he showed her: the shardlike cut of heroin in her nostrils, the bittersweet drain to her tongue. . . .

When she came out of her nod, the house was dark without lights. Rudy Black was gone.

In the hallway, Ace was trying to get in touch with the Italian, Puck. After dialing several times, he came back into the living room.

"Somethin's wrong with Puck," he said. "He's always home. I couldn't get him." His voice was almost fearful. "Somethin's happened! What do you s'pose happened, baby?"

Constance sat at the table, her head on her arms. Her dress was half pulled from her shoulders. In a while, she was conscious of his lips on the back of her neck, idly touching a shoulder blade.

"Let's go to bed, baby."

"Not now," she said, the words garbled.

"C'mon, let's go. I don't never say no to nothin you want, like drugs. Why you treat me so bad, baby?" His fingers found the tip of her breast and hurt her.

"I said *no*, goddamn you! Why do you pester me to death?"

"Baby—"

"I don't feel like it! I couldn't be like you want me, Tommy."
She sat up, the warmness of her belly nauseating her, as though she
had to throw up.

She took a deep breath, thinking of her mother, thinking of
what she might be doing at the moment.

"I don't want you to be no way," Ace said, his lips touching
her. "You don't have to, baby, you don't have to do nothin."

"Tommy—"

"Please, baby, please, please, please! Why do you treat me so
mean?"

"Can't you understand?" she said, rising up. "I don't *want* you!"

His fingers drilled into her belly violently, gripping the soft flesh.
He kissed her on the lips, twisting her head painfully.

All her strength left her in disgust.

. . . A long time ago she had been an extremely fast girl. She
would never have dreamed of getting a bee. The idea would have
been too impossible.

She had been brought up in the right neighborhood, with the
right playmates and school chums, with the right parents—although
her father had died when she was very young—with the right com-
panions of the opposite sex, with the right everything that was
necessary in the successful flowering of a bright, young, career-bent
Negro girl.

Everything had been ideal. Her life was to have been no question-
and-answer thing: it had been mapped out according to the new,
middle-class Negro social trend and left no room for deviation.

Yet she had got hooked.

And Newton had left for other gigs; left her with a bee and a
baby, born dead. Dead because of the bee, which allowed no other
life inside her body except its own.

To survive without selling her body was not easy, but she finally
found Thomas Carson, known as Ace—and the Scene. . . .

Somehow he had got her into the bedroom, across the unmade
bed, his breath whistling sourly into her face and his hands tight
around her limbs.

"Connie, baby," he moaned, dropping beside her, tearing away his clothes, baring the strongly jointed, muscle-packed little body. "Baby, ohh, baby . . ." His lips, warm and frantic, pasted themselves to her body, crawled sensitively over her flesh, arousing in her a faint glow of desire and disgust, mingled together and sickening, weakening.

"Stop, Tommy," she gasped.

"I'll do anything, baby. . . . I love you, baby. . . ."

"I said stop, you bastard!" Weakly she grasped his throat, moved her fingers to his thick, heavy hair and yanked.

"Unnnnh!"

"Let me *go*, Tommy!"

He sat up and looked at her. Tears began to form in his eyes.

"I give you my stuff," he told her. "What else you want me to do?"

In giving the narcotics, she knew he had given everything he had. He had lived in a lonely, insecure little world, without love or a chance to be really wanted or needed. Until now. And it cost her little enough to give herself to him.

She let him go on.

From somewhere near, through the sound of the rain, a record-player spun the refrain over and over, sad despite its swinging style of blues:

> *Let me go, baby, you ain't doin me no good.*
> *Let me go, baby, you ain't doin me no good.*
> *Lovin you, darlin, is like lovin a piece of wood . . .*
>   *Hey, NOW!*

Later she got up and went to the bathroom. She waited until her stomach quieted, then went back to bed, to sleep until tomorrow.

. . . A long time ago, she had not been a junkie. . . .

Davis met Patterson right after roll call that night. "C'mon over to the record office with me. I wanna show you a few things."

The record office—a converted interrogation room with a check-out cage—served a dual purpose as safe for confiscated evidence, and arsenal.

Behind the cage, a tallow-faced patrolman sat on a high chair, reading a pocket-sized novel. He looked up when they came over.

"How ya doing, Mance?" he smiled.

Davis shrugged a greeting. "Ken, this is my new partner, Virgil Patterson. I'm sorta breaking him in. Virgil don't seem to know much about junk. You got that stuff I took off the junkie a while back?"

The patrolman looked through a big, threadbare record book. "Don't know if I have, Mance. They mighta called it downtown as evidence. Let's see . . ." He perused several pages. "Yeah, here we go. No, they haven't asked for it yet. You wanna take a look at it?"

"If you don't have to dig," Davis said. "We gotta get going in a few minutes."

Swinging nimbly off the chair and going over to the shelf crammed with manila envelopes, head-high on all sides of the room, the patrolman selected a package and came back to the window. "Here it is."

Davis loosened the strings and emptied the contents of the package.

"This," he said to Patterson, selecting one of the items, "is what most addicts call a spike. You can see all it consists of is an everyday eye-dropper, a baby's pacifier, tightened at the top with a rubber band, and a size-25 hypodermic needle. You hold the needle on by tearing the edge of a dollar bill and wrapping it around the small end of the dropper. You call that the 'G.' We've got a regulation against selling needles without specific directions from a physician, but it's one of those things that aren't followed through, like spitting on the sidewalk." He fingered through the articles. "See this?" he said, holding it up so Patterson could take a close look. "What does it look like to you?"

"Why, just a bottle cap," Patterson said, trying to make out a trade name on the blackened bottom of the cap. "It looks like it might have come off a bottle of cleanser."

"That's just what it came off," Davis affirmed. "This is the cooker. An addict holds this thing between his fingers while he cooks the drug with several matches. It burns the hell out of his fingers, but he'll never drop it—he'd rather die. Here—see this on the inside?"

"Looks like crystallized sugar."

"Right again. That's milk sugar, used in chemical solutions. Sale of it is supposed to be tight." He grunted. "It takes an experienced hand to cut drugs up, college boy—I mean really cut 'em for the last hair of the dollar. If the drugs come pure, it's a ticklish operation, something a chemist or pharmacist has to do. That's why we know we're playing with a bunch of smart cookies, talented guys, professionals."

"It's pretty dirty," said the patrolman, shaking his head.

"That's the least it is," Davis said, picking up one of the three capsules in the envelope. "This is stuff." He eased the top off one of the capsules and held it out to Patterson. "Here, taste it. It's not going to hurt you. Just take a little bit on your tongue. There, that's it. Get that taste?"

Patterson made a face.

"Bitter as hell, huh?" Davis smiled. "Don't forget that taste. Nothing else but heroin tastes like that. The bitterer it is, the better. That's how a junkie tells what he's getting." He returned the capsules to the envelope and gave the patrolman a wave.

They started back out to the squad room.

"Think you get the idea, college boy?"

"I'm beginning to," Patterson said, bristling at what appeared destined to be a permanent nickname.

"I've got other things to show you," Davis said. "Things like morphine and cocain. We don't get those very often. Sometimes a Chink or wetback gets into the city with some: it doesn't last long. Those things are luxuries."

Before they left, Lieutenant Stuart called after Davis across the squad room. There was a half-smile on his lips when he came over.

"Thought you might like to know, Mance," he said. "Speer knocked off Pietro Telluccini in dago-town this afternoon."

103

"Puck?" Davis said, surprised.

"The same," Stuart said. "That leave only Clyde Lujack and Tony Caseri, the independents. They've been doing all right without The Man, but they'll wish they had his kind of protection before we're through with them."

"How'd it happen?"

"It's the damndest thing!" Stuart grinned. "We got a call in, said Telluccini had just made a purchase. Speer got over to his place in time to find him sitting."

"That is luck," Davis said. "Somebody big had to set him up. Purchases aren't something everybody has a line on."

"I'm thinking it was another dealer—some big shot."

Davis pursed his lips. "Could be. I've known The Man to do things like this before, cut down the competition."

"Think it's useful to us?"

"We won't know for a while," Davis said. "One little punk I know—Ace—he was copping from Puck because of the low bulk-rate. He'll probably go back to The Man now, and that's good for me. When it comes time to squeeze Ace, he'll be one more tack in The Man's back pocket."

"That's encouraging. What have you planned for the moment?"

Davis pointed a thumb at Patterson. "Gonna see if we can knock Bertha Travis off this morning. Her connect downtown got emptied two days ago, and I've got information she's setting up with The Man."

"I'll be in a car with Garver this shift. If anything hot turns up, give me a call. I'll see you later."

Davis and Patterson went out to the garage, and found a plain two-door sedan and got in.

"I've got some clothes in the back for you," Davis said. "I want you to look the part when we nail Black Bertha."

"Sure," said Patterson, his mouth still tingling from the lingering, bittersweet taste of heroin.

6

IN THE HOUSE on Ninetieth the ounces sat divided on the table like equal portions of pirates' booty.

Getting up from the couch, Sylvia Dutton again checked the supply on the table. Sixteen ounces, she counted. At two hundred dollars an ounce, that came to over three thousand dollars.

Sylvia lighted a cigarette and went back over to the couch. They were making more money than ever. Since The Man had gotten rid of Coke Prado, the new pipeline out of New York, Georgie Barris, had proved dependable and cheap. It was nice the way Georgie had it set up, alternating as connection and pipeline, which was better than being solely one or the other. Now that The Man had decided to monopolize the city, the thing was working out fine.

She thought of the phone call she had made earlier that day. It was a stroke of luck that Telluccini had had to make an emergency purchase from The Man so she could set him up. When the rest of the dealers saw what had happened to him, it wouldn't be long before they all came in.

She drew at the cigarette thoughtfully. It was high time for The Man to branch out; she'd been telling him to make the move a long time ago. But now somehow it all seemed ookey. She didn't like the new pusher, Rudy Black—his grandiose manner, his braggadocio. He was one pusher she felt The Man would have done better without. She'd never liked addicts—even though Dell Swiggins, one of the Scene's bigger pushers, was an addict The Man had a lot of confidence in.

But there were some things you just couldn't tell The Man. She had been with him nearly ten years, had been faithfully devoted— yes, loved him for that length of time, though remaining little more than a secretary in his eyes—and she had never known him to be wrong about anything.

She got up and went over to the mirror on the far wall and looked at herself: the wide snout of nose, the thick lips and heavy-lidded eyes. Even the good clothes she wore failed to lend the slightest bit of attraction; the beauty treatments for her short hair, dyed red, was money wasted, though money was the least thing she had to worry about.

She stubbed the cigarette out in an ashtray. No, The Man had never been wrong about anything yet, not even her.

She smiled grandly at the horror in the mirror and turned back to the couch. She couldn't ask for any more than she had, could she? Or could she?

A college education was useless here, except for the simple book-keeping and connections the business required. The pay was extremely high—a lot higher than what Uncle Sam used to pay her in the WAC ten years ago—and she had her own small business on One-hundred-fifth, a completely legitimate lunchroom.

The memory of the WAC made her pause. The recollection brought mingled pain and pleasure. At least in the Army she had not been baseless. Once having attained the rank of sergeant, she could act pretty much as she pleased. The travels had been wonderful, and Florida, where she had met Floyd, had been doubly exciting, because that was where she had met Evelyn also.

She felt her heart throb at the thought: Evelyn, her sweet, smooth brown legs, her questioning, little-girl stare . . . she and Evelyn alone in her room at the barracks. . . .

Grimly, she lighted another cigarette and paced the floor rest-lessly. A bad conduct discharge. At least that had been all. And not long after, Floyd had come along.

So what had she to kick about? She had no one except herself and Floyd, The Man, *her* man. All the dirty little people she came into contact with meant nothing to her. She was objective about them, as the world had been objective about her: there would always be prostitution and drugs; the world *had* to have something to forget with.

Sylvia went over the newest layout of the Scene. With Rudy Black covering the new demand, five hundred or more dollars a week would roll into The Man's treasury, especially if Black established any outside bulk connections. The Man had a score or more pushers like Black scattered around the city, not counting middlemen; and the money was coming in nicely.

Black Bertha was supposed to show up tonight with Dell. He had arranged for her purchases through The Man, since her downtown connection had been knocked off by the police. Sylvia rolled the possibilities around in her mind. Bertha wasn't a great puller, but she might do as well as Rudy Black—perhaps better, since she wasn't an addict and wouldn't be tempted to go through her own bag.

Now that Telluccini was out of the way, Ace and the rest of Puck's business would be knocking at the door. Sylvia made a note to squeeze them for higher prices the first few weeks, just to show them they weren't really needed.

Sonny Tubbs was a regular and virile producer, even though he operated from a wheel chair. She reminded herself to give him better deals on his bulk purchases.

Lou and Ella Tyler provided the perfect stash with their hotel. She had to marvel at The Man's ingenuity. A hotel overrun with junkies was the last place the police would look for The Man's mountainous hoard.

The only thing still lacking in her knowledge of the entire operation was the identity of the Big Boy, the man who received the narcotics directly from the borderside connection and diluted its potency, the man above The Man.

It doesn't matter, she thought. That's something I'd rather not know.

Everything was going smoothly, and it wouldn't be long before The Man hit that million-dollar peak he was always talking about. Then they could quit, disappear from the syndicate, and thank fate.

Their only nemesis thus far had been the Roller Davis. The Man had tried everything in an effort to remove him from the narcotics detail, but to no avail. However, with Captain Beeker locked up tight at Sixth Precinct, Davis was a man fighting windmills.

Yes, The Man had thought of everything.

* * *

Although their conference had lasted nearly three hours, it was still raining when Bertha and Dell left The Man.

"How'm I supposed to make my next connection?" Bertha said past the collar of her coat. "I live right down here on the corner, just two blocks away. Should I come around here the next time?"

Dell pulled her into an open doorway of one of the tenements lining the street. "Bertie, I don't like the way you talked to The Man," he said, his eyes flashing at her.

"What'd I say? I just told him two hundred was too much an ounce. Downtown I paid one-sixty-five."

"You ain't downtown no more—"

"I told him what I thought," she said hotly. "What the hell is he supposed to be? He don't look like no king to me."

Dell felt his position with The Man threatened. The Man didn't like obstinacy, Dell knew that better than anyone else. Because Bertha was his girl friend, The Man would probably blame him for the things she said.

"Listen, Bert," he said patiently. "When we cop from The Man we got to pay his prices. Whadda you wanna do, get me in trouble with him? One day I'm gonna get a big slice from The Man. You wanna hurt me by talkin too much?"

"*Hurt* my butt!" Bertha said. "Do you realize I lost nearly three bills when my connect got busted? What have you got to lose? I say two hundred is too much, and I'm gonna tell him so every time I got to cop!"

"You got two ounces," Dell said, holding up his fingers. "Two ounces you wouldna never got if I hadn't took you in to The Man! Why you gonna bitch about a few cents for? He's doin you a favor—"

"He's doin me nothin! The stuff shouldn't cost over one-sixty-five!" She shook a fist under his nose. "And another thing! That monkey-faced bitch of his better watch her mouth, tryin to tell me where 'it would be best for you to center your operations'! Once I leave The Man with my drugs, they're *my* drugs! Nobody can tell me where I ought to sell 'em or to who!"

Dell saw that it was useless. Once Bertha had her mind set, she was immovable. However, he was not about to fall out of favor with The Man, even if it meant giving up Bertha. The Man had promised him a big spot with the organization; and he wasn't getting any younger. Forty-five was old for a junkie. He hoped to stash away a nice bankroll, along with several ounces, by the end of the year. So even if nothing worked out, he could go to South America, one of the sections where drugs were plentiful and quasi-legal, to spend the rest of his life.

But lately it seemed as though The Man had been grooming him. He'd told him about Georgie Barris and a portion of the pipeline set-up. Why would he tell him all that if he didn't figure to put him into some big spot?

"I'm tellin you that any connect that charges two hundred don't mean you no good!" Bertha was saying.

"Looka here," Dell said, raising a hand to shut her off, "I got things to do, I gotta get on over to the Quality and cap my stuff up."

"You mean cap your arm up, trick!"

"Maybe you should start usin," he said, starting out in the rain. "That's one way to keep your big blabbermouth shut!"

"Hey," she called after him. "How do I connect again?"

"I'll get in touch with you," he said over his shoulder.

At the steps of Bertha's rooming house, on the corner of Ninetieth and Maple, a man and woman stood shivering in the cold downpour. The man was shabbily dressed, the frayed edges of his overcoat pulled up close to his eyes. The woman, dressed in a white trenchcoat, was fat and very light-skinned. Two moles stood out darkly, on her chin and right cheekbone. She stood with her back against the building, arms crossed, the turmoil in her body making her legs and thighs jerk heavily in recurrent spasms.

As Bertha started up the steps, they both approached her.

"You Bertha?" the man asked. He was hatless, and the neatness of his short-cropped hair made Bertha suspicious.

"Yeah," she said.

109

"I wanna cop," he said. "Can I? Are you straight?"

"I don't know you," Bertha said. Then to the woman, whom she knew: "Let's go inside, Carrie."

The fat woman came up anxiously behind her. The man followed too.

"I told you I don't know you," Bertha said, turning on him. "You'd better get the hell away from me."

"But I'm sick," he protested. "I ain't gonna do nothin. I got money. I just wanna get the sickness off so I can go to work."

"I haven't got anything, I told you!"

"You didn't tell me—"

"I'm tellin you now! Get away from here. You'll make my place hot just standin here."

The man pointed at the fat woman. "You're gonna sell her some stuff. I know you're gonna sell her some. Why freeze on me? I never did nothin to nobody."

"Get away from here," Bertha said.

"Ask anybody on the Scene," the man pleaded. "Ask any sono-fabitch you want, they'll tell you. I live on the west side, I come over here all the time."

"They sell drugs on the west side," Bertha said unpityingly. "You better cop over there—don't come here buggin me! I don't know nothin about you!"

Bertha turned her back and went through the swinging, one-hinged front door, followed by the woman called Carrie.

The front hall was without lights, almost like night, no different from the outside except that the wind and rain did not disturb the coldness here. The stairs they ascended squeaked beneath their feet like animals. At the top of the stairs a child's voice could be heard singing.

> No, Mama, no, the baby she say no.
> Go, Mama, go, the baby she say go,
> go, go, go . . .

Near the end of the upper landing was a garbage can piled high with refuse; rats scrambled madly at the sound of footsteps. Bertha let herself into a room at the darkest end of the hallway, a room which seemed strangely yellow in spite of the white bareness of a huge bulb over a new kitchen table.

In an overlarge bed in the next room, two young girls lay sleeping, the covers pulled up to their throats, their bodies intertwined together in one high lump, their eyes closed and peaceful in warmth.

Bertha wrinkled her nose. "Edna!"

One of the girls moved slightly, but did not answer.

"Edna!" Bertha said again.

"Yeah, Ma?" One of the bodies unlinked itself and sat up slowly, brushing dark, natural curls away from sleepy eyes, gracefully unaware of itself as a body.

"Don't you Yeah-Ma me!" Bertha cried, overcome by a sudden fear. "Get out of that bed!"

"Aw, Ma—"

"I said get up!"

Edna Travis stood up from the bed, the movements of her slim body, immature but budding beautifully under the thin slip, insolent in a way that made Bertha stop to think nowadays. She was almost fifteen, the same age Bertha had been when her husband, Howard Travis, had turned her out to work the streets.

It seemed to Bertha that Edna was stacking up the same way she had, but with a body that had more determination, would turn her into something that would mark her for a shot by every hustler in the city.

Carrie put her hand on Bertha's arm. "I just want four things, Bert," she said sickly. "Just give me four things. I'll split then. I got other things to do."

"Wait for me or go somewhere else and cop!" Bertha shouted at her. She turned back on Edna. "Where'd you get the pot?"

"Pot?" Edna shook her head innocently. "I ain't got no pot, Ma. I got what you give me to keep, that's all."

"I don't mean that," Bertha said sharply. "You know what I mean—you been smokin pot! Where is it? Give it to me!"

"Honest to God, Ma—"

Bertha went over and slapped her across the mouth. "I'm no crazy damn fool!" she screamed furiously. "You give me that pot before I beat the hell out of you! Me, your mother, I'm crazy, huh? I'm a damn fool?" She trembled violently with emotion. "I don't know pot when I smell it, huh? I come in here and I'm so damn dumb, I can't smell the room is full of it?"

"Ma, listen—"

Bertha slapped her again, knocking her onto the bed, where the younger child awoke and watched them, eyes still clouded with sleep.

Edna's eyes burned sullenly, but she did not cry. "Honest to God, I ain't had no pot. Please don't hit me no more, Ma. . . . I ain't done nothin wrong. I only tried to do what you told me."

Bertha was not touched. She saw no innocence here. She saw instead two years in the future: her daughter, like the daughters of other women, overripe with life in thick thighs and hard, high breasts, standing on a corner and being a whore. Day after day the Scene showed her these things, and her own life served as a living testimonial. She knew. She knew the Scene as well as the narcotics she sold. It too could kill.

She knew her husband Howie and his kind, the mud-kickers, the stars, the stables and occasional white call-girls—she had been part of these things.

Then, smelling a new waft of the sharp marijuana scent, reminiscent of burning autumn leaves, she felt confused. Edna saw it on her face, and a childish loathing flashed quickly in her eyes and vanished.

"I told you I wasn't smokin no pot, Ma."

Tentatively, Carrie touched Bertha's arm. She held a five dollar bill. "Here's five for four, Bert. I *gotta* go, honey, I really gotta go." She had seen none of what had happened.

Bertha didn't hear her. "What—what is it?" she asked Edna.

"It's cookin," Edna told her.

"Cookin? What—"

"Cookin, Ma." She tried to smile at her mother's ignorance, but her eyes became dull as she remembered the violence of the moment before. "The house smells this way all the time—it ain't no pot." Her eyes became pleading now. "I wouldn't smoke no reefer, Ma, you know I wouldn't. I don't even know *how* to smoke."

"Bert—" Carrie insisted.

"People cook every mornin," Edna said. "People cook all over the place. Why, Ma?" she asked, reaching out to her mother as though gentleness could breach the wall between them. "Why you just gotta believe I'd do somethin wrong? I try to do everything you tell me, but you still don't believe I do. Why, Ma? I'd never do nothin you didn't want me to do."

Bertha didn't know how to make the hurt go away from her daughter's eyes. Where there had once been a woman in her mind, there was now only a lovely, dark, too-thin child, half frightened and unjustly accused, hurt more by the thought of her mother not believing her than by the blows suffered.

Knowing that she had been wrong, Bertha still clung to the thought that she had done best, that the blows were for the best, that even the hate Edna might feel for her was best: for then she would hate everything about the place she lived in and the people she lived among, and then she would be safe.

"Hurry up and get your clothes on, Edna," Bertha told her, trying to take some of the coarseness from her voice. "Take Ginny with you and fix some eggs and coffee and toast, and don't waste your damn time."

"Mama, tell Timmy Jones to quit singin in the mornin so's people can rest," Ginny said. She was nine years old, with a fat face and owl-like brown eyes.

Bertha whacked her half-playfully on the bottom. "You get in the bathroom and clean up. You couldn't hear Timmy, anyhow, you was sleepin so sound. Now get! Get outta here like I said, before I whop you a good one."

She allowed a tiny streamer of pride to course to her heart as she watched them go, her daughters. They had no part of Howie in them, save for his light complexion; it was as though she had impregnated herself, like a flower. Howie, though she still loved him with the same self-sacrificing intensity, no longer existed where her daughters were concerned. He was all the things she was trying to protect them from: the hustler, the pimp, the regular, the thoroughbred, the junkie, the weakling. . . .

For some reason, she had shied away from narcotics, and now she was glad; for if she had been a junkie there would really be no hope for the girls.

"Bert—" Carrie still held the five dollars. "Please, baby, come on through for me! I'm sick as hell! Bertha, honey—"

Bertha dug between her big breasts and counted out four pills from a penny matchbox.

"From now on, meet me on the corner," she said.

"O.K.," Carrie said quickly, anxious to leave.

"If that rum is still outside, tell him I said to get the hell away from here."

At the deserted corner of Ninetieth and Maple, Patterson waited in the shelter of a store awning, his eyes fastened on Bertha's rooming house. Across the street, just rounding the corner, he saw Davis wheel the unmarked sedan expertly and pause slightly in front of him.

In spite of himself, Patterson felt a jab of anxiety. Davis had told him specifically to make a buy from Bertha Travis, and he had muffed it! Nevertheless, Davis couldn't blame him; it was Patterson's first time out—could he help it if he couldn't quite fall into the right mood for the act he'd rehearsed with Davis?

Again, he could imagine Davis' ire.

The window came down on the right-hand side of the car, and he saw Davis' big red mustache peek out at him. "What the goddamn hell happened?"

"She said she didn't know me," Patterson said hoarsely. "She wouldn't sell me anything."

He heard Davis curse; the window shot up. The car pulled up

to the corner and parked, and its big driver got out ponderously and seemed to blend into the rain.

Nervously, Patterson looked at his watch, then back to the entrance of the rooming house.

A trolley bus whirred by, popping blue bolts, wheezing like a sick old man as its air brakes were applied at the corner. Near the bus stop, Davis appeared as though he had just gotten off the bus and was seeking shelter from the rain under the awning where Patterson stood.

Patterson kept his silence as Davis stood a few feet from him. "I did exactly as you told me—" he began.

Davis kept his face to the rain, staring off at the rooming house. "I told you I didn't like excuses."

"This is no excuse," Patterson said defensively.

"It's well on the goddamn road to being one," Davis said. "I told you what to do, all you had to do was *do* it! Seems to me an idiot could have done that."

"Then why didn't you get an idiot!" Patterson said before he knew it.

Davis glared at him. "That's what I thought I had me, college boy, but it appears I ain't a very good judge of character."

Patterson lost his temper. "You know one thing?" he said, stepping up to Davis. "I guess I'm pretty goddamn lucky! I get a chance to get soaked to the bone this morning; a pusher refuses to sell me drugs because she's never seen me before—on top of all that, I get you!"

Davis straightened up before him, and Patterson was struck with how big the man actually was. "Maybe you better clarify yourself, college boy."

"I don't think there's any need for clarification," Patterson said hotheadedly.

"Maybe not for you, but there is for me. All you bare-assed college boys come out here after two or three years on the force and think you know it all! If you'd done exactly as I told you, you'd have made that sale! I know more about these people than you'd know if you lived around them fifty years. They're not the same

115

people as you and me; they're the same color, and it ends there. What I know about 'em I didn't learn in books about criminology. I learned it by busting them flat-footed with hundreds of caps in their hands, by bribing and pushing and kicking their filthy butts in. You don't learn that in books, *Detective* Patterson," he said. "You learn it by dealing with these people day in and day out for more years 'n you can sneeze at. You get snitches and intuition. You can almost feel it when a new ounce gets into the city—or gets out. It's the sort of thing no wet-nosed fullback on last year's varsity can tell you a damn thing about. That's what *I* know, Patterson, and *you* don't do a bit of thinking, not a bit. You learn and you follow me and you do just as I tell you. And you consider yourself just like you said—pretty goddamn lucky!"

Patterson was speechless. Coping with Davis, with his overinflated ego, was too much for him. He's fighting me, Patterson thought; he's actually fighting me—and I'm fighting him!

It was monstrous; it made him feel hemmed in: on one side by Davis, on the other by the Scene.

When he spoke, it was with difficulty. "I'm willing to go on, sergeant, if there's any more we can do."

Davis seemed not to have heard. Instead he looked toward the rooming house again. "Here comes the woman you were standing with outside Bertha's place."

"Her name is Carrie."

"Yeah, yeah, I know," Davis said. "Pull over and beg her to sell you two caps—she knows me. She'll refuse, but seem desperate, offer her five dollars for two. That's a hell of a profit, but don't offer her any more. Any more would make her suspicious. If she still says no, offer her two-fifty for one." He drew back into the shadows. "If we can't go right to Bertha, we'll have to get her through one of her customers."

Patterson cut across through the rain toward the woman, arranging his face in torment, feeling more angry at Davis now than at the task he had to perform.

He liked to think that his reasons for being on the Narco Squad were altruistic, although he was fully aware of the material values:

the raise in salary, the detachment from the herd of bluecoats. Now it was becoming more than that. It was becoming a war he had no desire to fight, and yet a battle he could not possibly stand to lose. The Scene, the junkies, were beginning to take form for him; they were becoming actual people. The more Davis pounded the fact of their anonymity into him, the more they ceased to be anonymous.

Patterson walked up to the woman, his head bent low, his eyes watering. He became a junkie suddenly, feeling the actor's mask slide over his features.

"Baby, sell me two things. I'm so bogue I'll let my bowels go right here in the street if I don't have my fix. . . ."

7

IT WAS AFTERNOON. Andy Hooden was asleep when his sister Jacqueline came in. He stirred in bed as her voice chopped through his drugged slumber.

"Andy, get up, you lazy good-for-nothing!"

He turned over painfully, blinking the crust of sleep from his eyes. "I'm gettin up, I'm gettin up," he said.

"Then *get up!*" Her shrill voice broke off thinly. "What did you tell me this morning? You said for sure you were going out to find a job. What do you think I am?" she said desperately. "I come home and find you sleeping. You act as though you haven't got a thing in the world to worry about."

"I know," he said, shrinking at her words.

"You don't act like it, Andy. My God, what am I going to do? I can't beat you like Daddy did, I'm not strong enough, I'm too weak to be working like this without any help," she lamented. "You know I am!"

"Why don't you dry up and pull?" he said, running out of patience. He got out of bed, naked, knowing how she hated that, not giving her time to turn away. "I'm goin out to find a job—ain't that what I told ya?" he said. "I did *say* it, didn't I?" He went over to his dresser and started the record-player on top. After it had warmed up, he selected a long-playing record from the stack of albums next to the machine and put it on.

The rough staccato voice of an alto sax failed to drown out Jacqueline's voice.

"Nothing you say means anything any more," she cried.

His short, bone-punctuated nakedness made her nervous. She also was short, but her body chunked into large breasts and wide hips. Now her shoulders slouched tiredly under the tight blue waitress uniform, and her light complexion bore the traces of dried sweat. She watched him with a stare that was both frightened and accusing.

"Well, what are you gawkin at?" he said, still making no move to dress.

"Oh, Andy!" Her bearing crumbled and she began to cry. "Why don't you co-operate with me just this one time? You don't work, and you know you *can* work. It'd be different if you just couldn't find a job or something, but you could come downtown and work at my place. I told you the man who runs the place needs a—well, a helper—"

"Washing dishes?"

Her tears evaporated. "What difference does it make? Don't you think it's about time you started paying for your share of the apartment expenses, the food bill, the lights and gas? Andy, you're almost twenty, almost a man!"

"This *same* old crap again!"

"I hate this as much as you do—"

"Then why don't you act like it?" he yelled at her. "I'm *gettin* a job, didn't I tell you once? I *got* somethin lined up. Do you have to keep naggin at me every goddamn day?" He put his hands to both ears. "You're gonna make me *blow* wide open! You just keep it up! I swear I'll pop one day and I won't know what the hell I'm doin! I'll—I'll kill myself, that's what I'll do!"

"Andy—"

"Well, I will!" he promised. "People are always pickin on me, people are all the time drivin me, tellin me what to do !"

"Andy, I don't pick on you," she said, softened by his outburst. "All I want you to do is help me, that's all." She turned away from his nakedness and went to the door. "If—if you'd only leave that stuff alone, you—"

"G'wan, get out," he said.

"You know I'm telling the truth."

"Get the hell outta my face," he said, moving toward her threateningly. "Just get the hell on outta here and leave me alone!"

She stood her ground, looking at him pityingly. "It's that stuff—it's no good for you. For God's sake, pull what's left of yourself together and let's try to start over. We've got the apartment, and Daddy did leave us the car if he didn't leave anything else—"

"And a closet full of wine bottles," he said bitterly.

Her hand reached out and touched his shoulder lightly, testingly. "We can't blame him for that."

Andy drew away from her. "I don't see why not."

"But that doesn't mean anything now! It's us who're important." Her voice became sober. "Andy, I don't want to stay in this sickening, rat-infested apartment for the rest of my life. I want to go back and finish college—"

"Nobody's stoppin ya. You don't have to stay around and look after me. I'm a big boy now."

"You've grown into something that's sick. This neighborhood is no good, the people aren't like real people, your friends—Andy, they're sick, too."

"This *same* goddamn crap again!" He turned away, turned his body away but not his eyes, went over to the bed and felt under the pillow for the three things he had put there the night before. "You're all the time criticizin my friends," he said. "I don't ever criticize yours."

"You're never home to meet them."

"I've met that big sap you use for a boy friend."

"You keep Ernest out of this," she said tightly.

"Well, keep *my* friends out of it! Why is it, every damn day, it's this same old crap?"

"Because you make it like this," she said. "If Daddy were alive—"

"He'd be twisted nutty under the kitchen table."

"Andy!"

"Well, hell, it's true, ain't it? He never did me or you no good, and if Ma had used some of the money he spent on juice for doctor bills, maybe she'd still be alive!"

She started to cry again. "I never asked for this."

"But you're gettin it."

"Oh, Andy—"

"If you wanna get married, Jackie"—his voice became softer—"if you wanna go back to school, go ahead. You're twenty-five and you ain't gettin no younger."

"I would," she admitted, raising her eyes to him. "Andy, I would, if I only knew you'd be all right."

"Aw, what the hell—I'll be all right!"

"But how can I know that, seeing you this way? You've lost over twenty pounds in the last six months. You're scared all the time." She stopped, her eyes lighting up. "You can be helped though. I read about it in a magazine: there's a place, a government institution down in Kentucky—Lexington. They help addicts to rehabilitate themselves."

He moved past her impatiently and went down the hall to the bathroom. He could hear her following. The lock on the bathroom door was a useless hinge; he stood with his back against the door panel, stood limp, as though all his muscles had suddenly ceased to function.

He closed his eyes.

"Andy . . ."

He said evenly, "I am not a junkie. Lex is for junkies. I *ain't* hooked."

"Please, Andy, if you'd only listen—"

"I'm no junkie!" he said. "You can find better ways to get rid of me. Is that what you want to do? Get rid of me? Listen, if you want me to move outta here, I'll go any day. You don't have to ship me off to some goddamn hospital, so I'll be their responsibility. I can take care of myself, and I'm *not* hooked—I just joy pop. And a hospital wouldn't do me no good anyway."

"That's right," she said through the door, as if abruptly becoming aware of the words she spoke. "A hospital wouldn't do you any good at all."

Her reply almost maddened him. "Get the hell away from here!"

"I'm going."

"And don't come back!"

"I won't."

He could not hear her voice so well now. He listened intently for the sound of the door closing; he tightened, waiting for the sound. He closed his eyes hard, dug his shoulder blades into the wood of the door panel, praying for the click of metal that would release him.

It would not seem right until she was gone.

The gelatin began to melt in his hand.

Lexington.

He cursed.

"What right?" he said, the words reminding him suddenly of his father: *What right people got to tell me how much to drink?*

"What right's she got—" He stopped, for the click came unexpectedly; he jerked at the sound, throwing his thin body over to the toilet, kneeling on the seat, peering through the window.

Between the rusty crisscrossed arms of the fire escape reaching up to the third floor, he saw his sister make her way to a ten-year-old two-seater at the curb and get in. He waited for the painful sputter, the dirty explosion of smoke from the tail pipe, but the car didn't move.

Move! he thought. He held up his right hand, which nestled the capsules, and looked at the sticky objects. They were like the white excrement left by some huge insect. They were bound to his flesh

121

as though sewn; they were tantalizing, like penny suckers laid out unattended on a display counter.

"Aw, get the hell—" he said, watching the car.

She had to go before he had his fix; he didn't want her hanging around, then coming back to catch him in the midst of the operation and causing him to blow his shot. She does things like that; she can't mind her own business. She always has to be around, breakin through doors when I got the spike about a foot up my arm, then cryin and hollerin.

Then talkin about Lex.

He returned his gaze to the car, feeling his whole body suddenly erupt in goose pimples.

"Move, dammit!" His voice was not his own; it was like his father's.

It was funny how he was so much like the old man—and hated him so much. Hated him so much he used to get a sour taste every time he looked at him: the flaccid trembling of his hands, the perpetually idiotic incoherence.

When he was younger, he reveled in the taste of wine. He and an older buddy, Rico Walsh, used to drink it every day in school. And now he couldn't stand the taste of anything stronger than 7-Up—wine or anything.

He thought of what Carlisle, the director of the neighborhood Youth Center, said—that smack was the worst thing in the world to happen to a kid. (Andy had been sixteen at the time, and using.) He said, Would you smoke a joint if you were going in to fight for eight or ten rounds? All the chumps said no, of course not. He said, So you see? Smack and reefer is like knocking you down with the help of an opponent, cutting off your wind and timing and your desire to win. You've gotta remember, fellas, that every day of your life is a fight and you have to stay in top condition. *Stay away from narcotics*!

Now why did I think of Carlisle? Andy wondered. That Carlisle was a big, fatheaded chump. He never did anything for anybody, didn't everybody know that? All he was doing was pushing people around, building up the muscles and all that crap. Carlisle didn't

122

know that everybody just came around to the Center evenings in order to dance and rub tummies with the broads.

He was a big, square chump! Andy thought. But he could not deny he had liked Carlisle a little; liked the strength and sureness, liked the thing in his eyes that showed he wasn't afraid of anyone.

There was a movement on the street below, and his eyes shifted, found the grimy, impenetrable windows of the car, swung back to the snow-fuzzy path that led to the stairway of the tenement. He could not be certain he saw anyone. People were passing regularly on the street.

He stood up, and by chance his eyes came to the window of the wood-frame tenement across from him. Through the opposite window, a girl stood watching him with a gaze like that of a bronze statue, naked to the waist, her hair long, dark, thrown back over her shoulders, her cheekbones high, diving in vague depressions at the corners of her mouth. Her breasts were young and high; the nipples stood out like the near-pink color of orange rind. She watched him with a stare that was uninquiring, as though she were just about to pass him on the street. She made no move to cover herself, unashamed, unaware at this moment of the completeness of herself.

For a moment, they stood like that. Then she was gone.

He became ashamed of his nakedness, pulling down the shade over the window. He began to feel sick, and he got his works out of the metal grill in the floor, not caring whether Jacqueline came in now or not.

That evening he was sitting on the wall bench in the Garden Poolroom, watching Dell Swiggins and Rudy Black shoot a game of straight pool. He watched them, the big pushers. They were big, but they were afraid of him, little Andy Hodden; he could see it on their faces every time they looked at him. He stayed there mostly to irk them, to curtail any dope sale which might come into the poolroom.

He told himself he liked it this way, being alone, avoided. Boys he used to know in high school walked around him. Everybody knew him, knew what he had done and would still do. Flip. They had given him their own special name, and it was one he bore with a twisted sort of pride.

He'd been christened two years ago. He had been pushing drugs on the Scene for a sizable connection, Big Earl. The Feds busted Andy, then turned him over to the state authorities. The Rollers had beat him—not much of a beating, but enough to show they weren't kidding. That was when he'd met Davis.

We want the connect, Davis said; that's all we want.

It was so simple: Give us the big man next to the big man who's dealing directly with The Man next to the Top Dog, and we'll drop our beef and let you go. We'll even give you two or three fixes. Don't co-operate and we'll slide three to ten under your ass so quick you'll think you're on roller skates.

He had been frightened, so he co-operated, and Davis did just as he said he would. He let Andy go, with ten caps, and said a lot of dirty things as though disgusted at him for being so weak. That's when it began. . . .

Big Earl got four-and-a-half to ten, for possession. And the State didn't even make the arrest; the Feds did it, slamming in like knights on chargers to finish off the weakened foe, after the foot soldiers had done the real work. The Feds got the conviction, while the state stood by like Little Children Should Be Seen And Not Heard.

If you play you must pay, he thought.

That was the idea. He had teamed up with another exiled informer, Rico Walsh, to play and get paid at the same time, at no cost but people's hate.

He got up and went over to the juke, dropped a quarter in on "Whispering Grass," and everybody turned to look at him when the lyrics began.

> *Why do you whisper, green grass?*
> *Why do you tell all you know?*

They watched him as he walked back and sat down on the bench.

124

. . . Cause the breeze don't have to know.

It made him feel good to sit there and listen to the words and know nobody could do a thing to him for it. The song blandly symbolized his place on the Scene:

> *Now if you tell it to the trees,*
> *They'll tell all the birds and bees,*
> *And everyone will know. . . .*

He thought of Rico, long gone from the Scene, comfortable now in New York or Chicago, free to use narcotics without anyone pushing him to "tell."

It hurt to be a snitch. Flip the snitch: *He busted Big Earl, didn't you know? If you deal, don't deal with Flip—he'll leave you with a pocket full of hot money. . . .*

Freddy Arrujo, a tall, dark Puerto Rican of about Andy's age, came into the poolroom with two white boys, youngsters, looking for someone who had the bag. He stopped by the table Rudy and Dell were shooting on, but they wouldn't interrupt their game, nor would they make a sale in front of Andy. Arrujo came over to him.

"What do you want, mon?" Andy said.

"I want you to pull, mon, so I can cop," Arrujo told him.

"I ain't goin nowhere."

"I'm askin you nice, mon," Arrujo said, fire building up in his eyes.

"And I'm tellin you nice, mon, mon," Andy mocked. "What's it, huh? What the hell, you wanna cop? Whyncha say so? Is that all you want, mon? I got some drugs; buy my stuff, mon."

"I'm seek, I ain't got no time for goddim treeks."

"And I'm high," Andy said, smiling. "Do I look like I'm treekin? I got stuff. If you wanna buy, you can cop from me, but I'm not movin for nobody."

"You got stuff?"

"You wanna cop?"

Arrujo hesitated. "If you got, I buy, but I buy for other people, too."

"I don't give a damn. As long as it's green it'll spend."

Arrujo paused again, making up his mind. "You got twelve theengs?"

"What? What? Ask for twenty! You want twenty?"

"I wan twelve."

Andy held out his hand. "Gimme the bread."

Arrujo gave him the money, but stopped him before he could get up. "Look, mon, thees is not my money. Wherever you go, *I* go."

"I'm stashed outside. What's the matter, you don't trust me?" Andy shoved the money back to him. "Here, you cop somewhere else. I don't want nobody trailin me to my stash so's they can take it off. No, you take your money."

Arrujo wavered. "How long it take you?"

"Straight as the crow; right out the front door and right back in."

"Now you look out, mon," Arrujo warned him, giving him the money again. "Thees money you treat like your own. Sometheeng happen to it, I hurt you. Maybe I kill you."

"Nobody's gonna burn you. I'm not trying to con you out of your money."

The Puerto Rican's eyes quieted, regarding him. "You burn me, I burn you like fire."

"All right, all right." Andy got up and went past the white boys, who stood awkward and hunched over near the doorway. They stared after him hungrily.

Outside he got in a cab with the Puerto Rican's money and told the driver to take off. The perfect burn, he thought, humming to himself:

"Why do you whisper, green grass?"

He remembered Davis telling him to be at the rendezvous on Fifty-seventh at ten o'clock. From the cab window he saw a clock in a store front reading eleven-fifteen. He wondered what Davis would do when he didn't show up. Davis would probably go by his place, but he wouldn't be there. He'd make sure he wouldn't be there; he'd stay out until the police changed shifts. Then he could go home and sleep.

He closed his eyes in the cab, feeling the burn-money crisp and warm in his pocket. He was still high, and he felt like riding like this all night, feeling warm and good, with nobody shoving him around, with nobody telling him, "You'll set so-and-so up, or else. . . ."

Lately he had missed a couple of Davis' appointments. "Don't get useless to them," he seemed to hear Rico Walsh say. "When you get useless, you fall harder than anybody. Remember, you gotta serve time with the guys you busted." But this had no meaning for him. He had begun to hate everybody: the junkies, the people, the Rollers, the men with the bags.

He got out of the cab downtown and walked past the brilliant marquees along Pennsylvania, still beckoning for late shoppers. ONLY TEN MORE SHOPPING DAYS TO XMAS, the signs threatened.

His walk was filled with voices and faces of creatures from another world, creatures who didn't use drugs, who didn't raifield, who didn't even know he existed, so intent were they on their *ten more days* to that once-a-year brotherhood.

The thought of his father on a Christmas many years ago: the first toy train, a Roy Rogers gun-and-holster set, many peppermint bars and their sweet candy smell—these things brought an instant glow of sadness and shame.

For more than two hours he walked, covering sections of the city he had never known existed, seeing the Christmas things, the Christmas trees in windows, and he was excluded from it all.

At the window of one of the department stores, a group of people stood clustered, even though it was late, watching an animated Christmas display. He went over and stood behind them, fascinated by the puppets as they cavorted over a snowy landscape.

All fat and red and wind-blown, cheery Santa Claus was trying to mount Dumbo the elephant with his bulging sack. In the background, the eight tiny reindeer, attended by a red-nosed Rudolph in a nurse's uniform, were in bed with colds.

Santa was unsuccessful in his attempts to climb aboard the willing Dumbo; he kept sliding off with his sack. Rudolph went from bed to bed. Santa bobbed his head and grinned, hefted his sack on shoulder, and tried again, and again slid off the rounded back of the elephant. Watching from the window of their small, snow-covered cottage, Mrs. Claus shook her head woefully.

The scene touched Andy. He began to laugh. He laughed until his face tightened. The other people looked at him and then began laughing, too, and it struck him suddenly how good it felt to laugh; how good it felt to laugh with other people. He let himself go completely, and tears came to his eyes and pain to the laughing muscles of his belly. The laughter made him one with these people, these people who had seemed creatures of another world. He no longer felt excluded.

But gradually, one by one, they began to drift off. Andy looked about and found he was alone. He turned back to the window display, and it was no longer funny. He knew how terrible it was to keep sliding off the elephant's back.

He walked all the way home, gradually feeling the effect of the drugs he had used wear off, leaving him jerky and depressed.

When he came down his street from Pennsylvania, he paused at the corner. A black Ford was parked in front of his house. Someone sat in front, hidden by the shadows.

He turned back, feeling a brief stab of fear, and went into a wide-windowed, all-night dairy bar. He sat down on one of the stools and ordered a hamburger and malt, but he could hardly eat and drink when the order came.

He put a nickel in the coin-machine on the counter and pressed the green button next to "Dancing in the Dark." The music flowed out easily from the overhead PA system.

Getting up nervously, he went over to the door and looked down the long dark street. The car was still parked in front of his house.

Why didn't they leave him alone?

If you play you must pay . . .

128

"What right—?" he started, and bit his lips, and it was almost as though he tasted wine on them.

He was about to turn back to his stool, when she came in; he recognized her instantly. She was accompanied by three other girls, all between the ages of sixteen and eighteen. She tried to pass him in the doorway, but he couldn't move. He could only stare into the loveliness of her face.

"Excuse me," she said softly, trying to move around him.

"C'mon, Taylor," one of the girls called to her.

She was almost as tall as he; she had smooth brown skin, clear eyes and firmly rounded lips. She was bareheaded in spite of the cold, but her hair was done up now into two large plaits that came up the back of her head and tied in curly knots over her forehead.

"Excuse me," she said again, her lips barely moving. She stood waiting, her level brown eyes holding him, making him feel as naked as he had been before her that afternoon.

"I've never met you before," he said finally.

"We just moved on this street, my mother and I."

Andy shifted awkwardly. "You're out really late—it's almost three-thirty," he said.

"I'm used to it," she told him. "I work nights downtown. Today is my day off."

"My name is Andy Hodden," he said, trying to smile, not used to smiling, thinking: This ain't right, none of it is, it couldn't be!

"My name is Taylor Mayo," she said.

"Taylor—?"

"Miss Mayo."

"*Miss* Mayo?"

"Yes, Miss Mayo, not Taylor," she said. "You don't know me well enough—yet."

He became unreasonably angry. "Don't be a square!"

"I wasn't trying to be," she said, a sudden chill coming into her voice at his anger. "Maybe we shouldn't get to know each other."

"Why?" he said, desperately now.

"Because," she said quietly, "sometimes if you don't know people you'd like to know, it's better."

129

"Let me see you again," he said.

Her first smile was wan, almost helpless. "I can't stop you from seeing me."

"I mean—hell! I wanna talk with you."

She caught the curious glance of one of the girls and abruptly moved past him. "Excuse me."

He couldn't think; he didn't dare think.

If you play . . .

This love stuff, he thought. This kid stuff, he went on, hating his stupidity. This cocain-and-crackers stuff!

He left the place, and the air was cold on his lips. He heard Christmas bells in his head. TEN MORE SHOPPING DAYS TO XMAS.

The car was gone, but Davis came out of the shadows of the lower hallway when Andy started up the stairs. Patterson was with him.

"You think I'm playing games?" Davis said, snatching Andy back and slapping him across the mouth.

The pain did something to him—everybody pushing him, squeezing him back—and suddenly he rebelled.

"No," he said.

"No what?" Davis prompted angrily.

"No, I don't give a good goddamn," Andy said.

Davis knocked him down.

Patterson flinched. "Mance—"

"Goddamn you, Patterson, get off my back! I'll teach this lippy sonofabitch!" He pulled Andy to his feet and knocked him down again with such force that Andy could feel his scalp split against the ragged baseboard near the steps.

Davis pulled him up again, short-windedly snorting like an enraged bull. "So that's what you don't give, huh, little junkie?" He swung a big fist into the pit of the boy's stomach.

Pain on pain drove the scream of it away. Andy sat on the floor, blood in his mouth, his eye swelling where Davis' fist had crushed the flesh. He felt no movement above him, no attempt to make him stand. He got up by himself finally, slowly, tortuously.

Davis grabbed him by the collar and shoved him against the

130

wall. "Listen, you satchel-mouthed little punk, when I tell you to meet me, I mean for you to meet me! When I want something from you, I want it now, not when you feel good and goddamned ready! You just remember what side your bread is buttered on. You just remember I can have you if I want you! When you wake up to that, we'll get along fine together! But when you think the sun rises and sets on you and you can say what you don't give whenever you feel like it, you're in for trouble, boy, you're really in for trouble!" He shoved Andy away roughly.

"Did you find out about that drop Caseri and Lujack are supposed to pick up, now that Puck's business has gone over to The Man?"

"Lujack's dropped out," Andy said in a surly voice. "He's copping through Rudy Black, from The Man."

"Black's getting up in the world, huh?" Davis said. But there was a glimmer in his eye. Obviously, the Lujack information was news to him.

"Black came around tonight in a Cadillac," Andy said. "He must be doing all right."

"Well, I'm still waiting," said Davis. "Did you find out about that drop?"

"No."

"No, what?" said Davis, going for him again.

"No, I didn't find out about the goddamn drop!" yelled Andy.

Patterson put his hand on Davis' shoulder to cool him down, but Davis shrugged him away. "So you loused up the drop thing. You better find something to replace it, and you better find something soon!"

He and Patterson left.

Andy stood hunched against the wall. His head was pounding. He raised a hand to his throbbing eye.

If you play . . .

"What? What right?" he asked the darkness weakly. "*What right?*"

8

FROM SOMEWHERE in the hotel, the deep strains of "Noel, Noel" awakened Davis.

He sat up in bed slowly, turning on the night-table lamp, illuminating the pictures atop the bureau. They were of his dead wife and his daughter, who now lived in Texas with her husband and two children.

The portraits stood on the bureau next to a bottle of bourbon.

He got up from the bed in his underclothes and went over to the washbasin, where he found a tumbler. Then he came back and took a stiff drink.

He sat down on the bed and began to dress, the whiskey making him wheeze heavily as he drew on his socks and trousers. He stood and pulled on his shirt without looking at the three citations tacked over the head of his bed, the "meritorious duties" of '43, '50, and '51.

He grunted to himself. Lorrie, his daughter, hadn't seen the last one. No, she'd been too married—just as her mother had been too dead.

Going over to the closet, he fumbled around, trying to find a matching sports jacket for his trousers. Something kind of flashy, he thought, just to let those bastards in the precinct know he wasn't as old as they thought. Especially that Ivy League misfit, Patterson.

Funny—in a way he admired Patterson. He was giving the college boy hell, but the kid was still sticking on. One thing about him, Davis considered—he was honest. If he was sore, he didn't try to hide his emotions behind a superficial intellectual shield. He had a little spunk, Davis allowed, but it took more than a little spunk to be a good Narco man.

He continued to fumble around in the closet, unable to find the jacket he was looking for. It hadn't been like this when Bea was alive, when they had the house together.

He checked his thoughts quickly and returned to the safer subject of his old age. Old age! As if a man were *old* at fifty-two! He could remember when he'd made more arrests in the Sixth Precinct than all the other flatfoots combined. He remembered that he *had* to make them, had to fight above the slush pile—even if it took him seventeen years to do it.

He'd show them how old he was when he dragged The Man in. Let 'em talk about age then!

He found the jacket at the end of the rod a bit wrinkled and a little outdated with its too-long slit in the tail. A second look told him that it wasn't exactly what he'd expected to see. There was too much jazz in the cut of the shoulders, too much drape, too much "jitterbug" about the lapels.

He hung the thing up with disgust, wondering when he'd let himself be conned into purchasing it. It must have been a long time ago, maybe ten or twelve years, when there were still Bea and Lorrie, and they still had their home.

He went back over to the bureau again and got himself another drink. The second shot did something for him, flooding his face with warmth, his feet with anxiousness. There were still better than two hours before roll call, and he had no place to go, no friends to drop in on, not even some female. . . .

He sat back down on the bed, the bigness of him drooping against his will, a hand coming to his face to saddle the big nose and wire-brush mustache.

All right. He *preferred* being alone. He didn't owe anybody anything and they didn't owe him a damn thing, he could be damned sure of that!

He got up and went over to his hotel window, looked uptown toward the Scene, lit up for Christmas.

A distorted sense of pride came over him as he gazed at the Scene. He'd be damned if he didn't have that, at least! It was something he knew better than those other bastards like Stuart and Speer.

Yes, goddamn if he didn't have that! He could do his job better than anyone else in the precinct because he *knew* his job better than anyone else. That's why he was a sergeant; that's why he was one of only three Negro sergeants in the city.

O.K., O.K., so maybe all he had to sergeant was one dumb bastard with a college degree, but still that's something that doesn't happen overnight.

The Scene was bitterly precious to him, even as he asked himself: Who gives a damn about those scum? If they want to suck up that stuff in their arms, why should he give a damn? He had a *job* to do, no more no less, and he was determined to excel at it despite all odds.

Too old? Him? He'd never give it up, not ever! They might take it away from some lesser man, some youngster like Patterson—a guy who wanted to bounce up the stairs Davis had fought his way up—but they *wouldn't* take it away from him! He'd had enough taken away from him!

His mind went blank suddenly and he found himself looking at the pictures of his wife and daughter. He started to touch the bottle again, but remembered that in a little while he had to go in. He wanted to have his head about him. You could never tell; he wouldn't put it past Captain Beeker to make him stick out his tongue and say "Ah," right in the middle of the squad room.

He sat on the bed again, reached over to the night stand and got his holster and revolver, strapped them on.

Those sonsabitches.

He looked over at the pictures of his wife and daughter again, and at the whiskey bottle.

Ah, what the hell! he thought, and got up to get another drink.

Patterson caught him as he came in that morning.

"We picked up the Travis woman," he said. "She's here now. We had a matron come down and search her. Found her in possession of twenty-three capsules."

Davis started moving quickly through the squad room. "Where's she at?"

"Room three," Patterson said, hurrying to keep up with the big man's long strides.

They went down a hall until they came to a door Patterson had to unlock with one of the keys on a big ring. Bertha Travis sat at the rear of the windowless cubicle, eyes burning defiantly.

"Well, well," Davis said, coming out of his overcoat, "if it ain't Black Bertha!"

"You finally got a chance to pin somethin on me, huh, Davis?" Bertha said. "You come to my place and drag me and my kids off, then you have 'em plant some stuff on me. Where're my kids?" She stood up threateningly. "You better not let nothin happen to my kids!"

"Sit down," Davis said. "You should've thought of your kids when you started kicking stuff around. Just sit down and shut your big mouth!"

Bertha sat down. "I wanna see my lawyer. You can't keep me from seein my lawyer if I want to."

"You ain't seeing nobody," Davis said. He turned to Patterson. "You got that thing?"

Patterson handed him a sheet of paper from a manila folder.

Davis took it and went over to Bertha. "You see this, girlie? Along with that possession beef, we've got you for a sale!"

Bertha tried to grab the paper, but Davis held it out of reach. He went over and sat down facing her behind the plain table next to the wall.

"What the hell is goin on around here?" she said. "I know my goddamn rights, I know I got some rights!"

"You got a right to be in jail, Bert," Davis said. He motioned Patterson over. "Don't you remember this guy?"

She looked at Patterson, then back to Davis angrily. "I never seen this sonofabitch before in my life! I just wanna see my lawyer, that's all I know."

"You remember your friend Carrie?" Davis said. "You remember that day in the rain a week ago, when Carrie copped from you? You remember this guy coming up to you?"

"Yeah, I remember now," Bertha said, suddenly recognizing

Patterson. "I knew he was a cop. You ain't got nothin on me. I didn't sell him no drugs."

"You didn't sell him any, but you sold Carrie four things."

Davis saw the wild fear come into her eyes. "I didn't sell that bitch nothin! She's tellin a goddamn lie if she says I did."

"That's just what she said. She swore it," Davis said, waving the paper in front of her. "We've got four things in evidence against her. This officer swears he bought two things from Carrie, and she swears she bought four from you."

"You got nothin!" Bertha cried. "You only got me on the possession rap, and I'll get probation for that!"

Davis grunted with a show of satisfaction. "You'd be surprised. We arraign you tomorrow on this evidence, we hold trial two weeks from now—next month you're doing twenty to life in the hen mill."

Bertha knew he was telling the truth. She looked at each man frantically. "Just let me get to my lawyer. I bet you couldn't do that if I got to my lawyer."

The red mustache seemed to blaze over Davis' lips. "Listen, goddamn it, I'm not gonna play games with you, missy. Your ass is in the fire and there's only one way to pull it out—and you know what way that is. We could have you long gone before The Man's lawyers could flex their legal muscles."

Bertha fell into a frightened silence.

"Think about your kids," Davis said mercilessly.

"All right, *all right*!" she screamed. "But what can I do? I don't know anything. My boy friend, Dell, handles most of my business now."

"Don't give me that," Davis said. "You're not silly enough to put any money in that junkie's hand."

"Well, yeah, I pay my money . . ."

"To The Man?"

"No, to that broad, Sylvia. I only seen The Man once."

"You'd testify to that, wouldn't you?"

She hesitated.

"Well, *wouldn't* you?" Davis insisted.

"Yeah . . . I guess so."

136

"You fool with me," Davis said tightly, "and you won't guess—you'll give everything you have to testify."

"But I don't *know* nothin," Bertha pleaded.

"You know enough. You know it's The Man's stuff, don't you?"

"Yeah, I know that much . . ."

"Then when the time comes, you can say so. For the time being, I want you to get close as you can to this thing—" He broke off to ask Patterson, "Did anyone know we brought her in—anybody on the Scene, I mean?"

Patterson shook his head. "It was clean, I imagine. Speer carried through your pickup order and brought her and the children down. She's been here a couple of hours, though."

"Well, that's good," Davis said. "We don't want the rumor to get around that Bertha's paid us a visit. Now you listen, Bert," he said, turning to her. "I want information, and you're gonna get it for me. The slightest changes, anything. I wanna know where The Man stashes, I wanna know where the stuff is cut up. You play your cards right, you can do a lot for us. Understand?"

"Yeah . . ."

"Patterson, get the stenog in here to take a statement."

Patterson left the room, locking the door behind him.

"What about my kids?" Bertha said. "What about them?"

Davis looked at her with disgust. "You don't need kids. You got no right to have kids."

"They're *my* kids!" she shouted, getting up. "Who're you? God? Just 'cause you're a Roller? Just 'cause you happen to be a big guy what got all the breaks? You ain't got no right to say I don't need kids, you sonofabitch! I got much right as anybody, even you!"

"Shut up," Davis said quietly, somehow feeling disgusted with himself now. "Shut up and sit down."

Patterson came back in. "The stenog'll be down in a minute."

Davis got up. "Watch Bertie until I get back." He took the keys from Patterson and locked up behind him.

In the hall, he ran into Lieutenant Stuart. "Just coming for you, Mance. What about the Travis woman? Any results?"

"She's gonna cop out," Davis told him.

"I guess we can send the kids downtown, then. Juvenile bureau. They're down at the end of the hall."

"I'd like to keep that woman out in the street, chief. She's come closer to The Man than anyone I've busted so far. She could be very valuable when we drag that fish into court."

Stuart shrugged. "Do it your way, Mance. Let me know how it turns out."

They parted and Davis went down the hall to the room the children were in.

They were huddled together on a chair in the little room, their eyes bugged and frightened at the strange surroundings.

"Can we go home, mister?" the larger of the two girls said.

"I don't know," Davis said gruffly. "Maybe you can and maybe you can't."

"You better let us!" the smaller child told him. "I'll tell my mama on you if you don't!"

"What're your names?" Davis said.

"Edna and Ginny Travis," Edna said. Then, tentatively, she said: "My—my mother ain't done nothin, is she, mister?"

Davis caught himself. "You don't have to worry about that. You'll be going home pretty soon." He thought of Bertha's bitter reply, of his wanting to find justification in her children for his opinion of her, but it somehow seemed underhanded and small. He didn't give a damn, anyway, he told himself.

But the longer he looked at the pretty children, the angrier he became. It didn't seem right that a woman such as Bertha Travis should spawn such lovely things, have so much. . . .

He turned around quickly and left the room. The stenographer was waiting for him when he got to the interrogation room, an oversized cadet patrolman who looked better fitted to push logs than pencils.

He made Bertha run through the whole thing again, shooting her the customary leading questions. When they were finished, he had Bertha check it again for accuracy.

"Type up three copies," he told the stenographer. "Have her sign all of 'em," he instructed Patterson. He glanced at Bertha, who looked exhausted and drained in her seat. "You can leave after you're done here, Bert."

Her thankful look set him off again. "You keep your mouth shut about this, Bert; you don't say anything to anybody. You do, and it's your hind part, lady!"

"I understand," she said, unable to keep the joy from her voice.

"When we want you, we'll call you, and you better remember what side you're playing on from now on—who gave you your break." He turned to Patterson. "I'll be in the squad room. We'll take our tour soon's you finish here."

Patterson followed him out. He was looking at Davis as though he were crazy. "You mean you're going to let that woman out to sell more narcotics?"

Davis narrowed his eyes at him.

"Listen, Mance, we've got her," Patterson said, his lean face lighted up with bewilderment. "Why don't we just lock her up? I know there're a lot of things I don't understand about drugs, but I do know we're helping her kill people when we leave her on the street."

"Didn't you hear me in there?" Davis said.

"Sure, I heard you, but—"

"Then keep your mouth shut!" Davis said, a flush spreading out thickly under the roughness of his face. "When you get to be detective sergeant, then you can do things *your* way!"

He left Patterson standing there.

On his way down the hall, he looked in on the girls again. He wanted to make sure they were all right.

9

THE RECORDER'S Court Building was crowded Friday afternoon. On the ground floor, people moved slowly back and forth between the huge yellowed pillars; they packed the ancient elevators and walked in small, tired groups up the wide marble steps to the court-rooms on the second and third floors.

Over them, threatening in its hugeness, hung the regal aura of governmental authority, musty, impressing all the visitors, making them lower their voices in a respect they often were unable to feel.

An enormously fat man and his smaller brother pushed their way past the crowds and wedged into one of the elevators. "Second floor," demanded the big man, relaxing without regard for the other passengers, who were pressed painfully against the hard, vermicu-lated steel elevator walls.

The big, creaking box crept to the second floor, on which, the operator informed them, were the chambers of their honors Callum, Stanky, O'Callahan, Murphy, and Royal.

The big man surged out, walking surprisingly briskly for a man of his girth. His good clothes fell loosely about him as he walked, outlining the thick calves and thighs, the wide, copious strength in back and hips.

His brother, following behind, surveyed the wide back with something like hate in his steel-gray eyes.

Stopping abruptly near the stairway, the big man demanded of a guard the whereabouts of that sonofabitch O'Callahan in such a quick, chopping voice that the guard instantly pointed to the other end of the hallway. Over the portal of a massive double door was a long sign: *The Hon. Rice S. O'Callahan.*

The big man's lawyer saw him as he entered, hurried toward him and skillfully took him by the arm, explaining as they walked that it was only the arraignment. He led him to the front of the courtroom where some twenty half-interested spectators watched the proceedings.

The other brother watched them.

Richard D. Halsted, Sr., had arrived just in time to hear the prosecutor say something about "negligent homicide." He saw his son, Rickie, standing at the bar, and his anger swelled. The lawyer tried to calm him.

"If it please your honor," Halsted's lawyer broke in. "I think we can conclusively prove that the boy did not see the decedent. After all, the man was jaywalking! How can we possibly call this negligent homicide when the evidence proves beyond a doubt that the *decedent* was negligent?"

His honor sat with chin in hand, the big grizzly head seeming devoid of all comprehension.

"Your honor," the prosecutor said, "examination of skid marks by arresting officers at the scene shows that this young man was traveling over sixty miles an hour in a residential neighborhood. Not only that: a search of the defendant's clothing produced three capsules of heroin. We intend to prove that the defendant was incapable of operating a motor vehicle at the time of the accident because he was under the influence of narcotics."

Halsted had been looking at the bent, silent rigidity of his son, but at the mention of narcotics his head snapped up.

"You'll pardon me, but I'm this boy's father, and I'd like to know just what the—"

Judge O'Callahan turned a sharp-eyed gaze to Halsted. "You're this boy's father?"

Halsted stepped forward. "Yes, I am."

"Didn't you know he was being arraigned here this afternoon?"

"I've been out of town on business, your honor. When I arrived home last night, my brother Donald informed me that Rickie had been arrested on some ridiculous charge."

O'Callahan looked at him. "It's hardly a ridiculous charge. Your son struck a man two nights ago. The man is dead." He looked at some of the papers on the bench. "He died this morning, as a matter of fact. Your son may be tried for negligent homicide."

Halsted didn't understand. They couldn't be talking about Rickie!

"I see here that the Federal Bureau of Narcotics has expressed a particular interest in your son," the judge went on, "as to his possession of narcotics. However, since a death is involved, they've bowed out to the state. Your son's being a narcotics addict, nevertheless, will be considered by the hearing judge."

"Narcotics addict?" Halsted burst out. "Now look here—"

"Your honor—" Halsted's lawyer began, but the judge was whispering with one of the court aides.

"Considering the boy is only eighteen, with no record," Judge O'Callahan said finally, "I'm going to set bond. Fifteen hundred and two securities. Do you think that satisfactory, counselors?" he asked the prosecutor and Halsted's lawyer, and without waiting for their answers he affixed his signature to a document and handed it to the aide. "Will you be able to put up bond, Mr. Halsted?"

"Of course."

"That's fine," the judge said. "Mr. Halsted, I advise you to look into your son's recreation habits, his friends and associates." He nodded toward the defendant. "That boy is sick. Look at the way he's standing now—there's only one thing in the world to bring a youth before this court in that condition, and that's narcotics. If I were the judge hearing this case I'd recommend treatment, whether the verdict was guilty or not guilty."

"But, your honor—" Halsted's lawyer tried.

The judge cut him off with a nod toward the bailiff. "Next case."

Halsted saw his son being taken out a side door, saw the judge calmly continue on to other court business, completely disregarding the president of Halsted and Halsted Chemical Supplies. Halsted's face became red and he clenched his fists.

The lawyer placed a guiding hand on his arm. "That's all, Mr. Halsted. Come on, you'll see your son next door at headquarters while we arrange bond—"

142

"No one can talk to me that way!" Halsted said as the lawyer led him away.

Donald Halsted, who had been standing at the rear of the court-room, came over to his brother, his long angular face marked with concern. "Richard, take it easy! You're not doing yourself any good; you want that ulcer to explode on you again?"

"It's all lies," Halsted fumed. "By God, it's a dirty scheme to smear my company. The commissioner is a very good friend of mine, and I'll make damned sure he hears of this!"

They took the elevator to the main floor and went across a small walkway to police headquarters, which adjoined the court building.

A desk sergeant directed them to the Record Office, on the seventh floor, where Halsted's lawyer paid the bond and posted the securities. Then they went up to the ninth floor, where the prisoners were lodged, and waited in the quiet, stainless-steel lobby while Richard Halsted, Jr., went through the formalities and was released.

When the boy arrived, he didn't look at his father. He barely glanced up when his uncle came over and patted him on the shoulder consolingly. "You're going to be all right, Rickie. Don't worry about a thing."

Dandruff powdered the fringes of the boy's hastily-combed hair. The detective who came over with him was a big man, but beside the boy he was almost dwarfed; yet Richard seemed small and shrunken by some internal suffering, and his arms hung limply from his sides.

"Rickie!" Halsted said, shocked. "What have they done to you, son?"

The boy didn't answer.

The detective stepped forward. "Mr. Halsted, I'm Detective King. I'd like to have a word with you."

Halsted stared at him, puzzled. "My son—"

"Come this way, please," King said, leading the big man through a door marked Narcotics Bureau. Donald Halsted came along behind them, leaving the lawyer in charge of Rickie.

They went through an office where two women sat typing rap-idly, paying no attention as they went past, and into a rear office.

143

King sat down behind a small desk and motioned the men to chairs in front of his desk.

King spoke slowly. "You probably know I'm in charge of your son's case."

"Then maybe you can tell me just what the hell is going on around here!" Halsted said. "Maybe you can tell me what's wrong with my boy!"

"Your boy's a junkie," King said flatly; then, noticing Donald Halsted, he looked up at him questioningly.

"I'm Mr. Halsted's brother, Donald," he explained.

"We'd like to know what's going on, too," King went on without acknowledging the explanation.

"What do you mean?" Halsted said.

"Your boy had three capsules of heroin—almost pure heroin. Now the Feds wanted to know where he got that stuff, Mr. Halsted, and so do we."

"Just a moment—"

"Stuff like that doesn't walk into the state," King cut him off. "Somebody had to bring it in, either from the borders or from one of the seaports." He waited, watching understanding slowly begin to creep across Halsted's face. "Your son tells me he made frequent trips to Mexico—"

"That was only on business," Donald Halsted answered. "Richard here's been grooming the boy for a place in the business. He had to make all our Mexican connections regularly."

"Thanks," King said, with no note of gratitude, again directing the conversation toward Halsted. "That's what the boy told me. He told me he picked the caps up on his last visit, that it was his first time to use. Of course that was a damn lie."

"If that's what Rickie said," Halsted said hotly, "then that's just what happened. Rickie doesn't lie!"

King shrugged. "Maybe not to you, but he lied like hell to me. You see, Mr. Halsted, in this business you get to know things. You know that an amateur doesn't play around with pure stuff; that raw heroin your kid had could kill three men. A user's got to know how to bite off little pieces so he doesn't give himself an overdose.

144

For another thing, your boy's got tracks all up and down his left arm—"

"Tracks?"

"That's the spot on an addict's arm where he keeps shoving the needle in," King told him. "That's what your kid's got, and one of them is almost six inches long. So by that we can tell he's been using a long time, maybe a year, maybe better."

"This is unbelievable!" Donald Halsted said, sitting back in astonishment.

"It's impossible!" Halsted said.

King ignored them. "What kind of business are you in, Mr. Halsted?"

"Chemical supplies," Donald Halsted said.

"We furnish the necessary paraphernalia to nearly all the leading drug plants in this city," Halsted said, a bit reluctantly. "Equipment for chemists and pharmacists."

"Very interesting," King said. "Your boy was in a splendid position to be of service to a big wholesaler. Let's just suppose he was connecting over the border, for narcotics for one of the big labs or somebody in one of the labs you do business with—"

Halsted stood up. "Come along, Donald. I'm not going to listen to any more of this."

"That's your business," King said. "But I'm gonna keep an eye on your kid, Mr. Halsted, and I'm gonna find out everything about him. The Feds are mighty interested, too. From what I hear, they may be cracking down on this whole filthy operation very soon. Your son and others like him may get a Christmas present they never expected."

Halsted leaned over the desk, his lips drawn back over his teeth. "Say, what's behind all this damned stuff? Who's your boss? Who's making you hound my kid?"

King took a loose cigarette from his shirt pocket and lit it, squinting. He took his time before he spoke, as though he were pacing himself like a miler going around the first lap.

"It's strange you'd ask me who my boss is," he said. "You rich guys usually let a peon like me know right off you're my taxpaying boss." He opened a desk drawer and pulled out a makeshift hypodermic and a blackened, bent-handled spoon, and threw them on the desk blotter. "And you know how I feel about it? The same thing that happened to the kid who owned these can happen to your kid, and if you don't give a damn, neither do I. You could have my crap-pushing job and I wouldn't care, I've seen so many pompous bastards like you!" His voice rose, and Halsted backed away. "I got a goddamn stinking job to do, mister, and my chief tells me to do it the best way I can. If it means hounding your kid to do it, I'm gonna hound him till he's crusty! I'm gonna make sure I know where the hell that stuff is coming from, so maybe I can save a kid whose parents do give a damn about him." He stood up and shoved the eyedropper and spoon back into his drawer. "Now you go ahead and try to keep me from hounding him, Mr. Halsted; you start pulling some of those thousand-dollar strings. But I'll tell you this. If I ever find your kid down here again on a junk beef, I'm gonna do everything in my power to fix it up so he'll think heroin's a new dance when he gets out of the pokey!"

He walked out of the office.

"I strongly advise you to see the commissioner about that man!" Donald Halsted said, staring after King.

Back in the lobby, they were met by the lawyer and Rickie, who stood near the elevator, pressing the call button, waiting. He stood there, not moving, but it seemed as though his body did move, tilting slightly from one side to the other.

Halsted, followed by the lawyer and his brother, went over to him, but Rickie paid no attention to his father. Instead he clutched at his uncle.

"Uncle Donald, please help me!" he cried. "Make them let me out of here!"

His uncle could only pat his shoulder helplessly. "Don't worry, Rick. We'll be out of here in a minute. Everything'll be all right."

Halsted stood watching him, remembering the things King had said, remembering the things he had wanted to say and had been unable to, remembering the adage: There's nothing made that money can't buy.

146

Now, above all else, he wanted to buy back whatever the boy had lost. Couldn't he do that? He was an extremely rich man. Donald, of course, owned a few shares in the business, but he was little more than adviser and contact man.

There must be something he could do! He'd do anything for Rickie, no matter how much it cost. Yes! If it came to an emergency, he could give up everything for his son!

But would Rickie be worth it?

He hadn't wanted to ask himself the question, didn't want to come face to face with himself, not here, not looking at the tall, unkempt eighteen-year-old. He did not want to question his love or its limitations.

"Rickie," he began, "tell me they're lying . . . tell me you never used narcotics. Tell me, Rickie!"

The boy looked at him fitfully. "No . . . Dad," actually saying yes, saying yes in a tiny nervous voice. His finger punched the call button incessantly; he turned, frustrated at its uselessness, looking at his father and uncle and not seeing them, his face full of the lie he'd just spoken, his blue-gray eyes shining wildly. "Aren't there any *stairs* in this place!"

"Easy, son."

"Well, let's get the hell *out* of here! Let's go home, I want to get home."

"Rickie!" Halsted was seeing the truth, but even as he saw, it was colored by his mind so its edge was dulled. "Now slow down, boy! I know you've been through quite an ordeal, but have some concern for others. This hasn't been the best thing in the world for *my* health, y'know."

Chided, his son said, "I'm sorry."

The lawyer came over and spoke to Halsted, spoke of the coming trial (". . . might be a bit expensive because of the charge, which is very serious in this state, but we have youth and innocence on our side, and that appeals to any jury . . ."), sounded Halsted out, minimized the seriousness of the dope involvement, convinced him that his son was being made a scapegoat.

The elevator picked them up and took them down again to the

main floor. During the ride, they talked, the lawyer and Halsted and his brother, ignoring Rickie altogether.

On the ground floor, the boy bolted. They saw him dash through the swinging doors, rushing wildly to the street.

"Rickie!" Halsted yelled, realizing too late. "Stop him! He's not well!"

"Hey, kid!" somebody hollered.

Just as they reached the door, Halsted saw it happen, almost as if the action were slowed for his eyes. On stilted, fantastically moving legs, Rickie sprinted to the middle of the street. The fast-moving car put on brakes, but it was too late. The bumper and grill met the calf of the boy's left leg, and it caved and folded like a stick of wood. His torso bellied onto the hood with a sickening, fleshy sound. When he fell, the right front wheel of the automobile rolled over his chest with a loud bump, leaving it suddenly crushed and formless.

The sound of metal against flesh slapped Halsted across the mouth. He ran to the broken form of his son lying under the impersonal, murdering belly of the vehicle.

The car that had struck the boy was a police cruiser.

"Easy, don't move 'im!"

"Let me through, damn you, let me through! I'm his father."

"Get a buggy from Receiving," someone cried. "Give me your coat. You there, his father—take off that coat! Stand back. Quit crowding. Hey, stop that traffic up at the corner, keep those sonsabitches off the street."

"So quick," Halsted said dazedly, feeling the wind cut into him sharply as the commanding voice put equally commanding hands on him and removed the thick vicuna. "It all happened so quick!"

"Stand back. If you wanna help, get the hell out of the way!"

For once he did as he was told. He stood on the curb with other spectators and observed, not hearing the words spoken by the lawyer and his brother. He watched the strong men work purposefully, giving his son relief.

When the ambulance came he tried to get in back with the stretcher, but he was shoved back roughly.

"But I'm—"

The door slammed shut in his face.

Before the machine moved away he heard an imploring cry from the lips of his son. He saw the look in the dying eyes and heard the words:

"I'll get a fix now—won't I?"

*L*ou's Hotel was cleaned out in a vice raid early Sunday morning. The police broke in and ransacked every room, after having forced the occupants out roughly. Three squad cars and a paddy wagon stood ready in the icy morning air, and the arresting officers, white and Negro, as if angry at their task, angry for being there so early, went about their work with methodical destructiveness.

Lieutenant Stuart, Davis, and Patterson led the raid. They chose hotel characters at random, questioning them, examining their arms.

Davis bore down especially on the night clerk, a meek, frightened-eyed little woman whose voice rose extremely high.

"I just work here," she told him. "I don't know nothing more than what I have to do behind the desk." She pointed over to Lou and Ella Tyler, who stood behind the front desk in their nightclothes. Ella watched the confusion calmly, but Davis could see the bullethead of the dark little man jerk at each crash that came from the back rooms.

"You talk to them!" the clerk said. "They own the place. I don't know nothing more than what I have to do behind the desk!"

Davis caught Patterson's eye and waved to him. "Bring your notebook along." He watched for reaction from the proprietors as he and Patterson went over, but only Lou acted as though he were nervous.

There was something about the pair that alerted Davis. For one thing, they were an ill-matched couple: Lou was small, almost wizened, and the inaction of everything save his small darting eyes gave the impression of a snake coiled to strike; Ella, on the other hand, was broad of feature, with a wide, bold set of mouth. Standing an inch or so over her husband, in her early forties, she was clearly dominant. The lightness of her skin contrasted them sharply, a wild autumn peach alongside a black grape.

Davis noticed her edge forward to receive the brunt of his attack as he and Patterson came up.

He smiled at her with a shrewd graciousness, all but tipping his hat. "How do?" he said familiarly. "My name's Davis." He introduced his partner, who gave Davis a puzzled look at this departure from his usual approach. "Like to ask you all a few questions, if you don't mind."

"Go right ahead," Ella smiled amiably.

"You all lease this place, don't you?"

"We own it," Lou said over his wife's shoulder. "We own the whole buildin, paid good money for it. What's the matter? Somethin wrong with that?"

Davis appeared a bit surprised at the man's aggressive tone. "No, sir. I can say with a good bit of authority that there ain't nothing wrong in a man owning one nip of property. It's the best thing in the world!" He watched them closely. "But did you know your hotel was the biggest hangout in town for drug addicts and such?"

Ella nodded, a smile like granite on her lips. "Sure, we knew. Even tried to do something about it."

"Is that right?" Davis said interestedly.

"We called up the FBI last week," she said. "Told them about all these drug addicts. We even told Captain Beeker about it, over at Sixth Precinct. It's just something that got out of hand. My husband's been sick off and on for a spell now, and there's not much we can do when our hired folks let new tenants in."

"Who did you call first," Davis said, "the FBI or Captain Beeker?"

"Captain Beeker," Ella said. "I called Captain Beeker myself, about a month ago. He never did do anything until now, though. I called the FBI up last week. They sent a man over to investigate, but they didn't do anything."

Davis smiled unctuously. "I realize how hard it is for you folks to run a good, clean place, what with the people you have to put up with here in this neighborhood. I hope we won't have to bother you all any more."

"That's all right," Ella said.

Lou stuck an angry chin over her shoulder. "You better tell them cops to be careful. Everything they break, they're gonna pay for it! I'll take you to court if I have to."

"I'll sure tell 'em, sir," Davis said. "I'll tell 'em about that right now."

He and Patterson walked around to the rear, where Lieutenant Stuart was supervising the search.

"Just what was all that about?" Patterson said.

Davis gave him a sly smile. "That, my boy, was what us Southern folk call a julep—sweet and sticky. It makes people relax." He looked carefully over his shoulder. "Lou and Ella have never met me before, although they've probably heard of my busts on the Scene. I want their first impression to be a lasting one."

Lieutenant Stuart stood outside a room where two patrolmen were ripping a mattress to shreds.

"What have we got here?" Davis said.

"A junkie by the name of Rudy Black," Stuart told him. "When we shook them up, him and his girl friend, and brought them out front, a package full of dope magically appeared on the floor outside their door."

"Never thought I'd see the day Rudy Black would throw away drugs," Davis said.

Stuart carefully examined each bit of mattress stuffing thrown out in the hall. "Black was using his head. It'll be hard as hell trying

151

to pin a possession rap on him, and he knows it. I had him and the girl sent in, though. Maybe we can get one of them to crack."

"Don't count on it," Davis said. "That punk knows when he's holding an ace. Patterson and I'll give him a talking to, anyway. He just might say something incriminating."

Stuart looked up. "What's with the proprietors?"

"I don't know yet," Davis admitted. "But I got the feeling that something stinks around here."

Stuart paused at the tone of Davis' voice. "What is it, Mance? I've got that same feeling. With the exception of the dope we picked up on the floor, this place is clean."

"So I've noticed."

"Even with only one junkie around a place, you're going to find something. Maybe it'll be only a cooker or pacifier, but you're going to find something."

"If I didn't know better," Davis said, looking around him, "I'd say this place has been cleaned up."

"Exactly."

"But no one knows about raids but the police," Patterson said, beginning to get the implication.

"You're catching on, college boy."

Stuart motioned them out of earshot of the patrolmen. "We don't want to jump to conclusions. It's possible somebody might have said something unintentionally, you know. You mentioned you wanted to shake down this place some time ago, Mance."

"Yes, I did, chief, but we didn't synchronize ourselves until yesterday evening." He considered how to broach his suspicion to Stuart, then decided not to. Although he and Stuart were good friends, Beeker was the precinct captain. A month ago, Ella Tyler had said, Beeker was apprised of the situation existing in the hotel. Why hadn't he ordered an immediate raid of the premises?

"I'll string out a few feelers for leaks," Stuart said. "If somebody's been shooting his mouth off, they're going to catch hell, you can count on that."

152

*   *   *

After everyone had left, Ella went over to the wall phone and dialed a number. A woman answered.

"Sylvia?" she said. "This is Ella. Let me speak to Floyd."

"He's asleep," Sylvia said. "What's the matter?"

"The cops, they were just by. They picked up Rudy; they found some stuff outside his room."

"Rudy? What happened? I thought you were supposed to have the place clean!"

"I only got the wire from Beeker last night. Rudy came in sometime this morning and I didn't catch him."

"That's fine!" Sylvia said. "That's a wonderful piece of luck!"

"It wasn't *my* fault," Ella said in a strained voice. "Wasn't this suppose to happen way last month? Didn't Beeker say he'd give us plenty time?"

"The plan was to have this thing go smoothly! The reason we wanted to have you raided was because of this new batch. We didn't want to take any chances with it, and we figured if the cops knew your place was clean they wouldn't come snooping around." She sounded furious. "Now that they've found that stuff, they'll haunt the place!"

"Beeker should have done it on schedule," Ella complained. "He shouldn't have waited so late."

"Don't be a fool! Beeker didn't have anything to do with this— he's been sitting on his hands."

"Then who?"

"Probably Davis—this early morning shake-up looks like something he'd do."

"Davis? Lou and I met him this morning. He's pure yokel."

"What?"

"Davis is a fool. It's all over his face. And the guy he's got working with him is a kid. I think Davis has just been lucky with his busts."

"Are you out of your mind?" Sylvia said. "What sort of line did Davis give you?"

153

"Nothing, Syl, it's just plain to see. The guy was almost digging in his butt!"

"That was an act, you damn fool, and the copper sure made you fall for it! Keep out of his way, and make sure you know what you're talking about when he's got anything to say to you!"

"Don't get excited," Ella soothed. "We can go along on schedule. I don't think they're any wiser."

"We can't now. Something happened Friday that knocked the rocks from under us. We're going to have to wait until our connect cools down. We've got to be quiet for a while, and don't ask me why—that's all I know."

"What about Rudy?"

"Can't you bail him out, get a writ or something? Didn't you tell me they didn't find anything on him?"

"That's right, but I don't want to move on him myself. He doesn't even know I'm along, and I don't *want* him to know. Anyway, writs are almost impossible to get on Sunday, you know that."

Sylvia was silent for a moment. "I'll wake Floyd. We'll get in touch with Beeker. He'll do something—he'd better, for the kind of money he's getting."

"I don't like that Rudy boy," Ella said. "He's too swift. A Buick, then a Cadillac—you see what I mean? He's too weak, he's showy."

"Floyd says he's a hustler," Sylvia said noncommittally.

Ella picked up another line of thought. "So far we've had quite a free hand, but I've got a feeling things are going to tighten. There're signs. I suggest a raise in prices."

"Floyd thinks so, too. He thinks another four or five months would do it, then a freeze."

"We'll be ready, Lou and me."

"Good. I'll get right to work on the Black thing. Don't call me again unless it's something that just can't wait."

She hung up. Ella turned to find Lou hovering behind her, his dark little face pinched and worried.

"I've had this hotel fifteen years," he whined. "And now just look at it! Look at it!" He held up his hands in despair. "If I knowed

154

it was gonna come to this when I married you ten years ago, I never woulda done it!"

"That was ten years ago," Ella told him. "Ten years ago, you were scraping. Just look at the money we've got now."

"Just look at my hotel," Lou wailed, anguish strident in his voice. "Ella, I'm tellin you, you gotta quit this dope stuff. I never wanted to do it, and I still don't wanna do it. I don't care about the money."

"Well, I *do*," she said, seeming to billow over him. "If you want to be a poor nigger the rest of your life, that's your business! I told you when I married you, I intend to go someplace. I'm tired of back alleys and railroad tracks. I want me a fine big white house and all the fine big things. And you're going to do what I want, you're going to do what I want until I tell you to stop!"

"I picked you up from the gutter," Lou said, "right down there on Maple Street, and you wasn't nothin but a whore! I don't see how an everyday whore can come and rule me! You's my wife, and I say you better do what I say do."

"You just try and make me," Ella said softly but firmly. "If you're tired of living, you old sonofabitch, you just try and make me!"

At the Sixth Precinct, Rudy Black was called out of his cell for interrogation at one-thirty. He was gaunt and unshaven, and his hair stood out wildly stiff from its marcelled contours. He was beginning to get extremely sick; his joints were stiffening and his eyes were beginning to water. He was ushered into a small bare room off the entrance to the single tier of cells. The room had one small window with bars, two chairs, a table, and a scorched wooden ashtray.

He sat down, pressing both his knees together to ease the ache in them. He held his head in his hands and watched the tears drip from his eyes and soil the creases of his green, wrinkle-proof gabardine slacks. Somewhere, muffled but vaguely audible, two men were laughing. The sound of a cell door closing came to him, followed by the loud shrill screaming of a man. Another man could be heard shouting, then the screaming stopped suddenly.

The voices of the two men came again, laughing.

Someone was whimpering.

Rudy lit a cigarette and felt the hot smoke rake his throat. He tried to sit up straight; the bones snapped. He bent over with his head between his hands and watched the teardrops again. He yawned, then shivered convulsively. A tickle shot through his groin and testicles with a gnawing that brought sweat to his forehead.

I ain't this far out! I know I ain't!

He heard the doorknob turn but didn't look around. He felt too miserable to look up.

"Black?" a voice said.

He didn't answer.

"Black," the voice said, a little more firmly. "I'm Detective Patterson. I want to talk to you."

"I ain't got nothin to talk about," Rudy said, but he looked up and saw the young face, remembering the name, remembering, from the latest communiques on the Scene, the news that Davis had taken on a new partner.

Patterson sat down in the chair across from him, putting a blank envelope on the table. "Are you sick?" he asked, and Rudy was tempted to laugh at his manner, his voice, the slim, dignified cut of suit, the thick-soled shoes—a square.

"I'm feelin great," he said, "just great!"

"Let's not have any jokes. I don't think you're in the position right now."

"I'm not jokin."

"Would you like a fix?"

Rudy looked at him and smiled sickly. "For what? For the moon? Talk about jokes! Listen, my man, you cut me loose and I'll get my own fix."

Patterson strained against the barrier, repelled by the sloppy speech, the baked head of hair. He opened the envelope and took out two white capsules. From his pocket he took a book of matches and tore off half the back, following Davis' instructions. He offered them to Rudy. "Go ahead, it's your stuff."

Rudy hesitated. "Whadda you mean, *my stuff?* I never had no stuff. You tryin to make a joke?"

"I'm in no position to joke either," Patterson said, pushing the things into Rudy's hand. "Go ahead and snort it, get your sickness off. We'll both feel better if you do."

Rudy bent the match cover and emptied both capsules into it, then he placed it against one nostril and drew up loudly, choking as the drug bit into the tender tissues of his nose, tasting it warm and bitter in his throat. He took a draw on his cigarette and sat back, letting the taste of the drug fill his mouth and nose, relaxing. "Thanks, my man," he said. "That was real George."

Patterson nodded. "Don't worry; I know that fix doesn't buy you."

"It sure don't."

Patterson was stymied for a moment at the tone of the reply. "You were arrested with ninety-seven capsules this morning, Black—over a hundred dollars retail. That's as much as I make in a week."

"Wait a minute," Rudy said. "You didn't bust me with no drugs! Them drugs was outside my door, somebody else could've dropped 'em. For another thing, I don't give a damn how much you make in a week. I'm concerned about nobody but little Rudy, little Rudy Black."

Patterson frowned. "Just because the drugs weren't in your possession doesn't mean we can't go to court and prove they're yours—"

"Yeah, that's it," Rudy said. "You could take me to court and paint me on the wall, that's what you'd do. You cops like to send innocent guys to jail."

"We know for a fact that you've been pushing on the Scene," Patterson backed up his claim. "We know for a fact that you've been pushing for The Man."

"Well, you know a hell of a lot more than I know," Rudy said,

157

his belly warmed over by the drugs. "You cops like to *lie* on guys, you'd go to court and lie me into the joint, that's what you'd do!"

"Look here, Black, you're going to co-operate with us—or else."

Rudy's bloodshot eyes flickered. "Co-operate and send myself to the joint? Is that how you want me to co-operate?"

"You *will*, sooner or later."

"Oh," Rudy said, suddenly assuming the role of martyr. "So you're gonna beat me, huh? You're gonna wax me? You're gonna wax me and make me say I did somethin I didn't do?" He squared himself in his chair, the heroin adding a timbre to his voice. "Well, go ahead, copper, go ahead and beat me up!"

"I hoped this would be different," Patterson said between his teeth. "I thought a talking without beating would make you come to your senses. A beating is what you expected, and I'm almost tempted to do it."

"Why don't you?"

"Would you beat a drunk?" Then he felt silly after saying it, knowing full well that beating a drunk would mean less than nothing to Rudy Black.

Leaning forward, Rudy said, "Let me talk."

"Go ahead."

"You want me to co-operate, huh? Tell ya what, copper, I'm gonna co-operate, I'm gonna flip."

Patterson eyed him speculatively.

"You say them drugs you guys picked up is mine, huh?" Rudy said. "Okay, they're my drugs. You say I was pushin, huh? Okay, yeah, I was pushin 'em—right up my arm!"

"You listen, Black! You want a break, don't you?"

"What kinda break? I don't need no break!"

"You just admitted the narcotics were yours—"

"You just try to make me say that again in front of somebody besides you!"

Exasperated, Patterson got up and took a pair of cuffs off the clip at his side. "Hold out your hands."

Rudy looked at the cuffs suspiciously, his bravado deserting him for a moment. "What's this?"

158

"Shut up and put your hands in these."

Rudy obeyed. "So I get waxed now, huh?"

Patterson could visualize Davis' face when he brought Rudy out. He'd be smirking. He had practically begged Davis to give him a chance with Rudy, trying to make up for his fluff on the Bertha Travis thing, trying to show that he could come through with a little sensible police work—but even after a few minutes he knew that trying to get Rudy Black to incriminate himself was like trying to get an elephant to sit on a three-legged stool!

Picturing the wide, satisfied smile on Davis' face, Patterson tried again, this time feeling the fork in his tongue.

"I really don't want to see you go through all this for nothing, Black," he said. "I want to help you all I can, whether you believe that or not. The Man is the biggest dope man in town. As one of his pushers, you're in a position to kick the supports down and come out on top. Am I getting to you?"

"Listen—" Rudy said, eying Patterson slyly.

"I'm listening, Black."

"I've done time before," Rudy said.

"I know your record."

"So, dig," said Rudy, easing himself back in the chair, letting his hands fall to his lap, closing his eyes until they were small slits. "I'm bugged. Do you get bugged sometimes? Stuff gets you like that sometimes—it scares you."

Strangely, there seemed to be a note of truth in his words; Patterson was struck by the sudden change.

"Can I talk?" Rudy said, then continued after Patterson nodded. "You know my record? Dig . . . A long time ago I got hit by a car and wet my pants I was so scared. So I told myself I wasn't gonna ever get hit by no more cars, and I didn't. Then me and some more guys was raifieldin a radio shop and got caught, and I got sapped up and went to the Hill for eighteen months. I was so scared I never raifielded no more. I kept stealin but I never raifielded. But then I got hooked, after I got my woman, and I got scared again. . . ."

It was coming out like an explosion of a dam, yet Rudy couldn't help himself. More than anything, it was important that he say this, even if the Roller didn't understand. It was more for Rudy, this review of his life; in the warm surge of heroin he felt almost clean looking back on what he used to be, exposing the dirt of himself. And then he saw the look of sympathy on Patterson's face and knew that it was serving a double purpose.

"But you couldn't stop this time," Patterson nudged.

"Do you know how it was?" Rudy said. "It's like nothin—" He stopped; something inside him made him stop.

"Go on, Black, it's no secret. You got hooked and you couldn't unhook yourself even though you were afraid, isn't that it?"

"Let *me* tell it!" Rudy shouted. "What do *you* know?"

"Only what you tell me."

"I'm hip! You can't even *think* how it was the first time I kicked in the County Jail; it's nothin you, a Roller, would know anything about. All you do is bust a junkie and lock him up for thirty days or thirty years! What the hell do you care?"

"But I do care!" Patterson said inadequately. "I'm listening to you. If I didn't care I wouldn't listen to you."

"That's right . . . if you weren't interested, you'd be slappin my cap off, right?"

Patterson could merely nod, brought face to face with a strangely capricious monster.

"What's the use," Rudy said, retreating into himself.

"You tell me, Black, I'm listening. I swear to you I'm listening!"

Rudy was quick to receive the feeling that was communicated. Without actually thinking, he responded in an effort to gain Patterson's confidence.

"So this is the way it was, Mr. Patterson," he began. "I've never told this, the way I feel, to nobody, and the only reason I'm telling you is because people like me get bugged and they have to tell somebody—even if it's a Roller."

"Go ahead," Patterson said, ready to grasp any guide to Rudy's twisted psychology.

"Dig," Rudy went on. "So when I got hooked, I was scared too. There wasn't no way for me to stop. When I went and kicked the first time, I was so sick I couldn't see. So listen, man, what do you think I did? When I got out I said, 'Nothin—not me again,' but it wasn't so easy. I come right out and copped again. I was all the time around stuff. There was plenty smack around the neighborhood. I started usin again, one thing at a time. I had Nina and she was makin nice money, and with all that bread comin in I started buyin more stuff. Pretty soon I was usin two things, then three, then four, then I was usin five twice a day." He stretched his hands apart in the handcuffs. "Nina was hooked, too. Now this is what I figured. Here's a jinx I can't get away from, so what will I do? I'm gonna keep so much stuff, I'll never be scared no more. I'll keep the sickness off all the time. But there's just one thing against this. The Rollers. But I'm more scared of bein sick than I am of the Rollers."

Patterson waited, then stared at him when Rudy didn't go on. "You've told me?"

Rudy grinned expectantly. "That's it. All of it. Now I did have those ninety-some caps, but you can't make me say that on paper. Me and my woman use ninety-some caps a week, sometimes more."

"Black—"

"That's the truth, Mr. Patterson."

"Black, you're lying," Patterson said.

Rudy said nothing. He sat back in the chair and closed his eyes completely.

"I thought it'd be easier, talking to you like this." Patterson was becoming angry now at the thought Rudy had made a fool of him. "You don't even know when you're lying; that's typical of you addicts."

"Don't shoot me none of them words," Rudy snapped. "Either cut me loose or beat my ass."

"We know you're dealing with The Man. You're going to make a buy for us, Black."

Rudy looked at him hard. "No! Double n-o, Roller!"

A fine spray of heat seemed to splatter Patterson's face, "We don't even have to beat you. All we have to do is lock you up for a couple of hours and you'll be begging to make a buy. Why do all you junkies react this way?"

161

Rudy leaned forward in his chair, twisting the loose bands of steel into his wrists. *"Because!"* he shouted. "Because you guys bug us to death!"

"Who?"

"YOU! People like you! Why don't you set up a country for junkies and leave us alone? Have you ever heard that sayin, 'Once a junkie always a junkie'? Well, it's true! You Rollers keep bustin us and bustin us and bustin us! Don't you know it ain't doin us no good? Don't you know the sonofabitch who said that sayin was *right*? Say, man, *dig*: a junkie don't want your help! A junkie don't want no help at all!"

"What *do* you want?" Patterson asked angrily.

"Smack," bubbled Rudy. "Nothin but boy and more boy, with a little girl on the side to make it worth livin. Listen, daddy, *you*, you don't know what you're missin! If you did, you'd give up that tin badge and lay up in a crib somewhere and use your gun to blow anybody in two who tried to mess with you while you was usin!"

"That doesn't answer my question, Black!" Patterson shouted. "We've got you now and you *do* need help! What do you want? You must want something! What is it?"

"Nothin," Rudy said calmly.

"Nothing?"

"I'm sayin this, Mr. Patterson, Mr. Roller, sir," Rudy sneered. "I say you can lock me up for two months or two years, and I still won't flip! I'm a thoroughbred! I came up in the street with nothin! I had a father and mother and I still had nothin! I dragged my butt in the mud until I was big enough to drag it out and start kickin people the way they been kickin me! I started livin and usin drugs and buyin clothes, strides and stomps that'd set you back a whole month's pay! And I *like* livin like this, man, 'cause it's pure, like grade-A boy! I got my wings and bought a Cadillac, and it's paid for—almost paid for—already, the kind of car you couldn't buy if you didn't eat all year!"

Patterson lost control of himself. "This is living? Being a thoroughbred with a habit and a whore—this is what you consider really living?"

162

"You sure know what to say, copper," Rudy laughed. "You took the words right out of my mouth! And you know why, Mr. Police? 'Cause they're the kind of things you want and ain't got the nerve to get!"

Patterson stopped himself before he struck Rudy. He sat back and waited, easing the tension in his body. He said after a while, "You know, I've got a lot to learn, Black."

Rudy smiled. "Sure you have, sure you have. You gotta crawl before you walk, they say."

Patterson excused himself piteously. "I sat here thinking, this is a boy who can be helped; I can do something for him, not just bust him and send him away."

Rudy was not fooled. "I know that's what you were thinkin, Mr. Patterson—yes, sir."

Patterson felt maddened by this one-sided conflict. "I know this, too, Black. I know you're going to come back here, and when you do it's going to be for keeps!"

Rudy stood up. "Let's go see Mr. Davis. He's waitin, ain't he?"

"Yes. He knew."

"And now you know," Rudy said again.

Patterson got up and took him by the arm. "Let's go."

In the hallway they met Davis.

"Let him go," he told Patterson sharply.

"Why?"

"Beeker just called. Said he received a writ for Black's and the girl's release."

Rudy was smiling. When his hands were freed he smoothed back the daggers of hair at his scalp. He felt good now. He felt like there was a God. He felt the heroin Patterson had given him running through his body, every vein, making his whole system gurgitate with the desire for more.

He said, laughing deep in his chest so the officers could not hear, "Can I go? Am I free?"

"Go ahead," Patterson said ruefully. "You'll be back."

"If I didn't come back," Rudy said, starting off, "you guys'd be outta business and lookin for new haims."

Davis ran down the hall after Rudy and kicked him high on the leg. Rudy bent over in pain, smiling at Patterson, his mouth twisted, his body angled over like a broken piece of kindling wood.

"You see?" he said. "It's the same old crap all the time. . . ."

11

THE LITTLE cripple, his wheel chair slipping, sliding on the slick pavement and ice-rounded curbs, pushed himself through the night toward the Garden Poolroom.

The tiny, twisted, childlike body belied the strength of his movement, belied the wide mackinawed chest of a grown man.

He lingered in front of the poolroom, feeling the sting of the cold rush over him to stop at his waist where all sense of feeling ceased. He liked the cold because other people did not; it was his habit to take unto himself those things other people hated.

He imagined he could feel the cold on his legs, but it was pure imagination, for he had never walked in his life.

One of the countless figures from the Scene lifted his chair into the doorway of the poolroom—

"Thanks, man, come to my pad later on. I'll fix you up. . . ."

He could almost hear the objections of his mother. . . . *Sonny, you mustn't use dope, you and your friend. . . .* As if she gave a damn, with the money she brought home each day from her beauty shoppe with its pervading smells of collard greens and ham hocks and Dixie Peach hair dressing.

He hated his mother even more than he hated the nothingness that was his father. He hated his mother's strong arms lifting him on buses or beds or chairs or out of his wheel chair into a theater seat. He hated his father's power to impregnate and vanish and forget.

His twenty-six years were filled with hate against everything but the extremes of cold and heat. These belonged to him; these were his domain, these and the drugs he sold. . . .

"Got any stuff, Sonny?" the faces in the poolroom said.

"I got the bomb, baby, the bomb!"

Always he accommodated, with a smile. The junkies loved him, knew him to be generous and understanding of their plight.

But he hated them, hated their legs and movement; and with his drugs he controlled them, they came to depend on him and be manipulated by him. They bought him drinks he never drank, ordered him exotic Chinese dishes from the all-night restaurant which he only nibbled at; they did anything which might please him and keep him turning them on.

Almost all the women of the Scene he could have had at a nod of his head—the females with sharp tongues and red lips and pancaked faces like smooth brown masks from which their eyes glowed weakly, with dresses pulled up over their knees, oversmooth nylons and opera pumps and calluses from walking the street all night—sitting together after working hours in the all-night restaurant, listening to Sarah or Ella or Lady Day emote from the juke, smiling at him like beautiful brown dolls. . . .

He lifted his eyes to the poolroom, just as the anxious motion that was Rudy Black swirled before him, swerved, long arms swinging hard against Sonny's shoulder, his big body crashing against the chair, sending it against the front door with an abrupt smash.

"Why don't you get that goddamn pushcart out of the way!"

Then the ugly face was gone, and the hate suffused him.

"—stuff, Sonny?"

"—bomb, baby!"

Selling the explosives, accommodating, smiling, thinking: I'll get even with that bastard for that! I'll get him!

A bank game was in progress between Dell and Clyde Lujack from dago-town. He wheeled up as it ended, asking:

"How'd Rudy Black get out so quick?" To everybody at large. *"He fell yesterday."*

A big surprised look appeared on the yellow face of Dell. *"He didn't fall. He was just in here. He ain't fell that quick."*

His strong, gloved fingers moved the wheel chair around the poolroom. *"I thought everybody knew. Some guys at Lou's told me. He fell yesterday."*

Lujack, big black mustache on a white face, little finger glinting with a diamond: *"If he fell, how come he's out?"*

The wheelchair was on the other side of the poolroom, and in a voice loud so everyone would hear: *"I just know what I hear. Wonder how come he's out?"*

Lujack, looking at Dell: *"It don't smell right."*

"It's all right. . . ."

He felt his wide chest expand at the sudden power. *"Wasn't nobody hip?"*

Lujack, frowning: *"I got business with that man."*

Dell, trying to reassure: *"It's all right. I know."*

"It don't smell right." Worried. *"It stinks!"*

"He'll be back, he's just goin to connect for ya. Don't worry."

The power burst in the expanding chest: *"Maybe they got an indictment! Maybe somebody's set up!"*

"He wouldn't flip." Dell telling Lujack. *"I know that boy. He'd tell the Rollers what to eat."*

Lujack pulling the basket from under the table, putting on a white, double-breasted, cashmere overcoat. *"It's Christmas in three days. I'm gonna be home for Christmas, man!"*

Dell, pleading. *"Whyncha just wait? Ask him!"*

Big black mustache shaking. *"It's funky London Town, man. I don't like it. The word's out that the Feds are gonna clean up for Christmas. Like I said, I'm gonna be home for Christmas."*

Pleading again: *"Let Rudy talk!"*

"He shoulda talked, man. He shoulda said, 'Man, I got busted yesterday, but the Rollers cut me.'"

The Power smiling, wheeling up to the table, pushing past the big fat proprietor racking balls. *"Yeah, why didn't he?"*

166

Dell's eyes were now slits. *"Shut up, you crippled bastard! You tryin to rank Rudy, that's what you tryin to do!"*

He shoulda slapped me, the cripple thought, turning away, the smile still pasted on his lips. The sonofabitch shoulda slapped me!

"—stuff, Sonny?"

"—bomb, baby . . ."

He hit and ran like a marauding fighter plane, dropping his bombs and then roaring off on wheeled legs.

He was outside, helped out by one of the poolroom's junkies, and the cold clasped him.

He let the wind pound at his back, thinking of Rudy Black, and his mother. They shouldn't push me like that, he thought. I'll fix 'em when they push me!

He had been powerful, hurting Rudy. He could hardly wait for his next buy from The Man: he'd tell Sylvia about Rudy's bust, too.

Along with this warm, satisfying thought, he decided to hurt his mother. He'd use too many drugs and wheel home. Then he'd fall out of the chair on the pavement in front of his house and watch his mother rush out into the cold she hated, to help him in.

Suddenly a face perched high above him. *"—stuff, Sonny?"*

"The bomb, baby, the goddamn bomb!"

"Good. Good."

Strong hands reached, wrapped themselves around the back of his chair. *"Good."*

Another figure came and put handcuffs on his wrists quickly, bent down and breathed spearmint gum in his face. *"FBI, Tubbs. You're under arrest."* The badge was a little golden cup in the palm of a hand. *"I bet you're filthy, Tubbs."*

Clyde Lujack had said it. The word had gone out, but no one really believed it. The Feds were going to clean up for Christmas. It had to happen to him—to him!

Tough for him.

Yeah, tough for Tubby!

They pushed him over to a car on the corner, put him inside.

He saw a face come out of the poolroom, two faces, then three. Watching.

Instantly, he grasped the sensation of power again, wanting to leave something vivid and dynamic of his twisted little soul on the great Scene.

Awkwardly, he rolled the car window down, aiming his mouth at the watching faces: *"Rudy Black, Rudy Black!"*

But a hand come over his mouth and mashed his lips together.

The damage done Rudy Black was irreparable.

"**W**HADDA YOU want?" the landlady said, squinting down her long nose at them. "Whadda you want, wakin people up out the bed this time of night?"

"We're bringing him home."

"Nobody wants him here. I've had enough trouble with you junkies. Get away from here."

"He's weak."

"I don't give a damn."

"Please, señora . . ." Coke Prado wore only a hospital nightshirt and trousers.

"You're junkies," the landlady told them. "Get away from here!"

"Hey?" a woman's voice came from upstairs. "Is that a customer, hey?"

"It's that spic sonofabitch and those kids," the landlady called back. "You come down here."

"Can we come in, lady? It's cold."

"Why the hell don't you stay home and enjoy Christmas like

good kids should, insteada shootin that stuff all the time?" the landlady said.

"Who is it?" Adele's face showed in the doorway.

"Your old man," the landlady said. "I'm not gonna have no more fights around here. I'm not gonna let him in."

"Let him in," Adele told her.

"Now listen—"

"There won't be no trouble, I swear there won't!"

They came in. The warmth slapped their faces, made their stomachs turn with its deliciousness.

"*Look* at him!" The landlady smirked. "What happened to you, Paydro? You ain't got enough ass to last you out the rest of the year! Where's my old man?" she said, starting off. "He's gotta see the big-timer now!"

"Upstairs," Adele said, afraid to touch Coke.

"It wasn't easy," Frankie said. "We nearly got caught swinging him outta that joint."

Adele whirled on him. "Who told you to, you little snot? Everything was going O.K.!" She grabbed Coke by the arm roughly. "C'mon, let's get the hell upstairs."

They stumbled up the steps awkwardly with him, Tippy on the right and Adele on the left. Frankie kept his hands under Coke's armpits, lifting.

"You have to go easy with him," Tippy said. "Something's wrong with his insides."

"Madre de Dios," Coke said with pain.

They reached the landing and almost dragged him over to the door of her room. Inside they laid him on the bed.

They stood around watching him, horrified. The man's hair remained only in patches, outlining his bony features like the ringed head of a poodle. His long, twiglike fingers reached up from his chest at intervals, snatching wildly, grasping great handfuls of air and shoving the emptiness into the gaping mouth.

Tippy was awestruck. "He's *dying!*"

Coke heard him. "Call priest," he said. "Give me . . ." He was

169

wracked with yawns. ". . . stuff . . . you got stuff?" He looked at Adele pleadingly.

Tippy turned his back. "Give him some stuff."

Adele seemed unmoved. "I got some stuff," she said vaguely. "Get him off my bed. I don't want 'im dying on my bed. Get him in the bathroom. I'll bring the stuff."

They took him down the long, darkened hall to the bathroom.

Adele came in fifteen minutes later with a stamp-sized packet of heroin and a set of works.

Coke was sitting upright by himself. "Call padre . . ."

"I've called," Adele told him. "I've really called for you."

She looked at Frankie, who had started to prepare a shot for Coke, leaving enough for himself and Tippy.

"Why'd you get him out?" Adele said, a quiet but vicious hate in her eyes.

"Why?" Frankie said, his young face stricken by the interruption. "Coke said he's got stashes he put away when he was working for The Man; he said he'd give 'em to us if we just got him out of the hospital." Then, as a violent afterthought, "We're not getting burnt no more! That's all we ever get on the Scene, a burn!"

"Coke give us a big in with The Man," Tippy added. "That's another big reason. He told us about The Man's pipeline. He promised he might even tell us who the real top dog is. All we have to do is tell The Man what we know—"

"We can be as big as Coke was," Frankie said, "with the stuff he's gonna turn over to us. And if that isn't enough, The Man's gonna keep our bee straight and give us a chance to make some money. He's *gotta* do it, because of what we know."

Adele looked at him with disbelief. "You crazy? You wanna die or something? You don't stick up people like The Man. Coke ain't got no stash; if he did, don't you think I'd have it? He just wanted you punks to get him out the hospital so's he could do what he's doing now!"

They looked at Coke, who was weakly tying his upper arm with a shred of the nightshirt, almost exhausted with the effort, the needle clutched in his right hand.

170

"Whyn't you let him die?" Adele said shrilly. "Why didn't you punks leave me alone? Why didn't you just go ahead and kick if you couldn't keep up with the crowd?"

"Because we're junkies!" Frankie cried, trembling with his own admission. "Because when we need a fix, you don't matter, you or nobody else! If you can't kick, why should we!"

"Goddamn you!" Adele shrieked, beginning to cry.

"Why should you have your fix and we can't?" Frankie shouted at her. "On account of we're just little kids with the monkey and a couple bucks? Well, *our* monkey weighs just as much as yours, and it hurts just as much, and it takes the same stuff to get it off as it does yours!"

"You dead body!" Adele screamed at Coke. "You dead body, I hope it kills you!"

Coke had plunged the needle into one of the many worn tracks on his arm and emptied the fluid of the dropper into the vein.

Two plain-clothes men and a uniformed patrolman entered quietly. Tippy tried to run, but was slugged unconscious with a blackjack. The uniformed cop put handcuffs on Frankie roughly, then snatched Adele over to become the boy's partner.

One of the detectives pulled Coke up, while the other whisked the works and heroin into his pocket. "Boy! Talk about a dope den!" he said. "Who was it tipped this off?"

"I did," Adele said.

The landlady came with her short, bull-necked husband as the policemen dragged the parties out.

"I try to run a decent roomin house," she whined after them, "I swear to God I do. . . ."

At the stairway, half carried by the detectives, Coke stopped, made them stop with a strength that was unbelievable, snatched from some source deep within. A startled look came to his eyes, and a thick hoarse gurgling came from his mouth. Then he seemed to disintegrate in one of the men's arms.

The detective felt his pulse and looked up at his partner. "Must of been an overdose," he said. "The guy's dead."

Adele began to scream.

13

So this is it, he thought. Another morning. Another day.

He thought directly his eyes opened, still clouded with sleep, before all his senses came alive and warm under the bed covers and the thin slab of light beneath the window shade grinned at him.

So, he thought, not continuing to think after that. Only, *So*.

He heard his wife call from downstairs. "Virg, get up, baby! You'll be late!" and the voices of the children, Lonnie and Virg, Jr., their yelling over the breakfast table.

I'll get up. I'll get up. I'll get up.

But he didn't move. He closed his eyes against the light, bathing his body in the lush comfort that enveloped his thighs and legs and brain. . . .

In his dream he was hanging by his cuffs, the tips of his shoes barely touching the floor. He was two people, one watching the action and one participating.

All of a sudden, Davis came up out of the floor and started laughing at him. He laughed until he tired, then he started kicking him, again and again. Then Davis called Rudy Black over, and his mincing, grotesque figure glided ridiculously toward the hanging body. He and Davis started in together, kicking the defenseless body until it swung like a pendulum, screaming, screaming. . . .

He opened his eyes to see Maxine's face hovering over him worriedly, the smile wrinkles near the edges of her eyes drawn and tight. "Virg, baby, snap out of it! What's the matter, honey?"

He was startled at the sound of her voice, tried to smile. "Nothing . . . nothing's wrong."

"You were talking in your sleep; you never do that. And the look on your face . . ."

He rose up under her, placing his lips against her mouth. "I

172

should get to bed earlier. Probably will since the squad has swung on days for a while."

She smiled at him softly. "You need a shave, and you'd better get up right away. It's eight-ten. C'mon now, lazybones, get the lead out!"

"All right." He got out of bed and went into the bathroom. She followed and stood in the doorway while he removed his pajama shirt and prepared to shave.

"Virg?"

"Hummm?" He looked at her in the mirror.

"How's the job?"

"Oh, fine, I guess. . . . Where're the kids?"

"Downstairs, decorating the tree."

"Hey," he said, "I thought they were going to wait until I got home this evening."

"The way you guys have been going over at Sixth, I told them to go ahead. There's no telling when you'll be home."

"I'll *be* home," he said. "I've been home every other Christmas Eve, haven't I?"

"Sure, but you weren't at Sixth then. Your job was a lot more predictable."

He shook the razor at her mirror reflection. "Here's a prediction with certainty: nothing could keep me away from home tonight— Davis, the Sixth Precinct, or anything else."

She came over to put her arms around his waist, rubbing her cheek softly up and down his back muscles, and he could feel her breasts strong and sufficient against him. They laughed together, the soft, secret bubbling of lovers.

"Keep it up," he said, "and I'll call up sick."

"You'll do no such thing," she said behind him. "We need the money."

"Sometimes I think all you married me for was my money."

"Certainly not for your looks, Gargantua."

"I could have had any girl at Central, little lady. I guess you didn't know that when we met on the campus."

173

"You probably could have had any of them," she said, nibbling at his back, "but could you have *married* them?"

Again they laughed together, and the pause was significant.

"Virg, honey, will you tell me something?"

"I guess so. What is it?"

She looked over his shoulder into the mirror. "What's the matter?"

He stopped shaving. "What are you talking about?"

"I mean about the job."

He rinsed the soap and hair from his razor with a burst of hot water that shot steam over the mirror's surface, obscuring his face. "Well, I guess I might as well tell you now," he said.

"Tell me what?"

He turned to face her. "I put in for a transfer. It'll take a little time, of course, but—"

"A transfer?" she cried. "What are you talking about?"

"Listen, Max—"

"I've listened to you crab about this promotion all year long," she cut him off. "And now that you've got it, you're going to *transfer?* Where're you going to transfer to? Back to the squad car? You're going to voluntarily drop better than five hundred dollars a year?"

"There you go talking about money again," he said peevishly. "Listen, Max, it'd only be for a little while. Just till I got another assignment, another partner."

"You mean until another Negro makes detective?" She threw up her hands. "Fat chance! What's the matter with Mr. Davis? Aren't you getting along with him? What happened to all that enthusiasm when you first started with the Narco Squad? Where did it go off to, what rock did it crawl under to die?"

"All right, all right!" he said, raising his voice. "Let's just say I'm bored. The work is thankless. I don't feel like knocking myself out."

She looked at him keenly. "Did they give itty bitty baby a problem he couldn't solve? Is that it?"

"I don't think that was very nice!" he shouted.

"I didn't intend it to be!" she shouted back. "My goodness, Virg, don't you think I know when something's not going right with you? When you first started with Narco, I have to admit I was afraid of what the work might do to you—physically. But obviously it's not your health that's at stake. What is it? Pride? Has Mr. Davis stepped on your precious mental toes?"

"O.K., O.K.," he said, giving up. "It's that bastard I'm working with, Davis. He's my enemy, Max, my *enemy*! He doesn't *want* to see me make good. He won't give me any breaks!"

She refused to salve the wound. "The guy I used to know made his own breaks."

"It's not the same thing," he said. "This isn't a one-man job. He acts like I'm cargo, something he can toss overboard any time he feels like it."

"And you're going to let him beat you down?" she said quietly. "You're going to throw away everything you ever worked for, simply because of a clash of personalities?"

Patterson bit his lip. "Look, you don't understand—"

"I understand I'm not going to let you pin wings on this opportunity and let it fly off, that's what I understand!"

She made him feel ashamed, and for a moment he was angry at her for exposing his little-boy petulance; then he began to feel a bit angry at himself. He didn't tell her that he'd dropped his request for transfer on Captain Beeker's desk over the weekend, that it had probably been forwarded downtown by now.

Nor could he tell her about his sense of failure regarding the junkie, Rudy Black, who had become more of a nemesis to him than Davis since the day of that pitiful interrogation. That was the biggest burr, that feeling that he'd been defeated by an inferior enemy. It made him feel that he wasn't cut out for the work, and it further disturbed him to imagine that Davis had seen and recognized his inadequacy the first time they'd worked together.

He was becoming more obsessed by these things daily. He had vowed to become a better policeman than his father had been, remove himself far above the insignificance of a traffic cop. But for some reason Davis and Rudy Black were working malevolently against his aims, making him cease to care.

". . . And you've got to *care*," Maxine was saying. "If you don't care if you never amount to anything, you never will—never!" She tried a masculine affection, punching his bare chest with a tiny fist. "That's my boy! Now hurry up and shave. I'll have breakfast ready when you get downstairs."

The boys had just finished decorating a small pine, a brave little thing which tried valiantly to support the mountain of lights, tassels, and imitation snow, when he came down to the living room.

Virg, Jr., ran to his father and dragged him over to the work of art. Lonnie stood appreciatively viewing the whole effect.

"Whadda you think, Pop?" Virg, Jr., said.

"Well . . ." Patterson said with a critical eye. "It's kind of lopsided."

"That's Lonnie's fault. He put the star on crooked."

"You're crazy," Lonnie said. "You're just not looking at it right."

Patterson went over to tilt the silver star a bit. "Hmmm. Maybe you're right, Lonnie. It depends on where you're standing." He replaced the star in its former position.

"Now all we need is some real snow," Virg, Jr., said. "I wish the snow'd snow until it came up to the windows, then it'd really be Christmas."

"You don't need snow for it to be Christmas," Lonnie told him. "It's Christmas when you feel it in your heart; Mom said so."

"And it's Christmas when you get a lot of presents," Virg, Jr., said.

"Listen," Patterson said, pulling them together. "Your mother's right. It's Christmas when you know what you feel in your heart for other people is good. That's what Christmas really means. And when you feel like that, you don't have to wait all year on Christmas—you can have it every day of the year."

"But what about the presents?" Virg, Jr., said.

"Those are symbolic," Patterson told him. "That's just the goodness of people taking form."

176

"What about the kids that won't have any Christmas?" Lonnie said. "The kids who're too poor, I mean. They won't get any presents."

"That doesn't mean that it still won't be Christmas for them," Patterson said. "Listen, boys, remember that Christmas is love, not presents. The presents only stand for love."

Lonnie shook his head, puzzled. "I don't understand, Pop."

"It's simple, fellas," Patterson said. "You see, you guys are lucky, just plain lucky. Suppose I wasn't a cop with a regular salary? Suppose I couldn't feed or clothe you when it was necessary? Christmas wouldn't seem like much when it came around, would it?"

They shook their heads.

"But, still, if we were poor, I'd still love you as I love you now, and you wouldn't miss your presents as much as you think."

"We'd have them in our hearts," Lonnie said.

"Sure," Patterson said. "Now if you received presents from your mother and me without the love that goes along with it, the presents wouldn't mean very much, would they?"

"We don't need snow," Lonnie said. "People have Christmas all over the world in places where there's no snow."

Patterson straightened up at the thought of the Scene and its many helpless children. What kind of Christmas would they have!

Maxine came into the room. "You'd better hurry, Virg. Breakfast is on the table. You're going to be late."

"I don't much care this morning," Patterson said.

Lonnie tugged at his sleeve. "Hey, Pop."

"Yes, son?"

"I think you'd better straighten that star. It does look a little crooked."

14

*H*E WALKED quickly through the crowded squad room to his desk. Davis waited there for him.

"How come you're so late, Virg?" he said genially, and Patterson knew that something was wrong; Davis had a maniacal adherence to punctuality. Then he knew Beeker must have told Davis about the transfer.

"What's the matter?" Davis went on sweetly. "Can't get used to this day shift?"

Patterson sat down and began to sort through a file from the F.B.I. "Days are fine," he said. "I'll get to see my kids more often."

"That's right, you have got two boys, haven't you? I'd like to stop in on you sometime, meet your family."

Patterson was finding Davis' condescension annoying. "Is this all the info on that Coke Prado fella?"

"Thought you might like to look through that," Davis said. "One of Speer's squads picked him up with his woman and those two kids who've been haunting the Scene. He's dead, you know."

"Prado?"

"The guy had built up a tolerance for heroin, then he became allergic to it. The fix he had killed him on the spot. The boys were sent downtown. I really want to get to those kids," he said. "I can't figure out why they lifted Coke from Municipal."

Patterson sifted the papers on his desk. "How did the Federal cleanup go off the other night, the one we were alerted to?"

"The Feds don't tell us everything. Maybe it's a good thing they didn't." Davis rubbed his mustache thoughtfully. "I hear the catch was mighty small. The only real fish they caught was that little bastard, Sonny Tubbs."

Patterson looked at him. "The leak again?"

"Could be. Although Stuart said security was tight. Only a few of us knew about it."

"What do we do about it?"

"Nothing," Davis said. "We continue as usual. I'm gonna get in touch with Bertha sometime this week. I've pressured Andy Hodden, and he's come up with a big-sized buy for us tonight: two ounces from some new guy who doesn't know him."

"Tonight?" Patterson said. "But it's Christmas Eve, Mance! I want to be home with my family."

"Can't help that," Davis said. "We're not gonna miss this buy."

"If I remember your last meeting with Andy Hodden, you don't need my help."

"All right, college boy," Davis said patiently. "I'm trying to get along with you."

"It wouldn't be because Beeker let you in on my request for transfer, would it?" Patterson said.

A smirk came to Davis' mouth. "I can't help it if you can't take it, college boy, and I won't say I'm sorry."

Patterson stood up beside the big man, looking him full in the eyes. "Isn't it time for our tour?"

"Not until I tell you something. I don't like you, Patterson."

"I'm happy to say I feel the same way about you, sir."

"And that's not all," Davis said, the anger building up. "If I didn't think you had the makings of a damn good Narco man, I'd have blown you a good while back. I'm glad I waited. I'm glad I found out just what you're made of. You're a bastard and a snob, and I don't like anything about you, from your snappy college suits to your crew-cut nigger hair. You're too correct. So, brother, you just take your goddamn transfer and shove it in the best place, but for the time you've got left with me I'm gonna work you frazzled-assed!"

"I've been trying to stay on your dark side for almost a month," Patterson told him. "You couldn't begin to be as happy about that transfer as I am!"

"Merry Christmas!" Davis said, growing red.

"You said it!" Patterson agreed.

"Now that we've got an understanding," Davis said, "let's take that goddamn tour!"

It was seven-thirty, and very cold. Near a schoolground with high hedges in the front, Davis and Patterson had just rendezvoused with Andy Hodden. They went into a drugstore on the corner and ordered coffee.

"I don't want any," Andy said. He looked sick and cold. He was wearing a light-gray jacket.

"What's the matter?" Davis asked him. "Don't you drink coffee?"

"After—after a while, Mr. Davis. I don't want any now, that's all." His voice was thick with phlegm, his eyes unusually wide and darting.

"You had your fix?" Patterson said, feeling sorry and a bit responsible for the boy ever since he had watched Davis administer the terrible beating in the hallway.

"No," Andy said.

"You'll have one in a little while," Davis said.

Andy shook his head. "That's O.K., no."

Davis was surprised. "You mean to tell me you don't *want* a fix?"

"I haven't used stuff all day—" The boy shivered. "I copped some Dolophine this morning. I'm gonna kick."

Davis snorted. "Bull! Don't gimme that bull!"

"Maybe he means it," Patterson suggested.

"I don't care what he does as long as he sets this punk up for us," Davis told him. He looked at his watch. "C'mon, let's get the hell out of here."

They went out into the cold. A mild blizzard had just commenced, driving a dustlike spray into their faces. They stood back against the shelter of the drugstore.

Davis looked at his watch again. "That guy's supposed to be on time, ain't he, Hodden?"

"Yeah, supposed to."

180

"Then why's he fifteen minutes late? How'd you set this thing up?"

"One of those confidential things," Andy said. "A junkie cut me into this guy two days ago, in the Garden Bar. This guy is supposed to have stuff unlimited, says he was gonna off it and get right out. He never heard of me, the junkie said; besides, it's costin two bills an ounce because it's so good."

"That's a lot for an ounce," Davis observed.

"But it's worth it, Mr. Davis. I tested some myself, just one thing, and it almost knocked my head off."

"You told him tonight, huh?"

"That's right, on the playground—that's what I told him. He's supposed to be here with two ounces, but I don't know. Maybe somebody told him somethin about me by now."

"If he's as confidential as you say he is, he hasn't talked to many people. What's his name?"

"I don't know," Andy said. "He wouldn't tell me. He seems kinda leery of me, but he wants to off that stuff. This junkie who cut me into him called him Popeye."

"You told him you'd have the money?"

"I told him I'd have to get myself together." Andy nodded. "You know—like I was stallin. But I told him I'd be here for sure."

Davis took eight fifties from his wallet and gave them to Andy. "Don't let anything happen to this money; it belongs to the city." He slapped the boy on the back. "Take this off smooth, and you'll get a cut of the drugs."

Andy took the money. "No, thanks, Mr. Davis. I'm tryin to kick."

Davis looked at him suspiciously. "If you got some crazy ideas, boy, you'd better get rid of them. I'd kick your ass pastel green if something went wrong."

"Everything'll go all right if the guy shows up, Mr. Davis." Andy shivered again and looked away. "All I want to do is get this over with and get away from here, that's all I want."

"You be sure that's all you want!" Davis warned.

Andy looked at both of them. "There ain't no way for me to win, is there?"

"There sure ain't!" Davis said.

Andy crossed the street through the increasing snow, head bowed. Almost hidden by the flurry, he sat down on one of the benches in the schoolyard, next to the powerhouse for the school building. He bent his head dismally, eyes on the ground.

"Let's get in the car," Davis told his partner.

They went over to the Ford at the curb and got in. Patterson got under the wheel and started the motor. In a few moments he turned the heater on. The heat flooded comfortably over their chilled knees and feet. Through the splotched windshield, they could still see Andy on the playground, the darkness gradually surging around him.

"I hope this doesn't take long," Patterson said.

Davis grunted. "It won't, college boy, you'll be home in due time."

"There's a chance he won't come."

"I think he'll be here," Davis said. "He's not gonna pass up four hundred bucks just because it's snowing." He squinted his eyes, trying to make out the image of Andy on the playground. "I don't like these free-lancers. Something funny's going on, that little stoolie not wanting any drugs. . . ."

Patterson shrugged to himself. "Maybe he does want to kick."

Davis looked at him. "Since when did you become an authority?"

The anger he felt for The Man was frightening, even for him. Though a young man, Georgie Barris had been in the business of dope, in and out of New York, for more than eight years. In that time he had come up against some pretty tough dealers. Still, he had never met anyone like The Man.

He had been the direct connect, but now that the kid had been taken out of circulation in the accident, he was both connect and contact for The Man.

All right. Since The Man couldn't see his way clear to come up

182

with more cash, he'd make it up himself! He'd sell to anyone who had the cash—like that kid he was supposed to meet tonight. He had the bulk, nearly a kilo, of pure stuff, and if he had to make his get-away money by chopping it, he'd chop it!

In the back of his mind, he considered taking the whole bulk load and going back to New York. With that much dope, he could really set up, perhaps one day become The Man himself. But he was afraid of taking the chance. He was aware that The Man paid tribute to the syndicate, that if he were fouled the syndicate had ways and means to deal with the offending party. Even New York wouldn't be big enough to hide him.

He neared the corner, the snow smashing into his face heavily, and saw the playground across the street. Then he noticed the car in front of the drugstore on the next corner; it looked harmless enough to him, but he watched it closely for a few moments before he continued.

That kid had better have the money! He didn't know him, and took a junkie's word that the boy was all right. He had the dope with him, but he wasn't afraid of a stick-up, not from a small nothing like the boy.

The bench near the powerhouse, he thought, as he caught sight of the figure. He started over quickly.

The boy got up as he approached. "How ya doin?" he said.

"You got the money?"

The boy went into his pocket. "Here you go, but where's the stuff?"

The package was held in his hand, ready all the time. He stretched it out to the boy, taking the money as he released the drugs. "You're gonna be satisfied," he said. "Real satisfied, man."

He was a big, slow man, and he didn't know what was happening until he saw them coming.

Instantly he saw the trap. With one blow he knocked Andy down, his eyes bugged and white in the almost-darkness, his body hunched in such a way that he could not go forward or retreat; he could only stand there, petrified. Unthinkably, he released the

183

money, as if that action might save him. He froze, not so much with fear as with surprise, waiting until they were close and reaching for him, reaching their hands toward his overcoat, digging their fingers into its thickness.

Then he erupted like high explosive, the panic making him a great, wide-eyed animal, his arms lashing out, the big fists like great sledges slamming out to meet them.

Davis fell like a tree, his nose broken. Patterson had time to swing an ineffectual fist over the man's ear, a short, chopping blow which sounded out through the cold silence like the snapping of wet, soggy wood. Then he was caught under the heart with a solid punch, and he seemed to cave in the middle, aware that this was probably a boxer, this junkie, a man possessed by something far more terrible than heroin: fear.

Patterson had just got to his knees as the man started off, running. He reached to the holster at his hip and brought forth his service revolver. Bracing himself in the regulation crouching position, he squinted over the sights, his finger tightening around the trigger.

"Stop it, Patterson, goddamn you! Let him go!" Davis wobbled to his feet, his hand held high on his crushed nose, his mustache red and shiny with blood. "That's one bastard I want alive!" Davis said. "Get on the radio and put out an alert for him! He'll be picked up in half an hour. Boy, I can *taste* that sonofabitch! It'll be just like his goddamn birthday when I get him down to the station!"

Patterson got to his feet, thankful that he had not killed the man, thinking of his sons and what Christmas meant to them. Thank God, not tonight!

He reholstered his gun. Before he started across the playground, he looked for a moment at Andy Hodden's prone body on the ground, the flesh over the ridges of his eyes pulling tight.

Then he hurried away, feeling as though he would throw up the next instant.

184

15

AYLOR MAYO was very tired when she climbed the stairs Saturday morning. She carried a loaf of bread and leftover turkey and dressing from the holiday meals they had been serving ever since Christmas in the restaurant where she worked. Though the turkey carcasses were free, the bread was bought with the following night's bus fare. I'll walk to work, she thought. It's not far, if I don't think about it.

Tomorrow night she would be paid: thirty-five dollars for seven days' work, nine hours a day—for working in a basement of steam with grimy dishes shooting past on a wooden conveyor, for stacking them and drying them and carting them up a ladder through a hole in the floor, where fresh white-clad blondes and brunettes stood ready to take them from her hands. . . . "Dishes, ma'am . . . your cups and dessert dishes, Maggie." . . . "Thanks, kid. Gee, you look beat! Why don't you give this up, Taylor? Why don't you marry up with some nice fella and get out of that hole?"

She formed the picture of the chubby cheeks and round lips, the flaming hair and soft blue eyes. She clasped these to her, thinking, *Somebody* cares.

Her legs seemed so heavy; she could feel pains shooting through them as she trudged up the tenement steps.

She finally reached the door of her apartment and knocked. It was her aunt who answered.

"Hello, Aunt Fay." She came inside, and her aunt, a light-skinned, frizzy-haired woman in a green housecoat, watched her, not answering, her thin lips locked together in a straight line.

"Is Mother up?" Taylor asked her.

"I don't know," her aunt answered stiffly.

Taylor shifted the packages in her arms. "Can I use the stove?"

"You been usin it, ain't you? Maury lets you use everything else, doesn't he?"

"I—just thought I'd ask."

"No harm in askin."

The girl went into the kitchen, a small closet that had been built onto the back porch. Windows had been added, but the wind found its way through the crevices with great force. The radiators did not work.

Through one of the dirty windows, Taylor could see the stiff, gray, impersonal back of the box factory.

She went over to the old gas stove and prepared the food. She took two plates from a drawer in the kitchen table and put most of the food on one plate, then she went into the room she and her mother shared together.

"Mother . . ."

Her mother sat by the window, looking out on the street below. She was a small, delicate-faced woman, and her dark hair had begun to gray over the forehead and temples. She wore only a soiled, wrinkled slip against the coldness of the room, and her feet were bare.

"Mother, here's your breakfast. Try to eat something, won't you?"

Her mother looked up blankly. "All right."

"Have you been doing all right?"

Her mother looked strangely askance at the solicitousness. "Yes."

"Do you need anything? I want to go to bed. Tell me before I'm in bed."

"I'm O.K. You go ahead."

Taylor looked down at her feet. "Where are your house shoes? I bought you a new pair last week, for Christmas."

"My feet hurt."

"But, Mother—"

"I'm pregnant. I just know I'm pregnant. Some man has made me pregnant." The woman looked up and smiled in a childish manner.

186

"Mother—"

Her mother's eyes blazed suddenly. "Don't look that way! Stop your staring! Bring me my Bible!"

Taylor went over to the dresser and brought back the tattered book, its cover split and marked with age. "Here . . . You're tired, dear. Why don't you eat and then rest?"

"I shall rest with Jesus," the woman said. "He is my Saviour. He is my soul, He is the food to make my spirit bold."

Taylor took off her coat and seated herself on the unmade bed. She took her plate and began to eat, watching her mother as she read, watching the moving lips and blank eyes, and she thought: I shall never be like other people. Simply, with knowledge, without any rebuke of others. She had lived this way for more than five years, ever since she was fourteen. She was content to live this way for the rest of her life.

"And the Lord saith . . ."

She regarded her mother like one of the winter birds she saw flitting irrationally about the park walks and monuments when she went to work in the evenings. Lost and hungry, but still clinging to life.

"He who spurneth the children of God . . ."

My mother is crazy, she thought, reminding herself.

Her father, a weakling and a gambler, had deserted them five years before. There were relatives who helped, an aunt and two of her mother's brothers. But one of the uncles had died two months before, and they had to give up the hovel on Sixtieth to move in with the remaining brother.

And here it was no better. It was worse. Here people hated them for breathing and sleeping, for living. . . .

"Take her to one of them crazy houses," her uncle Maurice had said.

"I can't. They're full up. They won't take her until they have space."

"Well, do *somethin* with her!"

"What?"

"Anything! She ain't so crazy she don't eat. Get a job so's you can help with her. You's got a high-school education; you can find somethin."

"I will," Taylor said.

"You be sure you do. I got three girls myself."

"I will."

"If you can't get no job, get a man."

"What?"

"Get a man—a *man*. What's the matter with you, girl? Get somebody's gonna take care of you and Sis and be glad to do it."

"I—"

"You can do it. You pretty and built up the way men like, with all that long hair."

"I—I'll get a job."

Man. That way. She had never thought in such terms before.

Men. She found herself watching them on trolley buses, and on the street corners. When she asked for bus tickets, she reacted to the drivers' voices.

She saw them as she worked alone in the steam room: tall men with long fleshy arms and muscles and the horrible little slants of hair across their upper lips. She fell into fantasies in which she was approached by men and touched by their hands and faces. She could see their white teeth between thin, grinning lips and smell the harshness of their bodies close to her own.

Alone with her thoughts, she recoiled slightly but excitedly as her mind made her do things with them, things she had never done before with anyone, the thrillingly secret obscene acts that she had heard about from other girls, or from the vivid word pictures of her mother who awoke at night screaming of men lying across her stomach and thighs and breasts.

"Preserve us, Lord, for without us You do not exist." Her mother was looking out on the street below. The Bible lay on the floor, spread like ragged fat wings.

"Mother . . ."

Her mother snatched around and kicked at her violently. "Don't get behind me! Get thou not *behind* me, Satan! Stay in front, where I can watch you!"

"Mother!"

"Yes," the woman said calmly.

"I was only putting my plate on the dresser. Please, Mother dear, let's try to get some rest. I'm so tired."

Her mother nodded meekly. "All right, Taylor."

Taylor took a towel and washcloth from the dresser drawer and went into the bathroom. She brushed her teeth, then sat down on the side of the bathtub, relishing the warmth of the small, three-piped radiator in the corner. The bathroom was the warmest place in the apartment. Absently, she wished she could stretch out on the floor and go to sleep. She could imagine the warmth and hardness of the floor against her back, and all at once her body became rigid with a foreign ecstasy. For she had imagined a man's body ensnaring her own, stretched against her, yearning, the strong arms banding her arms tightly, his lips on her lips, fleshy and raw and hot, his tongue pushing against hers.

She gasped, her eyes snapping open, terrified, her breath coming in quick, animal-like sounds. She got up quickly from the tub and washed her face in cold water. Her heart was beating fast. She was trembling, and she felt a deep tingling within, still unsatisfied.

She wiped her face again with the damp washcloth and felt suddenly driven to make her entire body cold. She removed her clothes, her fingers awkward and unresponsive, until she stood naked before the washbasin. Filling it full with cold water, she immersed her cloth and put it to the hotness of her breasts, the flat, hard twitching of her smooth belly, repeating the action until the floor was drenched, until the fire retreated from her flesh, nestling in her mind, mocking her.

Her eyes widened and, almost frantically, she thought, *No!*

Then, drawn like a magnet, she turned to the bathroom window, her eyes seeking out the adjoining window of the next tenement, hungrily visualizing the slim brown naked body.

No, she thought. My mother is crazy!

And it became too much: she could not stand the ignorance of not knowing.

She put on her clothes.

"Where you goin?" Her aunt stood in the kitchen with one of her daughters.

"Down—to the corner. I'll be back in a minute."

"I want them dishes you used washed," her aunt told her. "I don't want no dirty dishes around here."

"I'll be right back," Taylor said.

The aunt followed her to the doorway and watched as she went downstairs.

Her feet were tired in the flat little shoes. She had to buy new ones. She had to get Mother a pair that didn't hurt her feet. She had to get Mother in a hospital where she could get care. . . .

She rang the bell a long time before he came.

"Hello," she said.

He didn't say anything. He looked frightened, and there was a crushed and bluish look about his face.

"You like this?" he said, following her eyes. "Some guy started it. Then the cops—the Rollers—finished it. They did it to make me look pretty."

He knew she respected law and order, but she hated it now that it had done this to him.

"Can I come in?" she said.

He let her come in. "My sister's gone out. I guess it'll be O.K."

With the door closed, she too was frightened, and she tried to smile. "How are you, Andy?"

He watched her. "I'm all right."

"Would you like to—to talk with me for a while?" she said. "I'm on my way to the drugstore. Would you like to come with me?"

"It's too cold out."

The house was warm, much warmer than the one she lived in. She felt the warmth touch her legs and cheeks. She smiled to keep her voice from sounding jerky when she spoke.

"Let's sit down," she said.

"How long can you stay?"

"Not long."

"Why did you come here?"

190

She tried to keep smiling, but her lips pulled down, her heart beat faster. "I just wanted to talk."

He shook his head. "Why did you come?"

"Just to talk. We're neighbors. Is there anything wrong in— talking?"

"I don't dig you," he said. "Ever since I met you, Miss, I been goin crazy!" Then he gripped her hand tightly. "What is it? What's makin me feel this way? Can you tell me?"

She could find no answer. Watching him, she could only think of his closeness, his hands, his lips and body, his eyes which proved he wanted and needed her. She could feel the heat growing in her again, but it was the most wonderful thing she had ever felt.

"Kiss me," she told him, the breath leaving her with the words. "Kiss me, Andy, kiss me, kiss me. . . ."

His hands dug into her back, clawed a handful of her thick hair, made her body mould and come alive against him, into him.

His lips set her face afire. "Oh, Miss, you don't know how I been feelin! You don't know what I been doin!"

"Let's love each other, Andy," she said against his throat. "Let's just love each other!"

"I prayed," he said, his hands exploring the softness of her. "I swear I'll never use no more again! Please, I'll never use no more!"

Somehow they found his room, and when the door closed they found a new world, the joy hidden in their young bodies. Their flesh and lips meshed, and they were shocked and awed by the completeness of themselves.

They lay together, and their bodies married in repose brought back full consciousness. She told him of her life, all the things that made her life.

It was a while before he began to speak, but when he did he found that he could not lie. He told her the evil of himself and it meant nothing to her, because she had seen the good.

"I don't know," he said, puzzled. "I do know, I think I love you."

"I love you, Andy."

"But what can we do?" he said. "Where can we go? Somebody'll bother us. They always bother you when you've got somethin good, somethin you wanna keep!"

"We'll get married," she resolved. "Then we'd be together. We'd be strong enough together."

He kissed her smooth cheek, pulled to it irresistibly, and the touch of it coursed through him like electricity. "Yeah, Miss, we'll get married," he said. "But would you marry me?"

"I'd marry you."

"But we don't have any money."

"I have a job. I could work until you found something."

"I'd *find* somethin," he assured her. "I'd break up bricks!"

"My mother is dying."

"We could take her with us."

"We'll take her, then."

"Where could we go? We gotta go somewhere. I don't want you around the Scene."

"Then we'll go," she said. "But, Andy, there are places like the Scene all over. If we have enough faith in each other, we don't have to be afraid of them."

"I don't want anything buggin me, and when you're around somethin like the Scene, somethin's always buggin you."

She put her hand over his mouth. "Don't think about it. Let's stop thinking about bad things."

She sat up in bed suddenly, looking out the window. "Andy, I've got to get home. I've been over here for hours!"

They got up and began to dress. The phone rang, and he went out in the hall to answer it.

"Hello?" he said.

She hurried into her clothes, worried about her mother.

"Rudy?" he said from the hall. "Nothin right now. . . . Who'd you say? Rudy Black. Oh yeah, what you want, man? . . . What? . . . I don't know if I can. What do you want to see me for? . . . Well, I don't know what could be that important to me. Anyway, I'm sorta tied up right now, man. Maybe I can make it later on. . . .

192

Yeah, tonight. I'll try to.... But don't wait too long for me....
O.K. See you later." The phone clicked in the cradle.

She finished dressing. "Andy, I've got to hurry. Mother is probably hungry. I've been gone almost all day."

"Miss," he said suddenly, "let's go out—just me and you! Let's go somewhere."

"But, Andy, I can't. I've got to see about my mother. I've been gone all day. I haven't had any sleep."

"Can't you just tell her you're gonna take a walk or somethin? Please, Miss . . . I got a little bread, three or four dollars. Let's go down to the dairy bar and have a couple hamburgers, then we could go to the show."

"I don't think I want to go to the show."

"Then—" He was frantic with lack of suggestions. "Let's just ride the trolley bus. Let's just ride over the city—everywhere, all over the city."

A bit reluctantly, she nodded her head. "I've got to make sure Mother's all right."

"Wait a minute," he said happily. "Lemme get my jacket."

Together they left the apartment. The evening was cold and it nipped briskly at them.

He waited impatiently for her in front of the tenement, and as the time drew on, he began to fear that he had lost her. Lost her . . . *Please, God* . . . He would die if she didn't come, for he had never had a dream come true before, and knowing dreams he dreaded their inevitable anticlimax. No dream was as horrible as the Scene and stuff, and no dream was as good as the Miss. He could not lose her now, because then he would never be able to kick his habit.

"I'm back," she said in the darkness. "My aunt is mad, but I don't care. I told my mother we wouldn't be gone long."

"You told her—about me?"

"No. But I wanted to, I wanted to real bad. I just said I was going for a walk."

"Miss—Miss, I'm so happy!"

"Oh, Andy! I love you!"

"Where should we go? What should we do, Miss?"

"Don't call me 'Miss,' Andy. Call me Taylor."

"I like Miss better, 'cause you're a lady, just like them crazy broads you see pictures of in the society pages of the newspapers."

"Say it—say Taylor."

"Taylor," he said.

Her lips kissed his mouth. "It sounds formal when you say it. Just keep on calling me Miss."

They went down the street quickly, as though they would be late if they didn't hurry, as though the world were holding a party in their honor and they were late for it.

The wind howled tentatively out of the branches of the trees; behind them the Scene was already lighting up, but together they shut off the terror of its world.

"I love you, Miss. . . . I wish I could share everything with you. Remember the first time I saw you? Through the bathroom windows?"

"You're making me blush!"

"You got the smoothest skin a girl ever had, Miss."

They passed a store window, still brightly decorated for Christmas. It reminded him of the Santa in the department store and he told her all about it. He sighed contentedly. "I wonder if Santa ever got on Dumbo's back. Poor sucker, he should be me."

"Why?"

"Because then he wouldn't have to think about gettin on some dopey elephant's back."

"If he were you, he'd have someone to help him."

"Would you help me up, Miss?"

"I'd help you do anything."

"Will you help me now? Will you help me get over this hump?"

"You know I will."

"Let's go someplace where there ain't no people."

But there were people everywhere.

"Let's go to the overpass on Pennsylvania and watch the cars go under."

"O.K."

His thin jacket hugged his meager ribs tightly against the cold; her thick hair began to blow in the late-afternoon wind, whipping like black velvet about her face, covering her nose and eyes.

They reached the railing of the bridge and looked down on the cars, their headlights like eyes, their whizzing shapes barely distinguishable.

"You wouldn't think so many people had places to go," he said vaguely.

"I don't want to go. I want to stop. I'd want us to stop someplace, for good."

"We will. We'll have kids. And they'll never know about a city. I wouldn't let 'em come into a city."

"Oh, it seems so far off," she sighed.

"Yeah, it does."

"I wish it could happen tomorrow. I wish it could happen right now."

She leaned over and kissed him; his mouth felt cold, and she shivered.

"Andy . . ."

"Yeah?"

"Let's get married soon. Let's don't wait. We don't have to live together—just so long as we're married."

"When do you want to?"

"As soon as you want me. Tonight, if you want to."

"Miss . . ."

"Don't you *want* to marry me?"

"You know I do—but I want to have *somethin* for you. I don't even have the bread to pay for the license."

"I've got some money—"

"No, I wouldn't let you pay for it! I've got to pay for it with my own money. Maybe I might be able to borrow some money from my sister until I get a job."

"Andy, I've got a funny feeling. I don't want to wait!"

"Funny feelin about what, Miss? We could wait just a little while, couldn't we?"

She didn't answer.

"Please, Miss, I love you, you know that."

She turned her face to the cars, going, going.

He felt her shiver next to him, and he put his arm about her slim waist.

"I hate to go back," she said.

"Me too."

The cars sped under, *swoom*!

"It makes me dizzy to look," she said.

"Let's go back," he said.

They *had* to go back.

"Andy," she murmured, as they walked, "does it hurt to have babies?"

He laughed. "Now, why you ask me that? How'd I know?"

She looked up at him seriously. "Today was the first time for me. I never did before. Will I have a baby?"

"Is that why you want to get married in such a hurry?"

"No, that has nothing to do with it. I want to get married because I think we need each other right now. It wouldn't matter about a baby."

"I don't know. I guess it does."

"What? Matter about the baby?"

"Naw, havin 'em. I guess it does hurt."

She closed her eyes and leaned her head against him. "It hurts to make them, so I guess it hurts to have them."

"Don't you know anything?" he grinned. "It only hurts the first time."

"I guess you think I'm pretty dumb."

"Naw, Miss, you're the smartest girl I've ever met."

She looked up, surprised. "We're back already!"

"I didn't even notice."

The tenements loomed over them ominously.

"Kiss me, Andy."

He kissed her; his mouth tasted the funny, ripe sweetness of her mouth.

196

"Don't go, Andy. . . ."

"We'll see each other tomorrow, Miss."

"What are you going to do tonight?"

"A friend called me. I said I might see him."

"Andy—"

"Don't worry. I won't fool with no stuff."

Her hand squeezed his hand, then suddenly she came back and kissed him hungrily.

"I'm afraid, Andy!"

"Don't, Miss! Nothin's gonna happen."

"I love you, Andy. Please don't go away from me."

"Where could I go? See how small the world is: we were livin next door to each other all the time."

"Good night, Andy."

"Good night, Miss."

"I love you!"

"And I love you."

Rudy put the phone down.

From the lush living room of the apartment he could hear The Man's TV going. Somehow it seemed funny that The Man should watch TV.

He started toward the beaded curtains that divided the living room from the hallway, wondering now why he had made the promise, why The Man had become so afraid. Afraid—yeah, that was the way he was.

So Sonny was busted—so what? The Man had lost pushers before and it hadn't bothered him. Rudy didn't understand, but he wasn't a dummy; he could feel things. He knew he was under suspicion for Sonny's bust. The Man was testing him, figuring that if he *had* snitched out on Sonny, or was working for the Feds or the Rollers now, he wouldn't do what he was getting set to do.

The Man was smart: taking Andy out of the picture and making sure of Rudy at the same time. This flip had been slated to go, and setting up that Popeye creep had been the last straw. The Man had played it smart. Once he got word the Rollers nabbed Barris he bailed him out, even though he knew the meet with the snitch was a doublecross. Barris had been mussed up some by Davis, but he hadn't spilled. They'd put out an all-points on Barris when they found he'd jumped his bond, but they'd never find him. The Man would make sure of that.

The thought sat hard in Rudy's mind: it wouldn't have happened if that evil bad mouth hadn't gone out against him.

He hesitated for a moment outside the curtain. Hadn't The Man promised him a good spot, right alongside Dell, after Rudy straightened out this business? Maybe even the runner's spot that Dell had taken up when Barris cut out. Dell was too important to The Man in town. Anyway, he was old; he wasn't leery enough.

Nothing was worth risking that chance. If The Man wanted proof of his loyalty, he'd get it!

Rudy swelled with the thought. He was a thoroughbred, The Man had said so himself. . . .

"They ever catch up with Popeye, they can pressure him plenty on the stand with that snitch's testimony," he had said. "But no snitch—no testimony, no pressure. It's as simple as that."

"I'll kill the sonofabitch, Floyd; I'll snuff the bastard," Rudy had said.

"I'll give you a grand. I don't care how you do it, only do it clean."

"Don't worry, Floyd."

"If anything goes wrong, rely on me. Keep your mouth shut. I know you can do that. You're a thoroughbred. . . ."

Sure of his worth now, Rudy thrust out his mouth and called into the living room, "I'm on my way."

A deep, cautious voice came back. "Good. Watch your step, Black."

The TV played on.

Behind the wheel of the big automobile, Rudy tingled, fired with the importance of his mission. He had no doubts that he could carry it through.

In his pocket were thirty grains of battery acid, four caps of high-potency heroin, syringe and cooker, and ten hundred-dollar bills.

He was still high off the ounce he had promised himself for Christmas, and he had hopes that the new year would show him even greater riches.

All he had to do was kill Andy Hodden.

February

16

IN THE MIDST of the Scene there was a place the Panic could not reach.

Here boys and girls, both white and Negro, clustered together under the banner of the Youth Center; they swam, played basketball or volleyball, and participated in dances, cleanup drives and fund-raising for the good of the community.

Here they were taught the importance of pride and the values of competition. They were taught that no loyal member of his club should drink or take narcotics, that he should not steal, fight, lie, be promiscuous or lax in personal cleanliness, and that at all times he should show a respect for authority.

These youngsters, guided by the hand of a thickset Negro, were unaware of their enormous potential good in the evil vortex of the Scene.

The Scene was on all sides, but strangely it did not seek sanctuary in the Youth Center. Here the evidence of clean living was too strong, and clean living was as deadly to the Scene's people as the impersonal ruthlessness of the Panic itself.

And right now, the Scene was fighting for its life.

Davis and Patterson came into the gym quickly.

A short, dark, muscular man, in a T shirt with YOUTH CENTER curving over his chest, met them. "Can I do something for you guys?"

Davis, his nose bandaged into a flat, white boar's snout, showed his badge. "Want to ask you a few questions. Your name Carlisle Knop?"

"That's right."

"You're in charge of the Center?"

"Yeah. I've been instructor here since we first opened six years ago."

"I guess you get a lot of kids in here."

"Hummm, yeah, I guess so. Almost every kid in the neighborhood stops in here, white, colored, both. It's actually a youth *club* with membership, but if a kid doesn't want to join, we don't make him. We let him have access to all the facilities, boxing, swimming, basketball—you know. Then if he decides to stay, all we ask is that he participate in the Center's functions."

"Citizenship training, huh?"

"That's our purpose."

"What kind of attendance do you have?"

"Oh, I guess about a hundred, hundred and twenty a night. About seventy-five are regular members. The others, who come in just to pass the time, are generally known by us as 'drifters.' These are the ones we usually direct a stiff plea to; some of our members have infiltrated nonmember groups, and they put on the pressure to get them to join up. We only get two or three new members a week, but I think that's damn good."

"Yeah. You ever have any trouble?"

Carlisle grinned. "Nothing that I can't handle. Every now and then we have a gang fight around the neighborhood—the Rockets, Cool Daddies and Shakers—but I'm pretty sure none of our regular members belong to those groups. Around here, we usually keep things going smoothly."

"What about whiskey and reefer? Drugs?"

"That's specifically forbidden by our Center. We don't allow any violations, and anyone caught is either fined—if he is a member—or ousted, or both."

"How can you know when dope gets in this place or not?"

Carlisle shrugged. "Simply this: as long as a user is in this building, he is *not* using. The regulations see to that. And while he's not using, I have a chance to show him why he should *never* use again."

"How can you do that?" asked Patterson.

204

"By using arguments backed up by facts and figures a kid can understand. I can show them that thirty per cent of all the crimes committed last year were committed by drug addicts. I give them the statistics on the life expectancy and mental retardation caused by narcotics. I'm getting to some of them, I know that from those members I was telling you about who infiltrate the gangs. They keep their eyes open, and any time they spot a new youngster smoking reefer or using heroin, they let me know. Those kids are the ones I direct my arguments at."

"That sounds pretty weak to me," Davis said.

Carlisle frowned. "It might sound that way, mister, but how else can you fight dope? These kids can get heroin with less trouble than penicillin. I could ask five youngsters right now, thirteen-and fourteen-year-olds, to go out and bring me back twenty-five sticks of marijuana. So what can I do? Sometimes I can get to a user—some kid who really is scared by what he's doing—and he comes to me for help."

"Did Andy Hodden ever come to you for help?" Davis said.

Carlisle looked at both of them. "You mean Flip?"

"That's who I mean," Davis said. "Did you ever talk to him?"

Carlisle paused, remembering. "I knew the kid was on stuff. He used to come around the Center quite a bit, two, three years ago. He was one of our drifters, but he indulged a little more than others. He was a good forward in basketball, and I tried to get him to join the basketball team, but he was never too interested. I guess dope wouldn't let him be."

"Did you ever get to talk to him?" Patterson put in. "Did he ever act as though he wanted to stop? Did this"—he looked around the gym—"have any effect on him?"

Carlisle folded his arms, sensing Patterson's sincerity. He frowned, thoughtful. "You know, mister, that's a question I keep asking myself all the time, and I've come to this conclusion: if you can make a kid *want* to be helped, then this gym, this club, the games and dances and things, are effective. But you can't cure without the desire for the cure. Now take this Hodden boy, for example. I actually think he didn't want to be doing the things he

205

did, but the guy he ran around with, an older fella named Walsh, seemed to make dope a prerequisite of their association. To be regular, to be 'down,' Hodden had to indulge. To remain a regular, he had to continue using."

"You know the little bastard's dead, don't you?" Davis asked. He touched his bandaged nose.

Carlisle seemed angered, not by the words so much as by the way Davis said them. He uncrossed his arms. "I heard it, yeah. One of the kids told me. He got a hot shot?"

"That's right. We know why he got it; what we want to know is, who gave it to him?"

Carlisle smiled, stiffly. "*I* didn't. But I'll say this—he got his hot shot when he first put a needle in his arm."

"Who'd he fool around with? What girls? Who didn't like him?"

"Nobody liked him when he came around. There were girls, but I can't remember their names now or even their faces. That was over three years ago, mister."

"The reason I asked about girls was because I think our little dead friend was lured to a setting."

Carlisle's eyes squinted, watching Davis. He said, tightly, "You won't find Hodden's killer in my club, mister; you'll have to go somewhere else."

Davis shifted, interested. "Where do you suggest?"

"Anywhere—outside the building," Carlisle said.

Davis' mustache twitched on his upper lip. "Just what the hell do you mean?"

Patterson touched Davis' arm. "I think we'd better leave."

Davis snatched away, with a glare at him. "We're not leaving until I find out what this sonofabitch is talking about. He said himself that there are addicts who use this place. Maybe one of 'em slipped that hot pill in Hodden's fix." He turned to Carlisle. "Why are you trying to protect him?"

"If there's a murderer here, I *want* you to get him—I'm not trying to protect him. But you know well and good that no addict such as you describe would come here. Drugs would not allow them to swim, to box, to do any of the strenuous activities which they *must* take a part in the minute they walk in that door."

Carlisle spoke determinedly. "If you want Andy Hodden's murderer, look for someone who could gain from his death. Look for someone completely unscrupulous. And you can start looking out there, in the jungle, not here among decent kids playing volleyball and basketball. You do me a favor, mister, and just leave my young people alone!"

Davis' big body leaned forward. "Why, you fat-mouthed preacher! Do you think you're actually doing these young punks any good? You're wasting your time! If one kid here, just one, grows up to be worth the formaldehyde it takes to flush his belly out when he kicks off, I'll kiss your ass!"

Carlisle smiled, relaxing. "You wouldn't like to make a bet on that, would you?"

BEFORE THEY knocked off that evening, Patterson cornered Davis in one of the interrogation rooms.

"Look," he said, "about this Hodden thing, Mance. I know you're doing it your way and all that, but I'd like you to give me special permission to cover a few points."

"You feel I've overlooked a few?"

"That's not what I meant at all, but the boy's been dead a while now and we still haven't turned anything up. Flaubert's raising so much hell, I expect the whole Sixth to be purged if something isn't done."

"Listen," Davis said. "Flaubert or nobody else tells me how to do my job! I'm waiting for a damned good reason. I know these people, I know the Scene. Andy's killer has put a straitjacket on the Scene and that's something it isn't going to stand for; it's gonna cough our man up, you watch and see."

"I don't think it's the Scene that's in question here," Patterson said, looking at him oddly.

"I *know* that goddamned place!" Davis shouted, his nose shiny and blue where the bandage had been removed. "Where's the dope? Huh? Can you answer that? How come The Man's gas line is all choked up? Why's dago-town starving for dope?" He shook his finger at Patterson. "It's because that boy is dead, that's why! This is a vicious circle; you trying to tell me you can break it all at once?"

"You don't *want* to get rid of it completely, do you?" Patterson's eyes grew big with the question. "Mance, I actually think you're glad to have the Scene kicking around!"

"You're crazy!" But Davis was frightened by Patterson's biting insight. "Now listen here, you goddamn college punk—"

"You're scared to get rid of the Scene!" Patterson went on. "You *could* if you wanted to, but you're really scared to. What are you scared of, Mance?"

Davis stood up, his face contorted with anger. "You and your sonofabitching transfer, and you call *me* scared! If I run into something hard, brother, I don't chicken out! I take that goddamn thing in my hands and I crush it, I chew it up! I may be scared of it, but I tear it to pieces!" His hands made wild ripping motions. "What I'm scared of, I destroy! What do you do, you little nothing? You run, you run and hide!"

Patterson's head bowed. Having discovered the weakness of Davis, he discovered the weakness of himself.

Davis sat back down, deflated, it seemed. He had said Patterson was running, but the accusation more clearly applied to himself, although he couldn't bring himself to admit that.

"What do you intend to do?" he said quietly, almost defeatedly.

Patterson could barely get himself together for a moment. In the back of his mind he realized that it was a sense of obligation to Andy Hodden, a sense of responsibility actually, that made him want to bear down, to work to the point of exhaustion if necessary, to find the killer.

Even more, spurred on by his wife's attitude, he wanted to prove himself capable. During the past few days, that had become most important.

"I asked what do you figure on doing," Davis said.

"Well," Patterson stammered. "I'd like to go over and see Hodden's sister, take a look around the place. . . ."

"Don't you think that's been done already?"

"I guess so, but what's the harm in doing it again?"

Davis grunted, gingerly touching the darkened area of his nose. "What else you got in mind?"

"Well . . . I'd go up on the Scene, ask around, see some people who knew Hodden—"

Davis scoffed. "I'm gonna let you go ahead, college boy. You got my permission to run your ass ragged." He poked Patterson in the chest with a stiff finger. "But you just remember you got a lot to learn. You gotta crawl before you can walk."

Patterson recalled that someone else had said something similar to him, but he couldn't, at that moment, remember who it was.

The Scene eluded him. He canvassed without result, and the lights of the streets warned him away, like an enemy.

On his way home, he stopped at the apartment where Andy Hodden used to live.

Jacqueline answered the door.

"My name is Patterson, miss." He showed her his badge. "I'm from the narcotics division of the Sixth Precinct. I'd like to talk with you, if you don't mind. You're Andy Hodden's sister, aren't you?"

She nodded and let him come in.

He stood there awkwardly for a moment. "Do—do you mind if I look around, Miss Hodden?"

She shrugged listlessly. "If you want to. The other policemen have been here already."

He went through the rooms with their meager furnishings. Everything was neat and orderly if a bit shabby; every article seemed to have its own spot.

"Is this your brother's room?" he called to her.

"Yes. Next to the bathroom."

He looked about. "Would you come here a second, Miss Hodden?"

"What is it?" she said, coming in.

"Is this where your brother was found?"

"Yes. On the floor over there." She pointed near the foot of the bed.

Patterson went into the room. "Is everything just the way it was the night he was killed?"

Her eyes scanned everything carefully. "Yes . . . I guess it is. The other officers didn't take anything away."

He went over to the dresser, where a record player and stack of albums sat. He thumbed through the albums, then turned to her. "Your brother liked music, I can see."

She nodded. "He had that thing going practically all the time."

"Is that what prompted you to come in here when you arrived home that morning? I understand you found the body rather late."

"Yes, my boy friend and I had gone to several parties." She blushed self-consciously. "But the record player wasn't going when I got home. His door was wide open and the light was burning. I thought he'd fallen asleep, so I went in to turn it out. That's—that's when I found him."

Patterson was remembering some of the things about addicts he'd learned from Davis, especially a point about their making up where it was most comfy. Why hadn't Andy prepared his music, prepared himself for an airborne interlude of nodding?

He recalled the night they had tried to apprehend Georgie Barris: Hadn't Andy said he was trying to kick? He knew, without Davis' informing him, that most addicts were recidivists; but there seemed to be something about Andy's vow to reform that rang too sincerely. Why had he gone back to drugs? The answer was so simple, he cursed himself for not seeing it before: Andy had been *enticed* into using drugs again.

He came out of the room. The boy's sister seemed a nice enough girl, and it was apparent that she had some education.

"I know this is painful," he said, after they got to the front again, "but could you tell me anything about your brother, something that'd help?"

Her tiny laugh was mirthless and tired. "I guess Andy knew he was going to get hurt, Mr. Patterson, but he didn't seem to care. A little while ago, he came home all beaten up. I tried to find out who'd done it, but he wouldn't tell me a thing. It was almost as if he was glad he'd been hurt." She sighed. "He was little and afraid. It wasn't so bad when my mother was living, but after she died Andy seemed to get worse. Our father was a drunkard and Andy hated him for it." She turned, walked away from him slowly. "I don't know. After Daddy died, I was just too weak. I could see my brother going from bad to worse, but I just couldn't *do* anything about it."

Patterson twirled his hat in his hands awkwardly. "Well, I think that's all, Miss Hodden." He reached into his inside coat pocket for a card. "If anything else turns up, something you think we ought to know, I wish you'd give me a call at this number."

"Sure," she said.

"Well—good-by, now."

"Sure," she said again.

On his way downstairs, the shame he felt at her mention of Andy's beating was obscured by a stubborn nagging in his mind. Something was to be seen, if only he could find it. . . .

18

SONNY TUBBS was wheeled into the interrogation room at the county jail, where Patterson, Davis, and a Federal man named Mac-Mahon sat waiting. Sonny seemed shrunken, welded to his chair, a small lump of crooked flesh. He was crying.

"Shut up your slobbering, Tubbs," the Federal man said. "We want to ask you some questions."

Sonny's voice halted in the middle of a sob. "Ain't you through with me yet? You stuck me for three years already. Why don't you let me alone? I'm dyin, I'm sick!"

"He went to court today," MacMahon explained. "Three years in the federal hospital at Lexington."

Davis grunted. "You guys go too easy on 'em."

"Can I see my mother?" Sonny whimpered. "I want to see my mother."

"She's waiting downstairs," MacMahon told him. "Just come on and co-operate with us for a minute and we'll let you see her."

"We want to know about Andy Hodden," Davis said. "You know him?"

"I used to turn him on all the time," Sonny said.

"He's dead," Patterson said. "He got a hot shot."

"I don't care," Sonny wailed. "I don't care!"

"We wanna know who might have given it to him," Davis said.

"I don't know," the cripple whined. "I been in jail. How can I know who gave it to him?"

"You said you used to turn him on," Patterson said.

"That don't make me know who bumped him. Lots of cats didn't go for him because he was snitchin. Anybody could have give him a hot shot."

"Who do you think?" Davis asked.

"I don't know."

"Who do you *think?*" Davis insisted.

"It might have been anybody," Sonny said, his voice indefinite. "Ace . . . Dell, Bertha—"

Then his eyes flickered. "What about Rudy Black?" he said hopefully.

"He's got too much to lose," Patterson put in. "A Cadillac and a prostitute. He wouldn't risk them."

"Come on, Tubbs," MacMahon prompted. "You can think, you can think good. Just remember, you'll be getting out of Lexington one of these days. If you co-operate, perhaps you'll get some consideration, a whole lot of consideration."

"Man, there's a million junkies in the world!" Sonny moaned. "How do you think I should know which one slid the snuff powder to Flip?"

"Give us some names," Davis said. "That's all we want. Give us somebody to go after, somebody to put the heat on."

"I don't know. If Coke Prado was still operatin, I'd say he did it. Coke hated snitches."

"Coke's dead," Patterson said. However, Davis made a mental note to talk with the two kids picked up with Prado.

"There's always Georgie Barris," Patterson said. "Our boys can't pick up his trail anywhere since he was sprung on bond."

"We didn't even get a chance to sink our teeth in that guy," Davis said regretfully. "He's probably a thousand miles away by this time—he wouldn't have paused to give Andy a hot shot. Anyway, Andy wouldn't have let him get that close."

"What about your connect?" MacMahon asked Sonny. "What about The Man? Couldn't he have wanted Andy out of the way?"

"I give him more credit than that," Davis said. "He's certainly not gonna do something like that himself."

"Perhaps it was some gripe another junkie had against the Hodden boy," MacMahon said.

"Andy burned Freddy Arrujo a while back," Sonny said.

"A burn is always reason enough," Patterson said.

"Mance," MacMahon said, "that leak you called me about last week—got anything to go on?"

"All I've got is a hunch," Davis told him. "And I don't like it." He stood up slowly. "One thing, though: the streets are clean. You can't find a pusher anywhere, from Hundred-and-tenth to Fifty-fifth."

Patterson moved in his chair. "I was down on the Scene. The feel of dope is still pretty big."

"Can I see my mother now?" Sonny said. "What'll happen after I do that trey?" he asked MacMahon.

"You'll get what's due you," MacMahon promised.

"You've helped a lot, Sonny," Patterson told him gently. "I hope you make out at Lexington."

"And don't use too much stuff on your first day out," Davis encouraged wryly, moving toward the door. "*You* might get a hot shot."

The knife of heroin had cut a deep swath in the faces of Tippy and Frankie. Though their eyes were listless, a small gleam of physical awareness was returning. They were free of the habit, and the world around them was becoming a stark and brutal reality.

"What they got you boys booked on?" Davis asked after they had sat down in the interrogation room.

Frankie eyed the detectives with some hostility. "They say possession, but we ain't been to court yet."

"I asked the prosecutor to hold your cases up," Davis said.

"*You* did?" Tippy said.

"That's right." Davis looked at him. "If you boys are thinking like you should, maybe you won't have to go to court at all."

Frankie was suspicious. "What'll we have to do?"

"Tell me all you know about Coke Prado."

The boys looked at each other.

"Why'd you fellas take him out of Municipal Hospital?"

They clamped their lips.

Davis turned to Patterson. "You got your notebook?"

Patterson took it from his inside pocket.

Davis eyed the ceiling thoughtfully. "Put down, *Un-cooperative—recommend sentences of from two to five years . . .*"

"Who do you think you're kidding?" Frankie sneered. "Since when can anybody but a jury recommend sentences?"

"Since I've busted about two or three dozen punks like you," Davis said. "You'll meet a guy up at the reformatory named Benny Gibson. Ask him who recommended his five- to ten-year stretch."

The boys looked at each other again, this time fearfully.

After a respectable and face-saving silence, Tippy spoke. "Coke told us he'd do us a lot of good with The Man if we got him out of the hospital—"

"He said he could take us right to The Man after he'd had a fix or two," Frankie added ruefully. "He said The Man couldn't help but take us in after what he'd told us."

Davis straightened in his chair. "He told you something, huh?"

"Maybe he was lying." Tippy shrugged. "He was out of his mind most of the time—he probably was just talking."

"Maybe so, maybe not," Davis said. "What did he tell you?"

"Something about a pipeline," Frankie replied. "Coke used to be The Man's pipeline, said he even made the big connect across the border for The Man."

Davis motioned to Patterson, but his pencil was already busy in the notebook.

"How'd they handle it?" Davis said. "Did he tell you that?"

Frankie suddenly realized he was co-operating with the police, and bowed his head shamefully. "Coke—he said he was connect and pipeline when The Man first started."

"What happened?"

"The syndicate swallowed the operation, he said. Then he only became the line, until him and The Man couldn't get together about dough."

Davis' red mustache wiggled almost comically with anticipation. "So that was it! Who handled the connect after he got shoved?"

"You mean borderside?"

"Did he tell you that too?" Davis said, scarcely believing it could be possible. "I meant the pipeline, who took his place?"

"I don't know about that, but he told us some kid came in a little after he started the line. He was young, Coke said, and his

215

folks had a lot of dough. He said the kid made so many trips to Mexico, the customs knew him personally. That's why he didn't have any trouble."

"Did he tell you the kid's name?"

Frankie looked at Tippy for verification. "Balsom, wasn't it?"

"Balsom?" Davis said.

"More like Halston," Tippy corrected. "Yeah, I think that's it."

"Halsted?" Davis said. "Was his name Halsted?"

"That's it for sure," Frankie said. "I remember it now."

The big wide smile threw Davis' hard face out of kilter, and Patterson was surprised to realize it was the first time he had ever seen the sergeant grin. "Remember what I told you?" Davis said, thumping his shoulder with a hard hand of joy. "About the Halsted kid and that junkie Barris?"

Patterson's face lighted up. "There could be the connection, but the difference in social worlds—"

"I haven't figured that out yet," Davis said, "but I'm gonna find out just what the hell's going on!" He turned to the boys. "What else did Coke tell you?"

"That's all," Frankie said. "He said, with that information, we could go right to The Man and put squeezers on him."

"You be damn glad you didn't !" Davis told him. "Both you guys would probably be lying down in the morgue like another kid I knew!"

Tippy waved his hand at the men, almost like a student trying to attract the attention of the teacher. "You—you said we might not have to go to court."

"That's right," Davis said, "but after hearing what you boys have got to say, we're gonna have to keep you around a little while longer."

"It's a dirty doublecross!" Frankie yelled.

Davis glared at him. "I don't doublecross, kid. You may not know it, but you're safer in jail right now than out. Now shut your mouth and do as you're told, and you'll be out of here quicker than you think."

Frankie, calmed a little by Davis's brusqueness, stood in front

216

of him as they started out. "Look," he said hesitantly, "my old man—well, I'd appreciate it if you called my old man." The heroin look was dark and sorry on his face. "Would you tell 'im—would you—?" He struggled for the right words. "Well, would you ask him if he forgives me? Would you ask him if it's O.K. if I come home?"

Davis considered the request, squinting his eyes. "You're Wysocki, aren't you?"

"Yes, sir."

"If your old man says no to both questions, what then?"

Frankie looked down at the floor, and a small shudder passed over his shoulders. "I don't know," he said. "I guess I won't know until he does."

COLD SETTLED upon the city ruthlessly. The slush froze into sharp, jagged, miniature peaks in the streets, slashing at the tires that passed over them. The night was black.

In the house on Ninetieth, Constance Purtell finished packing her suitcase and carried it into the living room. Ace sat slumped at the table, a sick smile on his face, watching her. "You still goin?" he said.

"Yes." She went to the hall closet to get her coat. When she came back, Ace had not moved.

"You gonna change your mind fast, baby."

"I don't think so."

"Do you need some money?"

"No."

She felt so odd. She hadn't thought leaving Ace would be like this, so easy and calm. In her mind, this scene between Ace and herself had been so different, had been violent shapes that frightened her imagination.

She moved over to the table; she even touched him. "You—you understand why I've got to stop, Tommy? Can you understand?"

The smile was beginning to fade from his big mouth. "I dig."

"I want you to realize how I feel. . . ."

"You need a fix?" he said hopefully.

She shook her head. "I had one this afternoon. When I get to Municipal, I want to start right in kicking."

"Then start movin," he said harshly.

"I want you to know several things—"

"Get the hell out of here," he said quietly, the pain deep in his eyes.

She went over and picked up her suitcases.

"Wait a minute," he called. "Go ahead. What is it you want me to know?"

She came back over to the table. For a while she just stood there looking at him. "I know you've been real good to me, Tommy. I want you to know I appreciate it. If there were only some way I could show it—"

"You're showin it," he said.

She went on, as if not hearing his words. "But—you treating me the way you did—that was only natural to you. You expected and got nothing but my body for it."

He stopped smiling. "Listen, you whore, that's *all* I wanted from you!"

"That wasn't all you wanted," she said. "The other part I wasn't able to give you; what you paid for my body wouldn't allow me to give it to you. Maybe if things had been different, if we could have known each other without stuff—"

He looked away from her, his voice tight, the ugly little face shielded by a hand. "Don't give me that crap! On the street you never would've looked at me."

"Tommy, looks don't make up everything a woman wants in a

218

man. There're things about you a whole lot of handsome men could never have."

He looked up at her. "You don't ever think about me for nothin! You're leavin me right when I need you most. The Panic is gonna stay for a while. What will I do while it's on? I'll be here all by myself."

"I'm going to get rid of this habit," she told him. "Then I'm going back to live with my mother."

"And what about *me?*"

"The Panic will be over soon. You'll make out, Tommy."

"Connie baby—"

"Don't try to make me stay, Tommy. I won't let you."

"What are people gonna think?" he cried.

"I don't care what the Scene thinks."

His eyes grew misty with tears. "What about—about other things?"

"My body? You won't be losing anything. With stuff, you can have almost any woman on the Scene—you could have three or four at once. Maybe they can give you what I can't."

He began to cry, and it was frightening to her. "Baby, go on to the hospital and kick and come back—please!"

"Tommy . . ."

He clasped his hands together as though he were praying. "I love you, I swear to God I love you! If you want me to leave stuff alone all the way, I'd do it. I'd do anything. I'll go right out to the box factory in the mornin and get a haim! Only please don't leave me, Connie." He groped for her blindly. "I'd do anything for you, Connie."

"I don't love you," she said. She felt her heart constrict into a little ball, felt her lips chop the words off raggedly. "I don't even like you, Tommy."

"I don't care," he slobbered. "I don't care!"

She tried to keep from shuddering. "I couldn't stand living with you without stuff. Can't you understand that? Wouldn't you feel it? I'd have to start using all over again in order to stand you."

"Baby, I'd do anything!"

"I can't stand it, Tommy!" she said, almost screaming. "Heroin's got me so twisted up I—I can't think." She felt herself weakening. "The only thing you can do for me is leave me alone. I hate you!" She took her hand from him. Now there was no feeling. She went to pick up her suitcases once more.

"I'd do anything, Connie, anything!"

She started toward the door. She could hear him coming after her, the sound of his wild sobbing echoing through the house. "Connie! I got three hundred things. They're all yours, baby. Please don't freeze on me, baby! You can have anything you want, any goddamn thing in the world!" He ran around in front of her, his eyes wide and staring up, pleading at her, his gnomelike face streaked with tears. He held a handful of white capsules up to her, like a sacrifice. "All *these*, baby! Every one of 'em is yours. Everything I got, Connie. Connie, I'd die for you. Just name it and I'll do it."

"Just leave me alone!" she screamed, shoving the capsules out of her face. "That's all I want you to do—let me out of here before I go crazy."

She went past him through the door, into the night's coldness. She could feel him standing behind her in the doorway, the lights in the interior of the house stretching his crooked shadow out on the pavement.

The enormity of her leaving was as huge as death to him. When she got to the pavement, he hurled a quantity of the pills at her departing back.

"Go on, bitch!" he yelled. "I don't wantcha any damn way! Don't come back, you junkie bitch!"

He watched her fade away through the darkness, then he came down off the porch, suddenly realizing what he had done. Most of the capsules were lost, but he succeeded in finding some of them, groveling on his knees.

He got to his feet and began to run after the girl's figure, crying to the night. "Connie, Connie, come back! I'm sorry, baby! Please come back to me, Connie!"

He reached the corner of Ninetieth and Maple, but she was

nowhere to be seen. A cab pulled away down the long street, its lights blinking on top like a signal.

He stood with his head down, the tears dribbling from his eyes, the capsules of heroin dribbling from the prison of his fingers. Passers-by looked at the freakish sight, and they hurried away, they crossed the street from him.

A big hand fastened around his arm, then another hand around the other arm, and he looked up into Davis' face, then Patterson's.

Davis chuckled. "You got troubles, Ace, old boy. You got real troubles!" He took him over to the car at the curb while Patterson retrieved the fallen capsules. "Get in and let's talk 'em over, Ace. Papa Davis'll let you cry all over his great big shoulder!"

It was almost midnight. A transient couple had just left and Ella was cleaning up the room when the phone rang. By the time she got to the front desk, Lou had answered.

"Hello?" he said. "Yeah, this is Lou. . . . Ella? Who is this?"

Ella came over. "Who is it?"

Lou held her off, frowning into the mouthpiece. "Yeah. Well, what's supposed to happen now?"

Ella put her ear close to the receiver, drew back. "Sylvia?" she asked, becoming angry.

Lou nodded quickly. Then back to the phone, "Listen, I don't like this. I been tellin Ella I don't like it. You just don't count on us no more."

Ella reached for the phone. "Give it here," she snapped.

Lou pushed her hand away. He held the receiver to his chest and turned to her, jaw jutted. "Don't talk us into nothin else. I got my mind made up and I ain't gonna let nothin unmake it!" He shoved the phone at Ella and left.

Ella put her ear to the receiver quickly. "Hello?"

"Listen, doll, this is Syl. I want one of those pounds you've got, right away."

"Something big?"

"A guy here in the city thinks the Panic is a fine time to move.

He wants to set up around Hundredth Street, a little away from the Scene."

"He's crazy," Ella said. "The Rollers are all over since that snitch got it. It's too dangerous."

"I don't give a damn how dangerous it is to him. He's been dealing for a few days and he thinks he knows everything. We won't argue because he's got kilo money. When he turns this over, he plans to buy the supply, everything we've got."

"He's crazy," Ella said again, then she became conscious of Sylvia's last words. "Buy everything?"

"That's right. We're going to close up shop."

"I—I didn't think it'd happen so soon."

"Don't say you didn't have any warning. Everything's exploding. Popeye's taken off and run out with more than twenty pieces, Hodden's dead. Beeker called to say Ace has taken a fall."

"Ace?"

"It's getting too ookey! All the newspapers are playing it up."

"But—but I thought we'd wait a while."

Sylvia was surprised. "Don't tell me you need the money. You must be a millionaire right now!"

Ella pursed her lips. "Syl, let *me* buy the load. I can wait to do business."

"*I* can't sell you anything."

"Then let me talk to Floyd."

"He's not in, and if he was he wouldn't sell it to you. There's over ninety grand worth in your stash right now, retail. That's what he'd sell it to you for."

Ella thought for a moment. "I could—"

"No, you couldn't. Get that out of your mind. The Man is never wrong. You follow suit and do as I told you, you'll be in good shape."

"I—I'd still like to talk to Floyd."

"I'll tell him to call you when he gets in," Sylvia said. "Listen, when can your old man get over here with the quantity?"

"He says he's through. I can't get the old bastard to do anything."

222

"Where's Rudy?"

"In bed, him and Nina."

"Get him to bring it over."

"I told you I didn't want him knowing about me—"

"There's nothing else you can do, and I need that stuff right away."

"Can you trust him with all that?"

Sylvia's voice sounded sure. "Better than anybody else, I can trust him."

"Okay."

"Tell him to meet me on Hundred-fifth and Maple at two-thirty."

"This is your responsibility, Syl."

"I'll take care of everything. You just send him with that package."

"Tell Floyd to call me."

"Good-by," Sylvia said.

Ella hung up. She stood there a long while, a slight smile on her lips, the anger burning in her. Then she popped both her fingers loudly and went into the hall. Lou stood at the doorway of their room, watching her darkly. She went over to B-23 and knocked until Nina came. She wore only a pair of low-knotted stockings, and her breasts wearily over the apple of her smooth belly. All the shades were down and the room was dark.

"What is it?" Nina asked thickly.

"Your old man in?"

"Yeah."

"Tell him to come to the door."

"He's sleepin."

"Go wake him."

"He'll be drugged," Nina warned.

"It's important."

Nina left. Rudy appeared soon, keeping his face hidden in the room's darkness. "What is it?"

"A woman named Sylvia called and said a package would be

223

waiting here for you around two. She said you should bring it to Hundred-fifth and Maple at two-thirty."

Rudy grunted and shut the door in her face.

She turned and went over to her room. Lou still stood in the doorway.

"What happened?" he asked.

"Nothing." She tried to get past him into the room, but he barred her way.

"I *told* you," he croaked. "I told you I wasn't havin no more. You's my wife, Ella. You better do what I say do."

She shoved a hand up under his throat, and he tried to wrest away but she was stronger than he. "You're gonna do what *I* say do," she told him quietly. "You dumb old bastard, I married you for a meal. I did you a favor!"

"Let me go!" He choked, but she still held him firmly.

"I want *big* things," she said, "and I'm not gonna let you get in my way. I'm too good for you!"

"You—you ain't nothin but a whore!" he gasped.

"And you ain't nothing but a stupid old man! We got thirty-five thousand dollars, you fool! If you didn't have me, how would you get thirty-five thousand dollars? You *never* would!"

"Maybe I ain't had no ed'cation like you," he said, struggling under her hands, "but I know the difference 'tween right and wrong, and you can't tell me I don't!"

"You know the difference between being hungry and full?" she said. "You know the difference between sitting in a big fine house and sitting on the street? *I* know it! I had to be a whore to learn what good things were about, and I'm not going to let you mess it up for me."

His arms surged against her strength, and he broke away from her. "I'm tellin you, Ella," he said breathlessly, "somethin's gonna happen! I'm not gonna let you mess my hotel up, I'm not gonna let you take everything I worked for."

"And before I let you take what I've worked for," she said, her lips drawing back, "I'd kill you!"

He broke past her suddenly, going to the front.

224

She was clenching and unclenching her hands with the anger. First Sylvia saying The Man wouldn't sell her the stash, and now the crazy old man!

She turned and went into her room. She closed the door behind her and went over to look down the street. The neon sign, *Lou's Hotel*, blinked eternally at the side of her window. The Scene was dead below, and she could not see a whore anywhere. Thinking of Nina, she knew the Panic had driven them inside.

She looked over to her closet, where more than three kilograms were secreted in the ceiling. Over ninety thousand dollars' worth of dope. In a brisk period, that much dope would be sold in the space of two weeks.

She couldn't see why they didn't want her to buy the stash. If they were afraid to wait until the Panic was over, that didn't mean that she had to.

She leaned against the frame of the window, smiling to herself. Or . . . she could keep it and not pay a quarter, if she wanted to. When things got too hot, The Man wouldn't waste his time fooling around with her.

Then she could set up her own operation, she could get an army of pushers from the junkies who lived in the hotel. The only thing that could possibly hold her back would be Lou.

She cast her eyes over the deadness of the Scene, and began to wonder idly about Lou . . .

20

MARSHA LEE felt them too late. She tried to get past the wide plate-glass door, but they cut her off, the man and woman. The man was big, a Negro, wearing a dark, tight-fitting suit. But the woman was white, and Marsha Lee had first thought she was a teenager: she was boyishly slim, wearing bobby socks and brown-and-white bucks. A bright red babushka, with white bells swinging musical notes from where the clappers should have been, was tied around her head. But when the woman approached her, Marsha Lee could see the thin lines in her face; the hair lapping from under the babushka looked bleached.

She touched Marsha Lee lightly on the arm and said, "Let's go upstairs, shall we, honey? Don't make a fuss, and everything'll go marvelous for you."

The man came over and took Marsha Lee by the other arm. He smiled whitely. "How are you today, sweetheart? Your womb looks a little distended."

They took her toward the service elevator. The people, shopping at various counters, had noticed nothing.

They went up in the elevator and got off at the mezzanine. Marsha Lee kept her mouth closed tightly.

When they got to an office near the stairway, she stopped suddenly and turned to the woman. "Lady, I'se from Memphis and some man did me wrong while I been here and I got a baby and that's the only reason I'se stealin. Please, lady, you gone get your stuff back anyways. Whyn't you let me go on condition I'll never come back to your store no more?"

The lines went hard in the woman's face when she looked at Marsha Lee. "You got a better line than that, haven't you, sister?"

"Please, lady—"

"Just keep your mouth shut until I tell you to open it, and everything'll be just marvelous."

The man opened the door. "Get in here."

The room was very small, without any windows, and Marsha Lee had to stand with her back against the far wall. A desk, telephone, and three chairs with deep cushions were the only furniture.

The man and woman had a whispered conversation, then the man made a quick telephone call, telling someone, "This is the girl," his mouth full and grinning as the woman roughly stripped Marsha Lee naked. She put one ermine stole, two dinner dresses with sequins, three expensive blue silk slip-and-pantie sets, into a neat pile on the desk. She held up the hooks the goods had been secured with so the man could see.

"We've got a professional, Jonesey!" she said. Then she told Marsha Lee to get dressed.

The man finished his call and came over. "I noticed something. Let me see your arm, the left one."

Marsha Lee held back, but he snatched her arm out and looked at the tracks. He laughed. "Is this the baby that no-count man give you, sweetheart?"

"Sho 'tis," the woman laughed. "Her-un's from Tennessee, with fingahs like frog laigs, and just as jumpy." She sounded as though she had crackers in her mouth.

"What's your name?" the man asked.

"Tillie Belle Curry," Marsha Lee said. "And I ain't from Tennessee, I'm from Macon, Gee Ay, and I don't know what professional is, unless it's being a professional doorshaker. And those hooks are real harmless. I got 'em from a lady store-dick in California who used 'em to scratch the ants outta her hot pants. Maybe you oughta try 'em," she told the woman.

The woman grew red. "You're in trouble now, honey. You keep that trap of yours going and you're going to be in real hot water."

"Yes, ma'am."

The big man pushed her into a chair.

"You keep your goddamn hands off me!" Marsha Lee shouted.

"My, my, my," he said. He went over and dialed again, but got a busy signal.

"Let me get my lawyer," Marsha Lee said.

"Everything'll be marvelous," the woman said. "Just keep your damn trap shut, honey, and try not to put your foot in it."

"Where the other girls?" the man asked Marsha Lee.

"What other girls?"

"You know who I'm talking about, little lady. The girls who've been working this store and all the others with you."

She looked blank. "I don't know no other girls. Just let me get at that phone so I can call my lawyer."

The woman went behind the desk and began going through Marsha Lee's purse. She paused when she found the identification card in a wallet, and looked up. "So, you're Christine Smith, eh, honey? West Hundred-thirty-seventh Street, New York?"

The big man pushed a chair next to the door and sat down.

"That's phony; I bet it's a phony. She probably knows someone there who's hep on what she's doing, who'll put up bail long distance if she gets caught the way we caught her today. Ain't that right, sweetie?"

Marsha Lee's heart beat faster as she thought of Mickey. "That's really where I live, mister. Me and my mother stay there alone, and she's poor and there's nothin she can really do for me. Please, won't you let me call her? I'll call her collect."

"A minute ago you wanted to call your lawyer," the man said. He smiled broadly. "But mama, lawyer, or nobody'll be able to spring you out of this, baby. You're going to jail."

"Unless you talk," the woman put in. "Unless you co-operate with us fast. I'm Miss Neill, of the theft adjustment department here, and this is Mr. Jones, of the Bunco Squad, downtown. We've been watching you for over a week, honey, and we've really got the thing to fry your ass—photographs. You come on and co-operate with us and everything'll be just marvelous, I promise you."

Jones shrugged. "I've got all I need. I've seen all I want to see. Except for the other two. These girls've been burning the business section up for the past month. All I want now is for you to press charges against this little booster. If she wants to act snotty, good. That makes it that much better."

"I'm sure she doesn't want to act that way," Miss Neill said. "You do want to get along with us, don't you, Christine?"

"Just let me call my mother," Marsha Lee said, beginning to feel a deep fear all at once. This wasn't the first time she'd been busted, but it was the first time she'd fallen without someone else knowing of it, someone who could help her immediately.

And now she realized she couldn't call Mickey, not even if they let her. How could she explain to him why she'd been busted alone? He was probably enraged over the fact that she'd been working and hadn't sent him any money for more than a month. What could she possibly tell him?

Could she say, "Baby darling, you know I love you, dearest darling. The money's been in the mail. . . . *Haven't you been gettin it?* . . . It's those goddamn post office people, Mickey, I swear it is, I sent the money—"

No, he wouldn't believe her. And then there were Alice and Leslie. But she couldn't even call them, because they hadn't known she was going to boost alone. They'll probably freeze altogether and leave the city, she thought frantically. They'll leave me alone, without even bus fare to New York.

Baby darling, you know I love you. . . .

But there was nothing in the thought. Everything else had been excluded when she'd decided to put her need for drugs above the unity that was necessary for her to survive. She hadn't even sent Mickey a post card. She only worked with Leslie and Alice when she was absolutely sure her refusal to come along would make them suspicious.

The danger in her resolution to work alone, in order to keep all the money and all the drugs, was clear and frightening to her now.

"Well," Jones said. He looked as though everything were ended, as far as he was concerned.

Miss Neill tried to smile warmly at Marsha Lee. "You're going to act like a grown-up woman, now, aren't you, honey? We know you're a pro. We've had you and your girl friends fingered for a long time."

"She's not going to do anything," Jones said positively. "She's a junkie—did you see the tracks on her arm? She's not going to give us anything but trouble."

"I don't think so," Miss Neill said. "I think she's giving this thing a little thought. Aren't you, Christine?"

Jones went over and fingered the pile of stolen goods. "She's got somebody special buys this stuff. I'd like to know who he is. But if she won't co-operate, this is all we need to cinch the case."

"How about it, Christine? You will help us, won't you, dear? It'll be so much better for everybody, all the way around."

Marsha Lee held her breath, looking at them. "Let me talk to my lawyer first, please. . . ."

Jones put the articles under his arm. "Let's go, sweetheart," he told Marsha Lee.

"Wait a minute, Jonesey," Miss Neill said. "Maybe she wants to say something else."

Jones looked away disinterestedly. "She's had her chance. Anyway, I've called the bureau and they're all set to make a case. Everybody wants this girl, real bad. With the stuff I've got here, the photos, and a couple of I.D.'s at a few of the other stores, we're all set."

"Well, just let her *think* for a while," Miss Neill said. "She knows that this store won't be the only one to press charges against her. She could get a lot of time in the workhouse, all in all." She turned to Marsha Lee and smiled. "How about that, honey?"

Marsha Lee felt her throat tighten, and she began to sweat slightly on her upper lip. "Please . . ."

"*Please?*" Jones said. "You don't mean to tell me it's *please* again? Just a while ago you were as hard as a little boy's peter in a fifty-cent cat house."

"*Jonesey!*" Miss Neill blushed. "It's just that Christine, or whatever her name is, has been thinking. She's got exactly four dollars and a nickel in her wallet, and she's got a habit. That's not much to count on when you're faced with a jail sentence, is it? And poor old 'Mother' won't know what happened to her little girl and probably die from worry. Isn't that right, honey?"

Marsha Lee felt as though she would get sick in a moment. "Just let me use the phone—just one time."

Jones started toward the door. "You can see she doesn't want to play ball," he said disgustedly.

"I won't believe that," Miss Neill said, making her lips go grim. "I think I can really help this girl. People should help other people when they can, and I can help Christine by not pressing those charges, if she's willing to co-operate with me."

Jones came back and threw the clothes on the desk. "All right, I'll show you. Just ask her, just see if I'm wrong. *Ask* her!"

Miss Neill said sweetly, "You don't want to go to jail, do you, honey?"

"No . . ."

"Then just tell us where to find those other girls and who your fence is."

Marsha Lee held back, feeling trapped. The name Mickey was itching her mind, and she kept thinking of a small, big-eared mouse with short pants smiling weirdly in technicolor. Her eyes began to water.

Miss Neill leaned toward her confidentially. "They won't have to know you sent us, Christine; we could say we traced them down."

"What's the matter?" Jones said. "You getting sick? Just tell us what we want to know and we'll let you go."

"I . . ."

"Yes, go on, honey, we're listening."

"Just think about doing four years in the workhouse," Jones said. "They'll be free while you're doing time."

"C'mon, honey, be a good girl, so we can let you go home."

Marsha Lee felt something break inside her. Her voice rose. "Can I use the phone first? Please let me use the phone. . . ."

"We'll let you call later," Miss Neill smiled softly. "C'mon and answer our questions, and you won't even need a phone call."

They waited.

Marsha Lee put a hand to her nose and wiped away the stream that had begun to flow from her left nostril.

"All right," Jones said. "Where're the other girls staying?"

She lied instinctively, trying to gain time. "Three-twenty-five Eighty-first, an apartment house."

"Who's your fence? Where does he stay?"

Marsha Lee hesitated. She tried to think of something believable enough. And then she thought of Rudy Black. She remembered how much she hated him, and that he had some goods belonging to the trio that he had never returned.

"C'mon, who is he, sweets?" Jones said. "Where does he stay?"

"Rudy Black," Marsha Lee said. "He stays at Lou's Hotel, on Maple. Look in his closet and you'll find a lot of hot stuff."

"Good girl!" Miss Neill cried, beaming. "You're marvelous, honey! I knew you'd co-operate."

Jones went over to the phone and made a quick call. When he came back he was grinning. "They'll let me know in a few minutes," he told Miss Neill. "This might be a ring working out, something interstate. It could be real big."

Marsha Lee started to get up. "Can I go now?"

"Sit down," Jones told her.

"You can't leave now," Miss Neill said. "Everything's just beginning."

Marsha Lee looked at them. "You said I could go if I told you what you wanted to know."

Jones laughed. "Ever hear of the doublecross, sweetie? It's been played on you. You're in just as deep, if not deeper, than you were before. Don't think we'll let *you* back on the streets, not with your talent!"

"You sonofabitch," Marsha Lee said between her teeth.

Miss Neill smiled complacently. "You'd better shut your damn mouth."

"You dirty sonsabitches!" Marsha Lee said.

Miss Neill stopped smiling. "I'm telling you, you'd better shut up."

Jones came over to her. "You say one more word and I'll slap your mouth off."

After a while the phone rang and Jones went over and answered it. He listened without replying, and when he hung up he came over and gave Marsha Lee the promised slap across the mouth.

"You little bitch!" he said.

"What's the matter?" Miss Neill said.

"The boys found that guy named Black and some stolen clothes, but the place where she said the other girls lived doesn't even exist. She was lying."

Marsha Lee began to laugh, and the room blurred with her sickness. She knew it was all over, but she didn't even care now.

She felt that she had done something fine and good, and even Mickey no longer existed for her.

She fixed a watery gaze on Jones. "The doublecross can be played both ways, you dumb bastard!"

21

DAVIS HAD to scramble to get out of the way as Patterson's car pulled into the lot. "You trying to kill me, goddamn it?"

Patterson parked and got out; he could see Davis looking at his watch as he strode over.

"Does it take you thirty damn minutes to get a cup of coffee?" Davis said.

"I've been downtown," Patterson told him.

"Downtown? Downtown for what?"

"Well, I asked headquarters to have the lab boys go over Andy Hodden's room for latent prints—"

"You *what?*"

"Mance, we've been going on the assumption that Hodden was alone when he got the hot shot. Suppose there was someone else there with him?"

Davis watched him for a while, then said cautiously, "Go ahead. It's a thought. What made you think of that?"

"Well, I remembered you saying the crime boys didn't dust the place. Everybody seemed to figure Andy picked the drugs up on the street and brought them home, but what if someone came home with him?"

Davis shook his head. "That's a mighty slim hunch to roll that crew out on."

"Well, I had a reason. Remember you told me an addict always makes up where it's comfortable—he likes to have all his conveniences while using."

Davis eyed him. "That's right."

"Hodden's sister told me that he listened to his record player perpetually, but when she found him the thing wasn't even on."

"What does that prove?"

"Well . . . nothing, I guess, only doesn't it seem funny? Hodden was at home, in possession of what he thought to be two capsules of heroin. He was a nut for music . . ."

Davis fingered his mustache. "You may have something, college boy. When will you get a report?"

"They said they'd be through later today. I want it done as soon as possible, before somebody gets in that room and goofs up anything of value."

Impressed by Patterson's fervor, Davis regretted that the younger man hadn't seen fit to tell him about his suspicions earlier. Then he remembered their argument of the day before and had to admit there was no reason he should have expected it.

"Well," Davis told him, "we've had our grace. We're going to clean up." They started walking toward the garage.

Davis went over to one of the Fords and glanced in the back seat. Patterson came over.

"A riot gun?" he said.

"We might need the heavy artillery. That new bunch on Hundredth Street is supposed to be a tough one. We're not taking any chances. This is all strictly undercover. Right now, nobody but Stuart and me and you know about it."

"What about the leak?"

"It's right here in the station, but I won't say what I think. I'm supposed to get a call from Bertha Travis later on today. I think she'll have some news for me."

Lieutenant Stuart and Detective Garver came out in the garage.

"Davis," Stuart called, "we've put a squad with you. Speer and his boys'll be here in a minute."

"What about The Man, chief?" Davis said. "Do we knock him off at the same time?"

234

"I've been thinking about that," Stuart said. "Maybe we ought to let him slide until you get that phone call today."

"That's all right with me," Davis said.

"Remember, everything goes off at the same time. Pick up everybody, anybody, in the building. We'll have wagons standing by. Shake 'em good. We need information, and we're going to get it! Take their breaths away; you can count on us to do the same."

"Don't worry," Davis said.

A black, plain, four-door Buick pulled up in the open driveway and stopped next to them. A big, red-faced man and three others, all wearing civilian clothes, got out and came around.

"I just came from downtown," Speer said, frowning. "How come we're getting all the work lately? The prosecutor sent my bunch over to some junkie's place on a complaint last night—somebody you boys picked up and let out on bail and now he's skipped town. The prosecutor's mad as hell because we turned up all this evidence after the bird's flown."

"What was it?" Stuart asked.

"The landlord of one of those dumps on Eightieth was cleaning up his room yesterday evening, and found about twenty-five ounces in a bedpost. *Twenty-five ounces!* How come the room wasn't searched when you guys picked the bastard up? I'm telling you, it's a pain in the ass!"

Davis said, "Who was it?"

"I think you made the arrest, Mance. Anyway, I found your report on him—Georgie Barris, alias Popeye."

Patterson started, but he didn't speak, not yet. He was letting his mind group all the assorted pieces.

Then Stuart was saying, "Let's move! Don't leave anything undone. Let's hit hard. Everything should be over within fifteen minutes." Then they were in the cars, the harsh smell of carbon monoxide rasping away at their nostrils.

"Those social worlds," Patterson said disbelievingly. "It seems almost impossible that they could be drawn so close together."

"But they were! And that gives us our tie-in!" Davis breathed deeply, and the satisfaction came sharply into his lungs. "The way

I see it, after Coke got pushed, the Halsted kid became the direct connect, making the border and probably a straight delivery to the chemist. Barris might have picked up and delivered to The Man. But after the Halsted kid was killed, Barris probably had to take over both sides, which accounts for him having that high-percentage stuff for sale. Boy, The Man must have been mad when he heard his connect was trying to pick up some pocket money on his own."

"That's why Hodden had to be killed," Patterson said. "Barris was a pipeline. He couldn't stand to go to court."

Davis gave him a broad, unusual wink of companionship. "That might have been part of the reason, college boy. Although Andy wasn't half so dangerous after Barris had skipped town. . . ."

"The most important thing," Patterson said, tingling with excitement, "is that we do have a definite connection: Who else in this town would need a pipeline but The Man?"

Davis finally allowed that he was glad to have Patterson along for the ride.

Now that the police had taken Rudy off, Nina's concern had turned to indifference. Automatically she had thought of getting a writ, knowing that was what he would expect of her now that The Man was so leery, but she paused over her actions almost deliciously.

Strangely, it felt good to know that she could get Rudy out when she *wanted* to get him out. She stretched herself out on the bed luxuriously. Her head came to the ledge of the window, and her eyes danced casually over the street below. Soon, when the Panic was over, she could return to the sidewalks, her will toward prostitution stronger now because of the wealth of drugs Rudy had left pasted on the underside of the top dresser drawer. She really didn't need to prostitute herself, for the drawer also held over five hundred dollars.

Then she sat up with the thought, and there was a queer movement at her heart. Rudy hadn't kept it from her about Andy Hodden. She'd kept telling him to get that old battery out of the closet; now the Rollers had taken it down with everything else. Just staying high all the time, just lying around . . . he'd had plenty time to get rid of the battery.

She smoothed her skirt down over her full thighs. What if Rudy told them *she* had something to do with it? What if he got sick and started shooting his mouth off, telling lies? Just to get a fix? The police weren't so bad on you when they thought you were just a whore, but when it came to murder . . .

She tried to shoo away her anxieties. The police didn't know who had killed the boy. They couldn't pin it down to Rudy. She'd even rehearsed the alibi with him: Rudy was here in the room with her all that night; Rudy hadn't gone anywhere; that's right, that's right, they hadn't even moved!

Sure, that's it. Even if the Rollers did start thinking after they got the battery downtown, they were safe. They had the alibi. She was clear.

The thought did no good. She ran over to the dresser and the stash of drugs. They were still there. She wondered if she should use now, but she decided against it. With an unusual force of will, she quieted her mind.

All she had to say was that Rudy had been with her all night; Rudy hadn't gone anywhere; that's right! I was layin right there next to him! I'd know if he went anywhere, wouldn't I?

Did you sleep?

Did she sleep? She grasped the thought slyly. Sure, I mighta went to sleep for a minute, a little while.

How long did you sleep?

I don't know. I didn't sleep with no clock.

Did Rudy go anywhere?

How would I know? If I was sleep, how would I know if he went anywhere?

You just said he hadn't gone anywhere. You said he was with you all night.

How would I know all the time if I was sleep? I closed my eyes. I can't see him with my eyes closed.

Yes, that was it, that was what she should tell them. She wasn't

237

to blame, and all Rudy wanted her to do was tell them what he'd told her. She couldn't help it if it came out that way, could she?

What about the battery?

Her heart contracted. The battery?

That's what I said! You knew he had the battery in the room.

I didn't know what he had the damn thing for. I thought he was fixin it.

You're lying!

I'm not, I swear I'm not! He brought it home that day. I don't know why he brought it home; I don't know anything about batteries. Ask me about how I make a two-minute trick, but don't ask me about batteries!

Yes, that was all right. She could tell them that if they asked. How would she know about batteries and stuff?

Where'd you get all the money?

Money?

You heard me the first time. Don't tell me you made it all tricking and you're saving it for your old age.

The money . . .

Where did you get it?

It's not *my* money. It's Rudy's.

Where'd he get it?

I don't know.

Maybe it's your money after all; maybe you lifted it off some trick. I'll just check the trick complaints for the last month. One of 'em's bound to have lost over five hundred, even if he's lying, and once he's looked at your face—

He'd be lyin! I never stole money from the tricks!

Grand larceny, over fifty bucks. . . . You could get a lot of time.

It's Rudy's money, I tell ya! Rudy brought it home that night!

I thought you said he didn't go anywhere.

She thought quickly. I woke up. Yeah! I was sleep and I woke up and he was just comin in, but he couldna been gone but a little while.

Where'd he get the money?

He—he said a guy give it to him for somethin. For drugs, maybe.

Did he say The Man gave it to him?

I don't remember him sayin that. I don't remember.

Did he say it?

I—I don't know. He coulda said so. Yeah, he probably said "a man"—you know.

There was a *man* in it somewhere, huh?

I think there was. I *think* he said "the man," but I can't be sure.

You know who The Man is?

What man?

You know who I'm talking about! You've been around on the Scene long enough to know who The Man is.

I—I mighta heard somethin like that, but I don't know nothin about the guy; I never seen him in my life.

Didn't Rudy get his bag from The Man?

I don't know nothin about Rudy's bag. I just take my joys from it, that's all.

You better come clean with us, sister. Right now you're mixed up in a murder rap right up to your pretty tricking neck!

She found that she was drenched with perspiration, and her hands were trembling. Rudy was a damn fool! He didn't have to *kill* anybody!

She turned to the walls of the room, looking for an answer. She was short of breath, exhausted by the sudden fear. The trembling became too much. She went over to the dresser and prepared a fix, straining for some fifteen minutes before she found an adequate vein under the plumpness of her arm.

The heroin quieted her body's involuntary motions with its warmth, but it failed to dull the fear. She went back over to the bed and stretched out listlessly, tormented by her indecision.

Could she afford to let Rudy stay in jail, even if it meant only a few months' time for receiving stolen goods?

She shook her head. If he went to jail without her raising a hand to help him, he'd kill her when he got out.

I gotta get a writ, she thought, getting up to go to the phone in the hall. It's the only thing I can do.

But she stopped. She was in mighty hot water herself. She

239

wouldn't be helping herself any by showing her face. Besides, she was aware that she liked being without Rudy. Once before she had spent almost a week at the apartment of a new pimp, a youngster who wanted to make good on the Scene by securing the prostitute of one of the more notable pimps. Suppose she just let things ride, ducked out for awhile—and went back to the boudoir of that young mackman?

He liked her a lot; he'd told her she didn't even have to work if she came in with him, since he already had one moneymaker on the street.

The temptation was almost too much. The young pimp could do a lot for her, keep the Scene from killing her and her body. She'd be a fool if she didn't take the opportunity.

If she stuck with Rudy, maybe she'd even go to jail for murder. What could she look forward to with Rudy? Did he really care about her?

Yet he was her man, she couldn't ever forget that. They'd been together just as though they'd been married.

She proceeded to the hallway, thinking of the drugs in the drawer, and the young pimp, the security, the ease of living without worry, without Rudy.

In the hall, she went over to the wall phone, but it was not for the purpose of seeking out a writ for Rudy Black.

Bertha had chosen the back side of the coalyard because it was shielded from the street. The tenements off Eighty-eighth cast a long, dirty black shadow over the high, crazy-leg gait of the coalyard's plank fence.

In one of its natural crevices, Bertha stood waiting, nervous and perplexed that Davis and Patterson hadn't arrived yet. But she had heard the grapevine gossip, and concluded that the officers were busy elsewhere in the general crackdowns on the dope combines around the city.

Her eyes traced both ends of the dismal street. She wished they'd hurry! Maybe she'd stuck her neck out a little too far this time, but she figured the information she had on the leak was sufficient to completely exonerate her of the indictment Davis held.

She bundled her collar against the evening's chill, turning her head to the far end of the street.

She didn't think to turn when she heard the footsteps, and she recognized the voice immediately.

"You're a long way from home, ain't you, Bert?"

Dell stood over her, and there was nothing of his usual smile on the grim lips. "I seem to remember you bein a long way from home one other time," he said.

Unconsciously, she backed away, but the drab, dirty planks held her tightly. "Dell—"

"Last time I saw you, Bert, you was gettin outta that car." He tilted his head at her. "You remember?"

"That was a long time ago," she said quickly. "I don't remember."

"Now that I think about it hard," he said, "that looked an awful lot like a cop's car."

"You don't know what you're talkin about."

He came closer, so that his chest was at her chin, his chin above her forehead. "I been doin a lot of thinkin about that time," he told her.

She became indignant. "So what if I was in a car? Would I be in a *cop's* car? What's the matter with you—crazy?"

"I ain't so crazy. Maybe I was crazy that I didn't think about it enough that first time."

She tried to come around him, but his hands shoved her back hard against the wall.

"You sonofabitch—"

His big hand came and left a great, stinging welt on her cheek. "You was about to get us all knocked off, huh, Bert?"

Her eyes were wild. "I don't know what you're talkin about! Let me out of here!"

"You ain't goin nowhere," he said thickly. One hand went into his overcoat pocket and came out with a long-handled knife, the blade of which he thumbed to position.

"You sure picked a fine place to meet them cops, didn't you?"
She was now truly afraid. "Dell, let me go! It was for the kids!"
"You know how we found out about you?" he said. "You know them coppers you so tight with? They got a copper over them, and that copper knows what you been doin!"

"Beeker's wrong!" she cried. "They just picked me up, that's all!"

He nodded his head. "It was kinda silly for me to tell you about him, huh? But that was before I knowed about you. Beeker just told The Man about you today."

"Dell, let me go! I swear I'll get out of town! I'll get so far away they'll never find me!"

And now she saw his smile return, but it was a smile she'd never seen before. "That's right," he said softly. "You're goin so far away they'll never find you."

The knife came back and made a bright, smooth arc in his hand, and the blade came up to meet the thickness of her coat, the soft challenge of her belly. The knife bit through easily, and at first it seemed as though he had only struck her in the abdomen. Then she felt the blade rake intestines on its way out, and it was almost as though an electric shock had gathered in the region of the wound. She suddenly lost all power to stand, her eyes bugged as the pavement came from nowhere to meet her face.

Then it was a smash, the ring-ding ringing of shock in her ears, the sound of running feet, the sound of things that couldn't be real:

Stop, stop or I'll shoot!

Bertha! Bertie, are you all right! Get that bastard, Patterson! He's knifed her!

Ring, ring, ring

Bertie, Bertie!

Mance—I—I shot him.

Good! Damn good shooting!

Ring, ring, ring

Why don't those bastards hurry with the wagon? Take it easy,

Bert, take it easy, you'll be all right.
He's dead. I killed him.
Good. Good.
Ring, ring, ring

THE SQUAD room was a hubbub of activity. The men who had so effectively squashed the new attempts of heroin to re-entrench itself were preparing to go out on a new raid.

A pencil rapped a hard cheekbone. *The way I see it, you can't knock this stuff out in sorties; it's got to be one continuous kick in the ass.*

A fist slammed. *Just like that! This Lujack guy, he comes running at me with the biggest goddamn forty-five I ever seen, and bam! just like that, I let him have it!*

In this room, the men learn some facts they never knew before. They learn that in the last four calendar years there were approximately fifty thousand addicts in the United States. But that figure accounts only for those arrested. No one knows how many addicts had never been caught.

They are further apprised that of each one hundred addicts committed to federal institutions, more than seventy are recidivists.

They learn that heroin is not the only habit-forming drug; that there are more than twenty-seven others, from Alphaprodine to Proheptazine, and that addicts have access to practically all of them.

Yeah, I know the Feds are doing an ass-tight job, holding the stuff down, but what I can't stand is them hogging the credit! Now you watch the papers tomorrow. I'll bet they say, FBN SNARES DOPE COMBINE, CONFISCATES OVER THREE POUNDS OF HEROIN—LOCAL POLICE AID IN SEIZURE. *That's what galls me!*

One of these men sat on the outskirts, his long face drained of color.

No matter what has happened, no matter how much good has been done this day, the victory has been won at the cost of a man's life.

Together, Stuart and Davis considered the problem. They sat facing each other in Stuart's small office, a look of pain on their faces.

"It's hard to believe," Stuart said, playing idly with a lead paperweight.

Davis took a deep breath. "I had an idea like that when I questioned Lou and Ella Tyler, chief. Ella told me she'd hipped Beeker on the situation, but he hadn't done anything. Why hadn't he done something? Bertha told me when she called that it was one of our guys, but she wouldn't tell me who, over the phone."

"How is Bertha?"

"It'll be touch and go for a while, but they say she'll live."

Stuart shook his head, kept shaking it. "I just can't believe it, Mance! Beeker's been a captain for more than eight years, over twenty years on the force."

Davis didn't reply. He could not begin to explain. There was integrity, but it was also true that most men had their price.

"How long has he been in with The Man?" Stuart said. "Did she tell you that?"

Davis shrugged. "Judging by how long the bastard has been operating in this district without a bust, I'd say from the very beginning."

The indecision burned in Stuart's eyes; his lips and face twisted helplessly. "How do you do it, Mance? How can you tell people about something like this?"

"I don't envy you," Davis said sympathetically.

"It's not only Beeker I'm thinking of," Stuart said. "What about the precinct? What about the men who haven't been paid off, the guys who're doing an honest job? Think of the demoralization when they hear about this, the publicity we'll get!"

244

"I know what you mean. The fact that we've cleaned up, that we've finally got The Man, all that won't make a bit of difference." He looked at Stuart. "I don't think we have a choice, though, chief."

After a pause, Stuart said, "You're right, of course. I'll call the commissioner, then I'll put in a call to Beeker. We'll get started on it tonight."

Davis got up. "We're all set to give The Man a shove. The Feds said they'd be out to give us a hand."

"Fine," Stuart said. "Make sure you have some of the boys cover all his places. We don't know which one he's in, you know."

"I doubt if he's in any one of them. He's probably got some of our hot wires and gone into hiding. When he comes out, you can bet he'll have plenty of legal cover."

"Oh, before I forget," Stuart said, handing him a sheet of paper. "Here's a report Patterson requested—just came in."

Davis read it. "From the crime lab, eh?" He began to grin. "Well, well, my college boy'll have a fit about this!"

"Where's Patterson now?"

"Outside brooding," Davis told him. "He had to kill Dell Swiggins and I think it sorta turned his stomach. Now all we have to do is find Rudy Black."

"He's in the lockup downtown. Receiving stolen goods! How's that for a laugh? But guess what we found in his closet? The runniest old battery you ever did see!"

"If I was twenty years younger," Davis grinned, "I'd dance a jig!"

"You should see that mustache of yours," Stuart laughed.

"I'm gonna get right out and let the college boy know about this," Davis said. "Maybe it'll give him a jolt." He started toward the door. "You'll be right out?"

"As soon as I make those phone calls," Stuart replied. "I wouldn't miss this night's work for anything."

It was a long time before Stuart could bring himself to pick up the phone. Then, in one motion, he picked up the receiver, dialed a number, and began to speak very deliberately.

245

* * *

Out in the squad room, Davis was surprised to find Patterson doing anything but moping. He was talking on his phone animatedly, pencil streaking across the pad in front of him.

Finally, the receiver clashed to the cradle and Patterson snapped to his feet.

"Mance, you won't believe it!" he said excitedly. "A girl by the name of Taylor Mayo just called. She said she read about the dope crackdown and thought we should know she was with Andy on the night of his murder, and that she heard him receive a phone call."

"So?"

"Just this: the phone call was from Rudy Black! He was supposed to meet Andy that evening."

"So what does it prove?" Davis said, hiding the report sheet behind his back.

"Well—well, it proves—It proves that Black might've killed the boy, that's what!" Then he remembered. "I just thought of it! The same night Andy was killed, we saw Rudy Black come off that street. He could have just left Andy's apartment. We've got no better suspects, and he was certainly near the scene of the murder."

"Don't get het up," Davis said, handing him the report. "Here's proof Black was around. Latent prints found a pair of beauties on the record player."

Patterson sat down quickly. "Then I was right." He read on farther. "Now all we need is a confession from Black."

"We'll go see 'im tomorrow. I don't think we'll have much trouble."

Patterson recalled his first meeting with Rudy Black. "I don't know, Mance. He might not be so easy to crack."

Davis grunted. "Ten or twelve hours without stuff'll soften him up. After we show him what we got, it shouldn't be too hard."

Patterson was not so sure. "Rudy Black's something different, I think. You ever seen anything so dirty it just wouldn't come clean? Black's like that."

Davis looked at him, beginning to get a little annoyed. "Black's no more than any other junkie—he'll crack."

*A*LL THE OTHER nights, liquor had helped him forget his wife Margaret and her cancer. It had helped him forget his needlessly extravagant life in the suburbs. It helped him forget Denise, his mindless daughter in a nursing home, a living testimonial to his carelessness during the First World War, in France.

Here in the sanctuary of his private den, his joints ached; the liquor helped some, but it couldn't reach the deeper ache that spread throughout his body.

He began to cry, and the tears dropped unevenly in his glass of whiskey, on the silken greenness of his smoking jacket. The sob stretched long and horrible from his throat, and his coward's body crumpled with the lamentation. The police captain fell to the floor, crying like a child. . . .

A little child he was, running down a country road with the wild smell of living things, with a butterfly lilting overhead, when a dog rushed at him like an angry bull and attacked him, his little hands, his little legs. . . .

Unconsciously, he felt his hands and legs, but they had healed.

How could he tell the dog he did not mean to do whatever it was that had angered him? How could he tell the dog?

The sobs had ceased, and the ridiculousness of lying full length on the floor came to him. In an instant, everything came to him, but he forced it back. He could not think of it! It was all too terrible!

But he had to do something.

What to do?

What to tell the goddamn dog?

What could he do tomorrow, the next day, the day after?

What could he say to Margaret, dying in the hospital?

He began to cry again. Oh God, have pity! Make it all a dream. Make everything go away so I won't have to wake up and see it tomorrow. Please, God, you could do it if you wanted to. I've been a good husband; I never whored around; I always went every Sunday to see Denise; and I went to church, too, God.

What can I do? What *can* I do?

His coward's hands touched the cowardly face, and the audacity of the thought relieved him of some stigma.

No . . .

That's not something you do right off. You've got to have time, days. You can't just think about it and then do it.

But there was the thought of tomorrow.

Please, God! Can't I do something else? Can't I get by some other way? You could *help* me!

He could not escape to the past. His unsteady legs took him to the desk. He opened the drawer, and saw the long snout of his service revolver.

No, I can't! he thought, shrinking away from it. I've got to have a drink first.

He had a drink, two, then three, but it was no use; his mind was numb.

Back at the desk, his hand faltered over the cold steel.

But you've got to! After tomorrow, you'll be dead anyway. But it'll hurt. It'll cave a little hole in my skull; the bullet'll rip through my brain, it'll tear it loose; the blood and brains and bone will gush out the other side. It's horrible, and it'll hurt like hell. But it'll hurt worse tomorrow.

He leaned on the desk to steady himself.

I can't do it! I *can't* kill myself! But you *must*! Not this way! Maybe if I hung myself . . .

Like all potential suicides, he examined the means desperately, searching for the one that would hurt least. Then his eyes narrowed.

248

Upstairs . . . Margaret had some of her medication left after the last operation. Just take them orally.

He stumbled to the wide doors of the room and flung them open. If he was going to do it, he had to hurry.

The neat expensive furnishings got in his way. He knocked over a chair in the hall. On the stairs he slipped. Upstairs, he rummaged through the drawers in his wife's bedroom.

Where is it?

He was glad that his hasty search did not reveal what he was looking for at once. Then he saw the box under a sheaf of letters.

There it is. Now open it. I can't kill myself! Open it. You must. It won't hurt.

He slid the box open with his nervous fingers. Ten tablets.

That should be enough. They're half-grain tablets; to help her sleep. He read the label: one tablet on retiring. *To be used only on doctor's prescription.* Take them out. Put them in your hand. Put them in your mouth. Now swallow them.

The white discs caught in his throat, and it was minutes before the last one passed down. Almost immediately he felt the pins and needles at his brain, and was terrified.

The sensation intensified, then he felt a warmth envelop him, and he ceased to care. Now he had no fears about tomorrow.

He floated on the mild feeling, amazed that it could feel so good to die. In his fog, he wondered if the dosage would be enough.

The stupor increased and he felt safer, knowing that soon he would be dead.

He did not know that his wife Margaret had purposely mislabled the medicine box, that he had just taken five grains of soluble morphine sulphate.

Though he had been involved with narcotics for years, never before had he tasted the strangeness of heroin—the principal ingredient in Margaret's pills, which were not sleeping tablets but an opium derivative.

*O*OOoo *bopsha bam*! *AAAaahcoogah Mop*!

The sounds filtered through to him. A youth with long shoes and pants with a frayed bottom walked the cell floor, his lips twisted around the phrases:

"SpleeEEE bee dah-OOOooo-yah, SpleeEEE bee dah OOOool yah Coo!"

He lay on the hard boards, his feet cramping in the soft leather of his shoes, the hundred and twenty-five dollar Benny rolled beneath his head as a cushion, his legs crossed lightly over one another to protect the crease of his slacks, thinking: *Nearer My God to Thee*, and remembering it was a song his mother used to sing far away in some distant squalor.

Absently, he watched the youth, who stood naïvely conscious of his fancied elaborate "downness," "hipness," high above the other sleeping drunks and petty violators of the law, all who lay like sick, exhausted pigs on the concrete floor. His hands were clasped together under the waist of his jacket, and his body was bent one-sided as he moved slowly among the sleeping bodies, hopping on the heel of his right foot as though it were malformed, his every motion in accord with the senselessness that emanated from under the fuzzy baby hair on his upper lip.

"My baby don't wear no draws; she's one of them high-class broads," in tune to "My Baby Is So Refined."

Lying back, resting on the softness of his coat, waiting for Nina to come with the writ, he called to the youth, "Say, my man," feeling suddenly, as he watched the boy turn, the sense of superiority, having once been like the boy. Perhaps it was the tinge of sickness beginning that made him feel like that.

"Yeah, baby?" the boy said.

"Come over here a minute."

The youth came over to the open cell door and stood watching him.

"You got a cigarette on you?" he asked the boy.

The youth fumbled through his jacket and gave him one from a crumpled pack, lighted it for him, noting the slim shoes, the good fit of clothes, the overall appearance of a regular. "When did they bring you in?" he asked Rudy.

"Yesterday morning."

The boy shook his head, somehow intimidated by the man's coolness, the good clothes, the thing about him that said Thoroughbred and Hustler. He grinned meekly. "I didn't notice you. I came in this mornin and I didn't see you."

"I been layin quiet. . . . I'm startin to get bogue."

"You use?"

"As much as I can shoot. I got an oil burner."

"I use myself," the boy lied. "But I ain't hooked."

"If you can't pay the dues, don't play."

The boy became indignant. "Look, man, I can pay as well as any other stud! Only, who wants to get hooked?"

"That's it. You got a good idea. Just go on and smoke that gangster and be real cool. Drink that juice and smoke that gangster and keep them needles outta your arm." Rudy was laughing at him.

"I can pay my dues," the boy said defensively. "I can carry my own weight."

The words made Rudy shiver as he tried to remember where he had heard them before. He thought hard, then remembered it was that Flip, Andy Hodden, and shivered again, imagining he saw a different face in the doorway.

"Sit down, man," he said, making a space on the hard boards.

The boy came over, sat. He dusted his shoes. As he moved, Rudy could smell the rankness of his body. The harsh human smell of the young body made him sick as he breathed it in.

The boy raised his shoes high in the dim light of the cell, dusting them, showing Rudy that they were new, shiny leather from the hide of some sick old cow or horse, brilliantly white stitches lining the soles in single thin evenness.

Hippy-dippy.

Just beginning. Seventeen or eighteen. Recently inaugurated to the ranks of the regulars; the tyro, as yet unversed in the matter of pimping, without a girl or the necessary combination of fortitude and ruthlessness which he would need to shackle the mind of some young, insecure female. . . . *A nice colored girl with a big ass and big tits? A trip around the world?*

Just beginning. Still smoking reefer for a thrill, for the thing that had been neglected or missing in his environment; a member of the Cool Daddies or Shakers, seeking in these organizations the security he had never known. One of the regulars, one of the No-Jonas-Tip-Played-on-Me personages. Because—because he was too hip, with twenty-five dollar shoes on his feet and no behind in his trousers.

The boy said, lighting his last cigarette and throwing the empty pack into the bowl of the evil-smelling toilet in the back wall, "What are you in for? Smock?"

"No."

"Me and another cat got run on when we took off a bar. We came in through the roof. My man got away, but I got busted." He bragged, not of the other boy getting away, but because he had got caught.

"The Rollers talk to you yet?" Rudy asked.

The boy smiled, in confidence. "Dig, baby, I don't think they got no case! They ain't talked to me since I got busted day before. I think my man is pullin some lines. I think I'll get out some time."

"You won't," Rudy said from experience. "They'll talk to you first."

"You think so?"

"Unless somebody got a fix in for you. They'll talk to you."

"They'll probably want me to flip."

"That's right."

The boy laughed nervously. "They can't shoot me no prop."

"They'll wax you, maybe."

"I can take a waxin, I don't care! I can carry my own weight. They—"

"Shut up," Rudy said. He couldn't stand the hippy-dippy voice any longer, nor the sharp, chopping gesticulations, nor the agitated scraping of the hard-heeled shoes on the concrete floor.

The boy looked at him with an odd kind of fascination. "What's the matter? You gettin bogue?" But he was not so completely fascinated that his voice, his eyes, did not show traces of envy.

Hippy-dippy, sometimes kiddy, cry for your bottle when you want your titty.

And magically, he became really sick when the boy asked him if he were.

Where's Nina with that writ? She knew I got busted!

All of a sudden, too quickly perhaps, the first tears rolled from his eyes. He closed his eyes to sleep, but it was too late.

The boy said, "Dig, baby, if you're bogue, I'll just go on and pull."

"I just told you to shut up, that's all I told you." To apologize any more than that was impossible now, as he thought of Nina and wished for her to come: big yellow girl with a lawyer and a piece of paper to set him free. And he continued to think.

How come I'm laying here in jail?

"How come *you* got busted?" the boy asked, and he was nearly mad with relief that the youth had asked his mind's question. It seemed now as though he had been locked up for thousands of years, but it was only a day. No one had told him the formal charge, but he knew it would probably be receiving stolen goods. How had they known where to come?

Piqued, he sat up. "I should call my man."

"What'd you get busted for?" the boy asked again.

"I don't know," he said, puzzled. "I was real twisted when the Rollers broke into my pad. Some broad stacked some hot stuff in my closet I shoulda got rid of a long time ago."

"That's no case."

"Yeah?" Rudy stared at him. "You think it ain't no case? You just try to tell the Rollers it ain't no case! If it ain't no case, why do you think I'm sittin here, you dizzy little sonofabitch?"

"Say, man, listen—"

"Shut up! Get outta my cell!"

The boy got up, scared. "If you're drugged—"

"Yeah, I'm drugged! Get the hell outta here!"

The suddenness of the mood shocked even him. His eyes began to water profusely while he sat upright; he stretched out again and closed them, thinking, What the hell'm I doin in jail?

He tried to do what he'd never done: to figure and evaluate step by step from past to present. But it was like a dream, like stepping on a sheet of water which seemed as solid as stone under your feet but suddenly caved in.

Jesus walked on the water . . .

A tall white man in a long white robe and a curly beard and bare feet, walking on the water . . .

Why didn't he fly?

Nina with the writ paper.

He thought of her, unable to remember her face, able only to remember her soft skin-color like a ripe lemon next to his own dark skin, lying in bed like two people of different worlds but with the same birthright of drugs.

He thought of her as he'd never thought of her before: lying beside or under other men, matching her body to theirs, all shapes and sizes, her body elastic to their lusts, a dirty, lemon-yellow glove. This also was difficult to do, this thinking of Nina, for his mind split her body into three different categories: her crotch, her mouth, her breasts—and only they really lived and were Nina. And if they were Nina, they could not come with the paper to set him free; they had no legs or hands or brain which could make them care one way or another whether he stayed in jail.

You listen, bitch, I'm your man—

And he was getting sicker, he could tell. Lying there, knowing all that about Nina, his body was forced to cease hoping. His eyes watered as though they had mouths, like eye-droppers, long full eye-droppers which extended to the very base of his skull, where a tiny, mad itching of fingers pressed the bulbs, softly, a big wet drop from each eye, one at a time.

He sat up. "Hey, my man!" The sharpness of his cry aroused

254

several of the other prisoners who lay on the floor, their bodies curled in soiled, comfortable humps.

The youth, still walking the floor, turned at the sound of his voice. His face restrained itself, but the callow gladness was plain to see.

"You mean me?" he said.

"Yeah," Rudy said through the bars. "C'mere."

The boy came back, hippy-dippy, dipping as he walked, grinning to himself smugly because Rudy had called *him*.

"Yeah, daddy?" he said, with such thorough, such complete smugness that Rudy wanted to rise up and strike him hard, knock him down and stomp him.

You think you're hip! You're what I used to be, years ago!

"What can I do for you?" the boy said.

"Sit down. I wanna talk to you."

The boy came in and stood over him, trying to appear big. "Don't treat me like no lame, man. If you sick, all right, but *nobody* treats me like a lame!"

"You ain't no square, I can tell that."

"You goddamn right!"

"I could tell by the way you carry yourself—you're a real speedy boy. You're quick as quicksand."

The boy softened, flattered. "You sure know what to say in a crowd, daddy."

"Sit down. Don't pay no attention if I get bogue again."

Needing someone to talk to, he begged of the boy, then forgot the need as he sat there, his mouth beginning to gape into huge yawns.

"When did you use last?" the boy asked, awed.

"Yesterday morning. I did about ten things before I got some nod. When the Rollers broke in, I was still made."

"*Ten* things?"

"Yeah."

"That's a lot of stuff."

"Sometimes it is, sometimes it ain't. It depends on how good the stuff is. My real shot is eight, just to get ready. I can get high off ten. I use about thirty, forty things a day."

"Damn! You musta had the bag."

Rudy yawned. "Yeah."

The boy said, proudly, "Every now and then I might use two, maybe three. But the way you are? Oh, man! I couldn't get that way out for a new Hog!"

"I have got a Hog."

"Yeah?" The boy didn't believe him. He opened up a new pack of cigarettes and offered Rudy one, which Rudy took. He knew the boy thought he was testing him, trying to belie his claim of owning a Cadillac, by offering the inexpensive cigarettes. But Rudy didn't care; it wasn't as important as it once might have been.

He had gone past the *hip* stage, the period of hero worship of notable pimps, hustlers, and con men. But he could understand the standard by which the boy measured him.

"Yeah, I got a Hog," he said, drawing in on the cigarette. *A Cadillac and a whore* . . . which were, of course, the prime requisites of any pimp worth his salt, so he could say to the nobodies, "This is what I got and you ain't, and it makes me better than you."

A sound like Patterson's voice seemed to jump at him: "Black?"

He shivered until his body snapped like taut wire against the boy, who held him up, his hard heels snapping on the floor as the leather drew no traction. "Say, man!" the boy said. "You're *real* bogue, ain't you?"

"*Black!*"

"Is somebody callin me? Somebody—" He was sweating. Hot and cold chills.

"Is that your name?" the boy said. "Black?"

He shuddered, wiped the sweat away from his forehead. He put the cigarette to his mouth and jerked his neck until the tendons stood out.

"RUDY BLACK! WHERE THE HELL ARE YOU!"

The boy sneered. "It's the goddamn hack."

Rudy stood up unsteadily, snatching his coat from the boards. "I'm Rudy Black . . ."

Nina with the writ! I knew . . .

"You sonofabitch!" someone said. He had stepped on him as he stumbled toward the gate. But it didn't make any difference, because he was leaving now . . . *Nina, lovely honey Nina, who could make the sickness go* . . . going to the door where the turnkey waited, a short man with a big voice and big key. "Get the hell on down the hall," he said, "The second door on your left."

There was something wrong. It was twisted. This wasn't the way it was when you were released on writ. This was the little room with the big men and their strong hands, with their telephone books and handcuffs and their voices saying, "You better talk, you sonofabitch! We'll—(*Wham*! over the head with the books)—teach—(*Wham*!)—you to—(*Wham*!)—steal—(*Wham, Wham, Wham*!).

His bowels felt loose.

"Go on, get in there!" the turnkey yelled at him.

Patterson and Davis and a white man stood waiting on him.

Nina . . .

"Sit down, Black," Patterson said, and he could see something different in the man's eyes, something that wasn't in his eyes the last time they met, something strong. "Sit down, Black!" Firmer this time, hard and forceful.

Nina . . .

He sat down. He waited, his eyes clouded with tears, his skin pimpling with goose pimples, cold.

I ain't this far out, I know . . .

But he was this far out, stretched like a long piece of rubber, his arms, his face, his hands itching for a fix. And it was worse now with them standing around, watching him like they were nuts, scaring him. Three squares standing, watching him, trying to bug him, their faces all tight and bitter.

It's crazy!

"All right, all right, what is it?" he said. "What do you want? What's this all about? I was picked up about some hot goods. Why are you guys here?"

Davis looked at his partner. "You tell 'im. It's your show."

Patterson took a deep breath. "I said you'd come back, Black.

257

It looks like you're back for good, this time." He took a couple of sheets of paper from the white man. "Have you ever been to Andy Hodden's apartment before?"

Rudy's flesh went cold all over. "Andy who?" he bluffed. "Andy? I never knew no Andy! Amos and Andy? What the hell are you talkin about?"

"I won't waste time," Patterson said. "We've got your finger-prints off the record player in Hodden's room, which proves that you've been there before. We found the dead battery that you used for the hot shot you gave Andy Hodden. It was right in the closet of your room." He glanced at the papers. "Our chemical analyst can prove the same acids which coat that battery were of the type administered to Hodden. We've also got a witness, Miss Taylor Mayo, who can testify that you called and made an appointment to meet Hodden on the night he was killed."

The fear shot up to Rudy's throat, and he almost heaved. "You got *nothin*, Roller, *nothin!* I was at home all night that night— Nina'll tell you!"

"It won't go, Black. Mr. Davis and I saw you on the Scene that night."

"It won't be hard to prove that The Man put you up to it," Davis said stiffly. "If Popeye had gone on the stand, everything stood a chance of going sky-high, didn't it? How much did The Man pay you, Black?"

Rudy didn't answer. He was sweating again. Patterson and Davis stood in front of him, their faces drawn and horrible. He became sicker, and a tickle developed in his groin, making him draw his legs together tightly until his testicles were mashed between his thighs and he sucked wind because of the pain.

"Talk, Black!' Davis shouted.

Black Rudy, talk!

A great yawn came, twisting his face. "I ain't got nothin to say!" He leaned forward, shifting, his stomach beginning to cramp.

Patterson pushed him back in the seat. "Don't you realize you're going to die for this, Black? Don't you realize that?"

"I ain't got *nothin* to say! NOTHIN!"

"Nobody can get you out of this," Davis said. "The Man can't get you out of it: he gave himself up voluntarily a few hours ago."

Stuff ran from Rudy's nose to his lips; he wiped it away with the back of his hand. "Busted? The Man's busted?" He was lying, Davis was lying! They were just trying to make him talk.

"Dell is dead," Patterson went on. "Lou and Ella are busted—Ace—all of them! We've cleaned up, Black. There's no one left."

"So?" Rudy said, making his voice calm.

"So you'll die if you don't talk and talk quick!"

"So what's dyin?" he laughed. He was sick and still he was strong! "I'm dyin now; I'll die if I don't have some stuff soon."

"You won't die," Davis rumbled. "Dying's too good for you, you little crud!"

"It's not you we want most," Patterson said. "We want The Man. Tell us the truth, Black, and you might beat the chair."

The test. A test. It was like a test, seeing him sick and weak, holding everything they needed, smug and warm with nothing to tickle their bellies except the knowledge that it was all over for him.

Nina, you bitch! You and my mother are bitches!

"Black, what are you going to say?" Patterson said, his voice and face fuzzy. "We've got everything we need to burn you. We know it was The Man who made you do it. Tell us the truth."

Rudy's laugh sounded insane. "You should know me, Roller!" he said. "I'm a thoroughbred. I wouldn't flip to save my mother."

"What about yourself?" Patterson said quietly.

Rudy laughed again, then he spat some mucus from his mouth which had blood in it.

"I don't care," he said. "I never liked me much, anyways."

Wouldn't flip to save my mother, or my father, or my brother, or my woman, wouldn't flip to save NOBODY!

Because nothing was wrong with dying. Everybody just put the bad mouth on it, that's the only reason it seemed like a drag. It was best to be this way, daddy: a Champ and little swimming pools in your head; a Champ and the itching in your clothes making them smooth-smelling steam baths, which soaked and soaked until you could swear they were soaking away your blood; a Champ and really righteous and the sweat freezing up on your skin, chilling you so deeply that your flesh turned bluish under the brownness; a Champ and small nobs in your belly, under your ribs.

A thoroughbred of the old school, where all the old pupils were dead.

Don't flip; you can't flip; Flip is dead!

"OOOL yak coobeee OOOoo Dah!"

"Shut up!"

"The hell with you, man!"

Somebody grabbed him before he got to the boy. "Man," they said, "what's wrong with you? You want the hack to come in and lock ever'body in them goddamn cells? We's got *freedom* in here!"

"Cut me loose! I'll kill you!" he screamed at them. They let him go and he went back to the cell. The Benny lay in the mess on the floor. The cell stank of him. He laid down, stretched himself on the boards, not on his back, on his side so that when the itch came he could brace his heels against the stone wall and push hard outward, straining all his muscles and bones, twisting his body in a half figure eight. He tightened his belt until the thin leather bit into his stomach like wire, establishing a new pain, one he could concentrate on to forget the others.

Flip.

The time stretched into hours.

Andy Hodden came in the cell. Andy Hodden said, "Dig, man, you got some stuff? I don't mean the kinda stuff you give me the last time, but I'll take some of that if you got some. I'm so bogue . . ."

He walked into the far wall, and the pain dashed through his vision like happy little stars. He didn't scream; he couldn't scream and remain a Champ. He laughed it off.

So I'm standin up . . . so what?

So he went over to the boards and sat down. He wouldn't lie down again; he couldn't sleep anyway. The tickle was best fought like this, sitting; he could bend over himself until his head hung between his knees and his body was jackknifed across his stomach,

mashing the lumps away. He began to shiver again; he picked up
his coat; it was covered with filth and stank. He had thrown up on
it, but he couldn't remember when.

Flip.

Somebody was *saying* that! He started to get up and find out
who it was, but he couldn't move. He was too comfortable like
this, with his body in a contortion and spittle and tears drooling
from his head. He had gotten hot again, but he could stand that
better than the cold. He forgot the tickle and itch for a moment.
Tickle and itch.

The tickle and itch is a sonofabitch.

Nina. We had good times, I know we did; I just can't think of
one. . . .

And so what if she didn't have a good time? She didn't deserve
any, the miserable bitch. Hadn't he dressed the whore up? When
he first met her and she was living with her sister, she was wearing
hand-me-down drawers, wasn't she? His fingers remembered the
harsh cloth, the touch of them, pink, with tiny wear holes.

"You'll do me like all the other boys. You'll just do it with me
and put me down."

"How do you know?"

" 'Cause everybody else—"

"This ain't everybody else, this is Rudy Black! Rudy Black's
gonna show you how to get along in this world. Rudy Black's gonna
be somebody. Rudy Black—"

His ankles were bending under his weight, and he couldn't stand
the tickle any longer. He stood up and opened his pants, dug his
fingers down deep inside, digging them into the soft flesh until the
pain was too much and he felt himself toppling, unable to see or
gain his balance. His forehead smashed into the wall and he fell in
a lump on the floor, his fingers still sunk like claws in the lower
part of his body. His forehead tingled, sang with the pain, and his
eyes seemed as though they were caught in the glare of a huge
spotlight, which shifted its colors from red to white, then to green
as his vision widened and he saw the dim insistence of the cell light
overhead. He put a hand to his forehead and brought it back sticky.

261

He put it to his mouth, tasted the blood, and spewed a warm greenness from his belly.

Several prisoners stood in the doorway, watching him.

"Somebody call the screw."

"What's wrong with him?"

"One of them damn junkies. He's gotta have a shot, I guess."

"Call the hack."

"HEY, COPPER, A GUY'S SICK IN HERE!"

He could hear the turnkey come to the door. "What's wrong with 'im?"

"I don't know."

"He's a dope addict," somebody said.

"Let 'im lay," the turnkey advised. "He'll get over it . . . I see 'em every day—they get over it."

Through a red haze he saw Andy Hodden come to the doorway and look in on him. "These people are beasts, baby, real dogs. I tried to get him to look at you, but—"

"Get the hell away!" he screamed. "GET THE HELL AWAY!"

The people moved away from his cell.

He tried to get up, struggling against the tickle. The tickle said, "Lay down," but he had to get up, had to remember how he'd got down there in the first place. He stood up, wobbling.

Floyd.

Floyd. Floyd could help him; Floyd had plenty money and plenty connections. Floyd would help him before it was too late; Floyd would send his fix-men down to put the fix in and get him freed. Floyd had all sorts of connections. He would take care of Rudy. That was the least he could do. He was the reason for Rudy being here, *he* was responsible. Why shouldn't he come through? He had promised. . . .

If anything goes wrong, rely on me. Keep your mouth shut. I know you can do that. You're a thoroughbred.

He moved toward the cell door with hope. Then stopped.

Don't you remember? Floyd is busted. Everybody is busted. You're gonna burn.

The tickle laughed at him. He put both hands to himself and

mashed. His stomach rolled up in knots and bent him over. He began to get cold chills. Sweat dripped from his forehead.

Nina and Mama, you're bitches! I'll make you do dirty things! I'll make you do it dirty!

He knelt on the floor and thought, Only two more days and it's all over. I can stand it that long. I'm a Champ.

Andy Hodden came back over to the doorway and said, "I'm tryin to kick, man. I haven't had no stuff for four days. I'm clean."

"Get away, you sonofabitch!"

He was standing, trembling, his body bent again. When he looked up, Andy Hodden was gone. He went over to the boards and lay down on his back, drawing his legs up by the ankles, containing the tickle. The light from the cell ceiling blinked at him dimly, then faded. He couldn't lie still; the tickle wouldn't let him. It was steadier and louder in him now. He turned his face to the boards, turned on his stomach, and pressed himself down hard, almost as though he were with a woman, a skinny, bony woman, her cheekbones biting into his face, her thighs and arms like sharp knives against him. He had an orgasm which was wonderful.

I couldn't be this far—

He pressed against the tickle, and another orgasm came, hurting him. He turned over on his back, breaking out in a new sweat, one that was profuse and stinging to his skin.

He saw Nina come to the cell door. "Baby daddy, sweetman, your mama's got the writ. C'mon, let's pull."

He got up, almost unable to believe it. "For real, mama? You wouldn't bullshit me, mamma?"

"C'mon, daddy," she said, "let's go get a fix."

"Don't bullshit me, mama, I'll KILL you if you do!"

When she laughed, he knew she was lying.

He stood looking at nothing. The other prisoners looked at him, looked at the wet in front, the wild pleading in his eyes.

"He said he's got a Cadillac," the boy told someone sneeringly.

He went back to the cell. He tripped over the door slot and fell to the floor, crushing a finger under him. The pain didn't touch him. He lay groveling on the floor, his body jerking uncontrollably,

263

his eyes twitching, his mouth yawning until the bones in his face felt as though they were slowly breaking, the mess from his nose streaking and drying on his face in tight, slick bands.

He crawled over to the toilet and threw up blood in it. As he bent there, the tickle came, slamming his body forward, making his intestines feel as though they had exploded. It shot clear to his head, made his hand come forward on the flush button of the toilet, pressing, pressing, flooding the bowl with swirling water, pressing, pressing, the cold making his thighs collapse under him.

He rose up, gasping.

THOROUGHBRED!

CHAMP!

MACKMAN!

BAGMAN!

NO MAN!

THOROUGH—

He came out of the cell and took a running start toward the wall at the end of the tier, head held down. Someone grabbed him before he got halfway. He straightened up, fighting, spitting blood. They held him so he could not move, so the tickle could attack him without interference.

He screamed, "Stop it! Stop it! Stop it! Send me a doctor! Send somebody with some stuff!"

"Boy," something whispered in his ear, "boy, boy, boy, whatcha gonna do? Do? Do?"

The tickle rose, knifing through him, and he felt the blood gush in his throat, draining back toward his empty stomach. Something kept saying Flip Flip Flip Flip, and he couldn't stand it any longer until he opened his eyes and saw Dr. Patterson bending over him.

25

HE HAD HAIR that was naturally curly, and it had distinguished streaks of gray above the ears. His skin was smooth and tanned and well cared for, with a perpetual glow from heat packs and massages. He was chubby from good living and his expensively-tailored clothes fit his body like soft-colored folds of outer skin. His eyes were big and bright, with childlike innocence, and his spine straightened against the chair pushed his wide chest outward, made his back seem broad as a board. His head was proud and high, like a plaster statue.

The arrogant, self-made aristocracy of The Man.

Around him sat a battery: white man, white man, Negro, Negro, white man, fat white woman with pencil poised. Flanking him were the Brothers Columbo, two of the city's most resourceful lawyers.

The Man looked around him assuredly, his hands clasped in his lap, the diamonds glinting on his fingers.

"I must say, this is all a puzzle to me," he picked up where he'd left off. "But my lawyers have assured me that a statement at this time can do nothing but establish my willingness to co-operate."

The pencil dipped, the eyes watched.

"I'm innocent of the charges, of course, but I'm ashamed to admit that I've been duped by the one person I so completely trusted. Miss Dutton, you know, was hired as my business manager a good many years ago. The woman has an incredible ability for bookkeeping, and she was invaluable to my business. I'm in shipping, you know." Certainly they knew, but why not say it again? And again? Reiterate, muddy the issue—that was the way to do it.

"I'm a terribly busy man. If you were to check my date book, which I happen to have along"—he drew it from his inside coat pocket—"you'd get some small idea of my fourteen-hour day. So you can see I had no way of knowing just *what* Miss Dutton was doing while I was away from the office, although I had complete confidence in her integrity."

"It's clear enough," one of the Brothers added. "Mr. Angelo was exploited by this woman. He had no way of knowing she used his business as a shield for this nefarious drug traffic."

"I've known Miss Dutton for more than ten years, gentlemen, from Florida," The Man said. "I engaged her as my private secretary, following some difficulty she had in the WAC. I never inquired into this business, but I might have done well to investigate." His brow creased benevolently. "I felt sorry for Miss Dutton, and noticing that she was a woman of education I thought I might make good use of her services."

"Miss Dutton's character may be judged from this service record I have here," the other Brother said, waving a paper. "She was found to have been indulging in homosexual activities. Well, now, a woman like that . . ." He let the opinion pass unspoken.

"I'm a legitimate businessman," The Man said. "What should I know of these things? However, as I said, I trusted Miss Dutton implicitly. I barely noticed the people she received in the apartment where she worked for me; I always thought them to be clients of some sort. I rarely came in contact with them."

"Mr. Angelo was totally ignorant of these shady characters," one of the Brothers said.

"I shudder to think of what might have happened to me," Mr. Angelo said, "alone with one of these men. I keep a good deal of cash around the apartment, you know. There's hardly a day passes that I don't have several thousand collected from my trucking firm or one of my land holdings." He watched the pencil dashing, the men watching him. "I remember the words of my dying father as well as if they were spoken yesterday: 'Boy,' he said, 'you just be studying about the matter at hand and let the little things take care of themselves.' I have made it my personal philosophy ever since to ignore the minor, irrelevant things and let the big problems occupy my time."

"You can see how it was," one of the Brothers said. "Everything but business was shut off from Mr. Angelo. He was completely unaware of Miss Dutton's ingeniously concealed dope empire."

Floyd Angelo agreed, for the first time showing anger: "And as for those people who say I was the figurehead in this infamous thing—those people who own the hotel, that Bertha person, that Black fellow—"

"Nobody said anything about Black." Somebody had said it, all right. They were trying to be mysterious!

The fat woman waited, pencil pointed toward the pad like a spear.

The Man spoke indulgently now. "I must forgive the police their suspicions. It's only natural to conclude that it was I, and not Miss Dutton, who headed the whole thing. But, gentlemen, I am a man who has never seen the inside of a jail or prison. I have tried, in every way, to abide by the law. I want to see this dope thing stamped out as fervently as any other right-thinking man. As a businessman and a good American, I know there can be no common ground between narcotics and law and order. My only regret is that I have been drawn so closely into this net by a woman I trusted."

His body was alive with a tingling. The Brothers watched him, twirling the tips of their slim fingers.

"I think Mr. Angelo has covered everything very thoroughly," one of them said.

"Yes," said the other.

"Not quite."

The objection came from a big burly Negro. "This guy could've made a fortune on the stage!" His laughter aroused a fear in The Man. "Show him those affidavits, Virgil!"

One of the Brothers was saying, ". . . my client on bond right away. You have no case, gentlemen. You have no evidence of a sale. Mr. Angelo was innocent . . ."

The youngest of the Negroes shoved the papers at the lawyer. "Mr. Angelo might have had a chance yesterday, but today—uh-uh."

"Captain Beeker tried to knock himself off," the burly man said. "What he thought was an overdose of sleeping pills was really

267

morphine. His wife was an addict. You'll find a full confession from him among those things."

The lawyer glanced through the papers quickly. "Now just a minute! This is intimidation!" His brother came over to see. "We'll have to check these things thoroughly," he said.

"We'll give you copies with gilt edges," one of the white men said. "You'll need something durable, because Mr. Angelo is going to have quite a few trials, most of them for the government."

The burly Negro came over and took the papers from the lawyer. "We want Mr. Angelo first. Among other things, he's an accessory to murder. Rudy Black wasn't as hard as you thought he was, Mr. Angelo. He talked. And so did Lou and Ella Tyler—and Bertha Travis is gonna live, did you know that?"

The Man looked at the lawyers, who looked back helplessly. "What . . . I . . . there's no proof! It's all lies! I didn't—"

"You've got nothing!" one of the Brothers tried. "Sylvia Dutton will testify for us—"

"I'm afraid she won't," the young man said. "She knows she can die in prison if she attempts to set Mr. Angelo free. We've got her statement along with the rest."

The Brothers turned to The Man. "Floyd," one of them said. "Floyd, *compromise*! Let's compromise!"

"What do you want?" The Man yelled at them. "Tell me what you want!"

The young man waited, his eyes quiet, looking into Floyd Angelo deeply, under the expensive clothes, the fat, healthy skin, touching the fear in him.

"It's simple," he said quietly. "Who's bigger than you, Mr. Angelo? We want the chemist, the bulk man. We want him, and you're going to give him to us."

26

THE MAN WHO was bigger than The Man, the chemist, brain and nerve center of the whole operation, was convinced that it was time to close down the gates, and he had made extensive preparations.

In the spaciousness of his large mansion, he hustled as vigorously as the servants to get together the vital odds and ends he, his wife, and small boy would need on their trip to South America.

Hurrying through the lower floors, he gripped the passing, gray-haired butler by the arm. "The plane tickets, Jeffrey?"

"All ready, sir."

"Now don't worry. We'll make arrangements to send for you and the others as soon as we're settled. You'll have to make up your own mind whether you care to live in South America indefinitely."

"I'll talk to my wife, sir," the butler said. "We're getting along in age, sir, and I don't see where South 'Merica would be any different."

"Well, just hurry with the bags. The Cadillacs will be picked up. We're leaving in a cab."

"A cab, sir?"

"The Cadillacs are sold, Jeffrey. A man will be here directly to claim them. He'll show you the necessary papers."

"Yes, sir. Will there be anything else, sir?"

"No. If anybody comes around, just say you don't know where we've gone. Here, take this. It'll help you and Emily along until we send for you."

"A *thousand* dollars, sir. But—"

"Goddamn it, don't argue with me, Jeffrey! Just keep your mouth shut! You don't know anything!"

"Yes, sir."

He started through the house again and caught a bright fresh flurry at the top of the long staircase.

"Oh, darling!"

"What is it, Cynthia?"

"My furs. Sandra tells me you told her to leave them behind."

"Yes."

"Those minks are worth thousands; I won't leave them!"

"Well, we'll send for them later, dear."

"But the house will be empty; anything could happen to them."

"If you care so much about those goddamn minks," he shouted up, "you can damn well stay here with them! Now shut up and hurry down! We've only got fifteen minutes to catch the plane."

He stormed into the library. If only he could leave her behind! He went over to the wall safe in the fireplace, moved back the sliding bricks, and began to twist the dial: ten left, four right, eight left, six right, *click*.

He'd expected something like this ever since the boy had got killed. The little bastard, why couldn't he leave the stuff alone? Why couldn't he just do as he was told? What manner of inducement could have made him become an addict? Curiosity?

Well, at least he hadn't told how he'd brought in the drugs from Mexico, or how he'd assisted in the dilution at the laboratory. Nor could he tell of the millions that had been made, the need to make those millions.

He stuffed his briefcase with the logs of money, ten thousand, twenty, fifty, one hundred, fifty. Yes, fifty thousand from The Man's last payment. Altogether, one hundred and fifty thousand. That was nothing compared to the hundreds of thousands he had in the bank in the Dominican Republic. Just hope there wasn't another of those bothersome revolutions until he got it all out.

He turned away, slamming the safe shut. Then he had a thought and opened it to change the combination. The only way to get in it now would be with a blowtorch. That would hold them up some.

He hadn't wanted to deal with The Man directly, but after the Prado fellow was eliminated there was nothing else for him to do. And then those men who had come from the syndicate when he'd wanted to get out . . .

If it wasn't for them, maybe the boy would be alive today.

But again, if it wasn't for them, he wouldn't have had this head start. The connections they had! If he hadn't been tipped, he'd never have had the time to dispose of his home and the cars, and take some of his prosperity along with him.

They had the inside track, those boys!

The thought of his thoroughness made him laugh. If the police ever got wise, and when The Man inevitably cracked, he'd be long gone. If they only knew! The quiet little man, the meek little man, the mild little coat-hanger.

He was the actual monarch of the whole thing. Seven years ago, or thereabouts—before The Man—he had tampered with opium in his work with a drug firm. . . . *This is heroin, we destroy it. Its lawful importation into the United States was prohibited in 1924. It's useless medically. Only narcotics addicts find it of value.*

The stuff had made him rich. His closest associate would die of heart failure if he knew how rich!

The briefcase bulged under his arm. He looked at his watch. The cab would be there in a moment. He went out of the library quickly to the foot of the stairs.

"Cynthia!" he called.

Her high heels tapped rapidly to the railing of the upper landing. "Yes, dear?"

"What the hell are you doing up there? We've got to hurry."

"Well, I'm hurrying as fast as I can. Anyway, we can't go until we arrange to pick up Ralph at school."

"Drat! I clear forgot about that! I'll call."

He went back to the library and dialed the phone on his desk. These interferences could very well cost him his life.

"Hello?" Thank goodness it was the school mistress. Hurriedly he told her what to do, when to have his son waiting. There, that was done!

He grinned and went over to the liquor shelf. One last drink.

He couldn't get over it—he was getting away. He'd give a million dollars to see his partner's face tomorrow when he read the papers. Him and his thick, bull-headed pride! Would he remember the other days? The days of abject subjugation? Would he realize the patience and genius it took to bend before an inferior? Ah! When realization fought its way into that thick brain, he would have long since been out of the country.

He laughed, visualizing the other man when the police came to question. He would be hard put to explain how a man so domineering could have had no knowledge of the operation. They wouldn't believe it. They might even think *he* was mixed up in it! Wouldn't that top it all?

The door opened, interrupting his thoughts.

"Yes, Jeffrey, what is it?"

"Begging your pardon, sir—"

"What the hell do you want?"

"There are some men here, sir. They asked to see you."

The big men came past him. Their coats bellied open, their hands held badges outward for him to see.

"Mr. Donald Halsted?" one of them said. "You might remember me; I'm Detective King. We'd like to take a few moments of your time, if you don't mind. . . ."

March

27

*T*HE MEN, THE women, the drug people are leaving the city.
Baby, I got to move!
I'm so sick . . .
*—to New York, I'm goin to the Apple. This never happens in
the Apple . . .*
Frantic, with the same pleading, the ones who cannot leave
remain like wounded soldiers on a battlefield, left alone to face the
sickness, the bogueness, the being twisted.

Somebody says, "I got some smack—you can cop from me. Just
keep it real quiet." But it is only a burn for bus fare to New York.

The new day and new dawn listen to the music of the city as it
heaves and groans its way into awareness.

Without dope.

And because there is no dope, more than five thousand people
in the city endure suffering and agony.

In their pain, they pray for the resurrection of The Man.

Davis and Patterson were called into the office of the new captain, John Stonestreet. He was a big, gruff man, with watery blue
eyes and abnormally big hands.

He and Davis might have been brothers, Patterson decided, if
it weren't that one was possibly a little meaner than the other.

The two big men shook hands heartily.

"How the hell are you, Mance?" Stonestreet said, grinning.

"Fine, Johnny! Finally sucked your way up to captain, I see."
A big hand smashed playfully against Davis' shoulder. "You

haven't been doing so bad yourself, kid! After this thing you've pulled off, who knows?"

"The only thing left for me is a retirement," Davis said with a laugh.

Stonestreet noticed Patterson's inquiring stare and became more formal. "Er, sit down, won't you both?"

They sat in front of him.

"This is the first time I've had a chance to talk to you boys since the—excitement." He leaned back in his chair with an awkward air of authority. "But I always make a point to personally interview every man under my command. I understand you were instrumental in breaking up that dope combine." He directed the last statement to Davis.

"We worked on it with the rest of the fellas," Davis conceded. Then, a bit grudgingly, "I guess you could say Detective Patterson here gave one of the biggest pushes. If Rudy Black hadn't nailed The Man down to the Hodden murder, the whole thing might have folded."

Patterson hastened to put in, "That's not altogether correct, sir. I had a hunch, but it was Sergeant Davis who came up with the real meat. We'd all have been out in the cold if it hadn't been for him."

Davis seethed inside. Patterson was crazy if he thought he would be grateful!

Then he realized that the man was his partner, and it really was not as patronizing as it sounded. He felt a little pain at the word partner. He remembered the many partners he'd had during his lengthy tenure with the Police Department, the many faces; some a little shorter on guts than the others, but good men for the most part.

And, when he thought it over, he had to own up that Patterson was no slouch in the guts department. He was pretty good at catching hell with his bare fingers, even if it did burn a little.

Then he recalled the transfer and took it all back.

Stonestreet stretched his big hands out on the desk and betrayed a brief smile. "I hope you fellas won't fill my hat full of that modest crap. You know what you did, and so does everybody else."

He made them wait uncomfortably for a moment.

"What's the status of that area that was cleaned out, the Scene?" he said at last. "Does it look as though we've wiped the thing out for good?"

"Well," Davis said, glancing at Patterson, "we've been keeping a close eye on the street. There's some infiltration, but nothing syndicated as yet. Though I don't expect things to stay like that."

The captain's eyes shifted. "Patterson, how do you see the situation?"

Patterson was surprised. "Well—I guess very much the same way Sergeant Davis does, sir. I was thinking—maybe we could get the city planning commission up in the air about the Scene. It's costing the taxpayers more than it's worth."

"You may have something there. It's possible I can get some wheels rolling along that line." He paused. "Truthfully, the real reason I called you in here is a little more elevating. They seemed to think downtown that you fellas did a neat little piece of police work." He grinned widely at them. "The commissioner's bestowing citations on you next month."

"Citations!" Patterson said.

"I imagine it *is* quite a surprise to you, Patterson," Stonestreet smiled. "Your very first case as a detective too, isn't it? However, Sergeant Davis is no stranger to these things. I'll leave it up to him to shave the grass off the top of your head." He stood up, signaling the interview was over. "Mance, why don't you stop in on me later this evening? We can stir up a few stories you could stand to forget about the old days."

"Glad to, Johnny."

They started out.

"Oh, Patterson," the captain called after them.

"Yes, sir?"

"About that transfer. I was able to kill it as you requested. Let me say that I'm glad you decided to stay on with us here."

Patterson was surprised that Davis didn't say anything when

they were out in the squad room. He might have known that he couldn't keep it a secret forever, but he would have preferred that Davis think the transfer had been denied or lost somewhere in the interoffice mail.

Not that he wouldn't have left if he thought he could have got an equal or better assignment.

Anyway, he'd made up his mind during the Rudy Black episode to stick it out, prove that he could take it. He'd be a damned fool to let one broken-nosed old man chase him out of five hundred dollars a year, wouldn't he?

And when you came right down to it, Davis wasn't such a terror, he'd seen that. He was just a great big eccentric sonofabitch who wanted you to treat him like a man, and who treated you the same way in return—if you warranted it.

Maybe his methods were crude and a little rough, but you couldn't deny they got results. And he wasn't, as Patterson had suspected, really afraid. One thing Davis had taught him was to be firm; you couldn't wear kid gloves out there in the dope world. And maybe, if he stayed on long enough and didn't let Davis throw him, Patterson could teach him something he had forgotten: compassion.

"All right," Davis said roughly, "let's take that goddamn tour. I've got some groceries I've gotta drop off."

Patterson looked at him. "Since when did you become a delivery boy?"

"Since Bertha Travis has been in the hospital." His eyes softened. "You should see the way her kids take care of themselves. Regular troupers."

"How come you didn't leave them downtown?"

"Do you have any idea what it's like downtown, the cold rooms and the mush meal twice a day? No! You sure don't!" They started toward the garage, then he suddenly had a thought and looked at Patterson. "You got two boys, ain't you, Virgil?"

"Yes, sir. Eight and nine."

"Like to see them boys," Davis said, almost to himself.

"Why don't you stop off for dinner this evening?" Patterson

asked him. "We always have enough, and I'd like my wife to meet you."

The big face tried to mask its embarrassment. "Now—no, I don't think I should—"

"C'mon," Patterson said, gripping his arm. "We'd be more than glad to have you, Mance."

Softly, Davis said, "Yes," then quickly looked away from Patterson toward the garage. "C'mon, college boy, let's get on that goddamn tour!"

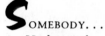OMEBODY. . .

He lay and sweated and cursed.

Somebody has put needles in my bed and let 'em punch me all over, 'cause I been bad, they say. The bastards, the stiffies—doin this to me. If I had some drugs . . .

The sweat drenched him; his eyes opened wide.

God, I didn't mean to curse; and Mama Mee was the goodest thing I ever dug too late. I'm thinkin crazy, seein Mama Mee, hearin her say, My baby, there's everything shoulda been given to you and wasn't . . .

They gave me life, what I had already, and left me without it here, the dirty sonsabitches. I'm well without sleepin. It ain't the first time I kicked, but it's the hardest.

He turned over in his sweat and pounded his fists into the helpless pillow, killing its softness into a wet, hard lump.

Snitch, snitch, snitch! My fault, everything! And I'm layin here, wantin a woman with soft breasts, like my Mama or Nina, just wantin a whore, just a woman for the first time in a long time, to

do everything with me I wanna to do. . . . Don't think about it. . . .
I'm twenty-one years old. Why didn't they give a woman life with
me, the square sonsabitches? Don't think about it. . . . I'll just go
on. I killed the snitch, Floyd! Don't think about it. . . . Somebody
put needles in my bed, the bastard. I wonder if—no, people are
always sayin it, all the stiff people, all the squares. I'll do it, every
day, because I'm strong enough and I'll push anybody, I'll killll
anybody, they'd have to killll me to stop me. They better leave me
alone, let me do my life. I'm so bogue, I still get sick, even this long,
I throw up. If I had just *one thing*! I can taste it in my mouth, just
thinking about—

*He beat his wet pillow; he slammed it against the wall and sat
up on the side of his bed.*

WHY, MAMA, WHY? . . . Stop being a chump! Stop being . . .
They better leave me alone, they better remember me, they don't
know I handled grands, GRANDS! and more pieces than they ever
saw. They don't know about stuff, they don't know about the *feelin*,
the *good* feelin, they don't know about speedin with stuff, when
the cocain and heroin seems like it's a man and woman inside you,
twistin on a big bed. They don't know about boy, REAL GOOD
BOY! they don't know how it saps your head down and gets into
your eyes and stomach and makes you itch and scratch and feel so
goddamn good you got to puke. The stiff, no-livin bastards! They're
dead, they're just dead bodies!

*He sat up straighter, the sweat drenching his body. Across a
deep chasm he could see tiers and tiers of cells, dark. Prisoners
sleeping. Experimentally, he rubbed the scars in the hollows of his
arms, thick, healing, marking him for life.*

Life . . . Mama . . . Mama Mee . . . These squares won't dig, I
just can't hip 'em, they keep puttin needles in my bed and sendin
me empty capsules and needles that're jammed and won't come
unclogged, and empty gum wrappers like what I used to carry my
stuff in, just for . . . Life . . .

*He sat looking at the Bible on the locker; he reached out his
hand and took it. He started to shred the pages into his toilet bowl.*

*Something struck him hard, like God, like stuff. He sat back upright
against the cold wall, sweating.*

Please please please please please please, I don't have to bend
under nobody! I'm me, Rudy Black, the Thoroughbred Hustler,
and I never snitched on nobody! I killed a snitch! Just leave me
alone, all you things! Just let me be me! Just let me outside again
so's I can get some stuff and get a broad, and leave me alone!

*A screw came along with a count sheet and asked him, "What're
you doing, sitting? Get in bed." But he didn't reply, and the screw
went along, recognizing the Lifer look on his face, the long look
of death.*

Hey, hey, I keep seein the Scene in my mind and all the lights
and every star whore from Hundredth to Seventieth, and the jams
in the poolroom and the bar, with cold beer in the summer on top
of some good reefer, and boy, and the girls sittin around in the
restaurants schemin on their men, and me with the bag, standin on
the corner twisted and sharp and my Hog at the curb, and Nina,
with my shoe marks on her ass, hustlin it when there ain't nothin
to hustle, and everybody hittin on me 'cause I got the bag, hey,
hey! This was mine! Coke parties and boy parties and the rest,
and me in cashmere and silk and kangaroo leather, to the tune of
"Dewey's Square" or "Dear Ol' Stockholm," now, now—and all
sorts of broads hittin on me, wantin to give me anything, just to
get their fingers in my bag! It was *mine*, my life, and they had no
right to take it or make me come where I wasn't wanted, like my
mother, layin on her back and makin me come where I wasn't
wanted. Why didn't she kill me? Why didn't she snuff me as soon
as I showed? Why didn't she just take vinegar or a dose of strong
laxative—or was she scared of upsettin her stomach? The bitch.
The whore. The garbage can. . . . Mama Mee, I keep seein you,
dear Mother Mee, my mother, help your baby to do his Life on a
string what's gonna cut him when he slides, and he'll fall fall fall
until he falls in the darkness Nearer My God to Thee Sweet Jesus
My God, and God takes and kicks him in the ass, right back out
again. . . . And I'll never use again, for real. Just one more time,
that's all . . .

And he picked up his soggy pillow from the floor and laid himself
down again, fell into a feverish sleep, until something awoke him,
God awoke him, a tall, glowing man up to the cell's ceiling, looking
angry. "You will never use drugs again," God said. "You will never
tear your Mother Mee's Bible again, you son of God."
And he screamed.

A YOUNG MAN named Phil is on a train; he is leaving with his
wife.

From the train windows, the city's expanse lies outstretched
against the night sky in humpbacked ridges down to the river.

Phil has been crying because he learned that his father died on
one of the nights when he was away from home. He has heard his
mother say, her eyes filled with disillusion, "Get away from me, I
hate you, get away."

Phillip is crying and feeling sick, and knowing he will have to
go back to the men's compartment in a moment and use a good
deal of the loose white powder he carries in an envelope in his right-
hand pocket. The needle he carries in his right pants pocket has
bitten through the protective wrapping of the woman's stocking
and imbedded its mouth in the flesh of his thigh. It hurts a little,
but he does not care.

"Honey . . ." His wife sits next to him, and presses his hand in
her own. "Honey, it's all over now, and everything's gonna be O.K.,
you just watch and see."

Because she doesn't know, because she can't understand, because
she is a big, dumb, blue-eyed female who is incapable of understanding, he lets her fondle him with her soft hands and hide his face

from the other passengers with her own, with the delicate, babylike fuzz of her hair in his wet eyes.

"We're going," she says in her silly, little-girl voice, her fingers stroking. "I knew something was wrong—all these months. But it's gonna be O.K., honey. Everything's gonna be hunky-dory for us." She looks at the other passengers defiantly.

"Lillie," he says, and for a moment he becomes as dumb and illogical as his wife. "Baby, I'm sorry, honest to Jesus Christ!" His voice is hoarse as he says it, apologizing for everything, in reality apologizing for only one thing: Lillie crying, saying, *What's wrong with me? We been married a year now, and you act like I got a disease. Why can't we ever do it? You know how I like to do it!*

"I'm sorry, honey," he says again, apologizing for his inability to sleep with her.

"That's all right, baby," she smiles down on him, understanding at least that part of it. "Stop your crying like a big kid! Those people down at Lexington'll make you O.K., and we can go right to a hotel after it's finished."

"Look, they don't do this in *one* day, Lillie—"

"Sssshhh—hush," she whispers.

They ride a little longer, and her breasts seem too hot against his head. He raises up.

"What's the matter?" she says, watching him.

"Papa—I was just thinking about Papa."

She tries to pull him down. "Sssh—*husssh*, honey, that's all over now. C'mon, now—"

"I'm sick," he says, starting to get up.

She looks worried. "Honey, I wish you wouldn't use no more of that stuff than you have to. Can't you just lay your head on me and rest till we get to Lexington tomorrow?"

He gets into the aisle, the sickness overcoming him. "I'll be right back. This is important, please believe it's important!"

"Phil . . ."

He goes down the aisle quickly, seeing nothing, seeing only the sign MEN at the far end of the coach. He goes in, not noticing that it is already occupied. The door slams hard behind him.

283

"What—" The other man turns. He is a young, dark-skinned Negro, with flashing eyes, and his left sleeve is rolled up as he stands before the washbasin. His tie is a red welt around the upper part of his left arm and the point of a needle is sunk in the soft, brown flesh in the arm's crook.

His face at once bares fear, amazement, and anger: a round, black knot has risen under the flesh just below the point of the needle.

"You sonofabitch," he tells Phil through tight lips. "Go tell the conductor, tell him I called you a sonofabitch and I'm usin dope in the craphouse—go on, you sonofabitch!"

The other man says, "I'm sorry," looking at the crude utensils on the washbasin, smelling the just-cooked odor of heroin.

The young Negro snatches the needle from his arm; blood drips from its tip and stains the floor in big red splotches.

"I'm hip, you're sorry!" he says. "You just made me blow my last fix, and you're sorry!" He begins to roll down his sleeve, his eyes burning. He cleans his needle and shoots the bloody water into the toilet in a thin stream. The water in the bowl looks completely red until he flushes the toilet. He turns toward Phil, looking as though he wants to fight. "All right, J. Edgar, go on and call the goddamn man—what're you waitin on?"

Phil shuffles, smiles, for the first time in his life feeling serene in his sickness. "I'm waiting for you to finish cleaning your fit and get away from the basin, so I can use mine."

"What—?"

"I said—"

"You said 'fit,'" the Negro says disbelievingly. "You use? You're a junkie?" He seems amazed that a junkie could be hidden under Phil's good clothes. "Listen—"

Phil smiles benevolently. "You'll get straight. Don't worry, I'll make up what I made you blow."

They lock the door and stand bent over the washbasin, their bodies touching in the operation of fixing up, their needles sucking the colorless powder of heroin, doing together with the steel biting their flesh and the eye-droppers sucking away their blood and delivering it again to the layer of underskin and veins. The heroin gets into their eyes and makes their flesh itch, white flesh and brown flesh; a common denominator is heroin.

They clean themselves and they clean their blood away from the whiteness of the bowl, ignoring the impatient knocks on the door, the somnolent click of the train wheels like a shutter on their minds, closing off the unnecessary thoughts and unnecessary words, making their lips smile in an involuntary peace and brotherhood.

They stand, their eyelids heavy, watching each other.

"I'm a musician," Phil announces without prompting. "I play bass for a living, but I don't have to. My folks are well off."

The Negro apparently hasn't heard, semiconscious from the heroin. "Man, that was the best stuff I've had in years! You must know a Chinaman. I know that's gonna last me to Lex."

"Is that where you're going?"

"Yeah, man."

"So am I."

"Goin to Lex?"

"With my wife, me and my wife. My wife is a way-out chick," Phil says. "My folks didn't want me to marry her. They said she was nothing. I met her in one of the joints I was gigging at, but she's a nice kid."

"Yeah, man."

"She didn't even know I was usin."

"How long you been married?"

"A year."

"She must be a dumb broad, Rollo."

Phil looks at him. "Why'd you call me Rollo?"

"You said you was rich. I'm not holdin it against you 'cause you're rich, though. I just said Rollo."

Phil nods away momentarily, but he comes back. "Yeah, my old man had a lot of green. We lived with him and my mother. It's a great big joint in the suburbs, and it's named Oak Haven because there's nothing but oaks all over the place."

The Negro sits down on the toilet. "I never did like oaks, man. They're so square. Where I come from, on the Scene, a guy next door to us had a willow growin on the edge of the alley. Give me a willow any time."

Deliberately invoking the pain, Phil remembers, "My old man—I called him Papa—he found out I was using. He couldn't take it. He died three days ago."

"And you're runnin to Lex now 'cause you killed him?"

"I didn't kill him!"

The Negro shakes his head sadly. "No, you didn't kill him, Rollo. Stuff killed him."

The wheels turn, the wheels click; a thousand miles pass between their numbed brains.

"Lex ain't so bad," the young Negro says.

"You been there?"

"Once every two years. I been hooked eight. I used to push stuff in the city for The Man, only I was downtown, out of the way of that big bust. I seen it comin. I even met that Rudy Black cat once or twice; I knew he wasn't right."

"Things are all twisted. You can't cop anywhere."

"It won't last. You can't kill stuff, Rollo."

Phil shook his head. "It's all over. Everything in the city is dead."

The flashing eyes survey Phil with surprise. "You think 'cause The Man is busted it's all over? Wake up, man! Things are just startin! When I left the city, I knew ten, fifteen guys had a bag, and all of it was different stuff. Right after a Panic, everybody is out to get that money. By the time me and you get back from Lex, there'll be a new Man; there'll be a new setup and a new coppin system. The only way the Rollers'll ever clean stuff up is to go to Italy and the rest of those countries. And *then* it won't be cleaned up."

"Nobody cares."

"That's it!"

"Nobody gives a damn."

"Nobody but the junkie. He's the one that hurts."

Phil's eyes fade, blur, and he opens them wider, wishing that he could sit down and relax and talk like this for the rest of the night.

"How's Lex?" he said. "Is it all right?"

"It's not so bad."

"What do they do? Do they give you a cold turkey?"

"They do it by steps. They find out what your shot is and give it to you in Demerol, then they cut down on the doses. It's kind of nice; you have your own room, and you can sign out any time you feel like it."

Phil props his buttocks on the washbasin. The other man is beginning to nod, so he raises his voice a trifle. "I've always wanted to ask—this is my first time to kick—is it—is it real tough?"

"No, not so bad. It depends."

"On what?"

"On how much hoss you use."

"I've got a big bee," Phil says, becoming frightened. "I don't use caps; I get sixteenths, and they last me about three days."

The young Negro looks at him and whistles, astonished. "You got a real fat arm, man!"

"I was playing gigs all the time. I used to cop like that so I wouldn't run out between dates. I'm a damn good bass man."

"That's crazy. They got some of the best musicians in the world at Lex, and they have sessions." He lights a cigarette and puffs for a moment. "How'd you get hooked?"

"A guy turned me on overseas, Japan. We were playing gigs at the USO clubs and some saki joints, and I got turned on." He closes his eyes, remembering. *"Man!"*

"Pure opium, huh?"

"It was lightning! I used all the way back to Frisco, and I was so gone I didn't know when we started or when we landed."

"And you never kicked, huh?"

"No. That was three years ago, when I started. This is the first time I ever felt I needed to kick. My old man—" He stops. Something invisible comes up and smacks him on the forehead, and he has to throw up. The Negro moves off the toilet quickly, stands until the other has emptied his stomach.

"Feel okay?" he asks Phil.

"I really feel all right now," Phil nods.

"What happened? Too much stuff?"

"No, I always throw up."

"Oh. Oh. I know a lot of guys who do that."

"I always feel better when I throw up."

"Yeah, you always do."

"Well, I better be getting back to Lillie. She'll be wondering."

"We'll be seein each other, I guess."

"Sure, we'll be there together."

"After we kick, we can sort of sit down together and talk this thing over."

"Sure."

"When are you gonna sign out?"

Phil shrugs. "After I kick, I guess. I'll let you know."

"Be sure you do. I know a cat lives outside of Lex who can turn us on when we leave."

"Turn us on?"

"That's right. All the cats stop by his pad when they leave the hospital."

"But we're going there to kick," Phil says. "It don't make much sense to go right back on, does it?"

"You'll see," the Negro says knowingly. "You'll want a fix so bad when you come out of Lex, you won't know what to do."

"What's the sense?" Phil says.

The Negro shakes his head. "I don't know, man. Do you? Can you tell me why we shouldn't?"

"No," Phil says helplessly.

The Negro laughs. "That's just the point. Nobody can ever tell us why we shouldn't."

Together they go out into the coach.

The train thunders on through the night.

Toward Lexington.

Printed in the United States
64372LVS00002B/216

9 780393 314632